THE CEO BUYS IN

D0963868

ALSO BY NANCY HERKNESS

A Bridge to Love

Shower of Stars

Music of the Night

Whisper Horse Novels

Take Me Home

Country Roads

The Place I Belong

A Down-Home Country Christmas (novella)

THE CEO BUYS IN

Wager of Hearts

Book 1

NANCY HERKNESS

Text copyright © 2015 Nancy Herkness

Published by Montlake Romance, Seattle

www.apub.com

Amazon, the Amazon logo, and Montlake Romance are trademarks of Amazon.com, Inc., or its affiliates.

ISBN-13: 9781503944091

ISBN-10: 1503944093

Cover design by Elizabeth Turner

Printed in the United States of America

In memory of Grandmuffy

PROLOGUE

"Scotch, straight up." Nathan Trainor settled into the leather chair and yanked the end of his bow tie loose. Ripping the black silk out from under the collar of his tuxedo shirt, he tossed it on the brass-topped table in front of him. One of the things he liked about the Bellwether Club was that the dress code was relaxed, no ties required.

"Here you are, Mr. Trainor." The waiter set a cut-crystal glass filled with golden-tan liquor in front of him and disappeared back behind the bar.

Nathan tossed it back, all of it. It was a twenty-year-old single malt and should be treated with more respect, but Nathan was soul weary. The scotch spread a welcome pool of warmth in his gut.

He held up the empty to the waiter, who arrived with a freshly filled tumbler. Sipping it this time, Nathan stretched out his long legs and glanced around the room. Not surprisingly for the late hour, it was virtually empty. However, he spotted another tuxedo-clad patron in the far corner, nursing his own glass of forgetfulness. He'd seen the man at the club before, of course. The membership was highly exclusive, so he suspected he had seen almost every member at some point.

Nathan frowned as a stronger sense of familiarity nagged at him. His fellow drinker was blond and took up a lot of space in his chair. Maybe an athlete. The Bellwether Club included a few, since they tended to be men who'd started with nothing and had succeeded on their own merits, one of the requirements for admission.

The other requirement was to have a net worth in ten digits, so the man must be a world-class athlete with some hefty endorsement contracts or he wouldn't have that kind of money. Nathan had neither the time nor enough interest to waste it on following spectator sports.

The mahogany door swung open to admit a third man, also wearing a tux. He had dark hair and walked carefully, as though he had to think about where to put his feet. Nathan had seen him drinking at the club more than once before tonight. The blond athlete glanced over and nodded politely to the newcomer. The man nodded back and headed for the bar, sliding onto one of the tall, leather-topped stools. "Bourbon, no rocks," he said into the silence.

After the bartender placed the glass in front of him, the new arrival swiveled on the stool and lifted it to the room. "To my fellow late-night tipplers. Bottoms up!" He tossed back the bourbon and turned to plunk the glass down on the counter for a refill.

Nathan took another sip of scotch and wondered if all of them had been at the same fund-raiser that night. That reminded him of Teresa Fogarty, and he finished his drink in a single gulp. The waiter materialized beside him with another glass. "Bring the bottle," Nathan said. "It'll save you steps."

He'd thought Teresa might be different. She wasn't a model or an actress. She was a lawyer, close to making partner. She didn't need Nathan or Trainor Electronics to succeed. They'd met at a charity dinner like the one he had just escaped. Her beauty was undeniable, but it had been her intelligence that intrigued him . . . and the fact that she hadn't known who he was when they both reached for the same canapé—her long, slim fingers brushing against his. Or so he'd believed until tonight.

They'd played a little game where neither introduced themselves, deliberately hiding in a corner of the balcony outside the party room. The attraction was electric. He had bribed a waiter to bring a table and their dinner outside to keep the bubble from bursting too soon. Only at the end of the night had they exchanged names and phone numbers.

Tonight one of her friends had overindulged with champagne and described how carefully Teresa had engineered the meeting, right down to the subtly sexy shade of nail polish she'd chosen for that moment when their fingers touched. The friend had treated it as a joke, now that Teresa and Nathan were a couple, but Teresa had sensed his disgust. She'd drawn him out onto the terrace behind the ballroom and wound her arms around his neck. "Melissa's exaggerating," she said. "I was kidding around with her about meeting you."

"You claimed you didn't know my name," he said.

"Because I was afraid you'd think I was just another woman throwing herself at you," Teresa said. "Does it matter how we met? We love each other now." She stretched up on her toes to touch her lips to his.

He put his hands on her waist to set her away from him. "You might have told me yourself."

"I was embarrassed." A shadow of concern crossed her face. "You do love me, don't you?"

"The first words you said to me were a lie," he said, wondering how many more were. He released her. "You can take the Rolls home."

She'd made a small sound of distress, but he was already halfway to the exit leading out to the anonymity of the New York City streets.

Too many people said only what they thought he wanted to hear these days. He didn't need his lover doing the same thing. She could have told him about the ruse of their meeting and he would have laughed about it. But she'd kept it a secret.

Now he wondered whether she'd been after his money or his influence.

His glass was empty and he poured himself another one. The scotch was beginning to seep into his brain.

"At this hour of the night, I'm betting it's a woman."

Nathan looked up to see who the man at the bar was talking to.

"I know what *his* problem is." The barfly tilted his head toward the blond man in the corner. "He threw an interception with five seconds to go against the Patriots."

The alcohol had lubricated the connections in Nathan's brain, so with that hint, he could identify the broad-shouldered drinker as Luke Archer, longtime quarterback for the New York Empire. You couldn't go anywhere in New York City without seeing his face on a billboard. Archer ignored both of them.

The bar stool occupant took another swig of his bourbon and brought his gaze back to Nathan. "So am I right?"

"I don't see that it's any of your business," Nathan said.

The other man laughed. "Everything's my business. I'm a writer."

Nathan scowled. The last thing he needed was to appear as an item in some gossip column. He relaxed when he remembered this was the Bellwether Club, where the dress code was laid-back but confidentiality was strictly enforced. A lot of high-level business deals got done within the thick walls of the club's tall brownstone. Probably a lot of government deals too, but he wasn't privy to those. Didn't want to be.

"What do you write?" he asked, to turn the conversation back on his overly talkative fellow drinker.

The man's posture went tense. "Novels."

"You're Gavin Miller." The quarterback spoke, a noticeable Texas twang in his voice. "I read your Julian Best books on planes. When's your next one coming out?"

Miller stared down into his glass as he swirled the bourbon around. "My original deadline was three months ago." He looked up with a mocking smile. "I missed it. My deadline extension was today. Missed it too. Writer's block."

"So what happens when a writer misses the deadline?" Nathan asked.

"The same thing that happens when a quarterback throws a bad pass. The coach isn't happy. And I get no royalties." He took a swig of bourbon. "But there's nothing they can do about it, because I don't have a backup."

"No ghostwriters?" Nathan asked.

"Don't think I haven't considered it, but I have enough respect and gratitude for my readers to believe I owe them my own efforts." He shook his head. "The truth is, I could keep myself in style on what I earn from the Julian Best movies for the rest of my life and beyond, but good old Julian has become a small industry in his own right. The editors, directors, actors, film crews—hell, even the movie theater ticket takers—all depend on him."

He grimaced and looked at Nathan again. "So we've established who two of us are. What about you?"

"I'm just a businessman," Nathan said.

"Not if you belong within these hallowed walls," Miller said, gesturing with his glass to the dark wood paneling that lined the room. "Frankie Hogan doesn't allow 'justs' in her club."

Nathan shrugged. "Nathan Trainor."

"Computer batteries," Archer said.

Miller saluted the quarterback with his glass. "So you're not just a dumb jock."

Despite the slight haze the scotch had cast over his brain, Nathan was shocked at Miller's bad manners. Archer, however, ignored the near insult. "I'm considering an investment in Trainor Electronics stock," the quarterback said. "No one has ever figured out how to make a computer battery as long lasting as yours."

"We've diversified," Nathan said. "Just in case they do." The truth was he no longer knew what products his research-and-development department had in the works. His job as CEO was to read endless reports and go to endless meetings. He didn't hear about new products until the paperwork hit his computer.

Another problem, right up there with Teresa. It struck him that he hadn't thought about her since Gavin Miller had started this odd conversation. "Why don't you all join me?" he asked, pointing to his table. "That way we won't have to shout at each other."

"Don't mind if I do," the writer said, staggering slightly as he eased off the stool.

Archer rose to an impressive height and strolled across the room, glass in hand. This was the guy Nathan had hated in school: the tall blond jock whom all the girls swooned over, while he and his fellow nerds were invisible. He allowed himself an inward smirk of satisfaction at meeting on an equal footing now.

Then he considered Teresa and her kind and decided that maybe the Archers of the world weren't so lucky after all. The high school girls had wanted Archer for the status of dating the star athlete, just like Teresa had wanted Nathan for his wealth or power. Neither was a good basis for a relationship.

"It's the beginning of a bad joke. A writer, a quarterback, and a CEO walk into a bar," Miller said, slouching into a chair and setting his glass down on the table.

"What's the punch line?" Archer asked, an undercurrent of amusement in his voice.

Miller shrugged. "I have writer's block, remember? That's why I missed my deadline."

"What does that mean, having writer's block?" Archer asked with a jab in his tone. "You can't type?"

Miller looked at Archer. "Why'd you throw a pass nowhere near your wide receiver?"

"It's harder than it looks," the big man said, unruffled, although Nathan noticed that he rolled his right shoulder slightly as he said it.

Miller laughed. "Exactly." He kept his gaze on the quarterback. "You must have some major endorsement contracts to be a member of this club."

"I've had some luck in the stock market. It's a hobby of mine."

"Luck, eh? Maybe I'll buy some Trainor Electronics stock too." He turned to Nathan. "So, a woman?"

"Maybe I just learned that my competitors invented a better battery," Nathan said. He gave his two companions a sardonic smile. "Which means you might want to rethink that investment."

"It's after midnight and you're wearing a tux." Miller let his head rest against the chair's back as he stared up at the coffered ceiling. "You weren't jilted at the altar, because it's a weekday. Maybe you caught your wife in bed with another man."

"Is this a way of trying to break your writer's block?" Nathan asked.

"Are you married?"

"No."

"You wear a look of cynical disgust," Miller said. "So her motives were less than pure."

Archer swallowed the last of the clear liquid in his glass. "Good luck finding a woman without ulterior motives when you qualify as a member of this club."

"What are you drinking?" Nathan asked, gesturing the waiter over.

"Water."

The writer laughed and picked up Nathan's bottle of scotch, sloshing slugs of liquor into Archer's glass and his own. "If we're going to discuss women, you need something stronger than water." Miller handed the empty bottle to the waiter. "Bring us one of bourbon and another one of scotch. And some nuts."

Archer picked up the glass of scotch and looked at it a long moment before lifting it to his lips.

"Attaboy," Miller said before he turned back to Nathan. "Did she break your heart or just injure your pride?"

Nathan had drunk enough to give the question serious consideration. "How can you tell the difference?"

"Now that is an excellent question," Miller said. "When my fiancée dumped me, I believe she broke my heart. But I was new to Hollywood back then and quite naive."

"Hollywood?" Nathan asked.

"She's one of the actresses in the Julian Best movies," Miller said. "I met her on the set."

"Irene Bartram," Archer said. "She plays Samantha Dubois, the double agent."

"A true fan," Miller said. "My thanks."

"You don't have a lot of women in your books," Archer pointed out.

"There's a reason for that," the novelist said.

Nathan snorted in agreement. "So, Archer, how do you handle women?"

"Full disclosure and keep it short," the quarterback said. "I don't have a lot of free time."

"None of us do," Nathan said.

"Full disclosure?" Miller asked.

Archer shrugged. "No strings, no rings."

"No gifts?" the writer asked, his eyebrows raised. "I hear Derek Jeter gives them signed baseballs."

"If they ask for a football, I'm happy to oblige," Archer said. "Seems kind of arrogant to assume they want my signature, though."

"I would think arrogance went with the territory," Miller said. "You're a quarterback."

For the first time, Archer smiled. "I've got plenty of arrogance on the field."

Miller turned to Nathan. "So have you figured it out yet?"

"You're damned annoying," Nathan said. "All right, pride. She played me and I'm pissed about it."

"What are you going to do?" Miller asked. The writer's eyes were half-closed as he lay back in his chair, but Nathan saw a spark of interest in them.

"Nothing. I don't care enough to expend the energy." It was depressing to realize how true that was.

Miller shook his head. "Disappointing."

"It's the only way to go," Archer said.

"Have you had your heart broken?" Miller prodded the quarterback.

"Half a dozen times," Archer said. "I got over it."

"Ah yes, the stoic, laconic jock," Miller said. "If I wrote you in a book, you'd be too much of a stereotype and my editor would complain." He gave a gusty sigh. "Since we agree that women are nothing but trouble, maybe we should play cards. It would distract us from our problems."

"Cards? Where the hell did you get that idea?" Nathan asked. Miller's conversational zigzags were beginning to irritate him.

The writer smiled crookedly. "Don't they say, 'Unlucky at love, lucky at cards'? Although it's hard to predict who will get the good luck in this group."

"I don't buy it," Archer said, leaning forward. "Everyone at this table knows you make your own luck. We wouldn't be here otherwise."

Nathan nodded. "Luck is the residue of design."

"We're all big on quotations tonight," Miller needled.

Archer made a sharp gesture to silence them. "How important is finding a woman you want to spend the rest of your life with?"

Neither Nathan nor Miller spoke, so Archer continued, "Pretty damned important. How much effort has any of us put into the search?" He gave them each a hard look. "I'm guessing not a lot. We see the same women at every event. Friends or colleagues fix us up. Maybe we even get a napkin slipped into our pocket and call that number."

"Speak for yourself on that last one," Miller said. That surprised a huff of laughter out of Nathan.

Archer acknowledged the interjection with a tight smile. "Our problem is lack of focus. We aren't making this a primary objective in our lives, so we're failing."

Nathan grunted in disagreement. "So we should be wife hunting instead of running a business or winning football games or writing the next bestseller? If you're that desperate, hire one of those executive matchmakers."

"That's like using a ghostwriter," Archer said.

Miller barked out a laugh.

"At least the transaction would be honest," Nathan said.

Archer sat forward. "How badly do you want a wife and family?"

Nathan considered the unhappy dynamics of his own family. Maybe there was a reason he had a hard time finding love. Maybe he couldn't recognize it. But yes, he wanted it, if only to do it better than his father had. "I'm listening. Miller?"

For a moment the writer looked downright sober. "Hell, yes, I'm still looking. What's the point of all this if you've got no one to share it with?" He waved a hand around at the expensive liquor, the ornate paneling, and the antique bronze chandeliers before he turned back to Archer. "And of course, you need a passel of sons to toss footballs with in your white-picket-fenced yard."

"I'm hoping for daughters," Archer said. "But yeah, I want kids. So what I'm saying is, we need a game plan."

The writer held up his hand. "I have a better idea." His eyes glittered with sly intent. "Gentlemen, I propose a challenge."

Nathan and Archer waited.

"We go in search of true love. We keep looking until we find it."

"This challenge is a load of garbage," Archer said. "How do you prove you've found true love?"

"A ring on her finger. Sorry, Archer," Miller said.

"A ring doesn't prove anything," Nathan pointed out.

"I've spent—what?—a half an hour with you gentlemen. And I'm confident you would not put a ring on a woman's finger unless you believed you would spend the rest of your life with her." Miller sat back and shifted his gaze between the two of them.

Nathan shook his head. "You've had too much to drink. And so have I."

"I say we make it a bet," Archer said, his pale-blue eyes intense. "We need to stake something valuable on the outcome."

The writer gave him a bleak smile. "The stakes are our hearts."

"We need to bet something more valuable than that," Nathan said, sucked back into the discussion in spite of himself.

A gleam of malevolent excitement showed in Miller's eyes. "All right, a donation to charity."

"Too easy," Archer said.

Miller lifted a hand to indicate he wasn't finished. "Not money: an item to be auctioned off. It must have intrinsic value, but it must also be something irreplaceable, something that would cause each of us pain to lose."

"Who chooses this irreplaceable artifact?" Nathan asked. The alcohol fumes must have been clouding his brain, because he found himself intrigued.

"You do," Miller said.

"So this is an honor system," Archer said.

Miller laid his hand over his heart. "A wager is always a matter of honor between gentlemen."

"A secret wager," Nathan said, his competitive spirit aroused. "We write down our stakes and seal them in envelopes. Only losers have to reveal their forfeits."

"I think we require Frankie for this," Miller said, twisting in his seat to address the bartender. "Donal, is the boss lady still awake?"

"Ms. Hogan never sleeps, sir," Donal said. "I'll call her."

"Miller, it's well after midnight. Leave the woman alone," Nathan said.

But Donal had already picked up the house phone. He spoke a couple of sentences and hung up. "She'll be here in ten minutes."

"We'll need three sheets of paper and three envelopes," Miller said before turning back to the table. "I've done a lot of stupid things when I was drunk, but this may be the most ridiculous one." He looked at Nathan and then at Archer. "We can cancel this right now before it goes any further."

Teresa's face floated through Nathan's mind, and his anger came to a boil. "I'm still in."

"You backing out, Miller?" Archer asked.

The writer shook his head. "Pardon my moment of sanity." He took a swallow of bourbon. "Gentlemen, I suggest we ponder our stakes."

Nathan leaned back in his chair, taking a mental inventory of his possessions. There wasn't much he gave a damn about. That was the problem with his whole life these days. Then an idea crossed his scotch-soaked mind.

"That's a downright unpleasant smile, Trainor." Miller was lounging in his chair, dangling his glass over one of its arms.

"I've decided on my wager," Nathan said.

"Are you sure it's something that would draw a high bid?"

"I guarantee it." Nathan tossed back the rest of his drink.

Miller turned to Archer. "Have you made your decision?"

"Made it five minutes ago." Pulling a silver pen out of his pocket, the quarterback sat forward and scrawled a number with multiple zeroes following it on his napkin before reversing it for Nathan and Miller to read. "Just to sweeten the pot, we should add a significant monetary donation to the charity."

"Done," Nathan said, impressed by the scale of the quarterback's suggestion. The man was a competitor.

The door to the bar swung open, and a tiny white-haired woman in a navy-blue pantsuit strode in. "Gentlemen, I understand there's illicit gambling going on in my establishment." She had a whiskey-hoarse voice with a tiny lilt of Irish. "I want a piece of it."

The three men stood and Miller laughed. "Frankie, we're wagering on matters of the heart, and you haven't got one."

Frankie's green eyes snapped with amusement. "Clearly, I can feel pity, because I let you join my club."

Nathan pulled a chair up to the table and held it for the club's legendary founder. Frances "Frankie" Hogan had started with nothing and had made a billion dollars, but had been refused entry to New York's most exclusive clubs. So she'd bought a magnificent brownstone and established the Bellwether Club, with rules that excluded most of the old-money crowd. Which meant, of course, that the old money wanted in.

As they all settled into their chairs, Donal brought over the stationery Miller had requested, along with three Montblanc Meisterstück pens.

"You're famous for your honesty and your ability to keep a secret," Nathan said to Frankie.

"Along with ruthlessness, cunning, and sheer cussedness," Miller murmured.

Nathan silenced him with a stare before turning back to Frankie. "So we're entrusting you with the personal stakes in our wager, sealed in separate envelopes. Each one of us can win or lose individually, but it takes the agreement of all three to declare someone a winner."

"I'll want to read them to make sure they're legit," Frankie said.

Nathan looked around the table. The other men nodded.

"What's the time frame?" Frankie asked.

"One year," Archer said. "Anyone who hasn't claimed their stakes back by then is declared a loser."

Frankie raised her eyebrows in surprise. "A long-term game."

Since they hadn't originally set a time limit, Nathan considered Archer's proposal. The quarterback was right; this project shouldn't be rushed. He nodded. "One year. Miller?"

"Agreed," the writer said without hesitation.

Nathan had the thought that they were all drunker than they appeared.

"I'll lock them in my private safe," Frankie said. "Who's going first?"

Miller picked up a pen and scrawled his name on an envelope before pulling a sheet of thick cream vellum toward him. "I'll trust my fellow bettors not to read over my shoulder." He scribbled several words on the paper and handed it to the club owner.

Frankie read it and gave him a long, appraising look before she folded the sheet and sealed it in the envelope.

Archer used his own pen to write his forfeit. Frankie whistled when she read the paper but made no other comment as she sealed the envelope.

Nathan addressed his envelope and wrote a description of the gift on the sheet. Frankie read it before raising a troubled gaze to his. "Are you sure?"

"Yes."

She slid it into the envelope. "You'll inform me anytime some-one is approved as a winner, or else we will meet in my office in one year's time." She stacked the envelopes in front of her. "I certainly hope whatever you win is worth what you all might lose."

Nathan thought about Teresa and the succession of women before her. "It will be life changing."

"That explains the stakes," Frankie said, gathering the envelopes and standing up. "Good night, gentlemen."

They stood and watched her stride out of the room. Miller raised his glass. "To our wager of hearts. May we be guests at each other's weddings."

Chapter 1

"Trainor Electronics. May I help you?" Chloe Russell smiled into her headset as she spoke, knowing it would make her sound friendlier. She nodded to the three middle-aged men who came through the office's front door carrying laptop cases and wearing button-down shirts and khakis. Middle managers. In the two days she'd been temping at Trainor Electronics, she'd learned that the high-level executives had their own entrance two floors up.

"Chloe, it's Judith. I've got a new assignment for you."

"But I've been here such a short time. Won't it look bad if you pull me out so soon?"

"It's still at Trainor Electronics, so, no. The CEO's executive assistant has come down with this darned flu. He needs a temp."

"CEOs of multinational corporations don't use temps. They take someone else's assistant and let their underlings deal with the temp," Chloe said, smiling at the twentysomethings sauntering by with their laptop carriers slung over their shoulders. Probably programmers.

"You've heard the word *epidemic*?" Judith asked. "Everyone's sick."

Luckily, Chloe never got sick.

"Besides," Judith said, "you're way overqualified to run a reception desk. You belong in the executive suite. And the pay is higher."

Higher pay was good. She needed it to hire a companion for Grandmillie so that she didn't have to go to a nursing home. "When can I start?" Chloe asked.

"As soon as Camilla gets there to replace you out front. Then head over to HR and they'll introduce you to your new boss."

"Got it," Chloe said. "Thanks for the raise."

"You'll probably get overtime too. I hear Mr. Trainor works long hours."

Not so good. She didn't like to leave her grandmother alone. Grandmillie always told her it was fine, but Chloe worried. That's why she was so determined to scrape together the money for a caretaker.

She glanced down at her outfit and frowned at the blue cotton blouse, beige trousers, and navy ballet flats. She'd dressed for entry-level clerical, not executive assistant. She'd gotten good at gauging those nuances of the corporate world after two months of temping for Judith's agency. Once Camilla arrived she'd take fifteen minutes to dash out and buy a faux silk scarf to throw on. There was a discount clothing store down a side street from Trainor Electronics' skyscraping office building. She could find something in her price range there.

Chloe made a slight adjustment to the red-and-blue striped scarf as she followed Roberta Stern, head of human resources, out of the executive elevator. Chloe had twisted her brown hair up into a sleek bun that mostly hid the blonde streaks and applied some red lipstick she'd found to match the scarf. Both adjustments made her look older and more sophisticated. The one thing she couldn't fix was her flat shoes. In her opinion, executive assistants should wear heels.

At least the carpeting on the top floor was so thick that it felt like her feet would be entirely hidden from view as they sank in. The receptionist behind the front desk looked like a model out of the pages of *Vogue*, with her perfectly fitting black suit and high cheekbones. Chloe's scarf suddenly reeked of bargain basement.

Roberta stopped at the desk. "Priscilla, this is Chloe Russell. She'll be working for Mr. Trainor until Janice is feeling better."

To be fair, Priscilla gave her a genuine smile that showed no judgment of Chloe's wardrobe inadequacies. "If you have any questions about where things are up here, just ask me," she said.

A resource. Chloe had learned to value those when she came into a new working environment. Some office workers were more willing to share knowledge than others. In fact, some were downright hostile to a temp, something that always baffled her, since she was no threat to their jobs. Judith said it was because Chloe was too good at hers and made them look bad. So Chloe tried to keep a low profile, although she refused to do subpar work.

Roberta led her down a long, wide corridor lined with paintings Chloe wished she had time to examine more closely. They were clearly originals and one looked like a Van Gogh, her favorite artist. Well, she would be able to admire them when she took a bathroom break. She assumed her new boss allowed those.

At the end of the corridor, massive double doors made of dark wood stood open. A beautifully sculptural wood-and-chrome desk sat just beyond them, empty.

"That's your workstation," Roberta said as they passed by the desk. "I'll get you set up with a password and show you the internal office system once you meet Mr. Trainor."

The head of human resources was going to show her how the computer worked? Usually she was lucky if a fellow admin told her which desk she should use. Were the staff members so intimidated by their boss?

Roberta knocked on the inner door, which was slightly ajar. "Mr. Trainor?"

"Yes, come in." His voice sounded muffled.

Roberta pushed the door fully open and walked through. Chloe fiddled with her scarf again and went in behind her.

No one was there. The burgundy leather chair behind the huge U-shaped desk with three widescreen computer monitors sat vacant. She glanced right, toward one wall of windows, to see a couch and four chairs comfortably arranged like a living room. All unoccupied. The conference table and chairs to the left were also empty.

"Mr. Trainor?" Roberta appeared as baffled as Chloe.

"Just a second. My processor needed an update," the voice said, this time emanating from somewhere in the vicinity of the desk. A large hand appeared on top of the desk, and then a man rose up behind it, his broad shoulders going up and up and up.

Chloe let her eyes skim over the tall, lean body, lingering a moment on the muscles the rolled-up sleeves of his white dress shirt revealed in his forearms. She checked out the shoulder breadth again. Definitely impressive. But it was the clean, sharp line of his jaw, the thick waves of his longish brown hair, and the intensity of his gray eyes that lit a spark of something irritatingly primitive deep in her belly.

She'd never met a CEO who looked like this before. They were usually older, balder, and chubbier.

"We have techs to do that," Roberta said.

"I like to feel a circuit board every now and then," her new boss said.

Chloe had to smother a spurt of laughter.

Roberta gestured Chloe forward. "Mr. Trainor, this is Chloe Russell, the temporary executive assistant who's filling in for Janice while she's sick."

Chloe stepped up to the edge of the desk and stretched out her hand across the wide surface. "Pleasure to meet you, Mr. Trainor."

"Chloe." He nodded and shook her hand before he turned to Roberta. "A temp?"

The HR manager spread her hands in apology. "There's a flu epidemic. The temp agency has total confidence in Chloe's ability to work at a high level."

"Right," he said. With a smile that was clearly forced, he looked at Chloe. "Well, we'll figure it out."

Squelching the little flare of annoyance at Trainor's assumption that she wouldn't be able to *figure it out*, Chloe managed a tight smile in return.

"I'm going to get her set up on the computer at Janice's desk," Roberta said. "Then she'll be ready to go."

Trainor nodded and sat down in the big chair, swiveling away from them toward a computer screen before they'd started to leave. So that was how it would be. All business. Chloe was good with that.

After Roberta gave her a quick tutorial on the executive e-mail and messaging system, Chloe smoothed her hair back, picked up a pad of paper and a pen, and knocked on Trainor's door.

"Come in." This time he was leaning back in his chair, contemplating one of the computer screens. He rotated to face her and gestured to the two square leather chairs set in front of his desk. "Have a seat. So all I do is answer e-mails, read and write reports, and go to meetings. You're in charge of facilitating those functions, particularly the meetings. I value punctuality."

Then he gave her a smile. It drew fascinating brackets at the corners of his very masculine lips. Chloe had a hard time breathing.

She sat down abruptly and sucked in oxygen as she tried to remember what she'd wanted to ask him. "Roberta showed me your calendar. Would you like an e-mail reminder twenty minutes before each item on your schedule if the meeting is in-house?"

"Good suggestion," he said. "How are you at proofreading?"

Feeling on firm ground now, she said, "I majored in English." Typos seemed to jump out at her when she read anything, something that often drove her crazy when reading articles on the Internet.

He turned his chair and swiped his fingertip over his screen first in one direction, then another, then a third. He had long, tapering fingers, so he looked rather like a magician casting a spell. "I've just sent you a report one of my associates drafted. It needs cleaning up. That's your first job."

"Yes, sir," Chloe said.

His brows drew together. "Sir?"

"Mr. Trainor."

He seemed about to say something, but instead shrugged and turned back to his computer screen.

Chloe returned to her desk, fighting down the mix of gut-punching attraction and mild resentment Trainor evoked in her. She didn't mind the resentment, but she needed to eliminate the attraction. He was the CEO of a giant, heartless corporation, just like the one that had sucked her father dry.

The report Trainor had sent her—an analysis of a recent marketing campaign written by someone named Richard Sinclair—needed more than just cleaning up. She debated a moment before she hit the intercom button. "Mr. Trainor, may I suggest some edits for this report? I'll use tracking so you know what I've changed."

"You want to edit the report?" His surprise came through her headset clearly.

"For clarity," Chloe said. In for a penny, in for a pound. "I've worked in marketing before, so I know the jargon."

She'd also worked in sales, accounting, and just about every other department a business could have. That was the joy and pain of working for start-ups; they were understaffed, so she filled in wherever she was needed. Unfortunately, she also brought the Russell jinx down on them. No fewer than three of the last four companies she'd worked for had failed. It had taken only three months from the day she was hired for the most recent one to close its doors. However, she refused to give up and work for a soulless corporation like Trainor Electronics except on a temporary basis. Her father's experience had convinced her to avoid that career path. His employer had used his brilliant mind and given him a pittance in return.

A moment of silence. "Go ahead," Trainor said and hung up.

She set alarms to remind herself to alert her boss about his meetings, and dug into the mess of charts and graphs and disorganized analyses. It got so bad that she created a whole new document with her changes. There were interruptions, of course, as the phone rang and a parade of visitors had to be vetted. However, the phone wasn't as busy as she'd expected because Priscilla screened all the calls first and only put through those she thought Trainor might have an interest in taking.

"This job is cake," Chloe muttered to herself as she attached the rewritten report to an e-mail and hit "Send."

Trainor's office door swung open, and the man himself emerged. Her gaze went straight to his sculpted forearms, then lifted as he ran one hand through the thick waves of his hair, making it look tousled, as though he'd just gotten out of bed. He frowned down at her from his considerable height. "Did you go to lunch?"

She glanced at the time on the computer screen: 2:03. She'd been so engrossed in the editing, she'd missed her one o'clock lunchtime. Her stomach growled. "Should I go now?"

"Could you order in sandwiches for both of us? I have a meeting in thirty minutes, and I'd like you to take notes."

"I don't know shorthand," Chloe confessed. Almost no one did anymore, but maybe he was old-school.

"Don't worry," he said. "You're just window dressing."

Maybe she should be insulted, but that reminded her that she was underdressed for her new position. She wasn't going to add any luster to her boss's reputation in this outfit.

But that wasn't a problem she could fix. Lunch was. Not that she knew where she was going to get lunch in less than twenty minutes. "What would you like on your sandwich?"

He hesitated, the first time she'd seen him do that. "Keep it plain."

"No food allergies? You're not a vegetarian?" Better safe than sorry.

Trainor shook his head, making one hank of waving hair fall onto his forehead. Her fingers twitched with a longing to feel the texture as she brushed it back. He removed temptation by striding down the hall to enter another office door. She couldn't help watching the way the fabric of his trousers shifted over the muscles of a very tight behind. Chloe shook her head. Not going there.

Chloe hoped Priscilla was at her desk and knew the drill. CEOs didn't like to be bothered with mundane details like buying lunch. She'd had to pay for a few herself when she could ill afford it. Luckily, Judith always paid her back.

She pushed the intercom button. "Priscilla," she said in a low, urgent tone, "how do I get sandwiches for the big boss pronto?"

"Executive dining room," the other woman said in her musical voice. "I'll e-mail you the menu and phone number. Just tell them who the food is for and they'll get it here fast."

"Do you have any idea what he likes to eat?"

"Wish I could help, but Janice always handles that. He has cold beverages in his office refrigerator, so you don't have to worry about those, at least."

The promised e-mail appeared in her in-box. Scanning it, Chloe decided to go conservative and easy to prepare, although her mouth watered over lamb sausage on focaccia with chutney. However, she needed to be able to give him a choice of two. She would take the other one.

The executive dining room didn't let her down. The sandwiches arrived in minutes and were accompanied by beautiful green, leafy salads, fresh fruit, and a bowl of multicolored chips that looked healthy. "Mr. Trainor likes the taro chips," the young man who slid the tray onto her desk said. "And the chocolate chip cookies." There was also a carafe of coffee that gave off a heavenly aroma.

She had no idea how to page the office Trainor had gone into, so she followed in his footsteps down the corridor and knocked on the open door. "Lunch is here," she said, leaning in to see her boss with his hip propped on the low back of a chair as he scanned a piece of paper. A man wearing a boldly striped shirt and brilliant red tie watched him from behind a desk.

Trainor pushed away from the chair. "Phil, I'll look this over after my meeting."

Phil nodded. "It's preliminary, but the numbers seem promising."

"Agreed." Trainor folded the paper in half and joined Chloe at the door, falling into step beside her as she walked back toward her desk. "Meetings and reports," he muttered.

Chloe stopped by her desk. "Turkey and swiss, or roast beef and muenster?" she asked, gesturing toward the sandwiches.

He scooped the entire tray off the desk and headed into his office. "Join me."

She stared after him. CEOs didn't carry their own lunch trays or invite their temps to eat lunch with them. She realized that he'd disappeared from view so she jogged forward.

He set the tray on the conference table before pulling a chair out from the corner of the table and looking at her. She stopped again.

"Chloe," he said, angling the chair with a touch of impatience.

"Oh, right." She hurried across the expanse of plush carpeting and plunked ungracefully down into the oversize leather chair.

He lowered himself into the chair at right angles to hers and slid the tray so it was in front of him. "You believe in the classics," he said, lifting the clear plastic lids off the plates.

The scent of balsamic vinaigrette wafting up from the salads made Chloe's mouth water, but Nathan's jaw seemed to tighten with distaste. She thought he looked a little queasy. "Do you mind if I have the turkey?" he asked.

"Of course not. I like red meat," she said, taking the rejected roast beef. She glanced around the huge room, searching for the promised refrigerator. All she saw were bookcases and paneling. "I'll get you something to drink if you tell me where you keep the beverages."

"Ah, the hidden kitchenette," he said, rising again. She started to protest when he held up his hand. "It's easier to show you." He walked to a section of paneling. "Third panel from the right. Press the side at about waist height and . . ." The paneling silently slid sideways to reveal the entrance to a small kitchen with dark-green granite countertops accenting elaborately grained wooden cabinets. "And the refrigerator is concealed behind this one," he said, pressing the largest wooden door so it swung open to reveal neatly arranged cans and bottles. "Evidently, the fact that I might eat or drink in my office must be kept secret. What can I get you?"

"Water, please," Chloe said, not sure how to react to his oddly whimsical mood. What she really wanted was the coffee, but she would wait until he had some.

He was sorting through the drinks. "Aha! They concealed it behind the Kauffman vodka. Who the hell stocks this thing, anyway?"

Chloe smiled tentatively when he returned to hand her the water. She waited until he was seated and had picked up his sandwich before grabbing her fork.

"Please," he said, nodding for her to eat.

She plunged the fork into a perfect slice of tomato and brought it to her mouth. The flavor blossomed with a hearty, almost smoky, quality on her tongue. Not one of those vapid, store-bought atrocities. "Mmm," she said involuntarily.

Trainor nodded, taking the first bite of his sandwich. He chewed slowly and swallowed without noticeable pleasure. Then he put the sandwich down and pushed the plate away.

"Is there something wrong with your food?" Chloe asked. "Should I order something else?"

"No." He picked up the carafe of coffee. "Maybe this will help."

He must have seen the longing in Chloe's eyes, because he filled both mugs.

Chloe decided to get this strange interlude back on a business footing. "May I ask what sort of window dressing you need me to do?"

Trainor picked up his mug. "Your function is to be the guarantor of my integrity."

"The what?" Chloe put down her fork.

He took a sip of coffee and leaned back in his chair. "This meeting is a favor to a friend. He's got an associate who's developed some new software he thinks will change the world of computing. He wants me to bring out his associate's product under the Trainor Electronics umbrella. You're here to prove I'm not stealing his idea."

"How am I going to do that?" She felt as though she'd wandered through the looking glass.

"This is a meeting among friends, so I can't ask to record it. You're going to make it clear you're taking notes. I'll send him a transcript of your notes for his approval. There will be no question of what products and ideas we discussed, just in case he wants to claim intellectual property theft."

Stunned, Chloe sat back. This was the flip side of what had happened to her father. In his case he'd worked for a corporation that had laid claim to all his inventions and the enormous profits they'd made from them without compensating him as he deserved. Nathan Trainor was making sure he didn't get accused of stealing someone else's ideas. "Have you had a problem with that before?"

"On occasion." He took another swallow of coffee. He must have seen something unflattering in her expression, because his lips thinned. "I don't need to steal other people's ideas. I have one of the best R and D departments in the business."

How many of his employees' ideas had he taken as his own, and rewarded them with not a cent above their salaries? She went back to her sandwich. She wasn't here to right the wrongs of the corporate world. She was just here to tide herself and Grandmillie over until she got another permanent position.

When she glanced back up at Trainor, he was cradling the coffee mug in his hands and gazing out the wall of windows where the sharp verticals of the Manhattan skyline sparkled against the brilliant blue autumn sky like a postcard. With his face turned toward the light, she noticed half circles of fatigue under his eyes. His dark eyebrows were drawn down in a scowl, and his mouth was set in a hard line.

Wanting to soften the bad mood she'd provoked, she pointed to a flat rectangular object enshrined in a Lucite case on the wall. It had loops of wire sticking out at all angles, and rows of metallic boxes marching across its face. It reminded her of some of the odd gadgets her father put together in his home workshop. "Is that modern art?"

He started before turning to follow the direction of her finger. "Not art. Electronics. That is the first Trainor XL battery ever made."

Chloe dug into her memory for the quick summary Judith had given her when she'd assigned her to work at Trainor Electronics. "Didn't you make it yourself? When you were really young?"

Surprise was written in his lifted eyebrows. "You know more about the company than most temps. Yes, I created it for my own use in a friend's garage when I was a teenager."

"So that's the battery Trainor Electronics was founded on." She put down her sandwich and got up to examine the artifact.

"Don't get too close or you'll be arrested for industrial espionage."

Chloe took a giant step away from the battery and tucked her hands behind her back.

"That was a joke. The design secret is inside the casing so you can't see it," he said. "Although the battery's kept in here for security reasons as well as historical interest."

"So someone could steal it and reverse-engineer it to develop their own superbattery."

"They could if they wanted to deal with the battalion of patent lawyers we'd unleash on them." He stood up and walked over to stand beside her, his eyes on the prototype battery. A self-mocking smile turned up the corners of his mouth and carved lines in his cheeks. "Its value is more sentimental than real. It changed the direction of my life."

He turned his head so their gazes met as he said, "It's unusual to be able to mark a turning point so clearly."

Chloe was held in thrall by the emotions roiling in his gray eyes and by the fascinating tilt of his lips. She pivoted back toward the battery because she didn't want to see the man inside the CEO.

Chapter 2

Chloe was typing the meeting notes when a tall brunette in a belted raincoat tried to breeze past her desk.

"May I help you?" Chloe asked in her best you-may-not-bother-the-boss tone.

The woman halted and made an impatient gesture. "Where's Janice? She knows who I am."

"Not available," Chloe said. "May I ask your name?"

"Teresa Fogarty."

Chloe checked Trainor's schedule. "I'm sorry. I don't see your appointment with him."

The brunette gave her a tight, fake smile. "That's because it's a personal visit. We're having dinner."

"I'll let him know you've arrived," Chloe said, pushing the phone's intercom button as the brunette started to protest. "Mr. Trainor, Ms. Teresa Fogarty is here to see you."

There was no response and Chloe tried again. "Mr. Trainor, Ms. Teresa Fo—"

"I heard." Trainor's voice snapped like a whip through the headset. Chloe actually drew back from the phone console before he continued. "She can come in."

When Chloe nodded to her, Ms. Fogarty flashed Chloe a triumphant look and turned on her heel. Which was shod in exactly the sort of high-heeled pump Chloe planned to wear tomorrow. Except Teresa's heels had the red sole that labeled them as coming from a very expensive designer. As the superior Ms. Fogarty stalked into Trainor's inner sanctum, Chloe rolled back from the desk and contemplated her simple, functional ballet flats. She sighed. She did like beautiful shoes.

She glided back in to finish the notes. Once that was done, she glanced at her watch and blew out a breath. If they were going to dinner, she wished they'd go, so she could get home to Grandmillie.

Courtesy brought Nathan to his feet as Teresa stormed through the doors into his office, her raincoat flapping open to show a deep red dress that clung to her body. That would have tempted him to run his hands down over her hips and up under her skirt until yesterday. Now he just wanted her out of his office.

"Nathan, you canceled our dinner date," she said, shedding her coat and tossing it on a chair. She perched on the chair's arm, crossing one long leg over the other so the narrow skirt rode up her thighs. The display had no effect on him. "Why?"

Her directness was one of the things he'd liked about her. Except now that he knew it wasn't real, it seemed more abrasive than refreshing.

The hangover headache he'd been battling all day jabbed at his temples. He and his two new drinking buddies at the Bellwether

Club had consumed more alcohol than he cared to remember. He considered blaming his hangover on Teresa, but he knew it was his own fault. As was the ridiculous wager he'd made with Luke Archer and Gavin Miller. He had fully expected one or the other to contact him today to call the whole thing off.

Now that he thought about it, he *could* blame the bet on Teresa. He walked around the desk to face her. "Since you're here, we might as well—"

Her face lit up and she started to gather up her coat.

"—talk about the end of our relationship," he finished.

Her expression hardened and her eyes sparked with temper. "I can't believe you're making such an issue out of the little joke I played when we met."

"Maybe if you'd told me yourself," he said, but he wasn't sure that was true anymore. For a brief, gratifying moment, he'd believed that a beautiful, desirable woman had wanted him just as a man. Not as a billionaire. Not as a CEO. Not even as a supposed genius. "I value honesty."

She stood up, her arms stretched out toward him. "I'm being deeply honest when I say that I am crazy in love with you."

The curve of her arms was pure grace, the tilt of her head was pleading without groveling, and the timbre of her voice vibrated with emotion. Every nuance was so perfect that he realized he was seeing a very skillful act. If Chloe Russell were in the grip of an emotion as powerful as Teresa claimed to be, the feisty little temp would probably hurl herself at him and pound on his chest to make her point.

He wondered where that image had come from, even as he dismissed it.

"Was it money or a job you wanted?" he asked.

"I wanted *you*," Teresa said in a throaty voice as she let her arms fall to her sides in an elegant arc.

"The company's legal business?" He was angry at himself for being fooled by this woman.

"Why can you not believe I love you for yourself?"

"Oh, for God's sake, Teresa, you're just digging a deeper hole."

"I read an interview with you in a business magazine," she said, dropping the mask of being insulted. "You said the rich don't have the luxury of falling in love like normal human beings."

"I don't remember having a philosophical discussion about love with a journalist."

"The article was dated about ten years ago. I was doing some research recently and found it."

He cast back in his memory and came up blank. Evidently he'd been smarter about women but dumber about the press back then. "What were you researching?"

"Trainor Electronics. I was going to court your business." She shook her hair back from her shoulders. "Only I found I wanted to court *you* instead. So I tried to create the illusion of falling in love like normal people. I thought you'd enjoy it."

The problem was that he had enjoyed it. Far too much. "I don't like illusions," he said. "They're just lies dressed up in fancy clothes."

"So, that's it?" she said. "You're just cutting me out of your life after five months of intimacy?"

"I'll send you a diamond bracelet as a parting gift," he said.

She couldn't hide the flare of greed in her eyes, even as she made a show of affronted virtue. "Keep your gift," she said, swiping up her coat and stalking to the door before she looked over her shoulder. "If you handed it to me now, I'd throw it in your face."

She slammed the door behind her.

He leaned back against his desk and rubbed his burning eyelids. The hangover and lack of sleep had probably made him harsher than he should have been. He'd send her the bracelet to salve his conscience. It would be interesting to see if she kept it.

His office door swung open a crack, and Chloe's head with its prim bun appeared in it. "I'm sorry to bother you, Mr. Trainor, but do you want me to stay?"

He glanced at his watch, surprised to find that it was after six. The poor temp wasn't used to working the longer hours of an executive assistant. "I'm sorry. You may go home. I assume they pay you extra for overtime."

She nodded. "Flexitemps is very good to its employees. Good night." Her head disappeared and the door closed softly.

The temp was a funny little thing. Her manners were flawlessly professional, but he got the feeling she disapproved of him. He didn't mind as long as she continued to manage his phone calls and calendar as competently as she had today. He'd hold all the high-level work until Janice got back.

That reminded him of the notes she'd taken at the meeting. She said she'd e-mail them to him when they were finished. He'd better doctor them up while the meeting was still fresh in his mind. The technical jargon had been flying, and he was sure she hadn't been able to keep up despite her mad scribbling.

Returning to his desk chair and finding the e-mail on his screen, he began to read. And read. And read. When he was done, he sat back, staring at the document in front of him in disbelief.

"Well, well, it looks like Flexitemps sent in a ringer."

"Sorry I'm so late, Grandmillie." Chloe bent to kiss her grandmother's soft, wrinkled cheek. "I got promoted to executive assistant by the flu epidemic and had to work late."

"I'm perfectly capable of fixing myself a bowl of soup, you know," Grandmillie said.

"But I like to have someone to cook for," Chloe said. She laughed as she put the takeout Thai food on the counter. "Or in this case, to buy for. When I walked past Boonsong, it smelled so good, I couldn't resist."

Grandmillie loved Thai food, but splurging on takeout was something they couldn't often do. Since Chloe was getting a higher wage for the executive assistant position, she'd decided on the treat. And she was too tired to cook after her stressful day.

Her grandmother stood up and followed Chloe to the dining area, using her brightly decorated cane for balance. The oak table was already set with Grandmillie's exquisite gold-rimmed wedding china. She said she couldn't take it to the afterlife so they might as well use it here.

Once the food was served, Grandmillie said, "What executive are you working for?"

"The big cheese. Mr. Trainor himself," Chloe said. "Mmm, this *pad see ew* is fantastic."

"Is he pleasant to work for?"

Chloe took another bite and chewed as she thought about that. "He's not *un*pleasant. I think he doesn't believe I can do much since I'm just a temp, so he kept it pretty simple today."

"That's considerate of him."

"I guess you could call it that." Chloe put down her fork. "It got very interesting this evening, though. Right as I was finishing up some notes from a meeting, this tall brunette wearing the most gorgeous Louboutin heels waltzed in. She claimed she had a dinner date with him. When I got him on the intercom, he was clearly not happy about her arrival, but he told her to come in anyway." She took a sip of water and leaned forward. "When she came out not long after, her face looked like a thundercloud. She stomped by my

34

desk so hard I was afraid she was going to break the heels on those beautiful shoes."

"Sounds like he canceled the date," Grandmillie said, her blue eyes twinkling.

"She muttered something about a bracelet, but she wasn't wearing one that I could see."

"Don't rich men give their mistresses jewelry when they end the relationship?" Grandmillie asked.

"I'm shocked. How do you know such a thing?" Chloe teased.

"I wasn't born yesterday, dear. And I read Regency romances."

In fact, Grandmillie was one shrewd cookie. She'd owned a bar with her ex-husband, even when he was ex. So she'd seen more of the gritty side of life than Chloe had.

"I don't think she was his mistress, though," Chloe said. "I'm pretty sure mistresses don't come to their sugar daddy's office during the workday. Unless they want to be ex-mistresses really fast."

"Maybe that's why he tossed her out," Grandmillie said, pulling chicken satay off the skewer with her fork. "She broke the rules."

"Technically speaking, wouldn't he have to be married to have a mistress?"

"He's not married?" Grandmillie's attention became very focused. "How old is the man?"

"Pretty young for a CEO." And pretty hot too. "He may be married, but I didn't see a ring."

"Google him on your phone," her grandmother ordered.

Chloe kept eating. "He's a billionaire. He's not interested in a temporary assistant."

"Not yet." Grandmillie put down her fork and looked at Chloe.

"Fine." Chloe got up and grabbed her handbag, digging her phone out of it and typing in Nathan Trainor's name. She chose a basic bio that appeared up-to-date. "Not married. Never has been. That's kind of weird."

"Why, dear?" Her grandmother resumed her consumption of the satay.

"Because he's so—" She'd been about to say "good looking" but decided she didn't want to give her grandmother any additional ammunition. "—rich."

"He just hasn't met the right woman." Grandmillie looked up. "Until now."

Chloe smiled at the woman who believed the king of England would be lucky to marry her granddaughter. "You are so sweet."

"Ha! The fellows trying to wheedle another drink out of me at closing time called me things that weren't anywhere near 'sweet.'"

"Well, I'll do my best to persuade Nathan Trainor to ask me out to dinner and see if I like him well enough for a second date," Chloe said, giving up.

"Just be yourself, dear, and he'll figure it out."

Chloe wondered how many dates you had to go on to get an expensive bracelet when you broke up. She could sell it and sock the money away in the bank.

Chapter 3

Chloe stepped off the executive-level elevator with considerably more confidence than she had the day before. She had on her Louboutin knockoffs, black linen trousers, a white blouse, and a gray tweed sweater jacket. The jacket had been marked down about four times at Nordstrom. The only reason no one had snapped it up was that it had fallen off the hanger and was puddled on the floor under the round clothes rack. Even then it had been a splurge, but it was a classic she could wear until it fell apart at the seams.

She greeted Priscilla warmly and received a welcoming smile in return. All the people she'd met at Trainor Electronics were surprisingly friendly and relaxed. Considering that it was a cutting-edge tech firm, she'd expected more tension and competitiveness. Or maybe that was just because the last tech firm she'd worked for was on the verge of bankruptcy all the time, so everyone was worried about their jobs. The Russell jinx at work again.

Even the mighty Mr. Trainor didn't give off a vibe of self-importance, just supreme confidence.

Chloe pulled out her desk drawer and dropped her bag into it before picking up a pad of paper. She knew she was old-fashioned, but she never quite trusted her notes to a computer tablet. Trainor's office door was closed, and she hesitated outside it. The privacy light on the phone console wasn't lit, so he shouldn't mind being disturbed. She needed to let him know that she was at work on time. Well, ten minutes early, actually, but she wouldn't clock in for that.

Chloe ran her hand over her sleeked-back hair and checked that her bun was firmly wound before she knocked on the door. There was no answer. Roberta Stern had said Trainor usually got in two hours before the rest of the staff, which made this seem odd.

She tried the doorknob. It turned in her hand, so she pushed the door open a crack and listened. No sound.

She opened the door wide enough to slip through it. The office appeared to be empty. Well, she'd just go back to her desk and wait for Trainor to show up. Then her glance snagged on a man's raincoat tossed over one of the chairs in front of her boss's desk. She looked more closely and discovered a briefcase leaning against the arm of the chair.

So he *had* been here.

Chloe turned to recheck his schedule, thinking she'd missed an early-morning appointment, when she heard a low, drawn-out moan coming from the direction of the desk.

The high-backed chair was swiveled so its back faced her. Remembering Teresa Fogarty's presence the night before, she debated whether she might witness something she didn't want to see if she walked around the desk. However, the chair hadn't moved the entire time she'd been there, and judging by Trainor's impressive physique, he would probably be fairly active when in the throes of passion.

She tiptoed around the corner of the desk and peered into the chair.

"Oh my God!" she gasped.

Her boss was slumped on the seat, his long legs sprawled out in front of him, while his head sagged to the side and his forearms hung limply over the armrests. His eyes were closed, and his skin bore a hectic, unnatural flush. "Mr. Trainor!"

She hurled the pad of paper onto the desk and dashed to his side. His eyelids fluttered open as she bent to look for injuries. "So hot," he mumbled. "Who are you? Wait, the ringer."

His eyes closed again. She laid the back of her hand against his forehead. His skin was on fire. She grabbed the phone and dialed Priscilla. "Mr. Trainor's really sick. Is there a nurse's office in the building?"

"I'll send someone right up," Priscilla said.

Chloe wasn't sure if she should leave her boss alone, since he looked to be in danger of sliding right out of the chair. However, she decided the best thing she could do was try to bring down some of that temperature. She raced into the kitchen and improvised a couple of ice packs at high speed.

Jogging back to the desk, she held one pack against the side of his neck and put one on top of his head.

"Ahh," he breathed out. "That feels good. You're smart, little ringer."

"I'm Chloe Russell, the temp," she said, trying to pull him back to reality.

Priscilla raced in. "The nurse is on her way up, and they've called Mr. Trainor's doctor. What's wrong?"

"He's burning up," Chloe said. "I guess Janice's flu germs got him."

"He looks terrible," Priscilla whispered. "Why didn't he stay home?"

"I'm not sick," Trainor mumbled. "I never get sick."

"The bigger they are, the harder they fall," Chloe said, shifting the ice pack to the other side of his neck. He nuzzled his cheek against it with another blissful sigh. "I'll bet he's a difficult patient."

The nurse came flying through the door, followed by Roberta and two male executives. Chloe stepped back as Trainor's staff took over.

The electronic thermometer beeped. "His temp is 104," the nurse said, her voice sharp with worry. She looked at the executives. "I can't handle this. He needs to go to the hospital immediately."

"No," Trainor said, struggling to pull himself upright. "I'm not sick."

The nurse gave him a professional smile of disbelief. "Your doctor will be here shortly. He'll make that decision." She glanced at Chloe's homemade ice packs. "We'll keep those on him."

"I can make some more packs," Chloe volunteered. It figured that Trainor would have a doctor who showed up on demand at his office.

The nurse nodded and Chloe hurried off to the kitchen again. She was holding a pack against the pulse point on one of Trainor's wrists when a lean young man with dark-red hair strode through the door.

"Dr. Cavill." The nurse's voice brimmed with relief. "His temp's 104. He's hyperthermic, but I didn't want to give him anything until you arrived."

"And I'll bet he claims he's not sick," the doctor said.

Chloe could see the effort it took for Trainor to open his eyes. "Damn straight. Just hungover. No, that was yesterday. Maybe I am sick."

"Well, that admission means he's on death's door," the doctor said. Chloe watched for signs of concern, but Cavill kept a poker face. "You should have taken that flu shot I recommended. Now you're suffering the consequences."

Trainor turned away from the doctor, his gaze stopping on her face. For a moment he looked puzzled. Then his face cleared. "Chloe Russell, the temp."

She nodded. "Yes, sir."

"Feels good," he repeated and drifted away again.

The doctor looked around the little group circling the big office chair. "Does anyone know how long he's been feverish?"

"I found him like this when I came in to work at 7:50," Chloe said.

"When did you start the ice packs?" Cavill looked at the nurse as he asked.

She nodded to Chloe. "She already had two on him when I arrived."

"Quick thinking," the doctor said. He lifted his bag and set it on the desk. "If you'll give me some privacy, I'll examine the patient."

Chloe set the cold pack on the desk and followed the group out of the office, closing the door behind her. Priscilla returned to her post in the reception area, but Roberta and the two men hovered by the door. Chloe sat down and checked her boss's calendar, finding virtually wall-to-wall meetings. She looked up at Roberta. "Should I cancel the rest of Mr. Trainor's schedule for today?"

Roberta turned to the shorter man, the same one whose office Trainor had been in. "Phil, could you take a look at Mr. Trainor's calendar and see if anything's critical?"

Phil came around the desk to lean over Chloe's shoulder. "Poor bastard, he really doesn't do anything except attend meetings," he muttered after a few seconds, his voice holding a trace of a foreign accent. "You can cancel everything but the three o'clock. I'll take care of that one. If anyone has any questions, refer them to me. I'm Phil Riviere. Executive vice president." He held out his hand to Chloe with a smile that must have charmed a thousand women.

Chloe shook his hand and nodded. "Cancel by e-mail or phone?" she asked, not knowing what the protocol would be at this level.

Phil considered the calendar. "E-mail is fine. If you draft it, I'll approve it."

Chloe nodded and began to type. She'd come up with a satisfactory paragraph when the door opened and Cavill came out.

"How is he?" Roberta asked.

"I got him to the couch, but that's as far as he could make it," Cavill said. "I think it's just the flu, but I want to run some additional tests since the fever is so high. Let me set up transport to the hospital."

He pulled out his cell phone and walked away from the desk to stand by the windows, where he spoke in a low voice Chloe couldn't hear.

The office door opened and the nurse put her head out, glancing around until she saw Chloe. "Mr. Trainor is asking for you," she said.

"Me?" Chloe's fingers stilled on the keyboard.

"He says you make him feel better," the nurse said. "The fever is making him delirious, so it's better just to go along with his requests. It will calm him down."

"Okay." Chloe stood and smoothed her palms down the front of her thighs as the high-powered executives stared at her. She followed the nurse across Trainor's office to the big suede couch in the seating area by the window.

Her boss lay with his head on one of the striped pillows, his tie gone and his shirt unbuttoned far enough so that she could see a dusting of brown hair over the muscles of his chest. He shifted uneasily and looked around with an unfocused gaze. "Make it feel better, Chloe," he muttered. "Make it better, like the report."

Chloe looked at the nurse. "How?"

"Maybe an ice pack again? You were the first person to use one. He might be remembering that. Don't move. I'll get it."

Trainor rolled over so that one of his arms flopped off the edge of the cushions, making his hand hit the carpeting. Chloe knelt and wrapped her fingers around his wrist to lift it back onto the couch. It was like touching the wax melting off a candle. She'd never known human skin could feel that hot. No wonder he wanted it to feel better.

The nurse returned with the ice pack, and Chloe laid it against his neck as she had that first one. She was rewarded with a slight upward curve of her boss's lips. He lay still, as though savoring the coolness against his neck. As she held the pack in position, she became aware of the fact that her hand was inside his open shirt, so her forearm grazed the burning skin of his chest whenever he inhaled, and his breath tickled her as he exhaled.

Even worse, her kneeling position put her right at face level with the sick man. She could see the way the texture of his skin changed from his jaw where he shaved, to the smooth skin at his temple. She could trace the wave of his hair back over the curve of his ear. She could count the tiny lines radiating from the corner of his eye. It was like being in bed with him.

She jerked back at the thought, letting the cold pack slip down onto his collarbone. He opened his eyes. Now she could see the striations of dark and light gray in his irises. He was frowning, and she guessed he was once again trying to remember who she was.

She dropped her gaze to focus on resettling the ice pack when the doctor walked over to the couch. "All set," he announced. Chloe started to stand up, but he gestured for her to stay. Then he picked up Trainor's wrist to check his pulse, frowning at his wristwatch. He muttered something under his breath before he gently placed her boss's hand back on the sofa.

Much as she wanted to know how the sick man was doing, she didn't dare presume to ask. She was just a temp, stepping in to help for a few minutes before she went back to canceling his appointments.

But he looked so ill, she couldn't help feeling a tug of anxiety. After all, he was only human, despite all his money and power. When he was sick, he felt the aches and pains as much as anyone else did.

Without thinking, she reached up to stroke his hair away from his face in a gesture of comfort. Despite all these people milling around him, he seemed oddly alone.

She wondered if Teresa would have taken care of him, had they not had a fight. As she tried to imagine the sophisticated brunette's bedside manner, three men hauling a stretcher rattled through the doorway.

There was a great flurry of activity, which ceased abruptly when Trainor opened his eyes and saw the stretcher. "No!" he said.

"Nathan, your temperature is dangerously high," Cavill said, leaning over the couch. For the first time, Chloe saw real concern on the doctor's face. "You need to go to the hospital for tests."

"No!" her boss said again. "No hospital."

The doctor and Trainor locked eyes for a long moment. Cavill stood up. "All right, no hospital. But you're going home in the ambulance because I'm not going to carry you to your car."

Trainor closed his eyes. "Can walk."

Cavill laughed. "Like hell you can." He gestured the orderlies forward.

Chloe extricated herself from the knot of people helping Trainor onto the stretcher. Her boss made an attempt to stand up on his own, but his knees gave way and the orderlies barely caught him before he hit the floor. "Big guy," one of them noted as they wrestled him onto the wheeled bed.

As they wheeled him toward the door, Chloe started to take her melting ice pack to the kitchen.

"Chloe," Trainor said. "Come with me. Feels better."

"What?" Chloe squawked. She looked at the doctor, who was following the gurney. "I'm not a nurse."

"That's not a problem," Cavill said. "I'll be with him." He frowned suddenly. "Have you had a flu shot?"

44

"Yes." Chloe always got the shot, because she didn't want to endanger Grandmillie's health by passing on germs. "What difference does that make?"

"I don't want to have to worry about you catching what Nathan has."

She shouldn't have been so honest. "Am I even allowed to ride in the ambulance?" She was grasping at straws.

The doctor shrugged. "It's a private ambulance. You can do anything Nathan wants you to."

"Chloe." Now Trainor sounded like a CEO as his voice crackled with command.

"Humor him," Cavill said.

Chloe got a grip on the towel-wrapped pack and trailed after them, making a brief stop at her desk to grab her handbag from the drawer. As they passed Roberta, Chloe cast a pleading glance at the human resources director. Roberta misinterpreted it, saying, "I'll get Priscilla to cancel the appointments."

Then she was closed into the executive elevator, whooshing down to the waiting ambulance.

As the big vehicle lurched through the streets of New York, Chloe sat wedged in on one side of Trainor's stretcher while Cavill sat on the other. Despite the jarring of potholes, her boss had fallen into a fitful sleep.

She had discarded the melted ice pack and was sitting with her hands twisted together on her lap, staring out the back window and wondering where they were going.

Her head jerked around as the doctor spoke. "I don't believe I've met you before. Ben Cavill." He held out his hand.

"Chloe Russell," she said, putting her hand in his. "I'm Mr. Trainor's temporary assistant. Janice has the flu."

"Who doesn't these days?" the doctor said. His grip was firm and dry, but his eyes were assessing. Chloe felt like a germ under a microscope. "How long have you been with him?"

"I was assigned yesterday." Since the doctor had started the conversation, she decided she could ask. "Is he going to be all right? He's so hot."

The doctor's lips twitched slightly, and Chloe noticed her unintentional double entendre. She flushed but decided to ignore it.

"He's so rarely ill that I don't know if he's prone to high fevers, but I suspect that it's just his body's normal reaction to the flu. Of course, I'll keep a close eye on him to make sure it's not pneumonia or something more sinister."

"Have you been his doctor long?" Chloe asked.

"Since I graduated from medical school," Cavill said. "We were friends as kids, so I keep a close eye on more than just his physical health."

It sounded as though he was trying to send her some kind of warning, but she couldn't figure out why he would feel the need to. In fact, she felt better knowing Trainor had a friend watching over him during his illness. "He's lucky to have you."

Cavill's eyebrows rose and he looked taken aback. "I'm not sure he'd agree at the moment."

"Where are we going?" Chloe asked after a moment of silence.

"To Nathan's home on the West Side." Cavill continued to watch her closely.

To avoid his scrutiny, she looked down at the man on the stretcher. He still had that hectic flush in his cheeks but he had stopped tossing and turning as though every inch of his body hurt.

The ambulance swerved over to the curb. The orderlies leaped out and swiftly unloaded the stretcher. Cavill helped her out of the back of the vehicle and started to lead the cavalcade toward the front door of a modern high-rise building sheathed in granite.

"I'll just catch a cab back to the office," Chloe said. She was sure Trainor Electronics would foot the bill.

"I'd rather you stayed," Cavill said. "In his delirium, he seems to have fixated on you as a caretaker."

The doctor didn't sound particularly happy about having her involved, but then Chloe wasn't either. This was the strangest situation she'd ever found herself in.

As she followed the stretcher out of the elevator doors on the level marked P-2, Chloe gawked at the huge bronze-and-crystal chandelier hanging at nearly eye level with the gallery they walked onto. A beautifully carved wooden balustrade curled around three sides of the space before it plunged downward along a grand staircase, leading to an exquisite marble mosaic floor below. Cavill walked briskly toward a wide hallway, carpeted with a gold-and-blue Oriental runner, and Chloe had to jog to catch up.

The rich really were different.

A woman dressed in a crisp nurse's uniform came out of the door at the end of the hallway to meet them. "I've got the IV set up for hydration," she said to the doctor.

He nodded and directed the orderlies into the room before he turned to Chloe. "You can wait in that bedroom to the right. As soon as we've got him undressed and in bed, we'll see if he still thinks you'll make it better." He gave her a tight smile before he disappeared through the big door.

Chloe wandered into the bedroom the doctor had pointed out. It was decorated in a mix of modern and antique furniture that was surprisingly harmonious. "I guess he hired a really good decorator," she muttered, trailing her finger over the smooth curves of a Chinese ceramic horse sculpture. The room had no personal touches, nothing that said someone lived in it, so she assumed it was a guest room. Sliding doors beckoned her past the seating area furnished with a deep yellow chaise longue that looked perfect for a long session with a good book.

She tested the slider and found it unlocked. "Well, duh, no one's going to climb up fifty floors," she reminded herself. Stepping outside the door, she gaped. The terrace spread out in front of her and to her left and right. Full-size trees in enormous terra-cotta pots rustled in the considerable breeze, while everywhere she looked flower boxes glowed with brilliant fall blossoms. Lounge chairs sat on platforms, so their reclining occupants could watch the ships and barges pass by on the Hudson River or enjoy the autumn-burnished cliffs gracing the shore of New Jersey. There were tables to eat on, folded-up awnings and umbrellas to cast shade, and a couple of burbling fountains.

All Chloe could do was stare. This demonstrated a wealth beyond anything she could wrap her mind around. Pulling the lapels of her jacket together to combat the brisk wind, she walked across the big square tiles to the railing, took a deep breath, and looked over. The cars and taxis seemed like toys as they zipped along the narrow street below. She straightened back up and fixed her gaze on a tugboat laboring up the Hudson River with its bow nudged against a barge three times its size. There were times when she felt like that tug, trying to keep herself and Grandmillie moving forward against the current that kept thrusting her back toward the churn of the ocean.

"Ms. Russell!" Cavill sounded annoyed.

She scurried back across the terrace, hoping he hadn't been calling her for long. "I'm sorry. It's such an amazing view," she said.

He didn't bother to answer that. "Nathan wants you to read him a report," he said.

"A report?" This just got weirder.

"Some marketing report he said you'd worked on."

"Oh, the one I edited. It's on the computer at the office."

"You have a smartphone?" the doctor asked.

Chloe pulled her Droid out of the handbag she'd been carrying around with her.

"Get someone to e-mail it to you on that." Cavill spun on his heel and went back into the guest room, clearly expecting her to follow him. "What temp agency do you work for?"

"Flexitemps," Chloe said, jogging after him. Why did he care about that?

Cavill slowed as they approached the master bedroom. "His temperature has been coming down slowly, and he's sliding in and out of consciousness," he said in a low voice as he pushed the door open.

Once again, Chloe caught the anxiety in his eyes and forgave the doctor for his abruptness with her.

She stepped into the room and blinked. Across the room in front of her was a wall of glass, with a view similar to the one she'd been drinking in on the terrace. Cavill turned left, bringing her gaze around to the bed set against the wall facing the windows. She hoped there were some heavy-duty shades to block out all that light.

She forgot all about views when she saw her boss lying in the huge bed wearing a dark-blue T-shirt. A sheet was pulled midway up his chest, and an IV was taped to one arm. His eyes were closed and looked as though they had sunk into his head. The unnatural flush still tinted his cheeks, and his hands twitched on top of the covers. The nurse, a stunningly beautiful blonde who looked to be about ten years older than Chloe, stood on the other side of the bed, checking a monitor.

Cavill gestured the woman over to where they stood about ten feet from the bed. He spoke in a low voice. "Tricia Oliver, meet Chloe Russell."

The nurse shook her hand. "Mr. Trainor was asking for you just a moment ago."

The doctor's lips thinned. He pointed to a spot by the windows. "You can call about the report from over there."

Chloe retreated from the grumpy doctor and retrieved the report. When she approached the doctor again, he gestured for her to sit in an armchair pulled up beside the bed. "Go ahead and read."

She enlarged the print on her phone and began. "'Analysis of Marketing for Product Number Seven-Two-Two' by Richard Sinclair." She hadn't changed the title, even though she'd longed to. She glanced over at Trainor. His eyes were closed and his hands lay still. That must be a good sign. She launched into the first paragraph, mentally editing it even more severely as her oral presentation highlighted additional problems in the sentence structure.

She forgot about her audience and plunged into the second paragraph.

A weak chuckle emanated from the bed. She stopped and looked up. Trainor's eyes remained shut but a smile touched his lips. "Knew it."

"Knew what?" she asked.

"You're a ringer," he said.

"I don't know what you mean."

"Sinclair has never written a sentence that good."

"You gave me permission to do some editing," Chloe said, not sure if he was offended by her corrections.

He turned his head on the pillow and opened his eyes, the striking combination of dark and light gray sending a shimmer of fascination through her. "Didn't expect such a good job. You've been hiding your talents under a bushel basket."

"Thank you." Gratification sent a billow of warmth through her. "Shall I go on?"

"No," he said, turning his head back again. "Wanted to confirm my suspicions. Who are you, Chloe Russell?"

Chloe sent a questioning look toward the doctor. She didn't know if she should keep talking or let Trainor sleep. Cavill nodded for her to continue.

The problem was, she didn't know what to say. "I'm just a temp," she said. "But I've worked for several small companies, start-ups, so I've had to learn about every aspect of business. Even accounting, which is not my favorite." She gave a comic grimace and then realized his eyes were closed so he couldn't see it.

"Nor mine," he surprised her by saying.

Cavill stepped forward. "Nathan, I have another house call to make, but I'll check in on you in a few hours. Tricia will keep an eye on your temperature. And Chloe will keep you company."

Chloe almost exclaimed out loud. Sitting beside a sickbed was not part of her job description. The doctor looked amused. As he walked to the door, Chloe jumped out of her chair and followed him. "Dr. Cavill, I'm not a home health aide."

"Are you supposed to be working for Mr. Trainor today?" the doctor asked, stopping just outside the door.

"As his executive assistant," Chloe said. "In his *office*."

Cavill started down the hallway. "I'll have Roberta explain your new assignment to your employer. I suspect she'll be agreeable." His tone had turned sardonic again. "I'll see you later, Ms. Russell."

Chloe put her hands on her hips and glared at the doctor's back. She had no idea what to do.

Chapter 4

When she walked back into the master bedroom, Trainor was twisting himself into the sheets again. "Talk to him," the nurse said. "Your voice seems to help."

"Um, Mr. Trainor, it's Chloe Russell. I'm here." Chloe reached out to touch the back of his hand, hoping that would bring his attention to her. The heat from his skin practically singed her fingers. She jerked her hand away.

"Shouldn't have taken the bet," Trainor mumbled, yanking at the bed linens. "Why the hell did Archer make it?"

Casting around frantically for a way to distract him, Chloe noticed a paperback sitting on the bedside table, a spy thriller by Gavin Miller. "Why don't I read to you?"

He opened those incredible eyes again. This time they were clouded. "You're the temp with the cool hands."

"Yes." She grabbed the paperback and flipped it open to the bookmarked page. "*Best faced Pasternak across the table in the interrogation room. Pasternak looked at his watch. 'You've got two minutes to make up your mind.' Best smiled. 'I don't need two minutes.' Pasternak waited. Best kept smiling. Pasternak finally spoke. 'Your smile irritates me. I'll have Smeltin start with pulling out all your—"*

An electronic alarm shrilled, making Chloe drop the book in a flutter of pages. The nurse muttered something under her breath as she checked one of the screens.

"What's going on?" Chloe asked as the alarm vibrated through her skull and her pulse raced with fear. She checked Trainor's chest to make sure it was still rising and falling.

"His temperature is spiking," Tricia said, hitting a button that silenced the alarm. "We need to bring it down, stat."

"I can make ice packs. Do you know where the kitchen is?" Chloe rocketed out of her chair.

"A lukewarm bath will work better." Tricia pointed to a door across the room. "The bathroom's there. Run the water at room temperature, and I'll call for some help to move him."

Trainor was plucking at the hem of his T-shirt. "My clothes! On fire!"

Tricia clasped Trainor's wrists. "Mr. Trainor, remain calm. We'll get your clothes off. You'll be fine."

"Burning!" Trainor shouted as Chloe started toward the bathroom. "Get the temp!"

Chloe spun back toward her temporary boss. He had pulled his hands out of Tricia's grasp and was tearing at his shirt.

"Try to calm him down," Tricia said. "I'm going to disconnect the IV before he pulls it out."

Chloe approached the bed. Trainor had kicked the sheets off. She had no idea what she should do. "Mr. Trainor, I'm here. What can I do to help?"

He stared down at his pajama pants with a look of horror. He stopped yanking on his shirt and began to swat at his legs. "Put it out!"

Tricia was trying to catch the arm with the IV in it, but Trainor continued to flail wildly. Panic clutched at Chloe's throat. She needed to get his attention. What was his first name? "Nathan!" she shouted, grabbing his wrist and clinging to it as if her life depended on it. "You have to hold still!"

Whether in shock or obedience, Trainor let her stop his flailing. Tricia swiftly removed the IV and slapped on a bandage. "Keep him quiet while I get the bath going and make that call."

He began to tear at his shirt again. She put one palm on either side of Trainor's scorching-hot head and turned his face toward her as she leaned in close. "I'm the temp. I'm here."

Chloe found herself nose to nose with the hallucinating CEO of a multibillion-dollar corporation. She was half lying across his chest and could feel the heat of his fever searing through her silk blouse. She eased the pressure of her hands against his head, sliding them down to rest on his shoulders so she could push herself upright.

"No," he said, his arms coming around her back and crushing her down against him so her face was smashed into his shoulder.

She gave an experimental push to see if he would release her, but instead his hold tightened. "Mr. Trainor, please," she begged, turning her head. He had a chest like a steel plate, and his arms felt like cables tying her down. She could hear his heart beating at a frantic rate. "I can't breathe," she gasped.

"You stopped the fire," he said.

Chloe went limp, since struggling seemed to make him press even harder. Despite his feverish strength, she felt an odd sense of security as she lay against his heated body; his grasp was persuasive, not threatening. He simply wanted her to stay.

"It's my heart," he said.

"Your heart hurts?" *Could he be having a heart attack?*

"No, the asinine bet."

"You bet on something?" Relief and embarrassment flooded her as she heard the door open. Tricia had gotten help. Chloe hoped it wasn't the disapproving Dr. Cavill. Being caught half in bed with Trainor wouldn't improve the doctor's opinion of her.

"Okay, Chloe, you can get up now." Tricia's voice came from behind her.

"He won't let go," Chloe said, trying again to squirm free.

An older man with dark-brown hair graying at the temples, dressed in a navy-blue suit, moved into her line of sight. Giving her a quizzical look, he said, "Nathan, your office is on the line. You need to speak with Janice."

The bands across her back loosened as she heard Trainor mutter, "My office."

"The phone is in the bathroom," the older man said. "Come with me and I'll show you."

"The phone," Trainor muttered, his arms falling away from her.

Chloe righted herself and took a hasty step back from the bed. She wasn't giving Trainor a chance to change his mind. "Thank you," she said, inhaling deeply.

"My pleasure," the gentleman said before he turned toward Trainor again. "Let me give you a hand." He slid an arm behind the CEO's back and eased him into a sitting position before two muscular blond men in khakis and matching polo shirts stepped up to the bed. They got Trainor on his feet, supporting him as he staggered across the room, with Tricia leading the way and the man in the suit following behind.

Chloe blew out a breath and walked over to the window to stare at the Hudson River rolling on its oblivious way. No one had commented on her full-body contact with her boss, thank goodness.

She heard splashing from the open bathroom door and the soothing but authoritative voice of the older man. Which sent her imagination veering into the forbidden zone of what Nathan Trainor would look like without his pajamas on. The soft cotton T-shirt he'd been wearing had stretched taut over some darned impressive pecs and abs, although the loose pants hadn't revealed much about his legs. Her memory kicked in with those few moments when she'd simply relaxed into his embrace. Warmth sizzled inside her as she remembered how her breasts had been crushed against the solid wall of his chest while his hands roamed over her back.

It had been a long time since she'd been locked against a man's body. Clearly, too long, since she was fantasizing about her seriously ill boss. It was strangely flattering that he'd turned to her in his delirium.

"Where is he?"

Chloe spun around to see Cavill standing by the bed with a sleek steel case in his hand.

"In the bathroom," she said. "Tricia's trying to bring his temperature down with a bath."

Cavill leaned in to peer at the bank of monitors, grunted, and strode to the bathroom door.

Chloe could hear the doctor's voice in counterpoint to Tricia's, in a series of rapid-fire questions and answers.

She went back to her river gazing until her stomach growled. Glancing at her watch, she realized it was lunchtime. Trainor's penthouse undoubtedly had a kitchen somewhere, but she figured she'd better not leave while the distrustful doctor was around.

There was more splashing and voices. One of the blond gods dashed out, rummaged around in a dresser drawer, and carried what must have been fresh pajamas back into the bathroom. Did Trainor keep random strong men on his staff just in case he got sick?

Cavill interrupted her thoughts as he joined her by the window. "He keeps asking for you."

"I'm not going in there if he's naked."

The doctor raised an eyebrow. "I assumed you'd already . . . ?"

Chloe waited for him to finish and was flabbergasted when he let the question trail off. "Are you implying that I . . . that we . . . ?" She sputtered to a halt. "I met the man for the first time yesterday! At work!"

"Sorry. You seemed to be . . . never mind." Cavill raised a hand in apology. "I'm worried about him."

His tie was crooked and his shirt and suit jacket showed large patches of dampness. He'd gotten splashed by his difficult patient. Chloe noted the tension in his jaw and decided to give him a pass on his offensive assumption. "Just so you know, I have a hard-and-fast rule against dating the boss." A hard lesson she'd learned fast.

Cavill nodded and copied Chloe's earlier pose, gazing out the window for a long moment before turning back to her. "For some reason, you're the only person who can calm him when the delirium takes hold. I want you to spend the night here."

"What! No." She couldn't leave Grandmillie alone overnight. She'd have a knot of worry in her chest the entire time. "That's not in my job description."

"You're Mr. Trainor's assistant, aren't you?" the doctor said.

"I'm a temp, not a nurse."

"I'll authorize triple overtime pay."

An involuntary mental estimate made her sigh at turning down such a hefty sum. "More money isn't going to change my mind. I have responsibilities at home."

The gathering frustration on Cavill's face cleared, and he waved a hand in dismissal. "What do you need? A babysitter? A chauffeur? I can arrange all that."

Grandmillie would have a fit if some stranger showed up to stay with her. She insisted that she was perfectly capable of taking care of herself, even though Chloe had begun to worry that it wasn't true. "Look, my eighty-six-year-old grandmother lives with me, and I never leave her alone overnight."

"No wonder you don't date your boss," Cavill said with an amused edge in his voice. "I'll send a health aide to keep her company."

"That won't work. Grandmillie is very independent." Chloe hesitated, not sure how to explain how ticked off her grandmother would be.

"I understand." He really seemed to, because his expression softened. "I wouldn't ask you to do this if Nathan weren't so ill. His fever is spiking to dangerous levels, and he could hurt himself during a hallucination."

"But he's got you and all kinds of other staff members."

Cavill locked his blue eyes on her. "He needs you."

Chloe hesitated. Having a CEO need her was truly bizarre.

"You can give your grandmother my twenty-four-hour emergency number," the doctor said. "If she needs medical care, I can get it to her faster than you can."

She glanced at the enormous bed, its rich wood frame and leather inlays contrasting with the high-tech monitors arrayed around it, and realized Cavill was right. "If Grandmillie agrees, I'll stay."

The doctor ignored her qualifying statement and went into organizational mode. "I'll get a bed brought in for you." Cavill pulled a prescription pad out of his pocket and scrawled a couple of phone numbers on it before tearing off the sheet. "Here's my emergency contact number and the number here at Nathan's. Someone always answers the phone here."

"Which one, Romulus or Remus?" Chloe muttered, accepting the paper.

"What?"

"The matching blonds," Chloe said.

Cavill gave a snort of laughter. "They're personal trainers who work in the building. I don't know their names."

"And the older gentleman?"

"Ed Roccuzzo. Nathan's butler."

"Of course. Silly me, I should have known."

"Maybe *butler* is the wrong term," Cavill said. "He manages all of Nathan's houses and staff. It's a big job."

"I'm sure it is." She was beginning to understand how very far removed Trainor's life was from her own. He practically breathed different air.

For the next twenty-four hours she was going to be breathing it right along with him.

Chapter 5

Nathan came awake with a sense of relief and a raging thirst. Relief from what, he had no idea. He was lying on his back in his own bed, while a strange bluish glow washed over the ceiling above him. He turned his head on the pillow to see where it came from and found a bank of medical monitors. Beside them a male nurse dressed in immaculate white scrubs sat in a chair reading an electronic tablet. Ben had overreacted as usual. That was the problem with having your friend as your doctor.

Nathan rolled his head back to center and stared up at the eerie light, trying to piece together the fragments whirling through his memory. It was night. He'd gone to work that morning—at least, he assumed it was still the same day—despite feeling out of sorts. He'd convinced himself it was just the tail end of the previous day's hangover.

Evidently, he'd been wrong.

He gazed at the ceiling some more. He remembered Ben needling him over his lack of a flu shot, so it must be the flu.

Other than that, all he came up with was a kaleidoscope of what were clearly hallucinations that involved his clothes being on fire, drowning in his own bathtub, and towers of paperwork crushing him to death. He grimaced. What did it say about his state of mind that his fever brought out images of death?

The one pleasant delirium dream he'd had was his new temp being draped over him in bed. He went back to that one, remembering the softness of her breasts against his chest and the curve of her hips under his hands.

That was better.

A shiver shook him and he realized that both his pajamas and the bedding were soaked and cooling rapidly. His fever must have broken. He needed dry pajamas and a tall, cold drink of water. He was about to throw the covers off and sit up when he realized there was a tube running into his right arm. He turned his head in the other direction to follow it, and his gaze landed on a cot holding the sleeping form of none other than the temp. Chloe Russell.

"What the hell are you doing here?"

A voice like the crack of a whip smacked Chloe awake. She sat up in a strange bed and glanced around an unfamiliar room bathed in a weird blue glow, wondering where on earth she was.

"Chloe?"

The voice. She knew it from somewhere. She swiveled around to find Nathan Trainor lying in a bed next to hers, scowling at her, and it all came back to her.

"You're awake," she said, pushing her hair back from her face and bracing herself for whatever new weirdness her delirious boss would come up with now.

"And his temp's normal," Arvind the night nurse said as he looked up from checking the monitor. He moved to the bed and tested the sheets near Trainor with his hand. "You'll want dry pajamas and linens." He disappeared into the bluish gloom.

Chloe heaved a sigh of relief. No bizarre feverish behavior to deal with.

Trainor's scowl was still directed toward her. "Do you have any medical training?" he asked.

"No, sir." Chloe swung her legs over the edge of the cot and straightened her blouse.

"Then why are you here?"

She eyed her boss. His damp hair clung to his skull while sweat stains spread across the fabric of his gray T-shirt. Even though the fever was gone, he couldn't be feeling well. It would pay to tread softly. "Dr. Cavill asked me to stay."

He made a gesture of exasperation. "In case I wanted you to type a memo? What the hell was Ben thinking?"

She sent a prayer of thanks skyward. He didn't remember his fixation on her. "You found my voice soothing when you were delirious. It calmed you down."

"Your voice." His tone was skeptical.

"I think you associated it with coolness because I put an ice pack on you when I found you in the office this—I mean, yesterday—morning."

His brows were still drawn together, but he changed the subject. "I'm fine now, so you can go home. Ed can get you a car."

"Terrific," she said, standing up with enthusiasm. She could run home to check on Grandmillie, and since it was four in the morning, she'd still get some nice overtime pay.

Arvind cleared his throat politely. "If you'd step outside, I'll help Mr. Trainor change."

Chloe scooped up her jacket and handbag from the foot of the cot. "I'm very glad you're feeling better, Mr. Trainor. Good night."

Trainor turned toward the nurse with an irritable wave of dismissal. "I can change my own damn pajamas."

Cranky indeed. Chloe hustled out of the room, nearly colliding with Ed Roccuzzo in the hallway. He was wearing dark trousers with a knife pleat down the front and a white polo shirt. Surely he didn't sleep in those.

"Is there a problem?" he asked. Despite his calm tone, she could see worry in the creases of his forehead. "Arvind rang."

"Exactly the opposite. Mr. Trainor's fever broke, so he's sending me home. He said you wouldn't mind arranging a car for me." Ordinarily, she would get herself home to New Jersey, but at this hour she would accept the ride.

Ed still looked concerned. "Dr. Cavill felt you should stay until morning. Mr. Trainor's temperature could go up again."

"Mr. Trainor was pretty definite about my leaving."

"The doctor will be here soon. Why don't you take advantage of the guest bathroom's amenities while I speak with him?" Ed indicated the room Chloe had wandered into hours before. "Please help yourself to any supplies you'd like to use."

She smoothed a hand over her rumpled hair and thought longingly of a toothbrush. Walking into the guest suite, she pulled open a door and found a walk-in closet that made her sigh with envy. The shelving was made of some exotic, pale wood with a dramatic grain, and the hardware was gleaming brushed nickel. The rods were half-filled with clothes with tags hanging from them. She picked one at random and discovered it indicated the size of the garment and its fabric content. Men's clothes were ranged on one side, while women's hung on the other. Could these be for the use of Trainor's guests?

Shoe boxes were slotted into custom-made cubbies. She couldn't resist opening a Jimmy Choo box marked "Evening Sandals" with her size on the outside.

She breathed out an *ooh* of delight. Aqua and forest-green crystals sparkled on leaf-shaped straps that wrapped around the foot. A high, slender black suede heel added to the elegance. They were the kind of shoes she fantasized about as she trolled through shoe websites. And they cost nearly two thousand dollars. She ran her fingertip over a line of crystals, fighting the longing to find out what it would be like to see this work of art on her foot. She was in her stocking feet, so it would only take a second to slip it on . . .

She slammed the lid closed. It would just make her knockoffs seem cheaper and drearier if she tried on the real thing. Shoving the box back into its niche, she marched out of the closet and tried the next door.

It led to a bathroom fit for a palace—all gray-and-white marble with silver tile mosaic accents. The tub would accommodate four people, if they liked each other, and the array of toiletries made her sigh. Even the toothbrushes sported polished wooden handles. The thought of using one and throwing it away offended her sense of thrift, so she did a thorough swish with mouthwash, using her finger to scrub at her teeth. After brushing her hair and adjusting her rumpled clothes, she wandered over to the sliding doors that gave access to the huge terrace.

"The city that never sleeps," she murmured, scanning the lit windows of the skyscrapers beyond the terrace's parapet.

"Ms. Russell." Chloe spun around to see Ed hovering at the door. "Dr. Cavill would like you to stay the rest of the night, if that's all right with you."

Chloe gave him a shrug and a smile. "It's four in the morning. What better things would I have to do?" She started toward the door.

Ed cleared his throat. "Dr. Cavill and Mr. Trainor are not in agreement about where you should sleep, so you might want to wait a few moments before you go in there."

"Let me guess. Dr. Cavill wants me on the cot, and Mr. Trainor doesn't."

"That's correct."

She couldn't blame Trainor for not wanting a total stranger sleeping beside him when he felt lousy. "Let me know when they make a decision." She hesitated before saying, "I walked into the closet when I was looking for the bathroom. I just wondered . . . who do all those clothes belong to?"

"They're for Mr. Trainor's guests. Please feel free to borrow anything you'd like."

Chloe thought of strolling into Trainor's bedroom in the evening sandals and had to suppress a giggle. "Thanks, but I was just curious."

Ed nodded and withdrew, closing the door gently behind him. She sat down on the chaise longue, pulled out her cell phone, and checked for missed calls. There were none, so either Grandmillie was fine, or she'd fallen and couldn't get up. Chloe grimaced at her gallows humor. Grandmillie was undoubtedly sound asleep in her own bed and wouldn't appreciate all of Chloe's worrying.

She could hear muffled voices from the next room, their tones testy. Trainor wasn't giving in to the doctor's orders without a fight. She stretched out on the chaise and closed her eyes, listening to the rise and fall of the argument next door.

"Ms. Russell."

Chloe sat up abruptly. Cavill stood at the foot of the chaise, looking down at her. She'd nodded off while she waited. "Sorry," she said, swinging her legs over so she could stand up. "It's late."

Cavill nodded. "I'm not going to mislead you. Nathan doesn't want you in his bedroom, but I've insisted."

She had to swallow a nervous giggle at his phrasing.

The doctor looked away and then back at her. "I'm sorry if he's not as appreciative as he should be."

Once again, she read the strain on Cavill's face. "Is he still very sick?"

The doctor made a gesture of uncertainty. "Fevers often go back up." He wasn't indulging the whim of a rich and important man; he was worried about his friend.

"I'll do whatever I can."

Cavill gave her a tired smile and walked beside her into the master suite.

Trainor was sitting up in the bed, his broad shoulders and chest covered by a dry dark-green T-shirt. His damp hair was neatly combed, and his eyes were unclouded by fever. When his gaze fell on Chloe, his mouth tightened. "Your presence is entirely unnecessary. Please allow Ed to send you home in a car."

"Your doctor believes I should stay," Chloe said.

"My doctor is an infuriating ass." Trainor turned his glare on Cavill.

"You're too weak to throw her out bodily," Cavill said, "so you might as well be gracious."

"I can fire her," Trainor said, although Chloe detected a lack of conviction in his voice.

"Then I'll hire her," the doctor replied.

She felt caught in the clash of the titans as the two men squared off.

Trainor sagged back on the pillow. "You win this round, Ben. Just leave me the hell alone."

"Gladly," Cavill said, picking up his bag. "I don't envy Ms. Russell having to spend the next few hours in your unpleasant company." He turned to Chloe. "Arvind knows what to do medically. Your job is to calm the savage beast."

Trainor muttered something unflattering under his breath, and Cavill chuckled as he walked out the door.

Chloe stood beside the cot, wondering if she was supposed to talk to her boss or encourage him to sleep. Trainor lifted his head and locked his gaze on her. "You can sleep in the guest room. If I become uncontrollable, Arvind can call you in to the rescue." His tone became heavily ironic.

Now what was she supposed to do? "Dr. Cavill told me to stay in here." She cast a glance of appeal at Arvind. He nodded.

"Oh, for God's sake, sleep wherever you want." Trainor closed his eyes. Now Chloe could see the dark circles under his eyes and the way the skin stretched too tightly over his cheekbones.

She felt awkward lying down on the cot even though Trainor wasn't watching. Her gaze landed on the paperback on the bedside table. "Would you like me to read to you?"

His eyelids snapped open and he skewered her with a look of utter disbelief. "In the middle of the night? No, I would like you to let me sleep."

She was tired and worried about Grandmillie or she wouldn't have snapped. "I don't want to be here in the middle of the night either, but your friend is concerned about you, so I agreed to stay as an act of kindness. Clearly, that quality is wasted on you."

She heard the nurse hiss in a breath as Trainor stared at her. Now he would fire her, and Cavill wouldn't be around to rehire her. She squared her shoulders and met his eyes straight on, refusing to show how horrified she was by her outburst.

Incredibly, the corners of Trainor's mouth twitched. "It's completely wasted on me. Remember that in the future. Now go to sleep, my grumpy little temp. We're none of us at our best at this hour." He shifted downward on the pillows and turned onto his side so his back was to her.

She sank onto the cot, her eyes tracing the line of Trainor's spine under the form-hugging T-shirt. She could see his shoulder muscles flex and shift as he settled into a more comfortable position. It was weirdly intimate to listen to his breath begin to slow and even rasp in a near snore.

Dropping her head into her hands, she massaged her temples with her thumbs. He hadn't fired her. However, he wouldn't be going to work for at least a day or two, so that left her without a position in the executive suite. She sighed. So much for the extra pay she had been counting on.

She flopped over sideways and brought her legs up onto the cot, pulling the pillow under her head and giving it a frustrated punch.

As always, it was the people like her who lost out when the big wheels had a problem.

Chapter 6

Nathan rolled over with a groan. His arms and legs felt like they were made of rubber, and someone seemed to be rapping on his skull with a hammer.

With a Herculean effort, he opened his eyes, and once again found Chloe Russell asleep beside his bed, bathed in the pale light of dawn. At least this time he remembered how she'd gotten there. Too exhausted to move, he let his gaze roam over the not-unattractive picture of her streaked, sleep-tousled hair spread over the pillow, and the swell of her breast highlighted by her up-flung arm. Her lips, so firm and prim when she was awake, were full, and a soft shade of pink without their usual lipstick.

He felt an unexpected tightening below his waist and sprawled onto his back to fix his gaze on the ceiling. If he was lusting after the temp, he wasn't as sick as Ben thought. The surge of desire dissipated as he remembered the long list of appointments he'd missed the day before. Not to mention the ones he would miss today, because he wasn't kidding himself about being able to go into work. He'd barely been able to stagger to the bathroom last night, and he was probably contagious.

The thought made him turn back to Chloe with a frown. She'd been breathing in the germ-laden air around him, so she was likely to be the flu's next victim. Then he'd have that on his conscience.

On the other hand, she'd already been exposed, so further contact with him couldn't make it any worse. She could stay and help him work from home.

He felt more cheerful at the prospect and wondered why. He was accustomed to working from home without any assistance. It must be another sign of how badly the flu had undermined his strength.

One of the monitors beeped, and Chloe's eyes came open. Their gazes met, and for one moment, those full lips of hers curved into a smile. The smile disappeared as confusion clouded her face and she sat up, clutching the covers to her chest as though she was wearing something more revealing than the now-wrinkled blouse she'd worn to work the day before. Guilt jabbed at him; Ben had upended her schedule without much concern.

"Wha—?" Chloe shook her hair out of her face. He saw the moment her memory of the situation clicked in, and she said, "You look better. How are you feeling?"

"Since I don't remember much about the last twenty-four hours, I can't say I feel better, but I suspect I do."

The worry cleared from her expression, and she released the sheet. "I'm pretty sure you couldn't have put that sentence together last night, so the fever must be down."

So he'd been incoherent. "Did I babble like an idiot?"

"Well, you babbled, but since you were having hallucinations, I don't think you were being an idiot. You just saw things that weren't there."

The hallucinations were beginning to fade from his memory. Only one remained vivid, and that was the feel of Chloe pressed against his chest as he lay in bed. A quick analysis offered two possibilities: either his brain preferred the pleasant image and held onto it, or the event had actually occurred. He decided to embrace the former explanation because the latter would make working with Chloe awkward.

"I have a proposition for you," he said. The temp looked wary. "I'm sure Ben won't let me go to the office today, and I have a lot to catch up on. You've already been exposed to my germs, which I apologize for but cannot fix. Would you consider working here with me?"

Her eyebrows drew downward as she untangled herself from the bedding and stood up. She had her lips pursed again. Instead of looking at him, she turned her gaze to the windows, where the tops of the buildings on the river's western shore were just beginning to catch the early sun's rays. "I'd need to go home first," she said. She waved her hands down alongside her body in a movement that was meant to indicate her rumpled clothing but only succeeded in drawing his eye to her curves again. "To change."

"There are clothes in the guest room you can use."

A mixture of animosity and amusement scudded across her face. "I know."

"If you're tired, you're welcome to use the guest bed as well." She gave a tiny shake of her head, and he realized he didn't want her to say no. "I'll double your hourly rate."

She brought her gaze back to him. "Dr. Cavill tripled it."

"You drive a hard bargain." He made a gesture of agreement. "Consider your rate tripled."

She nodded. "But I still have to go home. It should only take about three hours, depending on traffic."

"Where do you live?"

"New Jersey."

"You can use the helicopter. That will eliminate the traffic and get you back faster."

The look of astonishment on her face was worth the price of the aviation fuel it would take. "Use . . . the . . . helicopter." She stared at him. "Where do you think it will land? I don't exactly have a helipad on my roof."

"The pilot can figure that out and set up a car to meet you." When her brown eyes went even wider, he began to enjoy himself.

"You're serious." She shook her head as though she was trying to wake up from a deep sleep. "I guess I should be flattered that my time is so valuable to you."

"You should be." He allowed himself to smile as he touched the control panel on his bedside table. "Good morning, Ed. Get Kurt to fire up the small chopper."

"I'll be back as soon as possible," Chloe told the driver of the black sedan that had been waiting for her at the airport. This trip was a commuter's ultimate fantasy.

"Take your time," he said, closing the car door he was holding for her.

Chloe jogged up the bluestone sidewalk and unlocked the front door of her small stucco-and-brick house. She loved the solid feel of the oak door. It spoke of security to her. Her grandmother got up early, so she didn't hesitate to sing out, "Grandmillie, I'm home!"

Silence seemed to shudder through the house, making Chloe bolt for her grandmother's downstairs bedroom. The door was open. Chloe sprinted through it to find the bed neatly made, with no sign that her grandmother had slept in it. She ran around to the other side of the bed, but Grandmillie wasn't lying unconscious or disabled on the floor.

She heard the sound of water running and the bathroom door opening, and closed her eyes in a brief moment of relief. The steady rhythm of Grandmillie's footsteps accompanied by the tap of her cane floated to her ears like the sweetest music.

"Grandmillie!" she said, walking into the hall and enveloping her grandmother in a hug.

"Good heavens, girl, you've only been gone for one night." Grandmillie hugged Chloe back before extricating herself from the embrace.

"It was a long night," Chloe said. Her grandmother was fully dressed, her hair neatly pinned into its usual French twist, her cane's colors matching the royal blue and yellow of her blouse. That made everything right with Chloe's world.

Grandmillie turned toward the kitchen. "You can tell me about it over some oatmeal and fruit."

"Tempting, but I have to shower, change, and go back to work." She didn't mention that she'd be working in Trainor's home. Although her grandmother mostly had moved with the times, on occasion she surprised Chloe with an old-fashioned reaction.

"I'll have the oatmeal ready for when you're done dressing." Grandmillie was a strong believer in the importance of eating a healthy meal at the start of the day.

"Well, er, here's the thing. There's a car and a helicopter waiting for me."

Grandmillie raised her eyebrows. "Did you say a helicopter?"

Chloe gave an embarrassed shrug, since she thought it was a ridiculous extravagance too. "My boss wants me back quickly."

"He sent you here in a *helicopter*?"

"Actually, we landed at the Essex County Airport, and there was a car waiting for me." Chloe was beginning to realize that Grandmillie wasn't happy about something.

"Young lady, if your boss has you riding around in a helicopter, then he certainly could have provided a shower and a change of clothes. I know how those corporate offices are with their fancy gyms and locker rooms. You didn't have to come all the way back to New Jersey just to freshen up." Grandmillie put her hands on her hips, her cane jutting out at an angle that somehow indicated her annoyance. "You came back here to check on me."

"That's not true." Chloe tried to deflect the lecture she knew was coming. "I wanted my own clothes after a night of sleeping on a cot in a strange place."

"Remember our deal, Chloe? If my living here begins to interfere with your life in any way, I will sign myself into an assisted-living facility immediately." Grandmillie gave her a stern look. "That persistent Dr. Cavill gave me his personal emergency cell phone number, and you made me swear to wear my medical alert necklace, which I am." Grandmillie held up the stylish pendant that concealed the call button she could push in case she fell or had another problem that required assistance when Chloe wasn't home. "I don't appreciate being treated like an invalid, but I know your concern comes from the heart."

"I'm glad you realize that," Chloe said. "I don't mean to worry, but after the insanity of last night, I needed to come home to you. I was feeling lost, and you're my compass."

"Nonsense," Grandmillie said, but her expression softened. "You've got a good head on your shoulders."

Chloe smiled. "That's what I needed to hear. I felt like I fell down the rabbit hole into Wonderland. You wouldn't believe my boss's apartment, if you can call it that. It's really a whole house inside a skyscraper, with a grand staircase and huge terraces and an incredible view of the river and New Jersey. He even has Jimmy Choo shoes for his guests to borrow."

Grandmillie snorted as she took her hands off her hips. "Why you are so taken with those outlandishly high-heeled, outrageously expensive frou-frou designer shoes, I can't figure out."

"Maybe I have a Cinderella complex." Chloe gave her grandmother another hug. "I've got to shower, but I'll take you up on the oatmeal, after all. The helicopter can just wait a little longer."

Chapter 7

Nathan felt his mood lighten as Chloe Russell walked into his bedroom, looking both refreshed and businesslike in a slim charcoal skirt, a deep blue blouse, and black high-heeled pumps. He gave himself the pleasure of letting his gaze skim down her legs to her elegant ankles.

His doctor was less appreciative. "What the hell is she doing here?" Ben rapped out.

"Your manners are appalling, Ben," Nathan said. "My apologies, Chloe. Ben thinks I should spend the day sleeping."

"He's a doctor," she said with a tilt of a smile, "so he's probably right. You were pretty sick yesterday."

Irritation flared. "It was the flu. Nothing more serious than that."

"People die of the flu, you stubborn ass," Ben said.

Nathan caught the little choke of laughter the temp quickly stifled. He quelled a smile. "She finds you amusing, which is more than I do. I'm fine, so you can stop hovering and go treat someone who needs it. Before you go, get this damned tube out of my arm so I can get up." He held out his tethered arm to his friend.

Ben's eyebrows drew down in a scowl. "If your fever spikes again, you're going to need the intravenous line."

"Luis can put it back in," Nathan said, glancing at the nurse who stood beside the monitors.

Chloe spoke up. "I promise to keep an eye on him. If he looks feverish, I'll go on strike." She gave Ben a smile that pissed Nathan off. He was her boss; she should be smiling at *him*.

Ben nodded to Luis, who removed the needle and tube so skillfully that Nathan barely felt it.

"Now I have work to do," Nathan said, giving Ben a hard stare.

The doctor turned to Chloe. "If he gets out of bed other than to go to the bathroom, call me immediately. He won't admit it, but he's as weak as a kitten." Ben's eyes gleamed with wicked satisfaction at his description.

"Kittens have claws, Cavill," Nathan said. "And I'm about to use mine."

Ben laughed and picked up his bag. "Force fluids. Sleep when you get tired." His expression sobered. "Take it easy, Nathan. You won't do anyone any good if you suffer a relapse because you pushed yourself too hard and fast."

That was the problem with Ben. He knew he could defuse Nathan's anger with genuine concern.

"Chloe has guaranteed my good behavior," Nathan said, enjoying the temp's alert gaze as she watched the battle between Ben and him.

The doctor walked to the door. "A task I don't envy her, you royal pain," he said as he left.

Nathan surveyed Chloe. He felt at a disadvantage since he was lying in bed in a T-shirt and pajama pants while she looked crisp and professional. Maybe a little too professional, with her hair yanked back into some sort of bun. He preferred it loose and bed-mussed as it had been when she woke up that morning, but he supposed he couldn't tell her that. "Let's get started," he said instead. "You can use the desk there." He pointed to a small workstation Ed had set up beside the bed, which was equipped with a laptop, a printer, and other office supplies.

A look of relief crossed Chloe's face as she walked to the desk and seated herself in the ergonomic chair, her back ramrod straight. Clearly, she felt more comfortable when the situation was all business. He could deal with that.

Chloe had worked in some sketchy offices in her career with start-ups, but sitting at a desk beside Nathan Trainor's bed was the strangest working experience she'd ever had. Her boss was propped up on a bank of pillows arrayed against the huge wooden headboard inset with deep blue leather tooled in swirling geometric patterns. As spectacular as the bed was, the man in it was far more magnetic, even with dark circles under his gray eyes. His shoulders did an impressive job of covering a fair amount of the width of the bed, and his hair was just rumpled enough to look slept on. She found her gaze sliding along the curve of his biceps and forearm, down to where his hand lay on the fine cotton of the taupe-colored quilt. He had square palms and long fingers.

"Let's start with my e-mails. Just read me the sender names and subject lines."

His voice jerked her back into business mode, dispelling her unruly brain's vivid image of his index finger tracing a line down her neck into the vee of her blouse. She stared at the computer screen a moment before she remembered how to open his e-mail program.

She began to reel off the list, starting with the oldest unread e-mails.

"Repeat that one," he commanded, stopping her.

"Koenig, Andrew. Status of Prometheus." She glanced over to see him frown at the windows across from him.

"Let's hear what it says," he said after a long moment.

She opened the e-mail and began to read. It was a combination of techspeak and code names for various parts of whatever Prometheus was. At the end of the memo, which was about ten paragraphs long, she had no more idea of what the project was than when she started reading. However, one thing she could pick up from the tone was that Prometheus was not going well.

She turned away from the computer screen to look at her boss. His head was tilted back on the pillow, and his eyes were closed.

"Are you all right?" she asked, starting to rise from the fancy chair.

His eyelids snapped open and she caught the blaze of anger in his eyes. "No, I'm not, but it has nothing to do with the flu."

She sank back down, letting the chair cradle her weight. She could practically feel the frustration vibrating in him. He picked up one of his pillows and slammed it against the headboard as though to prop himself up more securely, but he didn't fool her. He really wanted to hurl something across the room. After a few moments of scowling, he threw the covers back and swung his legs over the side of the bed so his back was to her.

"May I get you something, Mr. Trainor?" the nurse asked, coming to his feet.

"No!" Trainor barked before adding in a more civil tone, "Thank you."

Chloe watched the muscles of Trainor's back bunch and shift under the T-shirt as he shoved himself upright. The nurse subtly moved closer as the invalid swayed and grabbed for the headboard.

"Don't hover," Trainor snapped. "If I fall down, I won't hold you responsible."

"Yes, sir," Luis said, but he didn't back off.

Trainor steadied himself and let go of the headboard, padding across the expanse of thick blue carpet and polished wooden floor to the seating area by the windows. Chloe couldn't tear her eyes away from his bare feet; they were long and narrow with high arches. It was strange to see the powerful and intimidating CEO without shoes—it made him seem like a regular human being.

He came to a stop at the windows, staring out for a moment before he sank into one of the low-armed chairs upholstered in a richly textured pale cream cut velvet.

Chloe heard Luis breathe out a sigh of relief.

As her boss sat silent and unmoving, she hesitated. The room was too big to hold an entire conversation across. "Do you want me to join you over there, Mr. Trainor?" she finally asked.

He ran his palms over his face before he said, "No. Much as it pains me to admit it, Ben is right." He levered himself out of the chair and headed back toward the bed. Luis started toward him, but Trainor waved him away with an irritated gesture.

This time he came around to where Chloe sat and lowered himself onto the side of the bed. The ligaments in his neck stood out, and she realized how much willpower he'd exerted to get himself across the room without assistance. Trainor sat with his hands braced on his knees. "I would wish this flu only on my worst enemy."

"Weak as a kitten?" Chloe said.

"Weaker," Trainor said, lifting his legs onto the bed and resuming his previous position against the pile of pillows. "Even the desperate state of the Prometheus project can't generate enough energy to keep me upright."

"Why don't I let you rest?" Chloe said, noting the way his body seemed to slump into the bed.

"I may not be able to walk, but I can think," he snapped, turning his head to glare at her.

"Well, you might think about renaming the Prometheus project," Chloe said, tired of his crankiness.

"Prometheus gave mankind the gift of fire, enabling all progress." At least he sounded interested rather than grouchy.

"And ended up having his liver eaten by an eagle over and over again," she pointed out.

"So you think we doomed the project by giving it the wrong name?"

She thought it was nice to see the strain around his mouth ease. "I'm just saying that it's never good to tempt the gods." After all, she brought the Russell jinx to her jobs, even though she couldn't take the blame for the difficulties of the Prometheus project since it had been developed before she worked at Trainor Electronics. "What is the Prometheus project anyway?"

"It's the next generation of battery, based on nanotechnology to make it incredibly small and light. It can power an electronic device for weeks instead of days." His face lit up with the intensity of his enthusiasm. "It could bring power to remote villages that can only access the power grid sporadically. Long-distance travelers won't have to search for plugs in airports. Military outposts can carry smaller, more portable generators." The light in his eyes died. "Except it doesn't work."

"Yet," Chloe said.

He looked at her. "Are you trying to give me a pep talk?"

She shrugged. "You told me yourself that you have the best R and D staff in the industry. They'll figure it out."

"You're more optimistic than I am."

"Maybe you should help them. After all, you invented the original battery."

For a moment, he looked as though he was considering her suggestion. Then he waved a hand at the laptop on her desk and said in a voice heavy with weariness, "Then who would answer all those e-mails?"

Chloe decided not to point out that there was a long list of executive vice presidents in the company's directory who could handle some of Trainor's workload. His management style was his business. She turned back to the computer. "I'll start reading again."

The volume of e-mails he received was staggering. Many of them he told her to delete after she read them to him. Others he dictated short answers to. Every time she thought they'd reached the end, another batch would land in his in-box.

She skimmed down the new arrivals. "Well, here's one that's different. You've been invited to a wedding."

He shoved himself higher on the pillows. "A wedding? Those invitations usually come in thick envelopes with overembellished calligraphy. Who the hell sends one by e-mail?"

Chloe was beginning to think she'd made a mistake in picking out that particular message. Even though it had come to Trainor's business address, it looked to be from a family member. "Major General Joseph W. Trainor does."

Trainor's face turned to stone. For a long moment, there was dead silence. Then he said in a voice that sliced like a knife, "Hand me the laptop."

Chloe nearly dropped the sleek, cutting-edge computer as she scooped it off the desk and shot out of her chair. She stumbled over one of the wheeled spokes supporting the chair and banged into the bed, jarring it and her boss. "Sorry," she said, holding the laptop out.

Trainor took it without a word and swiped one long finger across the screen to open the e-mail. She stood by the bed, watching the play of emotions on his face. None of them indicated any joy about the upcoming nuptials.

"This is unexpected," he finally said, slamming the laptop closed and tossing it halfway across the bed on the side opposite Chloe. He pinched the bridge of his nose between his thumb and forefinger. Were his feelings hurt because he hadn't known a family member was getting married? Chloe shifted on her high heels as she tried to figure out what to say.

He dropped his hand. "No matter how old you get or how far away you go, your family can still get to you."

"Because they sent an e-mail instead of a paper invitation?"

He rolled his head on the pillow so he was looking straight at her. "No, because my father is getting married."

Chloe smoothed a wrinkle out of the comforter as she scrambled for a response. Although his father was obviously older, that shouldn't make his remarriage upsetting. "It's nice that he's found someone he loves," she finally managed.

"My father is sixty-one. He's getting married because his forty-two-year-old girlfriend is pregnant. He sent me an e-mail because it's a shotgun wedding, so there wasn't time to mail invitations."

That's when Chloe knew the Russell jinx had hit Nathan Trainor too. Two disasters in one day could not be a coincidence. Of course, she hadn't been aware that she could ruin people's personal lives too.

She swallowed hard and blurted out the first thought that flitted through her mind. "So you're going to have a baby brother or sister."

A look of revulsion skittered across his face. "*Half* brother or sister," he corrected her. "I won't be changing its diapers or dandling it on my knee."

"I've never been clear on what dandling meant anyway," Chloe said, relieved he hadn't exploded.

"I don't intend to find out." He retreated back into his unhappy thoughts, leaving Chloe to balance uneasily on her heels. She eyed the laptop he'd tossed to the other side of the bed. Should she risk attracting his attention by walking around to fetch it, or was it better to let him finish his cogitations?

Luis caught her looking at it and reached out to pick it up before walking around the bed without a sound. She nodded her thanks as she took it from him and held it in front of her like a shield.

Trainor exhaled. "I'm going to sleep. Chloe, I'll call Ed, and you can tell him what you'd like to do for the next two hours. He'll arrange whatever you need." He shifted his attention to Luis. "You can take my temperature and give me whatever medications Ben foisted on you. However, you will *not* tell him I couldn't walk across the room or that I stopped working to sleep." There was steel in his voice, and Luis instantly murmured agreement. Trainor looked back at Chloe and used the same tone. "You will not tell him either."

"No, sir," she said, feeling as though she should slam her heels together and salute. Evidently, the major general had taught his son something about command.

A crease appeared between his eyebrows as he considered something. "Chloe, you might as well stay in the guest room here tonight. That way we can make up for the time we're losing now."

Her burgeoning pleasure at the prospect of a two-hour break withered under a lava flow of exasperation. "I have obligations at home," she said stiffly. For some reason she didn't want to tell Trainor about Grandmillie. Maybe because she was having hot fantasies about him, and mentioning she lived with her grandmother would take that sexy edge away.

He looked genuinely surprised. "What kind of obligations? You're not married."

"How do you know that?"

"You're not wearing a ring."

He hadn't looked at her left hand before he said it, and she felt a guilty twinge of delight that he'd noticed and drawn his conclusion before this moment. However, that didn't mean she was going to desert Grandmillie for a second night. "I have *other* responsibilities."

He sighed and said in a long-suffering tone, "You stayed here last night, so clearly those responsibilities can be taken care of by someone else."

"In an emergency," she said, remembering how worried she'd been. "Dr. Cavill felt my presence was necessary for your well-being, so I made an exception. However, you are clearly on the road to recovery, and dealing with your e-mails does not constitute an emergency."

"We'll discuss it later," he said, sweeping his hand over the intercom control panel at his bedside before dropping his arm in a way that betrayed his exhaustion. "Ed will be here in a minute."

"I'm not staying." She started toward the door to waylay Ed in the hallway.

"You underestimate my powers of persuasion," Trainor said.

Chloe closed the bedroom door behind her with a slight bang, just to show Trainor she wasn't intimidated. Ed was coming toward her at a fast clip. "Is everything all right, Ms. Russell?" he asked. He spoke calmly, but she could see anxiety in the tight way he held his shoulders.

"It's fine. Mr. Trainor just wants to give you all sorts of orders about what I'm supposed to do, but I wanted to mention a couple of things to you out of his hearing."

The butler looked both relieved and guarded. He nodded for her to continue.

"He's still very weak. He tried to walk across the room and nearly collapsed. Even *he* admitted that he wasn't ready to get out of bed. And now he's decided he needs to sleep for a couple of hours." She paused. "I get the feeling he doesn't nap often."

Ed's watchfulness ratcheted down a few notches. "That would be accurate."

Chloe debated a moment but decided a butler was probably privy to his employer's social calendar. "He received an e-mail wedding invitation too. His father's getting married next weekend."

She got a kick out of Ed's expression of shock. He muttered something under his breath that she thought was a strong expletive. To her he said, "Thank you for letting me know about the invitation."

Since it was apparent that Ed worried about his boss, Chloe added, "Mr. Trainor was a little perturbed by it."

"It's somewhat unexpected," Ed said in an obvious understatement.

"I didn't tell you any of this," Chloe said, fixing him with what she hoped was both a commanding and a pleading look.

His control cracked as he gave her a near smile. "I understand. Would you mind waiting in the guest room while I speak with Mr. Trainor?"

"I wouldn't mind at all," Chloe said. "I'll be out on the terrace."

She felt the need for some fresh air after spending the morning cooped up with a sick man. She hoped her flu shot and her immune system were proof against all the germs floating around her boss. Sliding open the door, she stepped out onto the tile expanse and lifted her face to the Indian-summer sun. The warmth and light soaked into her skin like one of the luxurious creams in the guest bathroom. "Except this luxury is free," she murmured.

After basking for a couple of minutes, she pulled her cell phone from her skirt pocket, dialing Judith's direct number at Flexitemps. Her employer picked up and said, "Chloe, are you still working at Trainor's apartment?"

Chloe had called Judith from the car in New Jersey to give her a brief explanation of the change in circumstances. "Yes, and I'm out of my depth here. I have two hours free. Can I come to your office?"

The sound of a mouse clicking came through the phone. "Okay, I've cleared my schedule for a half hour starting in twenty minutes. Is that enough time?"

Judith's business was very successful, due mostly to her hands-on approach to customer service, so Chloe appreciated the significance of a cleared half hour. "I'll make it work."

Disconnecting, Chloe walked to the wall of the terrace and gazed at the Hudson River, the same view Trainor's bedroom had. A sleek sailboat glided upriver, the white of its sails almost blinding in the brilliant autumn light.

"May I offer you lunch on the terrace? We won't have many more days like this one."

Chloe jumped and turned as Ed's voice came from behind her. The butler stood a few feet away from her—his somber, tailored clothing looking out of place against the vivid fall flowers in the planters.

"I'm sorry if I startled you," he said. "Even this high up, the street noise can cover the sound of footsteps."

"I was lost in my own world," Chloe admitted. "Lunch out here would be amazing, but I need to go see my boss at Flexitemps. Could you call a car for me?"

"Mr. Trainor has put his car and driver at your disposal."

Chloe nearly rolled her eyes. Trainor just had to keep his hands on the reins.

Even without the eye roll, her exasperation must have shown on her face, because Ed said, "Mr. Trainor understands how unusual it is to ask you to work in his home, so he wishes to lessen the imposition in any way he can."

Chloe stifled a snort. Mr. Trainor wanted to make sure she was at his beck and call. "I appreciate his thoughtfulness," she said, an edge of sarcasm in her voice.

"I'll have Oskar, the driver, take you down in the elevator to the garage," Ed said.

Chloe shifted in the chrome-and-white-leather chair in front of Judith's glass-topped desk as she finished describing her experience with Trainor's lifestyle. "So the chauffeur—because he's wearing a black suit and a hat so that makes him a chauffeur, not a driver— ushers me into this elevator all trimmed in fancy wood and we go down into a garage that only Trainor's elevator has access to. It's a separate area from the rest of the parking under the building with a gate that you have to swipe a card to open. It's unbelievable. Then Oskar asks me which car I would like to use."

Chloe twisted the cap off the bottle of water Judith had handed her and took a gulp. Her friend lounged in her executive chair behind the desk, her red hair pulled back into a businesslike pony- tail, her signature pantsuit a dark-green wool over a tailored white blouse. Chloe didn't think she'd ever seen Judith in anything other than trousers.

"Isn't it interesting to see how the other half lives?" Judith asked.

"Trainor is not the other half. He must be in the top one-thou- sandth of one percent," Chloe said. "There were six cars to choose from, including a Maserati and a Rolls-Royce."

"Which one did you choose?"

Chloe grinned. "The Rolls-Royce."

"So you've ridden in a helicopter, been driven by a chauffeur in a Rolls, and worked in an apartment bigger than most people's houses," Judith said. "What's the problem?"

Chloe fiddled with the bottle cap. "It's weird to work in his home." She shook her head at herself. "No, it's weird working in his bedroom. I mean, the man is lying in bed wearing pajamas while I'm reading him his e-mails." The picture of Trainor's shoulder muscles under his gray shirt flashed through her mind.

Judith sat forward. "Has he done anything that qualifies as sexual harassment?"

"No, no, nothing like that!" Chloe was appalled that Judith would think that's what she meant about Trainor. For all her mixed feelings about his position and power, Chloe didn't want to imply that he was sleazy. "I don't think he even likes me much. I'm just convenient."

Judith looked skeptical but let it pass. "So what is it that makes you uncomfortable?"

Chloe frowned, trying to put her finger on why she struggled with the situation. She should have been grateful to take the extra pay as long as it lasted. Instead, she found herself fighting against the sense that she was sliding down a dangerously slippery slope with every additional hour she spent with Trainor. "It's supposed to be a professional relationship, but I've also sort of gotten involved with his physical well-being. When he was feverish, I could calm him. It was flattering."

"Sweetie, you're not falling for Nathan Trainor, are you? Not that anyone could blame you, but he's out of your league."

Chloe gave a rueful shrug while she mentally shook herself. "There's something about seeing a man barefoot that makes you look past the suit and the giant desk. He becomes human." And capable of feeling pain. She remembered his face after he received his father's wedding invitation. There had been shock and anger, but there had also been hurt. She felt a flutter of concern. This was treacherous territory she was venturing into. First she jumped to Trainor's defense, and now she was feeling sorry for him.

Judith stared at the ceiling for a moment before she brought her gaze back to Chloe, saying, "Here's some advice. Whenever you start to think he's just another man, remember the size of his penthouse and the fact that he has a doctor on call twenty-four/seven and the choice of six cars with a driver. The very rich are different because they are insulated from all the normal wear and tear of life. People like Nathan Trainor don't consider other people's needs because their own are met without any effort on their part. He'll just assume yours are too, so he'll run right over you without a qualm."

Chloe thought about Trainor saying he'd find a way to persuade her to stay overnight, proving that Judith was right. Chloe wanted to be adamant in her refusal, yet she found herself longing to share the strange intimacy with him a little longer. Once he and his regular executive assistant recovered, her presence wouldn't be necessary and she'd never see him again. The thought left her with a hollow feeling. Not good. She needed to shore up her resistance to this unhealthy attraction.

"I'd offer to send someone else in your place, but it's been made clear that you are the only person Trainor wants," Judith said. "And you would not believe what you're making an hour now." Judith quoted a number that made Chloe's eyes go wide. "You're getting triple the usual rate, and I expected only double, so I'm giving you all the extra."

"That's not right," Chloe said. "You should take your percentage from the total."

"Sweetie, I know you need to sock away money for when Grandmillie needs a companion, and you were the one who negotiated the increase."

Chloe sighed. "I wasn't trying to get more money, although I really appreciate what you're doing. I was trying to make Trainor send me home because I was too expensive and demanding."

"He likes expensive, demanding women. He dates models and actresses."

"Really?" Chloe was disappointed in her temporary boss. "I'm pretty sure the woman he just dumped wasn't either of those things."

"He dumped her, didn't he?"

Chloe slumped back in her chair. "You are such a cynic." And she would absolutely not spend another night with Nathan Trainor.

"I thought you came here for a dose of reality." Judith's computer pinged. "Sorry, I have to leave for a client meeting. I'll walk you out. I want to check out the Rolls."

Chapter 8

Nathan massaged his forehead, trying to stop the jabbing pain. "I think it's time to take a break." It was four o'clock, and they'd been working steadily since he'd woken up at noon.

Chloe looked up from the computer screen. Her expression went from focused to concerned. "Can I get you some pain meds?" she asked.

He hated his weakness. Despite slogging through his e-mails and sending out a few memos, he could feel the pressure of undone work piling up. But his mind wasn't clear enough to handle the larger tasks. Like the disaster of the Prometheus project. "Do I look that bad?"

"You look like a man who's still recovering from a nasty flu," she said, pushing her chair back from the desk and standing up. "I'll get you the medicine."

Nathan watched her walk to the table where Ben had lined up his various medications. She had a nice swing to her hips, probably created by the high heels she was wearing. She'd changed her wardrobe since the first day she'd worked for him, taking it up a notch with the straight skirts and silk blouses. He gave her credit for understanding the nuances of the workplace. She was one smart cookie, Chloe Russell. He suspected that he'd barely scratched the surface when it came to her abilities.

She'd already proven she made a good nurse, and she was more fun to look at than Luis. Ben had agreed to do without the private nurse since Nathan's fever had not risen again. Although Ben's staff was carefully vetted and bonded, Nathan felt uncomfortable discussing confidential business matters in front of Luis or any other nurse.

Yet he didn't worry about the same issue with Chloe. She was bonded as well, of course. Judith Asner at Flexitemps had assured Roberta of that. He examined Chloe's face as she came back toward the bed. What made him trust her without question?

"What? Do I have spinach stuck between my teeth?" she asked as she handed him a glass of water and two tablets.

"No, you look immaculately professional, as always."

She gave him a pleased smile even though it was barely a compliment. What would she do if he called her beautiful? She was, in many subtle ways. There was that sway in her walk. Her hair, when it was down, was glossy and thick. She had large, expressive brown eyes and a kissable mouth. He pulled himself up on that thought. "Let's talk about your schedule for the rest of the day," he said.

That wiped the smile off her lips. "I'm not staying overnight," she said, her spine stiffening. "Take your pills."

He liked it when she forgot to be deferential. As they'd worked together, he'd noticed she made her own suggestions more and more often. In his germ-fogged state, he appreciated the assistance. He tossed the pills into his mouth and washed them down with a gulp of water. "I'll quadruple your pay for the entire time you're here."

She opened her mouth and closed it again, clearly torn. It was an absurdly generous offer, and he was suddenly curious about what would make her even consider turning it down. "What are these obligations at home that require your attention?"

She looked confused for a moment before a frown snapped her brows together. "They're private."

"I'm just wondering what I can do to ease your worry," he said.

"You're wondering what additional bribe you can offer to get me to stay," she said, planting her hands on her hips.

Which made the fabric of her blouse pull taut over the curves of her breasts. He added those to the list of her attractions.

"*Bribe* is such an unpleasant word," he said. "I want to turn this into a situation where everyone wins."

"I'll stay late, but I need to go home tonight." She gave him a level look. "You don't have to send the helicopter. Oskar can drive me."

So she wasn't going to tell him what drew her home so strongly. He had a feeling Ben knew; he'd find out from the doctor. He nodded. "That works."

It didn't, though. He wanted her here, in case . . . what? He shook off the irrational urgency of his need to have Chloe nearby. It must be a weird symptom of the flu that his hallucinating brain had somehow become imprinted on the temp.

"I'm going to let you rest for a while," Chloe said, moving back to the computer and putting it into sleep mode.

The need surged. "Stay," he said before he could stop himself. "Talk to me."

Chloe sat down hard on the desk chair and racked her brain. What the heck was she supposed to discuss with the CEO of Trainor Electronics? She cast a quick glance at him. He looked so ill and drawn. She fought back a nearly overwhelming urge to reach out and smooth a curl of his tousled hair off his forehead. The paperback on his bedside table caught her eye. "Why don't I read your book to you?" she suggested.

"I'd rather you told me what books you like to read," he said, turning his bleary gaze on her.

She remembered he was reading a thriller. "I liked *The Bourne Identity*."

"Movie or book?"

"Both. I think the movie did a good job of capturing the essence of the book." This wasn't going well. He wanted her to talk, and instead they were playing twenty questions. "Why don't I tell you about some of my experiences as a temp?"

He shifted so that his head was supported by the pillows. "I'm all ears."

She always told Grandmillie about the funny or mind-bogglingly stupid things that happened at her temporary jobs, so she had a collection of stories. Of course, she changed the names to protect the innocent, the crooked, and the downright stupid. After about three of them, Trainor's eyes closed. She stopped talking and stood up to leave the room so he could sleep.

The murmur of his voice stopped her. "Why did he invite me?"

"Excuse me?" she said.

He lifted his head, looking surprised. "Did I say that out loud?"

"You said something out loud."

He made a gesture of frustration as he stared out the windows. "I haven't seen my father in two years. I've spoken to him maybe half a dozen times in that period. Why would he decide I should be at his shotgun wedding?"

Did he really want her to answer that? She waited.

Trainor turned to her. "Why?"

So it wasn't a rhetorical question. "You're family," she said. "Blood is thicker than water." She winced at how trite that sounded.

"You can do better than that."

"Okay, fine." Chloe flopped into the desk chair again. She was getting tired of its upright ergonomics and looked longingly at the comfortable armchairs in the seating area. Unfortunately, they were too big to drag over to the bed. "Family is one of the constants in anyone's life. You always have to deal with them, even if it's to decide you don't want to deal with them."

"Now you're interesting me," Trainor said.

She made a face at him. "However, most of us continue to stay in touch with our families because there is a history we share with them that we share with no one else in the world. They are the witnesses to our life at all its stages. I would guess your father wants you to be part of this new and probably nerve-racking phase of his life in some way." This was getting too serious, so Chloe shrugged. "Or maybe he just wants a really nice wedding gift."

Trainor gave a crack of laughter. "If you're thinking china, my father considers a US military–issued mess kit a more than adequate table setting."

Since he had started the personal conversation, Chloe found the nerve to ask, "Why haven't you seen your father in two years?"

His eyes went cold, and she thought she'd pushed him too far. Then he shook his head. "I don't like the Marines, and he doesn't like anyone but Marines."

"But you're his son, and you're not exactly a miserable failure."

Trainor picked at a fold in the sheet beside him. "I was the first male in my family in five generations not to attend a military academy. The general handed down the prized family sword to the son who will never wear a uniform. He can't forgive me for that."

"Seriously? You run a multinational corporation that you started with your own personal invention. How could he not be proud of you?"

"Not good enough. I've never risked my life for my country."

"But your batteries are used by the military. You've made soldiers' lives safer and better, both personally and professionally, by providing reliable, long-term power for their computers and cell phones and gizmos too secret for me to know about."

"I think you should tell him that. In person." A calculating smile that she distrusted drew up the corners of his mouth. "Come with me to his wedding."

She shot off the chair so fast that it scooted backward on its wheels. Her first thought was how thrilling it would be to spend a day as Nathan Trainor's date. Her second was that he was mocking her. She held a tight rein on her words and managed to come up with, "That's not funny."

Annoyingly unruffled, he nodded. "I agree, and because it won't be at all amusing, I would pay you generously for your time."

"Why do you think money will overcome my objections to everything you propose?" She was beginning to feel insulted, despite the fact that money motivated her very powerfully because of her worries about Grandmillie's future care. He'd found her vulnerability and was exploiting it for his own ends. She didn't like that about him.

He looked vaguely surprised. "Ben told me you agreed to come here after negotiating an increase in your pay. I assumed that would work on other matters as well."

She bit her lip, upset that he saw her as being so crass. "I'm not as mercenary as you think."

"*Mercenary* is another one of those unnecessarily judgmental words. You have a realistic idea of your own value," he said.

"Well, when you put it that way . . ." She shot him an irritated glare.

He returned it with a cool look. "I'd prefer to pay you for your time for my own private reasons, so you don't need to feel soiled by my offer."

"It's still weird. You can't hire a temp to go as your date to your own father's wedding."

He raised his eyebrows at her. "I need someone to stand by my side at a social event. You have a responsibility that requires financial support. I thought it was a logical solution to both of our needs, but I'll accept your judgment that it's weird."

"You will?" Chloe had expected a much longer argument.

"For now." He pulled out several pillows from behind him. "I'm going to sleep."

She stood transfixed by the long line of his back, by the way his muscled arm lay along the covers over his hip and thigh, by the unconscious curve of his long fingers. The intimacy of it slithered in to weaken her resolve again. She felt like she might have a won a battle, but she was in danger of losing the war.

Chloe stood at the top of the grand staircase, surveying the hall below her. So far she hadn't ventured off the path between the elevator on the second floor of the apartment and Trainor's bedroom. The tug of curiosity made her set her foot on the next step down as she slid her palm over the satiny surface of the gleaming wooden banister. Her heels sank into the Oriental runner pinned to the stairs by brass rods running across the back of each step.

She imagined herself in a long, full ball gown spangled with glittering crystals, her arms encased in elbow-length white gloves, as she swept down the staircase, drawing all eyes to her. About halfway down, she added a tiara to her mental image, her head held high on her swanlike neck. As she reached the bottom, she started when the sound of applause echoed through the hallway.

Looking around, she saw Ed standing in a doorway, his face creased in an appreciative smile. "That was quite an entrance," he said, walking forward.

"How did you know I—? Never mind," Chloe said. "Mr. Trainor is asleep."

Ed nodded. "May I offer you an afternoon snack?"

Her stomach rumbled as she remembered she'd eaten lunch early. "I think that's a yes," she said. She also hoped Ed might give her some insight into Trainor's problems with his father. She had a feeling she was going to need help navigating that particular issue.

"Come with me," he said.

They walked through what Chloe mentally labeled the showrooms—huge spaces meticulously decorated down to the last expensive paperweight—arriving in a more inviting room with a glass wall that looked out onto a terrace like the one upstairs. A round wooden table and four high-backed upholstered chairs stood on one side of the room. The other half held a big plush sectional sofa and large cushiony chairs arranged in front of a giant flat-screen television. The colors were sophisticated taupes and mossy greens, clearly chosen by some master decorator, but still the room felt lived-in, possibly because there were shelves of books that looked like they'd been read, not bought by the foot, and an array of magazines stacked on the embossed tray topping the padded leather coffee table. A sleek desk made of pale wood trimmed with aluminum jutted out into the room from one wall so the person occupying it could look directly outside.

She could picture Trainor with his laptop open, frowning out at the Manhattan skyline. Then she'd come up behind him and slide her palms onto his shoulders and down his chest, feeling the solidity of his muscles and the heat of his body. She would lean down and whisper something in his ear that would make him smile and close the laptop with a snap.

She pulled herself up short. She needed to stop these crazy daydreams before she started to think they might come true.

"Make yourself comfortable, Ms. Russell," Ed said. "I'll have the chef bring out some hors d'oeuvres. Would you like wine or another beverage?"

"Please call me Chloe, and just water, thank you. If I had wine, I'd be sleeping right along with Mr. Trainor." That hadn't come out right. She felt a blush scorching her cheeks. "I mean, not *with* him, but *like* him."

"I understood," Ed said, poker-faced, as he swept his fingers across one of those pad thingies like the one in Trainor's bedroom. He spoke a couple of orders and turned back to her. "Is there anything else you need?"

She threw caution to the winds. "Information."

Surprise sent his eyebrows up toward his hairline. He looked at her without speaking.

She strolled over to the couch and sat down, patting the cushion beside her. "Your boss is having an issue with the wedding invitation."

"An issue?" Ed was being cagey, but he sat down.

She decided to use her only leverage to get the butler off balance so he'd talk. "He asked me to go with him to the wedding." That much was true. She didn't need to add that she'd refused the invitation.

Ed gave her his polite but silent attention.

"He told me that his father has never forgiven him for not going into the military. Something about a family sword." That was to prove that Trainor had opened up to her. "But why haven't they seen each other for two years?"

"You'll have to ask Nath—Mr. Trainor that."

Chloe gave him a pleading look. "I need some guidance here. I'm going into this situation blind, and I don't want to embarrass Mr. Trainor."

Ed searched her face. "How long have you known Mr. Trainor?"

"Since Tuesday. His illness has accelerated our relationship, I guess."

"Something certainly has." He paused a moment. "I served under Mr. Trainor's father and knew Nathan as a boy."

This was even better than she'd hoped. She leaned in as Ed kept talking.

"General Trainor is the kind of commanding officer every Marine dreams of. He led by example and believed in the code and structure of the military. Nathan is brilliant in a completely different way. His mind works in great bounds of intuition." Ed shook his head. "Nathan couldn't please his father, so he went out of his way to provoke him. He grew his hair long; he wore sloppy clothes; he kept his room a mess. He even refused to polish the sword." A ghost of a smile played over Ed's lips. "He had a long list of page 11s."

"Page 11s?"

Ed went back to being a butler. "My apologies. That's military slang for negative comments on a Marine's record."

"But he invented a computer battery that helps the military as well as civilians," Chloe said.

"General Trainor and Nathan don't see it that way."

Chloe sighed. "It's so hard to break the patterns of childhood, no matter how out-of-date they are." She remembered the wedding. "Are Nathan, er, Mr. Trainor's parents divorced?"

Ed spoke as though he was weighing every word. "His mother died five years ago. It was hard on him and his father."

Chloe was puzzled by his carefulness. What he said was sad but not out of the ordinary. Her mother had died when Chloe was twelve, which had been very difficult for her and her father. That was when Grandmillie had stepped in to help. "But grief didn't draw them closer together," she said.

He hesitated, his gaze flicking away and back. "It was a difficult time." Again the strange precision.

"Mr. Trainor told me why his father is getting married so quickly. The whole situation seems at odds with such a straight-arrow military type."

Ed evidently decided to trust her with some extra information. "Mr. Trainor felt that his father's, er, wife-to-be caught the general at a vulnerable time after Mrs. Trainor's death. He had some concerns about the sincerity of her affection."

"Did he also feel his father was somehow being unfaithful to his mother's memory? Is that why he wouldn't even visit him?"

"He is not fond of the general's intended, so he prefers to avoid her."

"Yet his father invited him to the wedding, and Mr. Trainor is planning to go." Chloe thought about the level of tension there would be at the wedding. "Wow."

Ed kept his gaze on Chloe. "Mr. Trainor will need an ally beside him."

"Aren't you going?"

The butler looked down. "If Mr. Trainor plans to attend, I will."

Ed's loyalty warmed Chloe. He wasn't going to desert his boss in favor of his former commanding officer. "Then he'll have you as an ally," she said, smiling her appreciation.

"Two of us against an entire Marine expeditionary force? You're a brave woman, Ms. Russell."

She felt guilty that she'd misled him into believing she would be there too.

Luckily, a door opened and a young woman in a cream shirt and black trousers walked into the room balancing a large tray, so Chloe's conscience didn't get the better of her and force her to confess.

Ed turned. "Susan, please serve the hors d'oeuvres here on the coffee table."

She strode to where they were seated, gave Chloe a smile, and arranged the dishes on the table. The aroma of warm, buttery pastry cupping tiny quiches and miniature bowls of hot carrot-ginger soup set Chloe's stomach grumbling again.

"Not a moment too soon, it seems," Ed said with a lift of his eyebrow. He stood. "Enjoy, Ms. Russell."

"Chloe," she corrected automatically. She felt another jab of remorse about tricking Ed into thinking that she'd agreed to go with Trainor. Of course, their boss hadn't yet admitted defeat on that front.

Ed nodded but didn't use her first name. He and Susan went out the door together, leaving Chloe to her thoughts and her feast. She picked up the empty plate and placed a sample of each of the bite-size offerings on it. That way she would know which to have seconds and thirds of.

Her appetite was slightly dampened by Ed's revelations. He'd painted too vivid a picture of the young Nathan battling with a powerful and rigid father for enough room to let his unorthodox brilliance shine.

Did either one of them recognize that Trainor had ultimately followed in his father's footsteps? He dressed in neat, well-tailored suits that weren't all that different from a uniform. He was responsible for the well-being of hundreds of people, if not for their actual lives. He was a leader, both in his own company and in his industry.

She had the unsettling idea that her boss didn't want this role, but it was the model he'd grown up with, so he'd followed it.

Chapter 9

At eleven o'clock, Nathan watched Chloe hit "Delete" on the last e-mail in his in-box. Except for a brief break for dinner, eaten in his bedroom, they'd worked steadily with nary a complaint from her since he'd awakened five hours before.

She flexed her fingers and arched her back in a subtle stretch, drawing his gaze to the way her blouse draped over the swell of her breasts. He'd been noticing little things like that all day: the elegant whorl of her ear as she tucked her hair behind it, the supple arch of her foot when she slipped off her shoes under the desk, the tautness of her skirt's fabric over her thighs as she shifted in the chair.

It must be some residual effect of his illness. He'd never noticed those things about Janice.

Chloe's chair creaked, drawing his gaze back to her face as she said, "You know, you're really good at this."

He felt a wash of pleasure. Another sign of weakness. "A high compliment from Ms. Chloe Russell," he said, injecting a sardonic edge into his voice so she wouldn't suspect how much her comment gratified him.

"I shouldn't have said that." She fiddled with the mouse. "Of course you're good at it. You're the CEO."

"An elevated title doesn't guarantee competence. In fact, there's a law about that."

She let go of the mouse and lifted her gaze to his with a slight smile. "The Peter Principle. You're promoted to the level of your incompetence. That doesn't apply to you."

"Because I founded the company?"

She nodded. "You didn't have to rise through the ranks. You got pushed upward as the ranks grew beneath you."

He wasn't sure whether that was a compliment or a subtle insult. "You're not afraid of me at all, are you?"

She waved her hand toward him. "There's something about seeing my boss in his pajamas that makes me forget I'm a mere temp."

"There is nothing *mere* about you."

She gave him a sideways look of skepticism before raising her hand to massage the back of her neck. He imagined replacing her hand with his. He could almost feel the soft, vulnerable skin at her nape. Sliding sideways on the bed, he said, "You've been sitting on that chair staring at a computer screen all day. You deserve to relax and enjoy the view." He gestured toward the space he'd left open beside him.

She sucked in a quick breath before she gave him a look as sharp as a razor blade. "I'll just turn my chair around."

Her first reaction was enough to encourage him, but he decided to back off for the moment. He gave a nonchalant shrug. "The bed is more comfortable." When he touched the control panel, the lights dimmed so he could see stars glowing against a translucent sky of dark blue above the horizon of New Jersey.

Throwing a dubious glance at the darkened overhead light fixture, she swiveled her seat around to face the wall of glass. "Wow! I didn't know New Jersey could look so good."

He watched her as she drank in the landscape of the river and its opposite bank. Her dark eyes picked up little glints of the surrounding illumination, and her sun-streaked hair showed the luster of satin. She wasn't a knockout. She had the kind of looks that grew on you. Or maybe it was what was beneath the surface that was a knockout. Now that he knew her better, he could see the woman hidden inside, and he wanted her with a surprising intensity.

"Come to my father's wedding with me," he said without thinking.

Her gaze swung around to him, and he caught the indecision on her face. She hadn't said no, so he just needed to find the right leverage. Evidently, money wasn't enough of an incentive. "It will be a military wedding. Men in uniforms, crossed swords, pomp and circumstance." Didn't women love that?

She started to shake her head, so he tried a different tack. "We'll take my jet to North Carolina. No long drive. No security lines. You can even change clothes on the plane."

"It wouldn't—"

He cut her off. "I could use a buffer between my father and me. You'd be doing me a favor."

"Oh." She looked away toward the window, then down at her hands clasped in her lap. "There must be another woman who'd go with you, one who would be more at ease in that social situation than I would."

He couldn't think of a single woman other than Chloe he'd want by his side. "I've seen you handle everything from a jargon-laden technical development meeting to a grown man in the grip of hallucinations. You'll be perfectly at ease with my father."

"What about his bride?"

"Angel?" Why would she ask about the interloper? "Her opinions are irrelevant."

"Sometimes you sound like a typical CEO."

That clearly wasn't a compliment. "Maybe you should meet Angel before you judge my attitude toward her." He saw Chloe's spine stiffen and knew he'd made a tactical error. Driven to the wall, he switched to flattery. "My father doesn't approve of my usual dates, but he'll like you."

"Because I'm not a supermodel or an actress?"

Somehow he was digging a deeper hole. Exasperated, he spoke the truth. Or some of it. "Look, I don't want to walk into a tense situation with some high-maintenance type on my arm. I'll have enough to deal with."

That had probably blown his chances. He cast a quick look at Chloe. Her expression had gone from pissed off to sympathetic.

He'd found his leverage. He just wasn't sure it was the kind of leverage he wanted to use.

Chloe was getting whipsawed between insult and gratification. Every time Trainor opened his mouth, he surprised her. But his last statement undercut all her resolve. He probably hadn't meant it as a compliment, but implying she wasn't high maintenance pleased her. Ed had said Trainor would need an ally. Now Trainor himself was telling her the same thing in his own way. And they both saw her as the right person for the job.

How could she refuse? "I'll go on two conditions."

"Done," Trainor said.

"You haven't even heard them." She caught the gleam of triumph in his eyes and wished she hadn't given in so quickly.

"It's a sign of my desperation," he said.

"Thanks. I love being someone's last resort."

"Not last resort. *Best* resort."

He was smiling into her eyes in a way that made her insides turn molten. That just added to the flare of heat he'd provoked by inviting her to sit beside him on the bed. She'd tried to interpret the invitation as an unspoken apology for making her work for so long without a break, but this smile wasn't as easy to explain away.

She needed to go on the offensive to put this whole encounter on a more businesslike footing. "The first condition is that you pay for whatever I have to wear to the wedding. All of it: shoes, purse, wrap, whatever." She couldn't afford the kind of dress and accessories she'd need, and she wasn't going to embarrass herself—or him—with the wrong clothes.

"What about the lingerie?" he asked.

She swallowed hard, trying to decide if he was merely wondering how much he would have to spend or if he was being deliberately provocative. "If it's necessary," she said, trying to sound cool and sophisticated when she could feel the blush scalding her cheeks.

"Maybe I'll go along for that part of the shopping trip."

Surprise made her stiffen as she realized she wasn't imagining things. *He was flirting with her.* Why would Nathan Trainor flirt with a temp? He must be so bored with being confined to his bed he would do anything for entertainment.

"This is a business arrangement," she reminded him . . . and herself. "You're paying me to go to your father's wedding with you."

"That doesn't mean I can't enjoy it." He lounged back against the pillows with a bland look that undercut the provocation of his comment.

Her heart was dancing in a confused rhythm, but she skewered him with a hard, clear gaze. "The second condition is that you have to fill me in on your family's dynamics, so I don't make things worse."

He shifted on the bed and broke eye contact. "Trust me, nothing you do could make it any worse."

She had brought up a touchy subject to give herself a chance to wrestle down the feeling of fluttering exhilaration he was causing, but now she wished she hadn't. While it made her nervous, the knowledge that her boss was noticing her as a woman made her feel as though she'd drunk a whole glass of champagne in one gulp. It bubbled and fizzed inside her.

"Just give me a bare-bones outline," she said.

Exhaustion washed over his face, making the bones show sharply under his skin. "I suppose you're entitled to know what a minefield you're walking into." He closed his eyes for a moment.

Guilt nagged at Chloe and she wished she had the nerve to touch his hand where it lay inert on the rumpled comforter. "You can tell me another day when you're feeling better."

He opened his gray eyes. "Might as well get it over with." He pushed himself higher up on the pillows. "The elephant in the room is that my mother committed suicide five years ago."

"Oh!" *Minefield* was the right word. "I'm so sorry." She winced at how inadequate that sounded.

"She'd struggled with depression all her life, so it wasn't a complete surprise." His foot began to jiggle in a nervous tic. "She shouldn't have married a military man. Every time my father was assigned to a new base, she struggled to adapt to a new set of people. And my father was ambitious, so he needed his wife to be perfect. The strain was more than she could handle. Maybe if my father had been more . . ."

He stopped and frowned down at his twitching foot, drawing up his leg so the knee was bent and his foot was flat on the bed.

"That kind of pressure would be hard, even for someone without mental health issues," Chloe said into the silence.

"She deserved as many medals as my father, but no one paid any attention to the wives. It was all about the soldiers," Trainor said, an edge of bitterness in his voice. "Being the model officer's wife used up most of her strength. There wasn't much left for . . . other things in her life."

Chloe put together what Ed had said about Trainor's father with what Trainor was saying about his mother. That left the man in front of her emotionally abandoned by his parents throughout his child-hood. It also appeared that he held his father at least partly account-able for his mother's death. No wonder he felt so ambivalent about his father's upcoming wedding.

She couldn't help it: she needed to offer him comfort. That required leaving her chair and perching on the side of the bed so she could place her palm over the back of his hand.

His skin was warm but not scorching, as it had been when his fever raged. She felt the hard bumps of his knuckles against her hand, and she could smell the spicy citrus of the shampoo he'd used earlier in the day.

For a long moment he went silent and still. She held her breath, wondering if she'd misread him or if his mood had simply changed too drastically. Then he turned his hand and wrapped his long fingers around hers, letting her feel the strength in his grip. His response sent a thrill of nerves zinging through her. She'd made the first move in a dance whose steps she didn't know.

She kept her eyes on their clasped hands because the air between them had taken on a charge of awareness, and she was afraid to find out how he might be looking at her.

He tightened his grip and tugged her hand toward him. She knew she should pull her hand away and bolt out the door. Nathan Trainor was used to women who played the game at the same level he did, and Chloe was way above her pay grade here.

But she wanted to feel the bed sink under his weight, to touch his body heat on the sheets, to be close to him for a reason other than work. This was dangerous territory for someone without a road map.

"Come sit with me." The request spoken in his deep, resonant voice tipped the scales.

She slipped off her shoes and slid just far enough onto the bed so she could swing her legs up and settle against the pillows.

"You'll fall off if you don't move over farther," he said, amusement threading through his words.

"I'm fine," she said, keeping her gaze on the view.

"I'll put a pillow between us if it will make you feel more comfortable," he said.

She was acting like a teenager playing her first game of spin the bottle. She turned to look at him and nearly carried out his prediction of falling off the bed. He was much closer than she'd expected. She could see the reddish-brown stubble on his jaw, the gradations of gray in his eyes, and the strong line of his throat as it rose from the neckline of his T-shirt.

"You have to admit this is a little strange," she said, trying to balance on the edge of the mattress.

He shifted, his weight making the mattress dip so she had to brace her hand on it to avoid tilting into his shoulder.

"There's nothing strange about having a beautiful woman in my bed," he said.

"I, er, I'm not beautiful," she said, her voice pitched higher than normal. She turned back toward the window. Nathan Trainor was trying to seduce her. Otherwise he wouldn't have told her she was beautiful. She could stop it now and retain her self-respect. Or she could find out what it was like to be kissed by a billionaire.

"I disagree," he said as he lifted his free hand and traced down her cheek with the back of it. Brushing down along her neck, he splayed his fingers when he reached the hollow of her throat and slipped them just under the open collar of her blouse.

She reacted in places he hadn't touched, with a yearning in her breasts, a liquid curl of warmth low in her belly. She made her decision, letting her eyes drift closed so she could concentrate on how it felt to have his hand against her skin. .

The mattress dipped again and she could feel his breath stirring her hair. Then his lips were against her temple and on her eyebrow and teasing her earlobe. She let her head drop back on the pillow and nearly moaned as he took advantage and slid his mouth down to replace his hand at the base of her throat.

Now that she couldn't see his face, she dared to open her eyes, threading her fingers into the thick waves of his hair—the strong, silky texture satisfying her pent-up curiosity about what it would be like to touch.

She felt heat and moistness as he flicked the tip of his tongue against her skin. The surprise and pleasure of it made her arch against the pillows. His hold on her hand tightened. He lifted his head, his gaze locked on her breasts. His free hand skimmed down along the upper curve of her breast, and he circled his thumb over her nipple where its peak was outlined by the thin silk of her blouse.

"Oh, yes," she breathed as the friction sent flares of arousal through her. Now she wanted more than just a kiss.

He cupped her breast with his palm, and she pushed against him to increase the delicious pressure.

He made a strangled sound and dropped his hand, rolling away from her. "What the hell am I thinking?" he growled as he shoved himself to a sitting position on the opposite edge of the bed.

So he'd come to his senses and realized he was seducing his tempo- rary employee. What else did she expect? She stiffened with humiliation and started to scramble off the bed. "It's hard to remember that our rela- tionship should be professional when we're working in your bedroom."

As she stood, he turned to her with a look of surprise, before a deep cynicism hardened his eyes. "Are you planning to cry sexual harassment? I suppose I deserve it," he said.

"Wait, no. I thought you stopped because I'm just—"

"I stopped because I have the flu, and I don't want to infect you," he said, watching her.

"Oh, is that it?" Relief made her feel giddy. "Dr. Cavill knows I've had my flu shot. And I never get sick anyway."

"I never get sick either, and look at me." He swept his hand down his pajama-clad body.

She had wanted to do more than look at him, but his guilty conscience had saved her from that ultimate insanity. She wasn't sure if she was grateful or upset. "I think it's time for me to go home," she said.

He lay back against the pillows, although his gray gaze laid a trail of heat as it skimmed down her body. "I'm too sick to argue with you." He narrowed his eyes as they returned to her face. "You'll be here in the morning."

It hit her that she would have to face him in the light of day, laptop at the ready, knowing how his lips had felt against her skin and how his hand had felt on her breast. And knowing he knew the same things.

"You're not going to bail out on me, are you?" His voice held a rasp of challenge.

"We can discuss it tomorrow morning," she said. If she found she couldn't bring herself to come back into this room, she could call Judith for a replacement. That was the advantage of being a temp.

"You've got more backbone than that."

She stared at him. Had he read her mind? "I'll come back tomorrow on two conditions."

"More conditions." The corner of his mouth twitched. "You'd make a master negotiator. What are they?"

"We don't talk about this, and we don't do it again."

He shook his head. "Those terms are not acceptable."

"Neither one?" she asked, not sure what to do now.

He pretended to think for a moment. "In the spirit of compromise, I'll agree to the first, but the second is nonnegotiable."

She tried very hard to cling to some shred of professionalism, but excitement bubbled through her at the idea that he wanted to touch her again. And she knew beyond a shadow of a doubt she would be back in the morning.

No other temp was going to set foot in Nathan Trainor's bedroom.

After the door closed behind Chloe, Nathan threw off the covers and padded over to the door to his terrace. His knees felt like rubber, but he needed to get outdoors and let the wind and the noise clear the haze of arousal from his brain and body. It took more effort than he expected to shove the door open, even though it slid on a well-lubricated glide. The smooth terra-cotta tiles under his feet were still warm from the day's sun, and he stood for a moment, enjoying the contrast of radiant heat and chilly air. The faint sounds of squealing brakes and taxi horns wafted up from the street far below while a breeze ruffled through his hair. He sucked in a breath of air that combined the pungent smells of the crowded concrete jungle with the brackish marine scent of the river.

His knees gave way and he grabbed for the back of a lounge chair, managing to haul himself onto its seat before he crumpled onto the hard floor.

"Damned germs," he muttered.

And he'd nearly transferred them to Chloe in a moment of lustful madness.

He remembered the feel of her breast against his hand and the way she'd purred deep in her throat as his thumb circled her hard nipple. The one part of his body that seemed to be unaffected by the flu stirred. He huffed out an irritated laugh.

Better to think of something else. He settled against the chair's cushions and stared across the river, wondering where in New Jersey Chloe lived.

That was better than remembering the feel of her pulse beating against his lips.

"Get a grip, Trainor," he growled at himself.

Instead he'd wrestle with how this new development played into the wager with Gavin Miller and Luke Archer. Nathan frowned. If he was searching for true love, did that mean he wasn't allowed to take an occasional detour? In fact, how was he supposed to know he'd met the right woman until he'd gotten to know her?

During his two admittedly unusual days with Chloe, he had come to respect her abilities, and he sure as hell wanted her in his bed, but could he fall in love with her?

He let his head tilt back so he could pick out the few stars not obliterated by the megawattage of the city lights.

That's why Miller's challenge was impossible. There was no such thing as love at first sight. Just because Chloe wasn't the sort of woman he generally dated didn't mean she was a candidate for true love.

"You're being an arrogant asshole," he muttered at the stars. "Chloe might have an opinion too."

And he suspected Chloe's opinion of him wasn't very high. Just because she had responded to him physically didn't mean she was looking for a lifetime commitment. Another problem with the wager. What if one of the three of them fell in love with a woman who didn't love him back?

Clearly they'd all been too drunk to think through the implications of the bet they'd made. Nathan reached into the pocket of his pajama pants and pulled out his cell phone.

He needed to get hold of Miller and call the whole thing off.

"Are you serious, Trainor?" The amusement in Gavin Miller's voice came through the phone line clearly. "You're a billionaire and you think you can't make a woman fall in love with you?"

"Your logic is flawed," Nathan countered, crossing his ankles on the lounge chair. "If I use my money to make the woman fall in love with me, she's the wrong woman."

"The wager doesn't mean you can't use every weapon at your disposal to win your true love." Gavin's voice took on an edge when he said the last two words. "By the way, you work fast. I'm impressed."

Nathan shifted in the chair. "It was a hypothetical question."

"Sure it was. Who is she?"

"Look up *hypothetical* in your OED." Nathan redirected the conversation. He was starting to feel the cold. "Is Archer still on board with this?"

"I haven't been informed otherwise."

"Has the writer's block broken yet?"

"No." All amusement was absent from Miller's voice for that one word. "By the way, when you're ready to go ring shopping, let me know. I'm a friend of the manager at Cartier."

Nathan snorted and ended the call. He glanced up at the stars and had the whimsical thought that he could pluck one out of the sky to set in an engagement ring.

It seemed like an idea Chloe would appreciate.

Chapter 10

Chloe walked into her boss's bedroom to find Cavill and Trainor—who wore an unbelted navy bathrobe hanging open over his pajamas—facing each other with equally furious expressions.

"Am I contagious?" Trainor asked.

"Probably not." Cavill sounded as though he could barely speak the words.

"One more day," Trainor said. "Then I'm going back to the office."

Chloe considered pointing out that the next day was Saturday but figured Trainor worked weekends too.

"Do you want to have a relapse and end up worse off than before?" Cavill asked. "You need at least two more days of bed rest."

"Don't push it, Ben." Trainor spun on his bare heel to stalk away from his friend and doctor, which brought him face-to-face with Chloe. The anger still sparked in his eyes, but an odd mixture of surprise and gratification joined it. "You came back."

Standing, he seemed larger and more intimidating than when she'd been close to him in his bed. A flush climbed her cheeks as she remembered just how close they'd been. "I made a commitment." And it had taken all her grit and guts to honor it.

He cast a sharp glance at Cavill. "We'll work in my office here."

"Yes, sir," she said, responding to the air of command he exuded, even in his pajamas.

His eyebrows rose and a slight smile curled the corners of his mouth. He might be remembering last night too.

"Your father would be proud," Cavill said, his voice laced with sarcasm. "*Ductos exemplo*. Lead by example. *Semper fi*."

Trainor's face went dark as he half turned to the doctor. "You're lucky there's a lady present, so I'm just going to tell you to piss off."

Chloe decided it was time to break up the argument. "I'll make sure he takes frequent breaks," she said to the doctor.

"I was under the impression you reported to *me*," Trainor said, his eyebrows slashing down.

"I want to keep you in good health so you can sign my paycheck," Chloe said.

Cavill gave a little snort of laughter, and Trainor shook his head. The tension between the two men eased.

"If you collapse, find another doctor to call," Cavill said. "I wash my hands of you."

Despite his words, his tone was exasperated rather than angry, and Chloe let out a sigh of relief.

"I may find another doctor anyway," Trainor said.

"Not when I know where all your skeletons are hidden, not to mention the broken bones in them." The doctor's face softened. "Take it slow, Nathan. You may be Tony Stark, but you're not Iron Man."

Chloe stifled a smile. "Too bad. I could see myself as Pepper Potts. She has great shoes."

"She works for Tony, not Iron Man," Trainor said. "So you can still play her role." His voice took on a provocative edge, and Chloe remembered that eventually Pepper and Tony ended up in bed together. Of course, she'd been there, done that already.

"As long as I get my own bionic chest battery," she said.

"That would be a shame," Trainor murmured, his eyes dropping to her breasts. "But I could find a way to miniaturize it so it doesn't ruin the symmetry."

Heat burned in Chloe's cheeks. Cavill came to her rescue, snapping his doctor's bag shut. "Unless Chloe sends a distress signal, I'll be back tomorrow morning. Give me your promise you won't leave for the office until I've seen you." He locked eyes with his friend.

Trainor's back went ramrod stiff, and for a moment she thought he would explode again. Instead he pulled the open edges of his robe together and tied the belt in a firm knot. "If you're not here by seven, I'm leaving without the checkup," he growled.

Cavill reached up to grip Trainor's shoulder before he turned to Chloe. "Make sure he hydrates. And I don't mean with scotch."

"Got it," she said.

The doctor nodded and left the room.

Trainor stood with his hands still at the belt of his bathrobe, his gaze growing more intimate and intense as it rested on her. "You're a brave woman, Chloe Russell."

"Not brave. Poor."

Surprise joined the heat in his eyes. "How should I interpret that?"

"I need the paycheck. You're paying me four times my usual hourly rate now. I'd be a fool to turn it down." It was a perfect excuse, and only partially a lie. Chloe had spent the night drifting between waking and sleeping fantasies that involved Nathan Trainor and herself in various states of arousal and undress.

"Hazardous-duty pay." He dropped his hands to his sides, and the fire in his eyes went out as though she'd thrown a bucket of water on it. Now he looked more like the invalid he was. The shadows under his eyes were lighter but noticeable, and his skin still appeared too tight around his jawline. "Time to get something useful accomplished. Wait here. I'm not working in my pajamas."

Chloe was torn between relief and disappointment as Trainor walked across his bedroom to a panel in the wall that swung inward at his touch.

She took two steps forward to catch a glimpse of a walk-in closet the size of her living room, its walls hung with various articles of clothing positioned at precise intervals so that none touched another. The shelving was a different wood from the guest room's but equally exotic in its grain. Trainor was untying his robe when he caught her eye. The wicked gleam came back into his gaze as he shrugged out of the navy silk. "Feel free to watch."

Chloe stood her ground. "I just wanted to see what a CEO's closet looks like."

With a sudden movement, he crossed his arms and yanked his T-shirt up over his head. As he balled it up and tossed it out of her sight, she found her gaze riveted by the movement of muscles under taut skin. Her fingers twitched with the desire to trace the sculpted planes of his abdomen. It was a crime to conceal all that male beauty under a business suit.

He turned his head toward her, and she dragged her gaze up past the dusting of hair on his chest to meet his heavy-lidded eyes. He'd caught her looking at more than his closet. She brazened it out. "How do you have time to stay in such good shape?"

"I exercise at night." His voice was deep and seductive. He moved his hands to the waistband of his pajama pants.

Chloe's curiosity had its limits. She scurried backward far enough to have no possible view of the interior of Trainor's closet. She thought she heard a satisfied chuckle, but it was so low it might have been her imagination.

Deciding to make it clear she wasn't looking, she walked farther away to examine two paintings hanging on the same wall. Painted in bold colors and strokes, they looked as though they were of the same landscape but interpreted by different artists. Intrigued, she leaned in to read the signatures and gasped. One was signed "P Gauguin," and the other signature read simply "Vincent." She knew enough about art to recognize that meant Vincent van Gogh.

Having a Van Gogh was mind-boggling enough, but having a matching Gauguin must make the two paintings nearly priceless as a pair. She stared at the two masterpieces. If this was what Trainor kept in his bedroom, she needed to look more closely at the art in his living room.

"I bought those when I took Trainor Electronics public. They were my first significant purchases of art. I should donate them to a museum, but when I see them I remember ringing the opening bell at the New York Stock Exchange. Heady stuff for a computer nerd."

Chloe jumped as Trainor's voice came from directly beside her. The thick carpeting had muffled his footsteps. "It's amazing to see them side by side," she said.

She sneaked a glance sideways. He stood with his hands in the pockets of a pair of pressed khaki trousers, his eyes fixed on the artwork. His messy bedhead had been tamed into tidy waves that touched the collar of a blue-and-white-striped button-down shirt, open at the neck. Letting her gaze slide down to his feet, she felt a sense of loss at seeing them encased in shiny burgundy loafers. He was back in his version of a uniform.

"Like a high school essay," he said. "Compare and contrast. Which one do you like better?"

"I don't know enough about art to choose," Chloe said, dragging her attention back to the paintings.

"What? No opinion from the strong-minded Ms. Russell?" There was a teasing note in his voice that made her insides go soft.

"Sometimes beauty should be appreciated, not judged," Chloe said. "Besides, the two pictures belong together. Choose one and you lose all that extra resonance."

He ran his index finger along the carved gilt frame of the Gauguin as his expression turned serious. "You make a good point. I'll strongly suggest that whoever acquires them next hangs these together permanently."

"And I guess they'll listen to you."

"Until I'm dead."

"According to Dr. Cavill, that could be any day now."

Trainor gave a little snort of disgust and turned away from the paintings. "Let's prove him wrong."

For a moment Chloe thought he was heading toward the bed, and her heart gave a leap of anxiety and excitement. However, his path took him to the door, and she realized that Trainor's way of warding off death was not to make love but to work.

Nathan pressed his palm against a touch pad, and a section of the wood paneling slid aside. The lights glowed to life automatically, illuminating sleek desks and banks of cutting-edge computer equipment. At the same time, the window wall went from shaded to translucent, offering a view of Manhattan's towers. This room was all his; he'd designed it and equipped it, mostly with electronics of his own personal design.

"Holy Batcave!" Chloe said as she stepped into the room and turned slowly.

"Two superheroes in one morning," Nathan said. "I'm flattered." But he enjoyed watching the mixture of wide-eyed admiration and cynical amusement in her expression. She'd looked at his favorite paintings the same way, although there had been some extra element then, a cautiousness. She didn't trust him.

And with good reason. He'd brought her to his office via the internal elevator that served only the three floors of his home. Being in that enclosed space with her had tested every ounce of his self-control. The faint floral hint of what must be her shampoo entered his lungs with every breath he drew in. He could see the rise and fall of her breasts under the white blouse she wore. He imagined pushing her against the wall of the elevator, shoving her skirt up to her waist, and burying himself in her while she wrapped her legs around his hips—those spike heels digging into him as she moaned the way she had last night.

Instead he'd put his hand at the small of her back as the elevator doors opened, a gesture that could be attributed to courtesy rather than an overwhelming desire to touch her somewhere. Anywhere.

It was a mistake. The warmth and movement of her body went straight from his palm to his groin.

He scanned the room along with her until his gaze settled on the back of a leather armchair while he pictured bending her over it and sliding his hands up her thighs before he . . .

She walked away from him to touch a swivel-mounted computer screen, making it pivot diagonally. "That's cool, but I don't see what the purpose is."

"There's a built-in projector so you can display the screen image on a wall or a ceiling or any other flat surface." He came up behind her and reached around to flick on the device, throwing the twirling screen-saver image onto a corner of the room. As she tilted her head to look at it, the angle of her body shifted so that her behind brushed against the front of his trousers. He barely swallowed a groan.

She sidestepped away from him, and he couldn't decide whether to be grateful or to seize her wrist and spin her in hard against him.

When she turned to look at him, he caught it: a quickening of her breathing, a tension in her posture, an awareness in her expression. She claimed she had come back only for the paycheck, but she was not offended by his behavior last night, as he'd feared. She might be wary but she was not indifferent to him.

He contemplated ignoring the mountain of reports on his computer and trying to seduce Chloe instead. Overcoming the barriers she put up would be a pleasurable challenge.

And she was a temp, so there would be no long-term issues as far as the office went. Once Janice was back, Chloe could go on to her next assignment at a different company.

The prospect gave him less relief than he expected. Chloe's smart observations and snarky asides made the work seem less dreary.

The word brought him up short. When had he begun to consider his job in that light? And how had Chloe become so important to his mood?

"I'll assume the giant chair behind the giant desk with the giant screens is your workstation." Her voice derailed the unsettling direction of his thoughts.

"Yes, I use the size of my computer screens to indicate the size of . . . other things," he said, matching his tone to hers.

That forced a little choke of laughter from her, and he felt a sense of satisfaction out of proportion to her response. It struck him that he could combine the work and the seduction into one package. The idea gave him such a jolt of energy that he wondered that electricity didn't shoot out from the tips of his fingers.

He pulled a chair away from a workstation and wheeled it over beside his own chair, angling it to face one of the wings of the admittedly huge desk. "Sit here."

She gave him a look that said she'd rather sit by a spider, and he smiled inwardly. This was going to be fun.

After four hours of perching within two feet of Nathan Trainor, Chloe was in a state of seething physical turmoil and utter mental exhaustion. Keeping up with a mind as lightning fast as his was hard enough, but when she asked a question and he glided his chair over to look at her computer screen, her body compounded the problem.

He would lean in, bringing his cheek so close she had only to turn her head to kiss it. Or they would both reach for the same touchscreen icon and his fingers would brush over the back of her hand, leaving a trail of heat that lingered for minutes. The most exquisite torture was when he would stretch his arm across the desk in front of her to pick up whatever report or contract she was working on. The warm fragrance of starch and man filled her nostrils, making her want to thread her fingers into the heavy waves of his hair, so she could hold him there and simply breathe in.

Even during the midmorning break he finally agreed to take, he lounged on the couch and invited her to sit in one of the leather upholstered chairs beside him while one of his minions served them coffee and various brunch-style snacks. When Trainor stretched out his legs, the fabric of his trousers caught against the nylon covering her calf, and the contact zinged right up to a spot between her thighs.

When Ed appeared in the doorway to inquire where Mr. Trainor would like him to serve lunch, Chloe interjected, "Don't fix anything for me. I need to run some errands, so I'll grab a sandwich at a deli."

She was amazed to see a look of disappointment cross her boss's face. "I thought we would work through lunch," he said. "We've got some good momentum going."

So it wasn't that he wanted to spend some social time with her. He just wanted to keep working. Irritation at her stupid naïveté made her tart. "I'm entitled to thirty minutes of paid lunchtime."

Annoyance flashed across Trainor's face. "Take as long as you need. Have Oskar drive you wherever you want to go."

"Let me make you a sandwich to take with you," Ed said, his tone conciliatory. "There aren't many delis in this neighborhood."

Suddenly she felt stifled. All these offers of so-called help seemed more like attempts to keep her in Trainor's orbit.

She stood up, sending her chair rolling backward so that Trainor had to catch it to avoid a collision. "Thank you, but I prefer to walk and find my own lunch. I'll be back in a half hour."

She stomped out of the room and down the hall, only to stop in front of the elevator with its palm plate. Would the doors open for her, or did her handprint have to be authorized in some way?

Annoyed, she slapped her hand against the black square and dashed away a tear of relief when the doors slid apart. At least she could leave of her own free will while she had the strength to do it.

Nathan tilted back his chair and pressed his fingertips against his eyelids. He'd screwed that up royally.

"If you want to work yourself into a state of collapse, that's your call. But you need to let Ms. Russell come up for air every now and then," Ed said.

Nathan dropped his hand and looked at the man who'd been more of a father to him than his own. "It was an excuse."

"For what?"

"I wanted her to eat lunch with me."

"Did you consider just asking her?"

Nathan shook his head. "I'm her employer."

Ed's look of censure faded. "Not at lunchtime. You're just a man who'd like some good company."

Chapter 11

There were no delis within a five-block radius of Trainor's building, so Chloe was forced to spend twice her normal lunch budget for an artsy sandwich at a snooty bistro. At least she'd found a pleasant little park to eat in while she lectured herself about letting her boss get to her. He was bored because he was confined to his house. She was just a temp, which made it safe for him to toy with her. Once he got back to the office, his interest in her would evaporate.

A niggling little voice asked her why she didn't just give in to the attraction flaring between them. What would she lose? He wouldn't tell anyone because it wouldn't look good for a CEO to sleep with his temporary executive assistant. She wouldn't tell anyone for the reverse reason.

He was just a man. He put his pants on one leg at a time, although she hadn't actually seen him do it. So why did she feel out of her depth with Nathan Trainor? Maybe she was afraid he would ruin her for a lesser mortal. After all, it was hard to compete with helicopters, Jimmy Choo sandals, and a chauffeur-driven Rolls-Royce. In bed, all those would be stripped away. He wouldn't be wearing a custom-tailored suit, and she wouldn't be wearing a bargain-basement scarf.

He'd made love to movie stars and supermodels. She would be a minor diversion compared to those, possibly a disappointment.

What she had to lose was her self-respect.

She hung on to that thought as she walked back into Trainor's office twenty-nine minutes after she'd left. It was empty. She sat down at her workstation and picked up where she'd left off on the report she'd been editing, becoming so absorbed in the task that she was shocked to find twenty minutes had passed before Trainor sauntered in.

He'd rolled up the sleeves of his shirt so she could see the ridge of muscle along his forearms. The sight sent a thrill of heat up her spine. *Self-respect*, she reminded herself.

"Got all your errands done?" he asked, coming around the desk to seat himself. The scent of the expensive soap he must have just washed his hands with wafted past her, making the tiny hairs at the nape of her neck prickle.

"Errands?" She'd nearly forgotten her spur-of-the moment excuse. "A couple of them."

"I told you to take as long as you needed."

She decided it was better not to argue with him. "Yes, you did."

He gave her a long look before swiveling his chair toward his computer. She let out the breath she hadn't realized she was holding and returned to her report.

Out of the corner of her eye, she caught the motion of his hand as he swiped documents and e-mails on and off his screen at high speed. Then all movement ceased and he cursed under his breath.

She waited but he made no further comment. She heard his chair creak and sneaked a glance to see him leaning back with his fingers steepled in front of a ferocious frown.

"Problem?" she asked.

"The same problem. The Prometheus project has hit another wall."

Chloe discarded her newly instituted policy of not disagreeing with her boss. It had been a lost cause from the start. She couldn't keep her thoughts to herself when someone refused to see the obvious. "Who invented the original Trainor Electronics battery?"

He lowered his hands and looked at her. "What's your point?"

"You're trying to develop a better battery, but you're depriving your research-and-development department of the most brilliant mind in the company. Yours."

"I have a multinational corporation to run. I can't take time off to do R and D."

"You have a whole bunch of vice presidents. Let them run it for a while."

Astonishment froze him for a moment. It was still in his voice when he spoke. "You're telling me how to manage Trainor Electronics."

Chloe wasn't backing down. "All I know is you have a key project floundering, and you're the person best qualified to rescue it."

Longing crossed his face before he looked away. "I was young. I had no responsibilities and I didn't know what was impossible."

"So you're afraid you've lost your ability to innovate?"

His gaze snapped back to her. "Thousands of people depend on Trainor Electronics to pay their mortgages, fund their health insurance, and feed their families. I can't walk away from that."

She began to understand that he felt the weight of all his employees' lives on his shoulders. Trainor was more his father's son than he wanted to acknowledge. Something made her keep prodding him. "Look at it this way. Trainor Electronics can provide livelihoods for even more people if the Prometheus project succeeds because you pitched in."

"Why are you so interested in the well-being of Trainor Electronics?"

"I'm not. I just see the obvious solution to your problem." He needed some joy in his life, and she got the feeling that working on the new battery would bring it to him. "But I'm just a temp, so you don't have to pay any attention to me."

The tense muscles in his jaw relaxed, and an undercurrent of amusement ran through his voice. "You are downright impossible to ignore."

"Because I have a valid point." Chloe basked in the glow of Trainor's compliment. At least, she decided to take it as such.

"Because you are an unusual person."

That was definitely a compliment.

He continued. "Opinionated, outspoken, insubordinate, manipulative, mercenary . . ."

Or not.

". . . and Machiavellian—all qualities I admire."

Chloe couldn't stop her pleased grin. "You do?"

"Yes, I admire them so much that I want to do something inappropriate." He took her hands and stood, drawing her to her feet with him.

Her heart stuttered as he released her hands to slide one of his under her hair to the nape of her neck. He cradled her head and tilted it so he could bring his lips down on hers at a better angle. There was plenty of time for her to armor herself in self-respect and step away from him, but she didn't.

Because last night she'd been dying for him to kiss her and he hadn't. Now she wanted to know how his lips would feel against hers. That was all. Then she would bring this to a halt.

She kept her eyes open as he came closer, appreciating the gray-and-silver striations in his eyes, the grit of dark stubble along his jaw, the bold strokes of his eyebrows. Then the first brush of his mouth sent her eyelids drifting down so she could savor the firm warmth of the lips she'd been so curious about. His fingers wove themselves into her hair while he slipped his other hand to the small of her back to bring her whole body against his.

He traced the line between her lips with the tip of his tongue, not invading, just stroking lightly. Then he shifted his weight so his thigh pressed between hers, her slim skirt pulling tight around her hips to accommodate him. It was the lightest of friction, but it sent a ripple of tiny detonations through her body, making her breasts ache and desire pool inside her.

She slid her hands up his arms and gripped his shoulders, crushing her breasts against the wall of his chest. She wanted to rip open the buttons of her blouse and tear off her bra so her skin could graze the fine cotton of his shirt.

In response, his kiss turned demanding, and she opened her lips to him. As their tongues met, his hand slipped downward to cup her behind and half lift her so he could force his thigh farther between hers. The sudden full contact made her arch into him, and he growled low in the back of his throat.

At the sound, a surge of power ran through her. She had made him do that. Any hesitation melted away and she gave in to her desire to run her hands over the beautiful muscles of his back, the roping strength of his arms, and the rippled lines of his abdomen. Another sound of wordless arousal rumbled in his chest.

He dragged his lips to her earlobe, which he nipped. A laser beam of heat tightened her nipples and fed the arousal between her legs. Then his fingers were at the buttons of her blouse. She threaded her arms between his and tugged at his buttons at the same time. He finished first, opening her blouse and pushing it down her arms. She gave up on his buttons long enough to let him pull it all the way off.

His sudden intake of breath sent another wave of heat through her body. She unfastened the last of his shirt buttons and yanked his shirttails out of his waistband. As she exposed the planes of his chest, she remembered his response to her question about keeping in shape. He must have one heck of a sex life.

Distracted by the sight of his torso, she hadn't realized his fingers had found the clasp of her bra until suddenly it went loose and slid down to her elbows. Before she could react, his hands were on her breasts, his thumbs teasing the already sensitive nipples. Sheer, delicious pleasure rioted through her. She hooked her fingers into his belt and leaned away to give him full access.

Shifting his hands to her hips, he hoisted her up and pushed her onto the desk. Shoving her skirt up her thighs, he spread them apart and stepped in to wedge himself between them. Then he bent to take one of her nipples in his mouth.

All she could do was hang on to his shoulders for dear life because he was driving her to the verge of orgasm.

As he pulled at her breast, she felt his fingers trail up her inner thigh, over the top of her thigh-high stockings, under the lace of her panties, and finally slide inside the wet, aching hollow between her legs. He did something wicked with his thumb, and she convulsed in a blast of explosive release so intense she arched backward and sent the computer screen crashing to the floor.

He flexed his fingers, and the orgasm slammed into her again and again until she went limp, trembling with delicious aftershocks. Collapsing onto his shoulder, she felt him begin to slip his fingers from inside her and locked her thighs together to stop him. "I like you there," she mumbled.

She squeezed her inner muscles as another aftershock shimmered through her, and he huffed out a breath. "I want more than my fingers there," he said hoarsely.

Now she wanted more than his fingers there too. She let her thighs fall open.

"No condom," he practically groaned.

That startled her into opening her eyes and lifting her head. The tendons of his neck were taut, and his face was a study in frustrated arousal. He lifted the hand she'd freed and slid two fingers in his mouth, closing his eyes as he tasted her on his skin. "Perfect," he said.

The word vibrated into her core, making her frantically scan the room as though she could find a condom somewhere. Then a couple of realizations struck her. He hadn't planned to seduce her or he would have come prepared. And with all his wealth and resources, he didn't have something as commonplace as a condom when he needed it. That struck her as funny, and she had to quash a smile. "Maybe you could ring for Ed to bring one."

For a moment, he looked flabbergasted. Then a strained smile curved his gorgeously male lips. "Don't mess with a highly aroused but unsatisfied man," he warned. "Or you may find yourself in an awkward position."

She almost challenged him, just to find out what position he meant. Instead, she stroked her palm down the rock-hard erection tenting his trousers. "Let me ease your frustration."

He captured her hand and lifted it to his lips for a kiss, his breath caressing her skin as he said, "I want to come inside you the first time."

His words knocked her breathless. "Oh."

He swept her bra off the desk and held it up by both straps. "Put this on so I can undress you in my bedroom."

As she shoved her arms through the straps and he wrapped the elastic around to her back and deftly hooked it, she became conscious of the fact that she still sat with her skirt rucked up to her hips and Trainor between her splayed thighs. Yet his touch was so careful and attentive as he held her blouse for her to slide her arms into that she felt no awkwardness.

That would come later.

After buttoning her blouse and helping her find the pins to retwist the bun he'd set free, Trainor shrugged into his shirt and, without bothering to button it, took her hand to lead her out the door. He stopped at a touch pad to press his thumb against one corner before they stepped into the elevator.

"What's that for?" Chloe asked as the elevator soared upward to the third floor of the penthouse.

"Privacy. So the staff knows what part of the house to stay away from."

"I see." What she saw was that maybe having a horde of people at your beck and call had some drawbacks. "Have you ever been, er, interrupted?"

He looked down at her with a frown. "No."

"Good to know." Although she suspected that if a staff member wandered into a private moment, he or she would remove himself or herself without the boss being aware of it.

He must have heard some skepticism in her voice. "My bedroom is off-limits at all times, unless I specifically call for someone."

That made her feel somewhat better. "What about your office?" She imagined Ed walking in when she was half-undressed.

"The same."

At least she could relax in two rooms of his house.

Nathan decided not to mention the security cameras. Those got turned off by the privacy switch too, but he could see Chloe's mood beginning to shift. Some women found the display of wealth a turn-on. His temp was not one of them.

He picked up the pace, hurrying her through the door of his bedroom and locking it behind them. Anticipation burned through his veins. He wanted to bury himself deep inside her gloriously responsive body and let loose all the pent-up tension inside him.

She stopped just inside the door. Giving her no chance to change her mind, he stepped behind her so he could wrap his arms around to palm her breasts and pull her back against him. He bent to find the sensitive skin just behind her ear and felt her body soften against his. His erection was nestled against the sweet curve of her behind, and he flexed his hips to make sure she could feel it.

Her sharp inhale told him she had.

He massaged her breasts, savoring the weight of them filling his hands and the way she shuddered when he pressed against her hard nipples. He drew in the scent of her, a mingling of a lemony shampoo, warm feminine skin, and the tangy edge of her orgasm still lingering on his hand. The memory of having his fingers inside her made him slide one hand down to press the fabric of her skirt between her legs.

She hummed out a breath.

Now that he was sure she was in the right frame of mind, he slipped his arm around her waist and led her across what seemed a vast expanse to his bed. The medical equipment had been cleared out so it no longer looked like an ER.

He held her against him as he jerked open the drawer of his bedside table and grabbed a handful of condoms. Never again was he going to be caught without them when Chloe was around.

She turned and sat on the bed before holding out her hand. "Allow me."

All his good intentions about taking it slowly went up in a flash of smoke. As she ripped open the foil packet, he unbuckled his belt and wrenched down the zipper of his trousers. The relief of letting his erection spring loose was exquisite. Even more exquisite was the soft touch of her fingers as she tugged down his boxers and stroked her palm along his cock.

"The condom," he ground out, feeling his control slip.

"Right." She smoothed it on him and then he snapped, pushing her backward onto the bed so he could shove her skirt up her thighs and yank her panties down and off over her hot high heels. He took a split second to appreciate the sight of her sprawled back on his bed before he stepped between the thighs she opened for him, grasped her hips, and drove fully into the warm grasp of her liquid heat. She cried out as he seated himself inside her—a wild, inflaming sound.

But he didn't move. He was memorizing the soft flesh of her buttocks in his hands, the delicious pressure of her enclosing him, and the strange certainty that this was right in some way.

Then she kicked off her shoes and pulled up her knees, bracing her feet on the edge of the bed so she could lever her hips upward to give him better access. Her movement incited him to action. He withdrew almost completely and then drove into her again, watching the pleasure wash across her face.

"Say my name," he said, wanting to hear her voice.

"Trainor," she murmured.

He pulled back and thrust in as he spoke. "Nathan."

"Nathan." It came out low and breathy, as though it was hard for her to pronounce.

He lost any coherent thought as she rolled her hips up into him, her muscles squeezing around him as she called his name again. The world blew apart around him, turned him inside out, and he bowed back, sending her name echoing off the ceiling.

He had just enough sanity left not to collapse directly on top of her. Dropping onto the bed, he hooked an arm around her waist and snugged her up against his side. He could feel tremors running through her as she came down from her second climax. "I envy you," he said, his eyes closed.

"Because I had two orgasms and you only had one?" Her voice was drowsy with pleasure.

He huffed out a laugh. "Because you're still feeling yours."

"The gift that keeps on giving." She snuggled closer to him, draping her thigh over his. "I guess women are luckier that way. We get an afterglow."

"I feel entirely lucky right now," he said, shaking the pins out of her bun again so he could comb his fingers through the golden-brown fall of her hair.

"Right now, I do too."

He didn't like the emphasis she put on *right now*.

Chapter 12

Chloe wanted to lie there for the rest of her life, mostly so she wouldn't have to face the fact that she'd just had sex with a man she wouldn't ordinarily even be on the same floor with. As his fingers toyed with her hair and satisfaction shimmered through her, she could pretend that the big male body she was plastered against was just a lover, although not an average one. He'd played her the way he played his computer—with a deft, sure touch that got him the results he wanted.

She splayed her hand on his chest and tried to memorize the texture of his warm, smooth skin and the rhythm of his heartbeat as it slowed to normal. She moved her nose closer to his shoulder to breathe in his entirely male fragrance, with its undertones of starch and expensive soap. Opening her eyes, she studied the fine lines at the corners of his closed eyes and the way his thick, straight lashes lay on his cheekbones. This close she saw that his nose had a slight downward curve to it, like an eagle's beak.

She wanted to store all these tiny details about him in a treasured place in her memory so she could cherish them when he was gone. Because this couldn't last.

In fact, she should make sure it didn't last any longer than today. Or she would feel like something discarded.

She had a healthy sense of self-worth, but all she had to do was glance across the room to see the Van Gogh and the Gauguin on the wall. That kind of wealth changed your expectations of the people around you.

Not to mention his genius. Maybe her inventor father could have kept up with that incredible mind, but she'd graduated from community college. She loved to learn and she read constantly, but Trainor was light-years beyond her.

She must have unconsciously shifted because Trainor—no, Nathan—said, "I can feel you thinking, Chloe, and I want you to stop."

She sighed. "I wish I could."

He opened his eyes and turned his head toward her. "I guess I'll just have to distract you."

With that he brought his free hand to the thigh she'd rested on top of him and skimmed his fingers upward until he touched the spot that made her dig her fingers into his shoulder muscle.

Thought fled in the face of overwhelming sensation.

Eventually Chloe lay naked with an equally naked Nathan facedown beside her, his arm a heavy but delicious weight over her waist, in the aftermath of his distraction. Of course, the first thing that met her eyes was the pair of paintings. She went tense and shifted away.

His arm tightened around her. "You promised to make sure I get enough bed rest."

Guilt jabbed at her. She'd completely forgotten he was recuperating from a serious bout of the flu. He certainly didn't show any signs of it. "I've failed miserably because there has been no rest going on in this bed. Are you feeling all right?"

He pivoted both of them sideways so her back was spooned against his chest. Then he hauled the covers up over them. "Never better. Your powers of healing are miraculous. However, I could sleep for a while."

"I should get back to work." She regretted the words almost as soon as she spoke them. Having the bare length of him against her was heaven.

He hooked his leg around both of hers. "Sleep. Doctor's orders."

"*Your* doctor."

She could hear his jaw creak in a yawn. "I'll sleep better with you here."

What could she say to that? She let him pull her in closer, although she had little hope that she would be able to join him in his nap. But her body was so sated that she felt her eyelids drift downward as his breath grew deep and even, whiffling through her hair.

Chloe jerked awake to find Nathan still wound around her. Tilting her head, she checked the digital clock on his bedside table. She'd only been asleep for about forty minutes. She felt like she'd been out for hours.

Now she had to figure out how to disentangle herself without interrupting his much-needed slumber.

It turned out to be impossible. He was strong and he was heavy. When she tried to slip her legs out from under his, he simply settled closer against her so his weight pinned her to the bed. An attempt to lift his arm from around her waist triggered an almost breath-stopping grip.

She was going to have to wake him up.

"Nathan," she murmured, giving his arm a gentle shake.

"Yes," came the immediate, clear response.

"You weren't asleep."

"I was until you started squirming around."

"Sorry."

"I'm not." He released her waist and moved his hand up to her breast. His erection pressed against her bare bottom.

She grabbed his wrist and tried to pull it away. "You need your sleep, and I need to get dressed and go back to work."

His hand didn't budge an inch. "You like deals, so here's one. I'll let you up if you promise not to put your clothes on."

"How am I supposed to work?"

"The same way you always do. You sit in the desk chair and you type. Clothes have nothing to do with productivity."

She snorted. "We haven't gotten a darned thing accomplished since you unbuttoned my blouse."

"On the contrary, I'm feeling very accomplished."

She could hear the smile in his voice, and it undermined her already tenuous self-discipline. "Smug is what you're feeling." But she was smiling too.

All of a sudden he rotated onto his back and flipped her so she was lying on top of him, looking down into his glinting eyes. "Stay here with me," he said.

She levered herself up and braced her forearms on his chest. "I can't afford to."

"What do you mean?"

"I can't put in for the hours we're in bed together. I need to work."

His eyebrows drew down into a scowl. "You will put in for any hours you spend here in my home."

"Really?" She wasn't going to back down on this. Her self-respect hadn't vanished entirely. "You're going to pay me for sex? That makes me a—"

"Stop!" he snapped. "I'm not paying you for sex. I'm paying you for your time."

She could see the frustration in his face as he realized he wasn't improving the situation. Instead of making her angrier, that made her want to kiss him. "I rest my case."

Taking advantage of his momentary inattention, she scrambled off of him and the bed.

"Damn it, Chloe." He raked one hand through his hair as he sat up.

"A very persuasive and articulate argument." She retrieved her bra and panties from the floor, thanking her lucky stars she'd worn one of her few matched sets.

As she bent over to step into the beige lace, he gave an appreciative whistle. "Could you do that again but with your back to me?"

Knowing he was watching her dress made her self-conscious, so she snagged the rest of her clothes and turned toward the bathroom.

"No more comments," he said. "Just let me enjoy the view."

She clutched her clothes against her chest and looked back at him. "I'd like to take a shower."

"Of course. I'm an inconsiderate idiot." He threw back the duvet and rose from the bed in all his beautiful, uncovered glory. "You'll find plenty of clean towels. Use whatever soap and shampoo you like."

She wanted to stay and drink in the gorgeous lines and planes of his body, but he was already pulling on his trousers. Sighing, she continued into the bathroom.

Maybe she was becoming immune to luxury, but the fact that it was twice the size of her bedroom and had a tub you could fit six people in didn't even make her blink. The exquisite marble mosaics on the floor and walls demanded a moment's admiration, and she twisted the tops off several shampoos to sniff their perfumes before she chose a tangy citrus scent that reminded her of Nathan. Then she stepped into the room-sized shower and nearly shrieked when she turned the handle and got blasted from all sides by multiple showerheads.

After a fast scrub, she wrapped herself in an enormous, fluffy white towel and gave her hair a quick blast with the blow-dryer before she braided it. A bun was impossible because all the hairpins were scattered in Nathan's bed and carpet, and she wasn't going to go looking for them.

Tucking her blouse into her black skirt, she looked at her bare face and decided she needed to go to the guest room to redo her makeup. Otherwise, only her slightly swollen lips revealed what she'd been doing half the afternoon.

Self-respect was overrated.

Nathan plucked another hairpin from the tangled linens and added it to the collection in his hand. The blow-dryer had gone silent a few minutes ago, so he padded over to the bathroom door and knocked.

A neat and tidy Chloe greeted him, fully clothed, a tight braid falling over her shoulder.

"Ah, I see you don't need these." He held out the pins on his palm.

She looked at them as though they were emeralds and diamonds. "Thank you for finding them all." Her fingertips brushed his palm as she took them, and he felt himself start to get hard again.

"I'm going to use the makeup in the guest room," she said. "Then I'll meet you in the office."

So she was going to avoid him. He leaned forward and kissed her, savoring the softness of her lips. "And here I was looking forward to the elevator ride."

Her breath hissed in and she threw him a look that was half reproof, half arousal. It made him want to toss her back on the bed.

"We'll ride together on your way out, then," he said.

She just shook her head and walked past him.

He turned to watch the sway of her hips. Memories of sinking his fingers into the delightful roundness of her behind while he drove into her had his erection lifting his unzipped khakis. A cold shower was in order.

As the water cascaded over him, he acknowledged he should have waited until Chloe was no longer working for him before he slept with her. However, his brain had not been the functioning body part in this encounter. Furthermore, he might not have succeeded if she was no longer in close proximity to him. One of the reasons he found her so intriguing was that she did her best to resist him, so he needed face time to break down her barriers.

He frowned as he considered whether Chloe had felt pressured in some way because she worked for him. He just didn't see it. She was a strong woman who didn't hesitate to speak her mind.

The one chink in her armor was the need for money. He would say it was an inconsistency in her, but she didn't expect it to be given to her. She simply wanted to be paid well for her work. That showed no lack of integrity.

But what made her negotiate so fiercely for those pay increases? Ben knew something about that. He made a mental note to call the doctor later.

In the meantime, he found himself looking forward to getting back to his office with an eagerness he hadn't felt in years.

They'd spent two hours within five feet of each other, and Chloe thought she would go up in flames. He was back to his old tricks of finding ways to touch her in the guise of working. Except now she was onto him. And she needed to get home.

"I'm sending you the marketing plan for the Delta Plug," she said, sweeping it across her screen and onto his cloud drive. "I've distributed the financials to your executive VPs, and your e-mail is current. It's quitting time."

He swiveled his chair to face her, his eyes blazing with anticipation. "Have dinner with me."

Only the thought of Grandmillie gave her the strength to say, "I have to go home."

"Why?"

Hadn't they had this conversation before? "I have responsibilities."

"Tell me about them."

Right. She was going to tell her hot new lover that her grandmother lived with her. "It's personal."

He gripped the arms of her chair and pulled it close so her knees were sandwiched between his. Stroking the back of his hand down her cheek, he asked, "Have we not gotten very personal?"

"Not in that way." Unable to resist, she leaned forward to kiss him. "I'm going now."

He still held her chair so she had no room to stand. "You'll meet me here tomorrow."

"Temps don't work on Saturdays without authorization. It requires overtime pay."

He gave a ghost of a laugh. "We are far beyond overtime pay."

She had to admit the truth of that. "I need to be home tomorrow." She had spent so little time with Grandmillie this week because of Nathan.

"Then dinner on Sunday. Surely, your responsibilities can spare you then."

The temptation was nearly impossible to withstand. All she could force out was, "I'm sorry."

Instead of looking insulted, Nathan's face sharpened with the thrill of a challenge. "At least let Oskar drive you home. It will ease my conscience for keeping you late again."

She knew she shouldn't give in, but she was exhausted from the whirlwind of the day, and she'd have to wait nearly an hour for the next train home. "I won't say no."

His eyes went hot. "Good response." He pushed her chair back a few inches before letting it go.

"To the car, not to what you're thinking," Chloe said, standing up. Nathan stood as well, and she found herself looking up at him. "Judith will let me know if you still need me on Monday."

He swooped down to kiss the side of her neck. "There is no question that I will need you on Monday," he said by her ear. "And Tuesday and Wednesday . . ."

She shivered and closed her eyes as his breath tickled over her skin. His words fanned a flicker of hope that she had no business encouraging. "Janice may have recovered by then."

He stepped back. "My need has nothing to do with Janice."

She knew what he meant, but she couldn't go down that road with him right now. It was impossible to think clearly when he was looking at her as though he wanted to strip her clothes off. She started around the desk but stopped when he fell into step beside her. "I know how to get to the garage," she said.

"A gentleman always walks a lady to the door." His voice was smooth as silk, but there was an undercurrent to it that she didn't trust.

"You don't have to be a gentleman. You're my boss."

"As of right now, you're off the clock." He took her hand and tugged her into motion again, stopping briefly by the door to press the keypad. "Oskar will be waiting."

As they walked down the hallway, he twined his fingers into hers and stroked the back of her hand with his thumb. The arousal he'd been stoking while they worked burst into full flame. Her nipples ached where they pushed against the lace of her bra, and the tension low in her belly intensified to near pain.

The elevator doors slid open and she stepped inside, her breathing erratic. Before the doors closed behind them, Nathan had her backed up against the wall, his mouth on hers.

"I need one more taste of you to hold me for the weekend," he murmured.

She could feel his erection against her thigh, and she was desperate to have him inside her for the last time. She tilted her head back to catch his gaze, hoping he would read the invitation in hers. "Is there a way to stop the elevator?"

If she'd thought his eyes burned hot before, now they nearly scorched her. Glancing behind him, he thumbed the touch pad and the elevator came to a gliding stop.

There was a flurry of activity as he shoved her skirt up and ripped her panties down while she unbuckled his belt and trousers. When he produced a condom from his back pocket, she scooped it out of his hand and rolled it onto his cock.

And then he lifted her and impaled her and braced her against the wall so he could drive into her deeper and harder. She locked her legs around his waist as he gripped her bottom to support her, the fierce pressure of his fingers intensifying the sense of urgency. She returned the favor, digging her fingers into the bunched muscles of his shoulders to brace herself.

His rhythm was hard and relentless, and she reveled in it, wanting it to go on forever, even as she panted for the explosion he was building to.

Then he came, pulsing inside her as his shout of completion boomed inside the enclosed space. He shifted angles and ground his pelvis against her so an orgasm crashed through her. Every muscle in her body tried to tighten, but she was crushed between Nathan's big body and the elevator wall, so she couldn't move, only feel. She had the sense of a storm contained in a bottle, the glass sides forcing the power to fold back on itself, magnifying the fury.

Her cries reverberated around them.

Then Nathan was slipping out of her and lowering her feet to the floor. He smoothed her skirt down over her hips and retrieved her panties. "That was . . . unexpected."

"You started it." Chloe turned her back to work her underwear up under her skirt.

As soon as she straightened, his arms snaked around her waist, and her back was against him. "And it was a spectacular finish. Maybe I'll join you in the Rolls. It has a privacy screen."

"Not a good idea." She didn't want him crossing the Hudson River into her private life. It would just make their parting more painful.

His hands were drifting up and down her body. "I think it's one of my better ideas."

She stepped away from him and raised her hand to the elevator's control panel. "How do you start this thing again?"

He reached around her and sent the elevator soaring upward. It stopped again almost immediately, and the door silently opened. Nathan took her elbow and escorted her to the main elevator a few feet away before he turned her into his arms. "How am I going to survive two days without you?"

Her own silent question was harder to answer. *How was she going to survive the rest of her life without him?*

Chapter 13

"There's chicken marsala keeping warm in there," Grandmillie said, waving her cane at the oven. "I ordered in from Vinny's for dinner."

"Bless you," Chloe said, dropping her purse and jacket on the coffee table and leaning down to kiss her grandmother. "I'm sorry I haven't been home much this week."

"Don't talk nonsense. You were needed at work."

Grandmillie's choice of words evoked her last exchange with Nathan, and Chloe felt a flush of desire and guilt. "Shall I open the Chianti?" The wine would help calm her whirring mind.

"TGIF!" Grandmillie said with a nod.

Chloe took her grandmother's arm to help her up out of her recliner and thought how fragile the bones felt. Such a contrast to Nathan's powerful forearm. She shoved that thought away.

As soon as she was on her feet, Grandmillie gently tugged her arm free of Chloe's grip. "Got to keep my balance muscles strong," she said, starting toward the dining table.

Chloe carried food and wine from the kitchen and attacked the delicious chicken with gusto. She had good reason to be ravenous.

Grandmillie let her take the edge off her hunger before asking, "Where did you work today?"

Chloe choked on the wine she'd just sipped. "Swallowed wrong," she croaked before taking a gulp of water. "In Mr. Trainor's home office. Turns out his penthouse has three floors, not two. You get to the office in a private elevator."

"So that's why you came home in the fancy car. I saw it out the window."

Chloe had a hot flash at the memory of Nathan wanting to join her behind the privacy screen. All the way home she'd been picturing what they might do on the deep leather seat.

"How was Mr. Trainor feeling today?"

Thank goodness she hadn't taken another drink of wine. "Much better. He wanted to go to Trainor Electronics, but his doctor threatened to quit if he did." How different would her day have been if Cavill had given the okay for Nathan to return to work? Would the heat between them have flared up even there, or would it have remained at a simmer because they were in a real office? She had an erotic vision of Nathan making love to her on the conference table.

"But he got up and worked anyway." Grandmillie snorted. "Typical man. More muscle than sense."

"Exactly." Chloe swallowed the last of her wine in a gulp and refilled her glass. "Shall we celebrate our windfall with a shopping trip to the mall tomorrow? I need a couple of nicer blouses if I'm going to keep working in the executive suite, and you're due for a pretty new top too."

"I'm not done with Mr. Trainor yet," Grandmillie said. "So he wants you back on Monday."

Needed her back on Monday, according to him.

"I knew if you got your foot in the door, they'd figure out how smart you are. Here's to a permanent job offer." Grandmillie lifted her wineglass.

Chloe clinked hers against it and drank without tasting the wine. She'd completely screwed up any prospect of staying at Trainor Electronics. Even if they offered her a position, how could she accept it now that she'd slept with the CEO?

"He has an excellent executive assistant. As soon as she recovers, I'll be back on the reception desk." Unless the receptionist had already recovered, in which case, Chloe would be at another company altogether. The thought dropped her into a trough of depression.

Until she remembered the wedding. Her spirits soared again. If nothing else, she'd have one more day with Nathan, even if they couldn't do more than hold hands. Just feeling his long fingers wrapped around hers would be delicious. And she could brush her shoulder against his, and maybe their thighs would touch in the church pew. If the wedding was in a church. She frowned as she realized she knew very little about the upcoming event.

"There's something you're not telling me," Grandmillie said. "I can see the gears turning behind those brown eyes of yours."

Chloe tried to disarm her with a wry smile and a partial revelation. "It's kind of weird, but Mr. Trainor hired me to go to a wedding with him next Saturday. It's a family wedding, and he didn't want to take a real date because tensions are running high."

Grandmillie's gaze felt like a laser on Chloe's face. "A very sensible arrangement," her grandmother finally said. "More people should do that."

Chloe couldn't believe she'd gotten off that easily. She let out her breath and stood up to clear the dishes. "You're the best, Grandmillie."

"Oh, I know that's not the whole story, but you'll tell me when you're ready."

Chloe fled to the kitchen.

Two hours later she was pulling her cotton nightgown over her head when the cell phone buzzed on her bedside table. The screen said "Private Caller" and she almost swiped it into the dismiss side when a hopeful little voice in the back of her mind said, *Telemarketers don't call late Friday night. Answer it.*

"Chloe, it's Nathan. I wanted to wish you sweet dreams."

She hadn't really believed he would call. "That's very thoughtful of you."

"That's not my whole wish. I want you to have sweet dreams of me. Of us. Together."

"*Sweet* would be the wrong adjective for those dreams."

"What adjective would you use?" His voice had dropped half an octave.

She sat down on the side of the bed. "Steamy, hot."

"Keep going."

She swallowed hard. "Erotic."

"Did you think erotic thoughts in the Rolls on the way home?"

"You wore me out, so I napped," she lied.

His chuckle was smug. "I don't believe you."

"You really are a genius."

She heard the intake of his breath. "Meet me tomorrow. Anytime, anywhere."

Her plans to take Grandmillie shopping rose up in her mind. "I can't. I—"

"—have responsibilities," he finished for her. "My father will like you."

He hung up before she could respond. Now she'd never be able to go to sleep.

Nathan was about to toss the phone onto the bed beside him when it rang. It was his doctor.

"Ben, I'm in bed, as ordered."

"I'd better get there fast. You must be dying." Ben's voice turned serious. "Be honest, how do you feel? Any fever, aches, pain?"

"No flu symptoms. Just some fatigue. That's the God's honest truth." Of course, the fatigue might be due to his high level of activity that afternoon. Nathan felt a stirring in his groin.

"Not surprising, given that your body tried to cook itself from the inside out. Can I persuade you to stay home for one more day?"

"No."

Ben's sigh was heavier than mere exasperation with his friend would warrant.

"Tough day at the clinic?" Nathan asked. Ben worked as a concierge doctor in order to fund the free clinic he ran in the Bronx.

"The administrator quit. Again."

"I'll get Roberta to find you a replacement."

Ben gave a ghost of a laugh. "Thanks, but Roberta is too good at her job. The last two admins she found for the clinic were so skilled they got hired away for twice the salary."

"So why did this one quit?"

"One of the patients became violent and scared the heck out of her. I can't blame her."

The administrators reminded Nathan of Chloe—not that she was ever entirely out of his thoughts. "Ben, why does Chloe Russell need to rush home every night?" And stay home all weekend. Without him. "Ask her."

"I did. All she would say is that she has responsibilities. Is it a mad husband in the attic?" A thought struck Nathan, sobering him. "Does she have a child?"

"All I will say is no and no. After that you're on your own. If she doesn't want you to know, it's not my place to tell you."

"Your conscience has always been a problem in our friendship." Nathan considered a different approach. "I've become interested in Chloe as more than an employee."

A long silence met Nathan's announcement. "What happened to Teresa?"

"Our entire relationship was built on the lie that she didn't know who I was when we met."

"Ah." Ben managed to inject sympathy, disapproval, and comprehension into one short syllable. "Do I need to remind you that Chloe works for you?"

"I believe I included that fact in my first mention of her name."

"Don't you think that gives you unfair leverage?"

"Do you think I would use my position to force a woman to do something she didn't want to?" Nathan was getting a little angry.

"Not deliberately, but the leverage is there nonetheless." Ben paused a moment. "Consider this: you don't even know why she insists on being home at night."

"Because I haven't applied any undue pressure to make her tell me."

The next day Nathan remembered his words as he paced to the window of his office at Trainor Electronics yet again. He couldn't focus on the reports he'd put off reading while he was ill. He kept wondering what Chloe was doing and how she could so easily refuse to see him for two days after the explosion of desire that had brought them together.

Was it a ploy as Machiavellian as Teresa's? She would play hard to get so he would want her even more?

It seemed to be working.

There was no point in staring at the computer screen any longer. He strode back to the desk and signed off. He would go home and swim until he stifled the yearning in his body with sheer exhaustion.

In the elevator, he started to push the button for the ground floor when Chloe's voice floated through his mind. *You have a key project floundering, and you're the person best qualified to rescue it.*

His finger hovered over the array of numbered buttons for a long moment before he touched the one for the research-and-development department.

When the elevator doors slid open, he stepped out into the open-plan room with a sense of familiarity that gradually disintegrated as he looked around. The bundles of wires hanging from the ceiling at regular intervals and the worktables outfitted with triple-layered shelving were the same. But the electronics arrayed on them were all several generations newer than what he'd worked with. He recognized their general function, but the screens and controls were configured differently.

He'd been away too long. He pivoted on his heel to return to the elevator.

"Mr. Trainor?" The woman's voice held a mixture of incredulity and awe.

Turning back, he watched heads pop up from behind racks of equipment. Some people looked curious, some shocked, and most appeared nervous. He was impressed with the number of people working on a Saturday.

The woman stood up from a desk. She was short and thin, with long, straight black hair twisted into a sloppy knot at the back of her head. "Mr. Trainor?" she repeated. A low murmur filled the room. He could hear the repetition of the *T* at the beginning of his name ticking through it.

He combed his memory of the Prometheus reports and came up with the assistant project manager's name. "Ginnie Tsai?"

"Yes, sir," she said, surprise and apprehension skittering across her face.

"I've read your reports," he said. "I came to see what I can contribute."

"Yes, sir!" she repeated, this time in a tone of breathless excitement. "It would be an honor to have you work with us."

"It's been a long time since I've been in a development lab," Nathan said with a wry grimace. He unbuttoned his cuffs and rolled up his sleeves. "Why don't you show me what you've got so far?"

Chapter 14

Despite her X-rated dreams, Chloe slept well, probably because her body had been so satisfied by Nathan's lovemaking. As she dressed and fixed breakfast, a little smile kept tilting the corners of her mouth upward. She would purse her lips to erase it, only to find them in the same contented position five minutes later. Grandmillie kept giving her sideways looks, which meant Chloe needed to get her happiness under better control.

Grandmillie was waiting in her recliner while Chloe got organized for their expedition to the mall when the doorbell rang. Chloe pulled open the front door to find Oskar standing on the tiny porch, a flat brown gift box tied with a turquoise-and-gold satin ribbon clasped carefully in his big, square hands. "From Mr. Trainor," he said, holding it out to her. "With his compliments."

"Thank you." Chloe took the box from the chauffeur, finding it heavier than she expected. "MarieBelle" was embossed into the box's fancy cardboard. Thank goodness it was too big and heavy to be a diamond farewell bracelet. "Do you know what it is?"

"No, ma'am, but it must be perishable, because I had instructions not to leave it outdoors."

That relieved her. Receiving a gift of food wasn't inappropriate, even if it was expensive food. She thanked him again and Oskar returned to the car. Not the Rolls, but an elegant dark-green sedan that she thought might be the Maserati.

She walked back into the living room. "I guess I did a good job, because Mr. Trainor sent me a gift."

Her grandmother's sharp gaze said she wasn't fooled by Chloe's attempt to minimize the unexpected arrival. "Via his own chauffeur, not some delivery service," Grandmillie pointed out.

"It's something that can't be left out in the sun, so he probably didn't want to entrust it to FedEx." Chloe stared down at the box in her hands. Nathan wouldn't send something potentially embarrassing, would he?

"Are you trying to untie the bow with your mind?" Grandmillie asked. "Open it!"

Chloe sat down with the box on her lap and pulled the ribbon loose. As she opened the lid, the aroma of chocolate saturated the air. An envelope with her name written in her boss's scrawl lay on top of a layer of turquoise tissue paper. She snatched it up and slid the heavy cream-colored card out. It had Nathan's full name engraved on the front in a bold font that somehow looked modern and high-tech without being hokey about it. She flipped it open.

> Dear Chloe,
> Since you appreciate my taste in art, I thought you might appreciate the taste of these. You have very good taste yourself.
> Nathan

She exhaled a sigh of relief. He had been circumspect, even though his double entendre about her taste made her flush. She glanced up at her grandmother.

"If it's personal, don't feel you have to share it with me," Grandmillie said. She had a sly look that made Chloe uneasy.

"No, no, it's fine." Chloe put the card on the coffee table and folded back the tissue paper. Under a layer of cushioning plastic lay two large rectangles of chocolate side by side. Painted onto their surface were meticulous copies of the Van Gogh and Gauguin landscapes Nathan had hanging in his bedroom. "How amazing!" Chloe breathed.

She rose and carried the box over to Grandmillie. "It's chocolate."

"Well, I'll be a shot of whiskey in a wine bar, that is some very fancy candy."

"So now you'll understand the card," Chloe said, placing the chocolate gently on the table and reading the card aloud. "He has these two paintings hanging together." She didn't mention in what room. "And he asked me which one I liked better."

Grandmillie scanned the chocolate images. "Which one did you choose?"

"Neither. I told him they were like a great relationship. Taking one away would end it."

"You're smart, just like your dad," Grandmillie said, giving Chloe's knee a gentle tap of approval with her cane. "Smarter, in some ways."

Chloe shook her head. "Dad was a genius."

"His brain was full of ideas, that's for certain."

"And many of them were very valuable," Chloe pointed out. "To Lindell." She couldn't keep the bitterness out of her voice.

"Your father signed his employment contract knowing full well what the terms were."

Chloe sat back. Grandmillie had never said anything that blunt before. "They could have given him a bonus, Grandmillie. What kind of company makes millions from an employee and never acknowledges it in any concrete way?"

Her grandmother was silent a long moment before she spoke again. "I'm not saying Lindell treated him well, but they had no legal obligation to give him more than they did."

Chloe tried again. "There's obligation and there's honor. They had no honor."

"They were just a big corporation doing what big corporations do: making a profit."

"Which is why I don't want to work for a big corporation," Chloe said. She was surprised by Grandmillie's implied criticism of her father. Her grandmother usually just listened when Chloe got going on the topic.

She changed the subject by touching the chocolate with her fingertip. "Should we taste it or is it too beautiful to eat?"

"This beauty is meant to be devoured with more than our eyes," Grandmillie said.

The chocolate was unbelievable. Intense, smooth, not too sweet but utterly satisfying. Almost as good as sex with Nathan. Chloe choked on the bite she'd just taken as that thought crossed her mind.

Grandmillie sat with her eyes closed as she savored her piece. "I'm thinking that most bosses don't send their temps custom-made chocolate after a few days' work." She opened her eyes and turned her gaze on Chloe. "What's going on here?"

Chloe coughed again. "I spent a lot of extra hours there and even left you alone overnight, so I guess he feels extra thanks are needed."

"Left me alone, ha! I had six different phone numbers for Dr. Cavill and had to swear on the Holy Bible that I'd wear that emergency call-button necklace. I expected a nurse to knock on the door every hour on the hour. But that's neither here nor there." Her blue eyes skewered her granddaughter. "I don't want any details because your private life is your private life, but when a man sends you a gift like this, it's not for being a good executive assistant."

"Um, there might be some interest between us that's not just professional," Chloe said. "But that happened after he hired me to go to the wedding with him."

Grandmillie tapped her cane on the ground with a satisfied little thump. "I knew it. So why isn't he taking you out for dinner tonight? Men in his position go after what they want."

Chloe cast around wildly for an excuse. "He already had another commitment."

"Don't lie to me, child." Grandmillie's expression held both love and regret. "You turned him down to stay home with me."

"I've missed you and wanted to spend time with you." Chloe got up and knelt in front of her grandmother. "That's the truth."

Grandmillie ran her palm down Chloe's cheek. "I don't know what I did to deserve a granddaughter like you, but it must have been pretty darned good. You need a reminder, though. When you invited me to move in with you, we made an agreement. If my presence interfered with your personal life, I would move out."

"You're not—"

Her grandmother held up her hand for silence. "You call your Mr. Trainor and you tell him you've had a change of heart and would love to have dinner with him tonight."

Chloe barely got her mouth open before Grandmillie stopped her again. "If you don't, I will put myself on the waiting list for Crestmont Village today."

Crestmont Village was the three-stage elder-care facility Grandmillie had nearly moved into four years ago before Chloe convinced her they could rent their little house together. After Chloe's mother died, Grandmillie had become a strong maternal presence, so she and Chloe were unusually close.

However, her grandmother had been adamant that she didn't want to be a burden on Chloe and had made a list of the conditions required for her to live there. Since her grandmother was a fiercely independent woman, Chloe had respected and lived by all of them.

In the last year or so, though, Grandmillie had begun to walk more slowly and put more weight on her cane, so Chloe worried about her falling. Maybe it was time to talk about getting someone to stay with her while Chloe was at work. The problem was paying for it.

Chloe frowned as she turned over her options in her mind.

"Well, are you going to call him?"

"Call him?" She'd forgotten what had started her train of thought. "Oh, you mean Nathan, er, Mr. Trainor. He's probably already found another date."

"His chauffeur just delivered custom-made chocolate. He's thinking about you, not some other woman. Call him."

"Um, okay." She pulled her cell phone out of her purse, giving in easily because she wanted to see him again so badly.

"Go in your room and close the door so you can be private," Grandmillie said with a smile.

Chloe hated to do it, but she retreated to her bedroom and pulled the door shut. She didn't know what Nathan might say, and she didn't want to have to choose her words with two different listeners in mind.

As she scrolled to Nathan's number, she wondered where he was at eleven o'clock on Saturday morning. Maybe he'd taken his doctor's advice and stayed home another day since it was the weekend. She shook her head at herself. Not a chance of that.

She took a deep breath as she hit "Dial" and held the phone to her ear.

"Chloe! Just a minute," Nathan answered. He sounded distracted, which she found disconcerting. She'd hoped he would sound pleased to hear from her.

"Did I catch you at a bad time? I'll call you back later," she said.

"No." It was a sharp command. "I'm in the lab, so I need to move to a quieter place."

She could hear voices and a low hum in the background. "What lab?"

"The R and D lab." The other voices had faded, and his held a wry note.

Chloe did a silent fist pump. "Checking on their progress?"

"Helping them make progress. Don't say it."

Since she'd just been wondering how to broach the subject of dinner that night, she was taken aback. "What shouldn't I say?"

"The normal but annoying response would be 'I told you so.'"

Relief made Chloe smile into the phone. "I try not to be annoying. I guess I don't always succeed." Nathan's deep chuckle made her knees go rubbery, so she sat down on the bed. "Anyway, that wasn't even close to what I was going to say."

"You have my full attention."

"My, um, responsibilities have changed, so I'm free for dinner tonight if you're still interested. And you're not already committed to something else." Chloe closed her eyes with a grimace as she contemplated her lack of finesse.

A long silence made her wish she'd just told Grandmillie that Nathan was busy.

"What is your favorite food?" Nathan asked.

"Chocolate," she said, realizing she hadn't thanked him. "Beautifully painted chocolate."

"That's dessert, and I have a new favorite in that category."

"Er, really?"

"You." His voice was a low vibration of pure desire. It knocked the breath out of her. "I need a main dish so I can decide where to take you for dinner."

"Lobster," she managed to croak. "I love it."

"I'll pick you up at five."

"No, I'll meet you there. Wherever there is." She wasn't ready to allow Nathan into her private space yet.

She could almost feel his displeasure through the phone.

"I'll respect your feelings for now," he finally said. "But Oskar will come in my place."

"All right." Somehow he'd made her feel guilty, as though she'd hurt him. "What should I wear?"

"I'd prefer nothing, but that would shock Oskar."

Another breath-stealing statement that proved he wasn't so upset that he wouldn't flirt with her. "Not to mention our fellow diners," Chloe said, her mind spinning with the image of sitting naked across an elegant dinner table from Nathan. It made her insides turn hot and liquid.

"The male diners would count themselves fortunate. And maybe a few of the female diners as well."

Chloe sputtered out a half laugh. "Seriously, what level of formality am I aiming for?"

"Less formal than work clothes, but more than jeans. Just make sure it's easy to get it off."

"I might have something with Velcro seams." She needed to thank him for the chocolate. "Nathan, the chocolate is amazing. I can't believe I had the nerve to taste such a work of art, but it's as delicious as it looks."

"Just like you."

The heat inside her went molten. "Please stop."

"Do you really want me to?"

She didn't want him to stop for the rest of her life, but that was a pipe dream. "Only until dinner. Then you can start again."

He laughed and hung up.

Chloe sat on the edge of the bed, the phone cradled in her hands, as she took in several deep breaths to calm her racing pulse.

She wasn't sure how she was going to get through the next seven hours without exploding.

Nathan stood in the project manager's empty office, staring sightlessly out the window, as he considered Gavin Miller's comment that he should use every weapon at his disposal.

A smile of wicked glee lit his face, and he hit Ed's speed dial on his phone. "Ed, tell Kurt to have the jet ready to go at Teterboro with a flight plan to Kennebunkport, Maine. I need dinner reservations for two at the Weather Vane Inn on the jetty. Oskar should pick up Chloe at her home at five."

Miller was right. There was no point to having all this money if you couldn't use it for the important things in life.

Like having Chloe naked at thirty thousand feet.

Chapter 15

Lolling on the glove-soft leather of the Rolls's backseat, Chloe was caught up in daydreams of Nathan stripping off first her cream V-neck sweater, then her pleated lavender sateen skirt, and finally the sheer peach lace bra and panties she'd sneaked away from Grandmillie to buy at the mall. When the big car made a sweeping turn and came to a stop, she peered out the window to discover they'd driven directly onto the tarmac of an airport. Ten feet from the car, a sleek black-and-silver jet crouched with its door open and its steps let down.

As she squinted at the writing on the side of the plane, Oskar came around to open her door. "Mr. Trainor is already on the plane," he said, holding out his hand to help her up from the depths of the car. The deep hum of the jet's idling engines surrounded her as their draft flattened her clothes against her body. She hugged her gray silk bomber jacket around her.

Now she could make out the logo of Trainor Electronics on the jet's fuselage. "Why stop at a helicopter?" she muttered.

He was pulling out all the stops, and that should have flattered her. Instead it reminded her of the vast gulf between her and her boss. She grimaced as she realized she'd just thought of him as her employer. For the blissful hours between their phone call and this moment, she'd considered him as just a man—a very sexy, smart, fascinating man—but someone she could face as an equal.

She stopped to take in the massive Rolls-Royce with Oskar standing beside it and the elegant power of the company jet, and felt a clot of tears in her throat.

She'd better make the best of this date, because she wouldn't be able to hold the interest of a man who commanded these resources for very long.

Nathan watched Chloe come to a halt on the tarmac, her gaze directed toward the jet. He should have told her they were flying to Maine to get the freshest lobster in the world.

He jogged from his seat to the plane's door, running lightly down the steps to meet her. He did the one thing he knew would overcome whatever barriers she was building in her mind. He kissed her, pulling her body against him and tasting the delicious softness of her lips. The hell with the lobster. This was the feast he was interested in.

For a moment she felt stiff in his arms, and then she melted against him so he had the sense that they fit together perfectly. He wanted to stay like this, not changing a single angle or atom of how their bodies touched.

Until she wound her fingers into his hair and slid her mouth along his jawline, where she blew a warm breath against the side of his neck just under his ear. Heat slammed into him like a missile.

"On the plane," he said, turning her in his arms and half carrying her up the steps. He needed privacy.

He escorted her to a seat beside a window before he opened the door to the cockpit and gave the pilot the go-ahead. As he turned back around, the sight of Chloe sitting on this plane that he had flown on a hundred times hit him with a shot of pure joy. She had been craning her neck to look out the window, but now she caught his gaze and smiled.

There was no way they'd make it all the way to Maine without making love.

The look in Nathan's eyes sent a pulse of arousal through Chloe. On top of his welcome kiss, she was pretty well seething with need.

It didn't help that he was wearing silver-gray trousers that made his legs look long and lean, and a burgundy shirt in a fabric that draped over the muscles of his shoulders and arms in a way that emphasized their power.

Three fluid strides brought him to the leather seat beside hers. He dropped into it, fastened his seat belt, and reached across the six inches between them to lace his fingers with hers. "Once we're at cruising altitude, you can sit on my lap." His look was heavy lidded, and she knew exactly what he was thinking about doing to her.

"But the pilots . . ." Chloe cast a look at the young woman locking the jet's door closed.

"As soon as she goes back in the cockpit, I press a button." He flipped up the top of his chair's arm to reveal a control panel. "A privacy light goes on, and no one comes back here unless there's an emergency."

"Oh." It shouldn't have surprised her that he'd had sex in the airplane before. He was a red-blooded male whom most women would fall over themselves to be seduced by.

"I use it for business negotiations of a confidential nature."

"Exactly what I was thinking."

"You're a terrible liar." He lifted her hand to kiss her knuckles one by one, sending shivers up her arm. "One of the many things I like about you."

Chloe wanted to ask him about some of the others, but she refused to fish. Instead she looked around the airplane as the engines revved and it began to taxi forward. The cabin looked like someone's designer living room, with its cushy tan leather chairs and polished wood-and-aluminum tables and cabinets. You could tell it was a plane only by the seat belts and the fact that the furniture was attached to the floor. "This is a lot nicer than economy class."

"I should have offered you a drink, but I was in a hurry to get us into the air. My apologies." His smile spoke of wickedly hot intentions.

The engine sound rose to a roar, and the jet hurtled down the runway before tilting upward in a swift ascent. She found her grip on Nathan's hand tightening involuntarily as the nimble Learjet turned on a wingtip.

"Do you dislike flying?" Nathan's frown of concern made her want him more.

"I'm not used to how fast a smaller plane turns." She eased her hold on him. "By the way, where are we going?"

"Kennebunkport, Maine, to a restaurant where they take the lobsters off the boat and cook them right then and there."

"I'm pretty sure they have good lobster in New York City."

"You're a tough woman to impress."

Chloe shook her head. "I'm already impressed. All this"—she swept her hand around the luxurious cabin—"just makes me nervous."

First Nathan scowled. Then he shook his head with a sharp laugh. "That shoots Miller's theory all to hell." The "Fasten Seat Belts" light winked out, and he unbuckled his so he could turn to face her. "Why would it make you nervous?"

"Because it proves how different we are."

"All it proves is that I got lucky with something I designed for my own use."

"Please." She tossed him a skeptical look. "Your *apartment* could hold four of my *house*. Just one of your terraces is bigger than my backyard. If you want lobster for dinner, you hop on your jet and fly to Maine."

"Trappings, Chloe, toys. That's all."

"This level of trappings changes people."

Nathan looked away. "Not as much as you would hope."

That caught her attention. So he had wanted his wealth and success to change something in his life. She wondered if it had to do with his father. She longed to ask but her nerve failed her.

He reached over and flicked open her seat-belt buckle, letting his fingertips drift over her thigh. "Will you sit on my lap?" he asked, his voice pitched low.

Her breath caught in her throat as she met his gray eyes. They burned.

"Y-yes." Without breaking eye contact, she pushed herself up from her seat and moved to stand in front of him, looking down.

His head was tilted back slightly so she could see the strong line of his neck and the hollow at the base of his throat. She braced her hands on the armrests and bent down to touch it with her tongue.

Then his hands were on her, lifting her so she landed with her knees on either side of his thighs. He pushed his fingers into her hair to hold her for a long kiss that made her forget they were on a plane. All thought and feeling were concentrated on the way he felt under her and against her. She sank down so his erection rubbed directly against the ache between her legs. She pulled away from his mouth to increase the pressure by arching her back.

He found the hem of her skirt and worked his hands up under it, skimming along her bare thighs. Despite the coolness of the evening, she'd decided to dispense with stockings since she suspected dinner might lead to something more intense. The heat of his palms made her push down harder, and he muttered her name on a groan as his fingers worked under the lace crotch of her panties.

"They untie," Chloe breathed. "At the sides."

"Even better than Velcro," he said with a ghost of a laugh.

She felt a yank at each hip and the falling away of the lace. Nathan bunched her skirt in one fist and shoved it up to her waist. "I want to see my hand on you."

As he cupped her, she reveled in the way his arousal made the strong angles of his face even sharper. *She* made him feel like this. A sense of power spiked through her, and she began yanking open the buttons of his shirt. Leaning down, she licked one of his nipples as she rocked her hips hard.

He retaliated by thrusting his finger inside her. She was so wet already that there was no resistance, and she pushed against him again, wanting more. He slid two fingers inside her and flexed them while he worked his thumb on her clitoris, sending waves of pleasure surging through her. She braced her palms on his bare chest, savoring the satin of his skin over the wall of his muscle.

"Are we a mile high yet?"

In answer, he released her skirt to pull a condom out of his trouser pocket. As he ripped the envelope, she jerked his belt open and unzipped his fly. Before she could touch him, he had the condom on and his hands were wrapped around her hips. "Hold your skirt up," he commanded. "Now let me guide you."

She gathered her skirt up and held it at her waist. His fingers tightened on her as he shifted her into position over him. She felt the head of his cock brush against her and gasped at the electric zing it sent through her. Then he was slowly lowering her, impaling her on him with exquisite deliberation. The sense of being filled and stretched made her sigh in sheer bliss. He brought her down so she was spread open over his lap, the insides of her thighs brushing against the fine fabric of his trousers. He held her there, neither of them moving as they let the intimacy of being joined sink deep inside them.

She wanted more. She tightened her internal muscles around him, making both of them moan. "Do that again," he ground out. "Yes." He hissed out the *s* as she obeyed. She contracted a third time and his self-control broke. He raised her just enough so he could withdraw and thrust back into her, going faster and deeper with each stroke.

Pinning her skirt against her waist with her elbows, she grabbed his wrists and held on while he drove her to a climax that convulsed muscles she didn't know she had. When the shocks began to fade, he seated himself hard and fast and used his thumb on her to trigger another searing orgasm as he reached his release inside her.

She let go of his wrists and fell forward in a boneless heap on top of him, her forehead resting against his shoulder while she gulped in chest-heaving breaths. His arms went around her, and he turned his head to kiss her temple. "I've been thinking about doing that ever since you called," he said.

"That's a good use of your brilliance."

"I've heard the mind is an erogenous zone."

"Anywhere you touch me is an erogenous zone." Chloe felt him slip out of her, setting off both a ripple of lingering pleasure and a yearning at the loss. She shifted so he could dispose of the condom and then turned sideways to snuggle down against him. "Lobster is going to be an anticlimax."

"We'll have oysters too."

Chloe chuckled. "Because you need an aphrodisiac? I don't think so."

"They were for you. I don't need any aphrodisiac except this." He ran his hand along the curve of her hip before he turned her face up and pressed his lips to hers.

She had to remind herself that this wasn't a fairy tale where the handsome prince was going to marry her and carry her off in his Learjet to his penthouse. She needed to keep a proper perspective on what was merely mind-blowing sex. Burying her face against his chest, she allowed herself a grim smile. *Merely mind-blowing sex* was an oxymoron.

She felt him settle more comfortably in the seat and let her eyelids drift closed. She focused on the smell of his skin, a slight spice of spent sex underpinning the clean, warm aroma that was Nathan's. His breath tickled past her ear, and his heartbeat sounded a quiet rhythm against her cheek. She tucked her arm around his rib cage, appreciating the texture of muscle and bone. "How many hours can the plane keep flying before it runs out of fuel?"

"I'll have Kurt circle the airport until the gauge hits empty." His voice sounded drowsy too. "There's always a little in reserve for landing."

The hum of the jet engines and the hiss of the air circulating in the cabin spun a cocoon of suspended time around them. Chloe had no idea whether it had been minutes or hours when Nathan stirred and murmured by her ear, "The 'Fasten Seat Belts' sign just came on."

"Can't you just fasten your seat belt over both of us?"

"I could, but Kurt and Sarah would get an eyeful when they came out of the cabin after we landed."

She moved her hand to his chest to push herself upright. As she shifted her position, her thigh brushed against Nathan's cock and she realized he was hard again. "Oops, not much we can do about that right now."

"There's always the limo ride to the restaurant."

Chloe choked as she shook her skirt down and smoothed the crumpled sateen while he straightened his own clothing. The plane banked and she practically fell into her seat, hastily buckling the seat belt.

Then they were on the ground and Nathan was escorting her to a black limousine parked on the edge of the tarmac. She caught a brief whiff of the sea as he handed her into the car.

She slid across the seat to let him in beside her, shivering a little when the car's heater chased away the chill of the northern wind. As he sat and stretched his long legs out, he said, "I was joking about the limo ride."

Chloe relaxed. She was still dubious about that thin partition between the driver and the backseat providing any privacy. "Maybe on the way back to the airport," she said.

He put his arm around her shoulders to pull her close as the limousine glided into motion. Dropping a kiss on the top of her head, he said, "After the oysters."

Chloe let her hand rest on his thigh, feeling the hard muscle under her palm. She let her gaze trace down the length of his leg to the polished black loafers. A shiver of delight shook her as she felt his fingers playing in her hair where it fell over her shoulder. It was almost too much to bear, this sensual onslaught.

She forced her brain to begin to function on a less primitive level. "You said you were working on the Prometheus project. What happened?"

His fingers stilled. "I couldn't focus on paperwork so I decided to try a change of scene."

"Why couldn't you focus? Are you still not feeling up to par?" She kept forgetting he'd been ill only four days before.

A pause as though he was debating what to say. When he spoke, his voice was pitched low. "I kept imagining you. On the desk. On the conference table. On the sofa. Against the wall."

"Oh." She felt a warm, melting sensation between her legs as she imagined the same thing, only from her point of view. She cleared her throat. "So you went down to the R and D lab?"

"Since I was already frustrated, I decided I might as well."

She tilted her head to discover a slight smile curling his lips. That made her brave. "And what did you find out there?"

"The team is dedicated, brilliant, and young. They have some great ideas, but they missed a few key steps."

"So you fixed Prometheus?"

He laughed. "Your faith in me is touching. I made some suggestions."

"How did you feel about being there?"

"Feel?" Surprise colored his voice.

"Did you enjoy being back in the lab?"

She thought he wasn't going to answer her question. Then he shifted slightly on the seat. "Yes and no."

"That's definitive."

"It felt like my brain was firing on all cylinders for the first time in years. But the technology—" She could feel him shake his head. "I might have left it too long."

"You're not going to let a few new gizmos chase you away, are you?"

"Virtually every tool in there was four generations newer than anything I've used."

"So you just need a refresher course," she said lightly. "Geniuses can learn anything."

She sensed another head shake. "I won't stop you from calling me that as long as it extends into the bedroom."

"And your office," she said.

The limousine made a sharp turn and thudded over what sounded like a wooden bridge. Chloe leaned across Nathan's wide chest to peer out the darkened glass of the car. "Where are we?" She could see water beside them and a rocky shoreline dotted with bare trees and a few sprawling shingled houses.

"On the causeway leading to the restaurant."

The limo continued onward a few minutes and then stopped. As Nathan helped her out of the car, the sounds of seagulls crying and waves slapping against rocks surrounded her. The wind was even stronger here, and Nathan wrapped his arm around her shoulders as she shuddered in the cold. They stood in front of a building constructed of classic weathered New England shingles and white wood trim, but with huge arched windows that glowed with a golden light. "The Weather Vane Inn" was painted in block letters on a small wooden sign affixed to a white post.

"So you just have to know this is here," she said.

"It functions on word of mouth," Nathan said, leading her to the dark-blue front door. "Nothing more is necessary when the food and setting are this good."

Chloe inhaled, closing her eyes as the scents of ocean and haute cuisine mingled deliciously in her nostrils. "Mmm. Nothing more than smelling it is necessary."

The door opened as they approached. A small, wizened man in a perfectly fitted dark suit said, "Welcome, Ms. Russell and Mr. Trainor. We're so glad you could join us this evening." His accent was pure Maine.

He turned and led them through a whitewashed foyer furnished with a round polished wooden table topped with a huge vase of fresh flowers. Arched doors led out to the dining area that held widely spaced tables covered in cream linen under large, gracefully curved pewter chandeliers. Although the effect was meant to be elegant simplicity, something about the sheen of the tablecloths and the brilliant sparkle of the glassware exuded a sense of no expense being spared. Chloe eyed a place setting as they passed a table and was relieved to see all the utensils were recognizable.

The maître d' led them to a table by one of the arched windows. Chloe suspected it was the most desirable view in the restaurant, since she could see the lights of the charming seaside town, as well as the pink, yellow, and orange of the sunset sky reflected and fractured on the waves of the sea. "It looks like a painting," she breathed as Nathan waved their guide aside and held the chair for her.

"I timed it so we could arrive at sunset," he said, his palms briefly caressing her shoulders. His touch sent a ripple of delight dancing across her skin.

He sat down across from her. As she turned from the view to look at him over the low bowl of flowers between them, she could barely catch her breath. His hair shone like burnished bronze; the planes of his lean face caught light and shadow like a sculpture; and the clear, masculine lines of his lips made her want to trace them with her fingertips. But it was his eyes that knocked her sideways. Their gray depths held brilliant intelligence, banked desire, and a focus that was entirely on her.

Nathan frowned as Chloe seemed to freeze when he looked at her. "Is everything all right?"

He saw her throat move as she swallowed. "Fine. It's all fine." She still looked like a deer caught in headlights.

"I'm not convinced."

Chloe grabbed her water goblet and took a gulp. "Just a little overwhelmed."

Nathan looked around the room, seeing nothing but tables, chairs, and white-painted walls. The pewter chandeliers were shiny but not ornate. "It's just a restored seaport inn. Nothing fancy."

Chloe made a small choking sound and held up her water glass, turning it so the crystal glittered with tiny rainbows. "It looks simple, but it's the kind of simple that costs a lot of money."

Her reactions were so different from other women's. His previous dates pretended not to notice where he took them or how they got there, but he could always see the calculations going on behind their masks of indifference. Chloe was frank in her appraisal of what things cost, and faintly disapproving of extravagance.

"This place has the best lobster I've ever eaten," he said. "That's why I brought you here."

The rigidity went out of her posture. She reached across the table toward him, her palm turned up. "And I appreciate that."

He wrapped his fingers around her small hand, and suddenly the table was far too wide. He wished the Weather Vane Inn had banquette seating so he could pull her up against his side, feel the softness of her, breathe in her scent, and twine his fingers into the shining strands of her hair.

His thoughts must have shown on his face, because a blush climbed her cheeks and she tugged her hand free to fumble open her menu, breaking contact with his gaze to scan the inn's offerings. He saw her eyebrows go up, and somehow knew she was noticing there were no prices on her menu. For once, she made no comment.

"Would you prefer mine?" he asked, offering it across the table.

"Sometimes ignorance is bliss." She went back to studying the menu before she closed it. "In keeping with the theme of simplicity, I'm just going to have a salad and a lobster."

"You have a choice of how many pounds. And butter or some other sauce."

"No butter. I want to taste the lobster itself. How many pounds are you having?"

"I'd recommend two two-pounders. I think the meat is better in the smaller lobsters." He was surprised she had asked for his recommendation. She generally had her own ideas about things. "May I choose our beverage?"

She nodded.

The moment he closed his menu, their waiter appeared at the table to take the order before he sent the sommelier over with the wine list. Nathan already knew what he was ordering, partly because he liked it with lobster, and partly because he knew it would horrify Chloe's thrifty soul. He scanned down the wine list and said, "Bin thirty-three."

"What's in bin thirty-three?" she asked after the sommelier left.

"Dom Pérignon. It's excellent with lobster." He didn't add that it was a highly valued vintage. She might refuse to drink it.

All she did was raise her eyebrows at him.

The server brought two empty champagne flutes and placed them on the table. Chloe reached out to twirl hers between her fingertips. "We have to discuss your father's wedding," she said, lifting her eyes from the spinning glass. "Now that we're, you know, dating, you can't pay me to go."

She was so matter-of-fact about her desire to earn money that he was curious to find out why she was turning down a substantial paycheck. "We made that deal before we started our relationship, so it still stands."

She dropped her gaze to her fidgeting fingers. "It would make me feel like someone from an escort service."

He could see the logic in that. "You'll still allow me to finance your clothing for the occasion, though. Otherwise I will rescind the invitation." He wasn't going to have his father's shotgun wedding become a burden for Chloe.

Her glass spun out of her fingers, rolling toward the edge of the table. He caught it as it fell and returned it to its place.

She lifted her chin. "I'll accept only because I don't want to embarrass you."

He looked at her with her cloud of shining gold-shot hair swirling around her shoulders, her huge brown eyes glowing in the candlelight, and the soft curves of her lips compressed with stubborn pride. "I would be proud to have you on my arm, no matter what you wore. However, I look forward to taking you shopping."

"What? You're going with me?" she squeaked.

He hadn't intended to until this moment. "I have strong opinions on female attire."

She snorted inelegantly. "Female lingerie I can believe, but I'm pretty sure you wouldn't know a Prada from a Pucci."

"Granted, my expertise runs more to SQL and Python. But I know what I like, and I'd like to watch you model it."

The line of her lips softened. "You have a company to run."

"I get a lunch hour like everyone else."

"Ha! That shows what you know about shopping. It will take more than an hour to find the right outfit for such a special occasion."

Her look of triumph entertained him. "I can give myself more than an hour for lunch, but I'm not sure I can do the same for you, since you report to Flexitemps."

"I think Judith would understand."

"So I can pay you for shopping time?"

She went back to fiddling with her glass. "I'm not sure. I have to think about it."

The sommelier appeared with the champagne, silently twisting the cork from the bottle before he poured a splash in Nathan's flute. Nathan tasted it and nodded his approval.

After their glasses were filled and the sommelier departed, Nathan lifted his flute. "To Pucci and Python, a good pairing."

Chloe looked skeptical until she took a sip of the Dom Pérignon. Her eyelids fluttered closed and he could see her rolling the sparkling wine around in her mouth. He wanted to kiss her so he could taste it on her tongue.

She opened her eyes. "Wow!" She took another drink, her eyes narrowing as she concentrated on the flavor.

"It's one of my favorites." He liked being the one who introduced her to a new taste.

"Don't tell me what it costs. I want to enjoy it without guilt."

He put down his glass. "Chloe, what makes you worry about money so much?"

"I'm sorry. I don't mean to be so focused on price. It's a bad habit." She stared down into the bubbles in her glass.

"Maybe I can help."

That made her look up. "No."

He leaned back in his chair. "Will you at least answer my question?"

He could see the debate going on behind her eyes. Finally, she shrugged before taking a gulp of champagne. "My grandmother lives with me. I don't want her to go into a nursing home, so I'm saving money for the day when I need to hire help for her."

"I see." That kind of care was expensive, and she was a temp. No wonder she negotiated for a raise whenever possible. "You continue to impress me."

"It would be more impressive if I didn't kill every company I worked for as a permanent employee."

"Kill?" He let her deflect his praise with the new topic. "Should I be worried about the future of Trainor Electronics?"

"You may be safe. The Russell jinx seems to affect only start-ups. So far Flexitemps is still in business, although I warned Judith when she took me on."

"Start-ups are notorious for failing, so I don't think you're the sole reason they've closed down. Why would you work for those if you're concerned about saving money?"

She hesitated, rearranging the array of forks in front of her as she spoke. "I don't have any patience with corporate politics. I like to be rewarded for getting my job done well rather than for schmoozing the boss." She blushed and looked him in the eye, saying, "This is *not* schmoozing."

He laughed at her directness. "We are well beyond schmoozing," he agreed before leaning forward. Her revelations about her work background proved that his original instincts were correct. "I said you were a ringer. Tell me where you've worked."

At that moment the servers arrived, and he caught a look of relief on her face. He quelled the desire to curse and send the waitstaff away so he could unravel more about his intriguing companion.

However, he'd ordered a variety of appetizers before the jet left New Jersey because he wanted Chloe to taste the entire array of deliciously fresh Maine seafood the Weather Vane Inn offered. He wanted to see the moment the flavor burst on her tongue and she focused on it. What he really wanted was to have her lying beside him naked while he fed it all to her with his fingers. A man could use his imagination.

"We'll never be able to eat all this," she said, her eyes wide as the waiter placed a large, artfully arranged platter in the center of the table.

"Speak for yourself. I worked up a considerable appetite on my way here."

She slanted him a warning glance, but the corners of her mouth twitched.

The waiter spoke, gesturing toward each item as he named it. "As you requested, Mr. Trainor, we have included only Maine seafood here. Steamed mussels, scallops, soft-shell clams, mahogany clams, rock crab, and a selection of Damariscotta oysters—including those from Glidden Point, Pemaquid, and Cape Blue." Nathan got another pointed glance from Chloe at the mention of oysters.

"We are especially fortunate to have two Belons, the rarest oysters in the world, for your tasting pleasure," the waiter continued. He backed away with a hint of a bow. "Enjoy our sampling."

"The rarest oysters in the world, eh?" Chloe said, poking at one with the miniature fork the waiter had set down beside her plate. "Does that give them extra powers?" She arched an eyebrow at him.

"They have a powerful flavor, so that might equate to extra potency." He picked up a Belon in its shell and held it out to her.

She started to take it from him with her hand but he pulled it back. "With your mouth," he said, wondering if she would do it.

She hesitated only a second and then leaned forward, opening her lips to take in the edge of the shell before she sucked the oyster out of its natural cup and into her mouth like a pro. The whole time she kept her gaze locked on his in deliberate provocation. The sight of her lips pursed around the rough shell sent a fast burn through his body, tightening his cock to rock hardness.

After a couple of chews, she grimaced and swallowed in a labored gulp. "Ugh! It tastes like metal." She grabbed her water goblet to take a swig before she picked up the other Belon oyster and held it out with a wicked smile. "Your turn."

The nasty flavor of the oyster lingered on Chloe's tongue as she dared Nathan to eat the other one. He didn't hesitate for a second before angling his body in to suck it off the shell. His lips touched her fingers, so she felt the heat and texture of his mouth before he leaned back. Now she understood the flare of intensity she'd seen in his eyes when she took the oyster from him. It was a strangely intimate act to feed someone from your hand.

He chewed the mollusk slowly, his eyes always on her. She watched the muscles in his throat work as he swallowed. "It does have a coppery taste," he said. "Like eating a computer chip."

"Just what I want for an appetizer," Chloe said.

His gaze was still on her as he said, "Now I understand the aphrodisiac properties of oysters. It's all about how you eat them and with whom." His voice was husky and low, vibrating through her so she shifted in her chair.

"The good news is that I'm not likely to acquire a taste for rare oysters," Chloe said, trying to defuse the suddenly charged atmosphere.

"Let's wash the taste away with a milder flavor," Nathan said, reaching for another shellfish. Once again he held it out to her.

She had been daring enough to play his game once, but she began to feel self-conscious. "Do you plan to feed me the entire dinner?"

A half smile curled his lips. "I'm considering getting the rest to go."

Would he really do that? Did she want him to? A vision of Nathan feeding her chunks of lobster from his fingers while they were lying in bed naked danced through her mind.

She slurped the oyster off the shell, barely tasting it before she swallowed. "Does lobster taste different when it's a mile high?"

Chapter 16

Chloe lay in bed, luxuriating in the memories of the night before. Grandmillie went to church every Sunday with the devoutly Catholic family who lived on the next block, so this was Chloe's private time each week. She lay on her back, staring at the ceiling as she remembered the briny taste of the oysters and the crisp, dry bubbles of that amazing champagne.

But the best memories were of Nathan's hands and mouth and body. Sex on the way to Maine had been wild and explosive. On the way home, they'd taken their time. It turned out the sofa on the company jet folded out into a bed. Nathan claimed he only used it to catch up on sleep while he traveled, but she took that with a grain of salt. However, she refused to worry about the women who had come before her or the women who would come after her.

They had spread the containers of food out on the table beside the sofa bed and started to feed each other, but their appetites had quickly veered in a different direction. She moved restlessly on the sheets as particular moments and sensations floated up from her memory. They'd gotten all their clothes off, and she'd explored the feel of his skin over various muscles, of which he had an impressive supply for a workaholic CEO. She discovered that he swam in a lap pool daily when he wasn't recuperating from the flu, which gave his back a beautiful ripple when he moved and drew lines of power down his thighs and calves. She wanted to see him wet and glistening as he rose out of the water.

The doorbell ruined her daydream. "Shoot!" she said, bolting out of bed and grabbing her bathrobe.

Pulling the belt tight around her waist, she peered through the sheer curtain that covered the sidelights by her front door. Oskar stood on the porch, holding a vase of tall blue flowers in one hand and a carrying case in the other.

Chloe could feel the smile curving her lips as she pulled open the door. "Morning, Oskar," she practically sang. "Come on in."

The solemn Oskar stepped through the door and cracked a tiny smile. "Mr. Trainor sends his regards."

"Thank you. Why don't you put the flowers there?" She pointed to the narrow hall table. It could barely accommodate the large arrangement.

Once he'd placed the flowers, Oskar reached inside his pocket and pulled out an envelope with her name on it. The stationery was the same as the card that had accompanied the chocolates yesterday. He handed it to her before lifting the case in his hand. "This is heavy, so it's best if I put it on a bigger table."

As Chloe led him into the dining area, she brushed her fingers over the envelope, knowing Nathan had touched it not long ago. Oskar put the case on the table and gave her a little bow before he strode to the front door. She closed it behind him and ripped open the envelope.

Darling Chloe,

The lupines are the most famous wildflower in Maine. However, I did not raid a roadside patch for these, so your conscience can rest easy.

The rest traveled home with us on the jet. I did my best to keep your attention focused inside the limousine so you didn't notice the extra containers being loaded in the trunk.

Chloe snorted. They'd been entwined with each other almost from the moment the driver had closed the door. Nathan had brought her to orgasm on the leather seat beside him with his long, clever fingers under her skirt since she refused to bare herself even with the privacy screen raised. The memory sent arousal zinging through her.

I believe the medical community has under-estimated the aphrodisiacal powers of oysters. I may convert my lap pool to an oyster bed.

While most people dread Monday morning, I look forward to it with great anticipation. Please give your grandmother my warm regards.

Nathan

Chloe felt like a character in a sappy Hallmark movie, but she couldn't help herself. She cradled the note against her cheek, trying to feel Nathan's presence in it. After rereading his line about Monday morning, she walked to the dining room table to see what was in the elegant cardboard case. She flipped open the top flap. Nestled in padded compartments were two bottles of the same Dom Pérignon they'd had with dinner the night before, along with three champagne flutes, also like the ones they'd used at the Weather Vane Inn. Another note was enclosed.

> Don't chill the Dom until the day before you
> plan to drink it. The extra flute is for your grand-
> mother. I look forward to meeting her.
> N.

The thought of Grandmillie and Nathan face-to-face made her sit down hard in a dining room chair. She didn't want to introduce Nathan to her grandmother, like a single mother who didn't let her boyfriend meet her child until she thought it might be serious. As realistic as Grandmillie usually was, she had a blind spot about Chloe. She would see no reason why a billionaire entrepreneur shouldn't fall madly in love with her granddaughter. Chloe didn't want Grandmillie to be disappointed when Nathan went on to a woman more suited to his status.

So she would just keep her worlds separate. That shouldn't be too hard for the short period of time Nathan's interest would last.

Chloe picked up one of the flutes and flicked her fingernail against it, making the fine crystal emit a pure, high note. "Well, we can use the third flute when we break the second one."

She put the flute back in the box and stowed the whole case away in the kitchen. Then she retrieved the lupines from their precarious perch and pushed aside a pile of magazines on the coffee table to set them there. The magazines cascaded onto the floor.

Kneeling to pick them up, Chloe noticed that one wouldn't stack neatly because a folder of some sort was wedged inside it. She pulled it out and sat back on her heels when she saw the embossed white writing: Crestmont Village, the assisted-living facility.

"How on earth did that get in here?" She flipped it open and dropped the magazines back on the floor. A letter dated only ten days ago was tucked into the folder.

> Dear Mrs. Russell,
> Thank you for your inquiry about our elder-care facility. We have enclosed the information you requested about availability of . . .

Chloe stopped reading. Why would Grandmillie request information from Crestmont Village? Other than their discussion about Chloe going on the date last night, everything had been fine. In fact, Grandmillie had been indignant about having Cavill's emergency contact numbers foisted on her when Chloe spent the night away.

Chloe riffled through the sheets of paper in the folder. There was a multipage application form with its blanks still empty. She breathed a sigh of relief. If her grandmother were serious, she would have filled the form out and sent it in; Grandmillie didn't mess around once her mind was made up to do something.

Chloe gathered up the magazines again, leaving the folder on top of them this time. She intended to find out what her grandmother was plotting.

In the meantime, she had a phone call to make.

Nathan did a kick turn and knifed through the water again. He was doing three more laps if it killed him.

Of course, Ben claimed it would.

But he needed to work off the sexual haze that had enveloped him ever since the first time he touched Chloe. He'd been blaming his lack of focus on the flu, but it was caused by something more difficult to cure.

He couldn't even swim without imagining how he would make love to her in the lap pool. He pictured her breasts glistening with drops of water that he would lick off her peaked nipples. She would wrap her fingers around his cock and stroke him hard under the surface. He would lay her back to float on the water before he spread her thighs and held her open while he buried himself inside her.

He nearly swallowed a mouthful of water as a groan of arousal tore itself from his throat. His erection was not helping his aquadynamics either.

Hitting the opposite wall of the pool, he kick-turned again and forced himself to concentrate on the Prometheus project, figuring that would be the most effective buzzkill. However, it just reminded him of Chloe's advice to pitch in on the project himself.

How the hell had she gotten so embedded in every aspect of his life so fast?

The question didn't unsettle him as much as he expected it to. If Chloe was taking up all his attention, it wasn't because she demanded it. He discovered that giving his attention freely was surprisingly pleasurable.

Sending the gifts to her this morning had been pure fun as he'd tried to decide what her reaction would be when she saw Oskar at the door holding the lupines. When she opened the box of Dom, would she frown in disapproval at the cost or enjoy the treat?

The line about meeting her grandmother had come from his pen without thought, yet he had meant it. He was curious about the woman Chloe was so devoted to.

He finished the final lap and hoisted himself out of the pool with shaking arms, collapsing onto his back on the tile floor and heaving in great gulps of oxygen. Thank God Ben wasn't here to see him gasping like a dying fish.

As his breathing settled into a more normal rhythm, he went back to solving his newest problem. He grudgingly admired Chloe's refusal to take payment for her trip to the wedding with him, but he knew she needed the money. He just couldn't figure out a way to offer it that she would accept.

He'd gotten around Ben's reluctance to accept Nathan's donations for his free medical clinic by setting up a foundation using a front man. Ben had no idea the money flowed from Nathan. However, that wouldn't work for Chloe, since she didn't have 501(c)(3) status. He grimaced. Chloe would be horrified to know he'd considered her in the same thought as a charity.

His cell phone rang and he vaulted to his feet to swipe it off the marble-topped table by the pool. Dropping into a nearby chair, he checked the caller ID. The laps had just been a way to kill time until this call came through.

He answered with the word he'd been waiting to say all morning. "Chloe."

"Nathan." Her tone held a smile and a touch of mockery. "You knew I'd call."

"Your manners are always impeccable."

She laughed. "Well, that's not true, but when someone sends me a wonderful gift, I like to say thank you."

"The gift was our time together last night. What I sent this morning was my thank-you."

"Very smooth." Her voice softened. "The lupines are lovely, and you know I'll enjoy the champagne in those elegant flutes. Every time I use them, I'll remember where they came from."

There was a strange wistfulness in her tone that bothered him. "We'll use them together."

"Of course." Her words lacked conviction.

"Chloe, is something wrong?"

"How could anything be wrong when I'm sitting in front of a vase of gorgeous flowers with two bottles of Dom Pérignon stashed in my cupboard? Not in the refrigerator. And there's still plenty of chocolate left." She paused. When she spoke again, her voice was low and uncertain. "There is one thing missing."

He tensed. *What omission was so glaring that she would mention it?* "Tell me."

"It would be better if you were here too."

A sudden restlessness brought him out of the chair to pace over the tiles. "I was thinking the same thing. In fact, I was picturing you swimming with me here in my lap pool. Naked." Her little intake of breath made his groin tighten.

"Should you be swimming so soon after the flu?" she asked, her voice quivering the tiniest bit.

"I exerted myself far more last night."

"Good point. But maybe that means you should rest today."

"There's no rest for the wicked, and I've been thinking nothing but wicked thoughts about you since last night. Would you like to hear some of them?"

She choked, whether on a laugh or a gasp, he couldn't tell. "No phone sex. Grandmillie will be home from church any minute now."

"How would she know what I'm saying?"

"I'm pretty sure it would show on my face."

"You do have an expression of wanton bliss when I touch you in certain places." Teasing Chloe was better than phone sex. He was sure she was blushing now.

"*Wanton bliss?*" she huffed. "You have an expression of drooling lust when I touch you in certain places."

He chuckled. "I don't drool."

"You do. And you snore too."

"We haven't actually slept together, so how would you know?"

"I slept beside you the whole night when you were sick."

"Not a fair test. Sleep with me again, and I'll prove I only snore when under the influence of germs."

She sighed. "That would be nice. Oh, the Lombardis' car just pulled up in front of the house. I've got to go. Thank you again, Nathan. You're so . . . everything is just . . . so amazing. 'Bye."

She hung up before he could answer her. He suspected it was because she didn't want him to hear the tears in her voice, but he had.

He dropped his phone on the table and grabbed his towel, rubbing it hard over his nearly dry hair and chest.

What the hell had he done to make her cry?

Chapter 17

"Still in your pajamas, I see," Grandmillie said as Chloe opened the front door. She'd had just enough time to tighten the belt of her robe and take a couple of deep breaths to shake off the effect of Nathan's attempt to seduce her by telephone. She wondered if he really would have told her what he'd been imagining doing to her.

"You're looking very snazzy this morning," Chloe said. Her grandmother wore a turquoise linen suit with a frivolous little hat of net and straw to match. Her slender cane was made of carved oak with a silver handle. She'd told Chloe one should dress well to dine with the Lord in his own house.

As she walked slowly into the living room, Grandmillie spotted the lupines on the table and nodded her approval. "That young man of yours knows how to treat a lady."

Grandmillie's description of Nathan made him sound like Chloe's teenage prom date. She thought of him striding down the corridor of Trainor Electronics in his custom-tailored suit with a phalanx of executive vice presidents marching behind him. Nope, not your average young man. And not *hers* either.

"He sent champagne too," Chloe said as her grandmother settled into her lounge chair.

Grandmillie's eyes lit up, her professional interest as a former bar owner piqued. "What kind?"

"Dom Pérignon."

"A classic. You can't go wrong with that." She removed her hat and set it on the table. "Now tell me all about your dinner out."

"There's something I need to ask you about first." Chloe picked up the Crestmont Village folder. "Why did you send for information about this place?"

Grandmillie waved a dismissive hand. "Oh, that. It just came in the mail. AARP must have sold them a mailing list of local seniors."

Chloe kept her voice calm. "There's a letter inside that's addressed to you and thanks you for your inquiry."

Her grandmother looked away. "It's a nice place. I put my name on the waiting list."

Chloe's heart seemed to twist in her chest. "But we've talked about this. You're doing fine here. And you don't belong in that place."

Grandmillie sighed and brought her gaze back to Chloe. "Not yet, sweetie, but I'm afraid the time is coming. I love you too much to be a burden and a worry to you."

"You're my anchor. I need you here in my home." Chloe wiped away tears with the back of her hand.

"You need to live your life, and I like the folks at Crestmont Village."

Chloe thought about her tour of the elder-care facility a couple of years ago. It was clean and well maintained. The staff was kind and caring. But so many of the residents were in the grip of dementia or stared blankly at a television set. Grandmillie was as sharp as a tack and loved visiting with their neighbors of all ages. She was especially good with the teenagers, who often spilled their troubles to her when they would talk to no one else.

"Is this because I asked Dr. Cavill to give you his emergency phone number?" Chloe had guessed Grandmillie would be annoyed about that. "I did it just to make myself feel better, not because I thought there would really be a problem."

"Exactly what I'm talking about. You felt guilty, and I won't stand for that."

"But I'll feel so much worse if you're not here with me."

Grandmillie looked down at her hands folded in her lap for a long moment before she spoke in a low voice. "I didn't want to tell you this, but two weeks ago I may have had a very minor stroke."

"What! When? Why didn't you call me? Did you go to the hospital?" Chloe couldn't stay on the couch. She got up and knelt in front of her grandmother, resting her hand on the older woman's nylon-covered knee, more to comfort herself than Grandmillie.

Her grandmother's pale-blue eyes went misty. "You are the best granddaughter anyone could ask for." She put her hand over Chloe's. "It was two Wednesdays ago. I fell in the hallway for no good reason, so I got out my cell phone and called Lynda to come over. She drove me to the doctor. I would have told you if the doctor had said it was serious, but he checked me over and said everything was good. It was just one of those things. And don't you go yelling at Lynda. I swore her to secrecy before I would tell her why I called."

Chloe couldn't hide the tears tracing hot, salty paths down her cheeks. The idea of Grandmillie lying on the hard wooden floor of their hallway all alone nearly choked her with guilt and distress. She'd been ignoring the evidence of her grandmother's increasing frailty because she didn't want to deal with the implications, and that denial had caused her grandmother pain.

"I'm so sorry." Chloe rested her forehead on Grandmillie's knee as a sob shook her. "I shouldn't have left you here alone."

"And that's exactly why I didn't tell you about it." Her grandmother's tone was sharp. "I'm perfectly capable of knowing when it's time to change my living situation, so you're not going to take the blame on yourself."

Chloe straightened and rubbed the tears away. She took a deep breath to clear the tightness in her chest. "You're right. But I don't agree that it's time to go to Crestmont Village. You just need someone to be here with you when I'm not."

"Missy, you know as well as I do how much that kind of care costs."

"And the good news is that I have a full-time job offer with benefits, so I can afford it."

Grandmillie looked skeptical. "This is the first time you've mentioned any such thing."

That was because Chloe hadn't planned to accept the job. She hated everything about it, from the man she would be working for to the sleazy way he did business. She'd spent a week as a temp for Larry Clarke, the head of sales at Brandt Tech, and he'd liked her so much he'd offered her a permanent job as his sales assistant. He'd also propositioned her, right in front of the framed photos of his wife and twin two-year-old daughters.

Chloe could handle the sexual issue; Larry had barely blinked when she turned him down flat. What bothered her more were the false promises Larry made to prospective clients when he wanted to close a deal. So she'd refused his original job offer, only to have him come back with an increase in salary, a signing bonus, and full benefits from day one. She hadn't said no immediately because it was so tempting financially. Now she felt that fate had been guiding her.

"That's because I was negotiating for a higher salary and hadn't accepted it yet. But the new offer just came in, and they added a signing bonus to convince me." Chloe tried to sound excited.

Grandmillie wasn't buying it. "Where is this miracle job?"

Unfortunately, Chloe had described Larry Clarke's dishonest sales tactics to Grandmillie while she was temping there. At least she hadn't mentioned his disgusting proposition. As Nathan had observed, Chloe was a terrible liar, so she told a general truth, saying breezily, "Brandt Tech. They loved me there."

"Where you worked for the lying dirtbag of a sales manager?" Grandmillie gave her the gimlet eye and thumped the floor with her cane. "No. You will not compromise your integrity for an old woman."

Chloe knew how to fix this. She pushed up from the floor and stood. "It's not just about you. I'm tired of not being able to eat out or buy a nice pair of shoes when I want to. This job would give me extra money to spend on myself too."

"I wasn't born yesterday." Grandmillie's voice was kind. "Sit down, child, and listen to me."

Chloe sank down onto the sofa with relief, since her knees felt shaky.

"I know you adored your father, especially after your mother died and he was the only parent you had. But my son foisted his adult bitterness on your young soul, and that wasn't right. If I'd known what he was telling you during those evenings you two spent in his workshop, I would have given him a piece of my mind."

"What do you mean?"

"All that talk about how terrible big corporations are. How they stole his marvelous inventions and never paid him a penny." Grandmillie shook her head. "When your father went to work for Lindell, he signed a contract stipulating that they owned anything he developed. He knew exactly what that signified."

"Yes, but other—"

"Let me finish. Furthermore, he worked with a team. Those inventions weren't just his; they were the result of lots of brains put together. Not to mention that without the equipment and the laboratory and the marketing support, your father couldn't have turned his ideas into salable products. Kevin was a dreamer, a brilliant one in certain ways, but not a practical man. Lindell gave him a real-world structure to work in."

Chloe sat back against the cushions as she tried to absorb this new perspective on her father. In all the hours she'd spent sitting on her favorite high stool, watching him tinker at his worktable, she'd never questioned his claim that Lindell had exploited his genius without proper compensation. Grandmillie was right about the bitterness; she'd drunk it in along with her father's stories about the drama and excitement of creating a new product that sent the company's profits soaring but didn't budge his paycheck.

"But what about paying him a bonus when his idea made them money? Lots of companies do that," Chloe said.

"He got bonuses, but he thought he deserved more." Grandmillie fidgeted with her cane. "I wouldn't say these things about my own son if I didn't think you needed to hear them. Just because a corporation is large doesn't make it evil. You shouldn't limit your job hunt to those fly-by-night start-ups you always choose. Or work for some dishonest salesman. You're better than that."

But they needed the money now, and her other applications for permanent employment hadn't borne fruit yet. As far as she could see, there was nothing wrong with Brandt Tech's product; it was just Larry's lies about its capabilities that were the problem.

She rubbed her fingers against her temples, trying to massage away the headache that had begun to hammer at her skull. She would make a few phone calls tomorrow to see if she could goose along the other prospective employers. Maybe Judith had some leads on permanent spots.

"Don't look so upset, Chloe. Nothing I said takes away from what your father accomplished or how much he loved you."

"No, of course not. It's just . . . not the way I thought of him."

"He was your hero, but he had his human frailties, like us all. He was still a good man."

It rang true from her adult perspective, but Chloe wanted to cling to her old view of the world and her father. She'd believed in her father with a child's wholehearted acceptance. After her mother's death, he was everything to Chloe and his view of the world became hers. Now Grandmillie had pushed her axis off center, leaving her wobbly and uncertain.

Grandmillie's gaze was concerned. "You've got enough to think about for one day. And I still haven't heard about your date last night."

Chloe was grateful for the change of subject. "Nathan wanted lobster, so we flew to Maine." She was curious as to whether Grandmillie would be shocked.

Her grandmother thumped her cane on the floor again. "Ha! Now that's the proper way to court my granddaughter."

Chloe was putting the dinner dishes in the dishwasher when her cell phone rang, showing Judith's number. Not a good sign.

"It's Judith, my dear. You have a new assignment for tomorrow. Tallman and Hicks Accounting in Midtown. You'll be helping with a major audit they're doing. They need papers organized, copied, and filed."

Disappointment thudded into Chloe like a jackhammer. "I'm not going back to Trainor Electronics?"

"No. HR called to say all their flu victims are well enough to come in tomorrow. I know it's a pay cut from the executive suite, but I gave you the highest paying of the new job openings."

"You're the best," Chloe said, trying to shake off the blow, and sound as grateful as she should be to her boss and friend. But all she could think about was not seeing Nathan tomorrow morning.

"Just to double-check, nothing awkward happened between you and Nathan Trainor, did it? I know you were finding it uncomfortable to work in his home."

"Awkward?" Chloe heard the squeak in her voice and swallowed hard. She wasn't sure what to tell Judith. Now that she wasn't working for Nathan anymore, her personal life shouldn't be relevant to Flexitemps. "No, we ended up getting along well enough."

"Good. That's a very nice account for me."

"Um, speaking of accounts," Chloe said, "I might want you to look for a permanent place for me."

"I'm sorry, sweetie, but you know I don't handle start-ups. There's not enough money in them."

"I've rethought my position on large corporations," Chloe said. She lowered her voice so Grandmillie wouldn't hear. "And I need the job security and the higher salary."

"I'll see what I can find. You have a great resumé, but the job market is tight, as you know." Judith's voice went from businesswoman to concerned friend. "What made you change your mind? Is your grandmother doing all right?"

"She's going to need help when I'm not here. But it was some other things too." Not just her grandmother's revelations. Knowing Nathan had begun to undermine her negative attitude. How could she disapprove of a big company when the man she was having incredible sex with ran one?

"Update your resumé and send it to me tonight," Judith said. "I'll e-mail you the address and reporting info for Tallman and Hicks."

"Right. I'll do that."

Judith said good-bye, and Chloe slumped in her chair, letting the cell phone drop into her lap. She didn't want to work on her resumé tonight; she wanted to sit in front of the television set, letting Grandmillie comment on how bad the shows were while Chloe daydreamed about Nathan.

Nathan! Did *he* know she wasn't going to be at Trainor Electronics tomorrow? No, he would have called her if he did. HR wouldn't bother the CEO on a Sunday with personnel issues; they would make sure he had whatever he needed without him ever having to think about it.

She stared down at her cell phone. She was afraid to call him, afraid her absence from outside his office wouldn't matter to him. Even more afraid that his interest would fade when she wasn't right there in front of him, working through his e-mails.

No, there was still the wedding next weekend. She would have at least six more days of his attention.

She picked up the phone and hit his speed dial.

He answered on the first ring. "Chloe, I'm on the terrace, staring across the Hudson River, wondering where in that glow of lights you are."

The tension drained from her body. He'd care that she wasn't going to be there tomorrow. "Slightly south and three counties in."

"How's Grandmillie?"

She sucked in a breath as his words touched that fresh bruise on her heart. "She's doing fine."

"You don't sound fine."

Even though he couldn't see her, Chloe shook her head. "She had a little health issue last week that she just shared with me, but it's nothing to worry about."

"I'll have Ben take a look at her. It will give him someone else to badger, so he'll leave me alone."

The temptation to have the highly qualified Cavill give Grandmillie a thorough checkup nearly overwhelmed her, but it was a favor she couldn't accept. Nor would her grandmother want her to. "Thank you, but it's not necessary. She saw her own doctor."

"We'll talk about it tomorrow."

He was using his strategy of retreating to fight another day, but she was too weary to tell him she wouldn't change her mind. "That's why I called. I won't be there tomorrow. Everyone at Trainor Electronics is healthy again."

He swore, making Chloe's sore heart flip with delight. "Where will you be working?"

"Tallman and Hicks Accounting in Midtown."

"We'll meet for lunch. At my apartment. I'll send Oskar for you."

She laughed. "You'd have to come in the car with Oskar. Remember, I only get half an hour for lunch."

He muttered another curse. She loved his frustration. "Isn't that against some labor law?" he asked.

"Not for a temp. We're just hired guns."

"I'll be there in the Rolls when you get off work. We'll drive to New Jersey together."

She knew she should say no. She needed to keep him separate from her real world. But the thought of not seeing him tomorrow made all her good sense evaporate like dew under an August sun. "Okay. I'll send you Tallman's address."

His voice came through the phone in a low, sexy rumble. "I hope the rush-hour traffic is horrific."

Chapter 18

Nathan usually enjoyed the quiet of early morning on the executive floor when he was the only one in. Today it felt empty.

He paced over to the wall of windows and stared outward without seeing the skyscrapers spiking up into the sky. He wanted Chloe here.

He'd checked and there were currently four open positions—with generous salaries—listed on the internal job roster that she could fill perfectly. In one stroke, he could ease her financial problems and satisfy his own need.

He was well aware that it would be more appropriate to find her a job at another corporation, something he could do easily, but he had to know she was in this building somewhere.

They would have to be discreet. That might be the most difficult part for him, since he had an almost constant desire to see her. But he would not tarnish her reputation.

He looked at his watch for the third time since he'd started work. Another hour before Roberta got into the HR office.

Chloe had never been so grateful for a mindless temporary assignment. As she copied and collated sheet after sheet of numbers and legal jargon, she veered among worrying about how to keep Grandmillie from signing herself into Crestmont Village, redrawing her image of her father, and having her knees go weak in anticipation of what she and Nathan might do in the back of the Rolls. It was an exhausting roil of emotions.

Her cell phone vibrated in her trousers pocket, indicating a text message had come in. She finished putting together a packet of papers before she pulled her phone out. It was from Nathan.

`Call me when you break for lunch.`

She glanced at the clock on the wall of the conference room where she was working, the papers spread across the vast mahogany tabletop in neat piles. The executive assistant she was working for had told her to take lunch whenever she wanted, so she could start it right now.

She plunked down in one of the huge leather chairs and shoved it away from the table, swiveling toward the windows as she called Nathan.

He answered halfway through the ring. "I needed to hear your voice."

"That's the best hello I've ever gotten." Chloe felt her worries lighten.

"I didn't manage my expectations well." His voice held an edge of self-mockery.

"In what way?"

"I spent all day yesterday imagining you in my office today. When you weren't here, I had a problem with it."

The powerful and brilliant Nathan Trainor missed her. How could she not feel thrilled by that? "At least you have weighty executive decisions to distract you. I'm only using about a quarter of my brain to collate a bunch of audit reports."

"I'm interested in hearing what you're using the other three-quarters for."

Chloe felt heat bloom in her cheeks. "That's for you to find out when you pick me up this afternoon."

There was a pause before he said with a rasp in his voice, "Advance planning is always wise. I look forward to combining your ideas with mine, because I suspect the effect will be explosive."

His words danced along her nerve endings, making her squirm on the leather cushion. Before she could respond, he said, "You only have a half hour for lunch, so go eat."

"Because I'll need my strength?" It came out sounding as though she couldn't quite catch her breath.

"Be ready the moment you get in the car. I will be."

He ended the call, leaving her hot and aching in private places. She closed her eyes and imagined him touching her where she ached the most, which only made it worse. She hauled herself out of the chair, sending her cell phone thudding onto the beige carpeting.

When it rang, she jumped and then scooped it up, hoping Nathan wanted to continue their phone foreplay.

It was Judith. "Sweetie, I've got a last-minute interview for you. Are you free today after work?"

Chloe straightened in the chair. "Not really. How about tomorrow?"

"The cutoff for the hiring decision is today."

Her stomach clenched. "How good is the position?"

Judith quoted a nice salary and decent benefits at a medium-sized but growing corporation. "And the position has significant upside."

"There has to be a catch."

"This is your last chance to interview for it," Judith said. "Seriously, I found out about this by sheer luck. Their HR director called me to check one candidate's employment record because I placed him in a job before this. They wanted to make sure he wasn't violating his employment contract."

"Was he? That would eliminate some of my competition." Chloe was stalling as she struggled with the inevitable. She was going to have to tell Nathan she couldn't meet him after work.

"No. He cleared his commitment by forty-three days."

"Darn." Chloe sighed inwardly as she worked hard to inject gratitude and enthusiasm into her voice. "I'll rearrange my schedule so I can take the interview. Thanks so much for giving me such a great opportunity."

She glanced down at her outfit of a slim navy skirt, high-heeled black pumps, and a peach silk blouse. She'd dressed up more than usual because she was meeting Nathan, so her clothing would work for an interview.

"It's pure self-interest," Judith said. "You'll make me a nice finder's fee when you get the job. I'll text you the address and contact information. Knock 'em dead!"

Chloe hung up and sagged in the chair. She was a little nervous about calling Nathan. A man like him was used to getting what he wanted when he wanted it. He might understand her decision to take the interview, but he wouldn't be happy about it. She wasn't happy about it either.

She had to think long-term, though. This thing with Nathan would burn out sooner rather than later, while the job was a more permanent proposition.

She hit his speed-dial button and waited, her grip so tight the edges of the phone cut into her fingers.

"Chloe." His voice was warm with pleasure. "Have you eaten lunch already?"

"No. I got another call. I have an unexpected job interview right after work. It's for a great permanent position, so I couldn't turn it down. I'm sorry."

There was a long moment of silence and she held her breath. Then his voice came through, sounding calm and matter-of-fact. "Not a problem. I can use the extra time to finish the work from last week. Call me as soon as you're done."

"I, um, thank you for understanding."

"Delay will make our encounter all the more . . . satisfying."

The pause before his last word was loaded with the promise of mind-bending sex. Chloe felt the build of desire begin again. "You're a more patient man than I thought."

"Only when the end result is worth waiting for."

Focusing on the interview was going to take every ounce of mental discipline she possessed.

Nathan hung up the phone and let loose a string of profanity. It wasn't the postponement of his sexual gratification that had him cursing like a Marine. It was the damned job interview. He had hoped to handle the offer of the position at Trainor Electronics subtly so no one—and especially Chloe—suspected that he had set it in motion. This new development would force him to cut corners for the sake of speed. He would also have to make sure the offer from his company was so much better than the other one that she would have a hard time turning it down.

He swiveled around to his computer and began to type a private message to Roberta.

There was no point in being the CEO if you couldn't use your power for a friend.

Chapter 19

"We'll be in touch." The interviewer stood and shook Chloe's hand.

Chloe gave him her best professional smile. "It was a pleasure talking with you." She walked out the door and straight to the ladies' room.

The adrenaline surging through her was making her jittery, but the interview had gone well. The HR fellow hadn't commented on the fact that the last three companies she'd worked for had folded, so maybe he hadn't noticed the Russell jinx. However, she had found the catch: the job was dull and unchallenging, and the upside that Judith had mentioned didn't sound much better. However, she couldn't overlook the salary and benefits at this point, so she had given the meeting her best.

Yet part of her mind had been on Nathan the entire time.

"He's just a man," she told herself in the mirror. "And a temporary one. You have to focus on Grandmillie and your future."

She wished she could splash cold water on her face to snap herself out of the spell Nathan exerted on her, but she didn't want to ruin her makeup. She took three deep breaths and felt more in control.

Sitting down on a chrome stool in front of a vanity mirror, she fired off a text to Judith, telling her she felt she would be in the running for the job. Her friend responded with a thumbs-up and the promise to let Chloe know as soon as she heard something further.

She brought up a text box under Nathan's cell number and stared at the blinking cursor. Nothing clever came to mind, so she went with the facts. "Interview completed. Will be at the front entrance in ten minutes."

"Already there," was the near-instant response.

She shouldn't be flattered. After all, he could sit in his Rolls and use his laptop or his cell phone, but the thought of the workaholic Nathan Trainor *waiting* for her was as heady an aphrodisiac as any oysters.

She'd been debating all day whether she had the nerve to do it, but this made her decision. She put her cell phone in her big handbag and went into one of the stalls. She'd worn thigh-high stockings for the occasion, and now she hiked up her skirt and tugged her panties down so she could step out of them. Balling up the white lace, she tucked them in her purse before exiting the bathroom.

As she walked down the corridor, she had the sense that everyone she passed could tell she had no underwear on. It was ridiculous, because her hem stopped a very proper quarter inch above her knees. Yet she felt exposed and turned on at the same time.

Stepping into the elevator with four other people, she flashed back to vivid images of making love at Nathan's apartment in the same kind of enclosed space. She could feel the heat building low in her body. As the door opened on the ground floor, she took a firm grip on the strap of her handbag and stepped out into the lobby as though she wasn't about to go up in flames.

Her composure cracked when she turned and saw the Rolls parked directly in front of the glass doors. Nathan wasn't working on his laptop or making calls on his cell phone. He was leaning against the big car dressed in one of his perfectly tailored dark suits, his arms folded across his chest, his long legs crossed at the ankles, as he scanned the stream of people leaving the building.

She stopped as a shiver of nerves slithered up her spine. Whatever was going on between them was intensifying faster than she was prepared for.

Shifting her bag to her other shoulder, she started forward again, knowing she was walking toward something no longer under her control.

The autumn wind sent a chill through her as she stepped out of the revolving door. Nathan straightened away from the car and met her in the middle of the sidewalk, sliding his hand under her blazer to the small of her back. He bent his head to murmur beside her ear, "To avoid shocking innocent bystanders, I'm not going to touch you any more than this until we're in the car."

"You have more self-control than I do." She thought she might come just from the heat of his palm radiating through the thin fabric of her blouse. His breath rasped noticeably, and she felt a smug smile curl her lips.

He marched her to the Rolls, swinging open the door and offering his hand to her. She appreciated the steely support of his arm as she climbed into the dark interior, always conscious that an awkward position could reveal more to the public than she wanted to share. Sliding across the seams of the leather seat pushed her arousal up another notch.

Nathan settled on the seat beside her, his weight tilting her against his side as he pulled the car door closed. With a heavy, expensive thunk, they were shut away from the cold wind, the blare of horns, and the seething crowd. The opaque privacy screen between them and the driver was already raised—enclosing them in a warm, intimate cocoon of burnished leather, plush carpeting, and windows tinted nearly black.

"Chloe," Nathan said as the car began to move, and then his hands were in her hair and he was tilting her mouth to his, devouring her as though she were a gourmet feast and he hadn't eaten in weeks. He kissed her jaw, her temples, her eyebrows, her throat, and her eyelids.

She slid her hands under his suit jacket so she could feel the power of his muscles and the pulse of his heart against her palms. Then his hands were on her waist and he lifted her onto his lap, facing him. Her straight skirt rode halfway up her thighs as she straddled him, her knees resting on the seat. She didn't dare sit down because she was so wet he might feel it through the expensive fabric of his trousers.

He raised no objections to her position as he shoved her blazer down and off before his fingers went to the buttons of her blouse. She reached beneath his arms to work his tie loose from its neat knot and rip it out of his shirt collar with a hiss of silk on cotton. He slid his fingers under her bra straps, the first touch of his skin against her bare shoulders making her suck in her breath with a hiss. Then he yanked the straps down along with her blouse so her breasts were bared. Suddenly, she was aware of the people walking just a few feet from the car. Even through the darkened glass, she could see their indistinct faces.

She started to bring her arms up to cover herself, but his hands were already at her breasts, massaging them and pressing against her peaked nipples.

"They can't see in." He'd noticed her moment of self-consciousness. "From outside, the windows are a solid black." He pinched one nipple gently between his thumb and forefinger, sending a streak of electric pleasure directly to the yearning spot between her legs.

She grabbed his shoulders just in time to keep herself from arching so far back that she fell off the seat.

"It's a safety precaution to prevent kidnapping attempts," he said, doing the same to her other nipple, making her dig her fingers hard into his nearly unyielding muscles as she bowed back again. "If they can't tell who's inside the car, and how many, they're less likely to attack. The glass and the privacy screen are bulletproof too."

He stopped talking and took her now-sensitized nipple into the heat and wet of his mouth, using the slight roughness of his tongue to make her whimper with need. When he released it, the longing low in her belly intensified, and she needed pressure against it. Forgetting all about how she might stain his custom-made suit, she bent her knees and ground against the deliciously solid surface of his thigh.

His head was level with her own, and she let go of his shoulders to thread her fingers into the thick waves of his hair before she brought her mouth to his to feel that clever tongue against hers. While they explored each other's mouths, his thumbs circled her nipples and she rotated her hips against his thigh in the same wild rhythm.

He dropped his hands to skim up the outside of her thighs, pushing the fabric of her skirt upward until his fingers hit bare skin where her panties should have been. He pulled away from their kiss and shoved her skirt up to her waist. As he looked down between them, his eyes went incandescent. "You got into my car without panties." Sliding one finger inside the slickness of her, he smiled—a feral, tooth-baring expression of pure arousal. "And you're ready."

Pushing a button on the overhead control panel, he lifted her off his lap onto the cushion next to him. The seat facing them slid forward and unfolded to make a wider surface. "We'll be more comfortable there," he said.

Her knees were shaky from kneeling over his lap, so she put her palms on the edge of the opposite seat and crawled onto it.

"Stay like that." His voice came from behind her.

She realized her skirt was still up around her waist, so she was completely exposed to him. For a moment she felt uneasy, but then she heard the quiet hiss of a zipper and the tearing sound of foil. The thought of him entering her from behind made her eyelids close as she sucked in a deep breath.

"Do you trust me?" he asked.

"I want you," she said, sinking down onto her elbows to show him how much. It was a breathtakingly vulnerable position, and she waited with nervous anticipation to feel what he would do.

For a long moment, nothing happened and she started to shift. "Please," he said, "let me just look at you. Once I touch you, I won't last long."

And then his hands were stroking along the curve of her buttocks, his fingers slipping inside her, his thumb pressing on the center of all sensation. She bowed her back downward, her cheek against the leather seat, and moaned as the exquisite shock of his touch reverberated through her, driving her to the edge of orgasm.

His fingers slid out of her and he took hold of her hips, lifting and angling them higher. She waited for a breathless moment, anticipating what was coming next, and then he was inside her, the sides of his suit jacket brushing against her thighs as he moved deep and hard.

One thrust was all it took to set off the convulsive explosion of her climax. She arched again as muscles clenched and released, sending delirious pleasure spinning through her. She turned her mouth into the leather to muffle the sounds wrenching themselves from her throat.

He'd gone still, letting her feel him filling her so she could savor her own finish. She could feel the effort it cost him by the bruising grip of his fingers on her hips. As the ripples of afterglow slowly diminished, he moved again, taking a long, slow stroke out and in, then holding himself there again as he let out a low, carnal "Ahh." Now she could feel his muscles quivering as he fought to delay his own satisfaction.

His control broke and he began to move in a fast, primitive rhythm that made her pant as it built another coil of tension inside her. He seated himself deep within her and shouted her name as he pumped out his release, his hold on her nearly punishing.

She ground back against him, trying to reach the second orgasm he'd pushed her to. He slid his hand around and between her legs, flicking exactly the right spot to send her screaming over the edge.

She collapsed onto the seat, her bones melted by the double explosion. She heard a rustle of clothing and then he rolled her so he was lying beside her on the extended seat, his breath whistling past her ear, his arm wrapped around her waist to press her back against his chest. He crooked his knee behind hers so their thighs nested together.

She was shaken by how vulnerable she'd made herself to him without a qualm. This was dangerous territory because it involved more than just her body. She had given him her trust.

"Hello," he said, his voice rumbling near her ear.

She couldn't help smiling. "Aren't we beyond that?"

"We're back to that. Your missing panties robbed me of coherent speech."

"You have very eloquent hands . . . and other body parts."

"I'm trying to decide if I want to know if you took them off before or after the interview."

Chloe was enjoying her unexpected role of femme fatale. "I—"

"Don't tell me," he broke in. "I can enjoy the fantasy without wanting to kill the fellow who interviewed you."

"How do you know it wasn't a woman?"

"Now that's an interesting thought." His tone was rich with innuendo.

"You too with the lesbian fantasies?" Chloe lightly smacked his arm.

He retaliated by nipping her earlobe, which sent a little arrow of heat zinging down between her legs. "They're only fantasies, darling. I don't share, even with other women."

The heat blossomed at the raw possessiveness of his statement. And the *darling*.

His grip on her tightened. "How did the interview go?"

The question jolted her out of the delicious haze of sensual satisfaction she'd been drifting in. She became aware that she was lying on a car seat half-nude in broad daylight, wrapped in the arms of a fully clothed man whom she'd known for less than a week. "It went pretty well. I'm the last candidate they're talking to, so the decision should be made quickly."

She must have made a subtle shift away from him because Nathan's hold on her waist became like steel.

"What kind of position is it?"

She repeated what Judith and her interviewer had told her. As she talked, she realized how dismal the position sounded; all it promised was a good salary and benefits and a way to avoid working for Larry Clarke. She'd accept the job if it was offered to her, but she would be bored. "I'd rather talk about what's going on with the Prometheus project. Have you been back to help them?"

Now Nathan shifted. "I checked in on the team this afternoon between meetings."

She heard the longing in his voice. "And you wanted to blow off the meetings and stay to work on it."

"There was some temptation."

After his reaction to her going commando, Chloe felt brave. "Send one of your dozens of executive VPs to the meetings. That's why you have them."

"The meetings are my responsibility." His response was clipped.

"So is Prometheus."

"I have to let my R and D staff do their jobs."

"Why do you act as though working on Prometheus is some kind of guilty pleasure you should deny yourself? You would be doing your staff a favor by working on it."

The silence was filled with the muffled hum of the Rolls's engine and the occasional thump as they hit a pothole even the car's weight and suspension couldn't compensate for. Then he skimmed his hand up from her waist to cup her breast. "Speaking of pleasure," he said, "we should have time for at least one more."

He flipped over, bringing her with him so she was sprawled on her back on top of him, open to the exquisite invasion of his roving hands. Before the Rolls took the exit ramp off the Garden State Parkway, they'd managed two more pleasures.

As she felt the car slow down, Chloe untangled herself from Nathan's arms and legs. "We're getting close to my house. I've got to get dressed."

Nathan helped her sit up and retrieved her blouse, bra, and blazer from the carpeted floor before shifting to the seat opposite her. "I'll watch," he said, handing her the crumpled pile of clothing. Without taking his eyes off her, he shrugged into his own shirt and began to button it.

After what they'd just done, it seemed ridiculous to feel self-conscious about having him see her dress, but it marked the transition from lovers to . . . whatever they were. She half turned away from him as she slipped into her bra and fastened it before pulling on her blouse. Her skirt was still bunched up around her waist, so she squirmed to pull it back down to her knees. Now she had to get her panties out of her handbag and find a graceful way to put them back on.

"You can leave them off." Nathan's voice made her turn on the seat. His eyes held a wicked glint. "I won't tell anyone."

The waves of his hair were rumpled from being tangled with her fingers, and although his shirt was tucked in, he hadn't bothered to put his jacket or tie back on. He looked completely at ease, while she felt like a wrinkled, rumpled, deliciously used mess. "It's bad enough that I have to face Grandmillie knowing what we've just done. I'm not doing it without underwear."

He crossed his arms over his chest, his eyes still gleaming. "More entertainment for me."

Torn between amusement and irritation, she pulled the panties from her purse and bent over to get them over her feet and up to her knees. She faced the fact that she was going to have to pull her skirt back up to get the lace where it belonged.

"Now for the good part," Nathan said.

"You're not helping."

He leaned forward. "Would you like me to?"

She shot him a glare. He went back to his lounging but lowered his gaze to the white lace circling her knees.

She planted her feet on the floor, closed her eyes, and arched up off the leather seat as she yanked her skirt and panties up at the same time.

"Slow down." Nathan's voice held both humor and arousal. "I'm enjoying the view."

Chloe pulled her skirt back down. "You're enjoying bothering me."

"You bother me just by sitting there."

The intensity in his voice restoked the heat between her thighs. She hid her reaction by rummaging in her handbag again. When she pulled out a brush and lipstick, Nathan pushed a button. A mirrored panel dropped down from the ceiling. One glance and Chloe went into high-speed repair mode.

Nathan gave a loud sigh.

"What?" Chloe looked away from the mirror.

"You've lost that I-just-had-sex-in-a-car look."

"Then my job here is done." She dropped the brush and makeup into her purse and shrugged into her blazer.

He pushed the mirror back up before he reached across the space between them to pull her onto the seat beside him. He wrapped his arm around her shoulders and bent to imprint a hot kiss on the side of her neck before he murmured. "I'll pick you up after work tomorrow and we'll go shopping."

She stiffened as he reminded her of the upcoming ordeal of his father's wedding. She'd managed to shove that to the back of her mind.

"You agreed to accept my gift of clothing," he said, misinterpreting her tension.

"I know." That wasn't the problem. "I'd like to go to Saks Fifth Avenue."

She felt him shake his head. "I have a personal shopper coming to my home with a selection of whatever she thinks you'll need for the wedding."

The closet in his guest room flitted through her mind. All designer clothes. All expensive beyond belief. "I'd rather go to Saks."

"Fine."

Surprised by his easy capitulation, she tilted her head to look up at him. "Fine?"

He returned her gaze with a raised eyebrow. "She'll bring the clothes to Saks." Then he kissed her, long and deep, until she clutched at his lapel to pull herself in closer. She felt the warmth of his palm on her thigh as he slipped his hand under her skirt.

The car stopped and Oskar's voice came through the intercom, announcing they were at Ms. Russell's home. Nathan cursed softly.

Chloe felt a zing of satisfaction that his attempt to distract her from the shopping issue had been more successful at frustrating him. "Language," she said, laying a finger across his lips.

"But I need time to do this," he said, moving his hand farther up her thigh until his fingers just brushed at the lace between her legs. He found a way under the panties and slid one finger inside her, making her throw back her head. He flexed it once and withdrew, the friction sending exquisite heat curling through her. Locking his gaze on her, he licked his finger.

She was going to have to face Grandmillie with the image of Nathan tasting her seared into her brain. "I'll get you back for that tomorrow," she said, giving him a nudge since his long body was between her and the door.

"Retaliation can lead to escalation." He reached up to hit some sort of release before opening the door and unfolding himself out of the car. Turning, he held her hand to help her out of the car, his gray eyes lit with desire and a touch of mischief. "I look forward to it."

"Good evening, Chloe." Grandmillie's voice was like a bucket of cold water on the bonfire Nathan had lit.

Chloe spun away from him to see her grandmother standing on the front porch, the door open behind her. "Bring your young man inside for a minute." Grandmillie gripped the head of her cane with both hands. "I've baked scones."

Chloe turned back in time to see Nathan rake his fingers through his disheveled hair and yank his shirt collar higher. As satisfying as it was to find that he was not immune to Grandmillie's tone of authority, Chloe didn't want him in the house, invading her world.

"You don't have to come," Chloe said in a low murmur. "Say you have business to get back to."

Nathan looked down at her. "But I want to meet your grandmother."

"Why?" Chloe asked between clenched teeth.

"She's part of your life."

He said it matter-of-factly, but his words gave Chloe pause. She'd been telling herself that Nathan saw her as a fling, a few weeks' entertainment. That had allowed her to let go of her inhibitions, to consider this an acceptable deviation from her usual sensible approach to relationships, because it wouldn't continue.

But flings didn't want to meet your grandmother, did they?

"After you," Nathan said, standing aside so she could walk up the flagstone path. Chloe gave him a quick glare before trudging up to the porch, aware of his footsteps on the stones just behind her. She gave Grandmillie a matching glare before turning to say, "Grandmillie, this is Nathan Trainor. Nathan, my grandmother, Millicent Russell."

As Nathan shook her grandmother's hand, Chloe could only be glad it wasn't with the same hand he'd slid under her skirt earlier. "I've been hoping to meet you, Mrs. Russell."

"We'll see about that," Grandmillie said giving him a penetrating look. "I appreciate your giving my granddaughter a ride home, Mr. Trainor."

"Call me Nathan, please. I enjoy her company."

Chloe caught her breath, but Nathan's voice was clear of any innuendo. He smiled down at the older woman as he waited for Grandmillie to make her way into the house.

Chloe followed her grandmother, hoping against hope that she wouldn't subject Nathan to an embarrassing interrogation. The scones were a bad sign, because it meant they'd have to sit down in order to eat the warm, crumbly pastries with clotted cream and jam. As they walked into the living room, the fragrance of Grandmillie's baking wafted around them, making Chloe salivate in spite of her nervousness. She'd worked up a considerable appetite in the Rolls.

Nathan's nostrils flared as he inhaled. "I'd follow that aroma to the ends of the earth," he said.

"Don't exaggerate, young man," Grandmillie said, but Chloe could hear the gratification in her voice. "The proof is not in the smell, but the taste."

"So it is," Nathan said, casting a wicked glance at Chloe.

She jabbed him with her elbow, taking satisfaction in his barely perceptible wince.

Grandmillie directed them into the dining area, where the table was covered with an embroidered linen tablecloth and set with the good china, as always. She'd put on a full English tea, along with a decanter of some golden liquor and tiny stemmed glasses. Nathan helped her into the chair at the head of the table. When he was behind her pushing in the chair, Grandmillie caught Chloe's eye and winked.

That wasn't going to get her grandmother out of a talking-to about ambushing Chloe like this.

"Chloe, the scones are warming in the oven. I'll pour while you bring them in." Grandmillie hooked her cane on the table. "Nathan, you sit here to my right."

Chloe walked into the kitchen and stopped to take a deep breath. Atop the pristine countertops, a linen-lined basket and a well-polished silver tray awaited the scones.

She took another breath, trying to calm the jangle of her nerves. She grabbed the dish towel hanging on its hook and rubbed it over her damp palms before folding it into a hot pad and opening the oven. A cloud of hot, scone-scented air billowed around her when she reached in to retrieve them.

As she piled the scones in the basket, she listened to Grandmillie and Nathan exchange small talk about sugar, milk, and the offer of port. She emerged from the kitchen to find Nathan bent attentively toward her grandmother as she poured a glass of the fortified wine for him. He accepted the delicate crystal, holding it in his long fingers as though it were as fragile as a Fabergé egg.

"A drop of port?" Grandmillie asked her when Chloe slid the tray onto the table.

"Yes, please." She was tempted to tell her grandmother to make it a double.

Chloe took the stemmed glass and carried it to her seat to the left of her grandmother, who was directing the serving of the scones. Even with his shirt unbuttoned at the collar and his hair in disarray, Nathan radiated authority and control as he distributed scones and tea, his attention focused on following Grandmillie's instructions. His manner toward Chloe was that of an old friend without even a hint of sexual interest. She heaved a sigh of relief.

After they'd sampled the scones, and Nathan had paid Grandmillie extravagant but well-deserved compliments on her baking, the conversation veered into dangerous territory.

"So," Grandmillie said, giving Nathan an assessing look, "I hear you had a pretty bad case of the flu. How are you feeling now?"

"Fully recovered," he said. "Your granddaughter has a healing touch."

Chloe considered kicking his ankle, but once again he kept all insinuation out of his voice.

"I imagine your Dr. Cavill isn't happy that you're back at work so soon," Grandmillie said.

Nathan chuckled as he took a sip of the port. "And he lets me know about it. That's the problem with having an old friend as your doctor."

"Did he help you develop your computer battery?"

"Ben?" Nathan looked startled. "No, I had a hard time even getting him to play video games with me. He was always rescuing injured animals while I fooled around with electronics."

"Chloe's father was an inventor too, you know," Grandmillie said.

This time Chloe wanted to kick her grandmother under the table.

Nathan cast a sharp glance at her. "I wasn't aware of that. What sort of things did he invent?"

"Consumer products," Chloe said vaguely. "A better umbrella. That kind of thing."

"He felt he wasn't treated well by the company where he worked," Grandmillie said. "That's why Chloe likes to work at start-ups. She says they reward their employees' contributions more fairly."

What the heck was Grandmillie doing?

"Except the start-ups where I work become shut-downs," Chloe said, trying to stop Grandmillie from offending Nathan any further.

Nathan's gaze was focused on her in a way that made her wonder what he was thinking. "Trainor Electronics was a start-up not that long ago."

"But now it's just as corporate as Lindell."

"Is that where your father worked?" he asked.

Chloe realized she'd said more than she meant to, so she nodded and took a swig of port.

Nathan turned to her grandmother with a charming smile. "You've relieved my mind, Mrs. Russell."

Grandmillie looked taken aback. "I have?"

Nathan nodded. "When I was ill, and admittedly not at my best, I sensed a certain attitude of disapproval from your granddaughter. Now I understand that it was directed at my position as the head of a corporation rather than at me as an invalid."

Chloe wasn't going to let him get away with that. "It was because you thought all you had to do was throw money at me and I'd drop everything to be at your beck and call."

"I was hallucinating," Nathan said.

Chloe snorted. "You were cranky but perfectly clearheaded."

Grandmillie broke into their bickering. "Chloe worries about me being alone."

"She's a good granddaughter," Nathan said, his tone respectful.

"I couldn't ask for a better one." Grandmillie reached over to touch Chloe's hand.

Chloe felt a surge of tears at Grandmillie's public compliment. She glanced at Nathan to find him staring at the older woman's hand lying on top of Chloe's, his face tight with an emotion she couldn't identify.

He raised his eyes and met hers. "You're both very fortunate." He folded his napkin and laid it on the table. "I shouldn't impose on your hospitality any longer."

Grandmillie waved a hand of disagreement. "Sit. Have another scone before you go."

His strange expression evaporated as he leaned back in his chair with a groan, his hand on his washboard-flat abdomen. "I can't swallow another bite."

"You'll take some home with you, then," Grandmillie said.

"With pleasure," Nathan said.

Chloe stood, picking up the basket of scones and her own plate and knife. Nathan also rose, his head nearly colliding with the chandelier hanging low over the table. As he started to clear the dishes in front of her grandmother, Chloe said, "It's okay. I'll get those later."

He ignored her, deftly arranging the cup, saucer, plate, and flatware for easy carrying. "I have to earn my scones."

"Your mother raised you right," Grandmillie said.

Chloe caught the shadow that turned Nathan's eyes flat, as though he was hiding all emotion. She remembered Ed's description of Nathan's mother and realized Grandmillie had touched a nerve with her comment about how he was raised.

Wishing she could comfort him but not knowing how, Chloe led the way to the kitchen. "Just put the dishes on the counter," she said as she pulled a plastic baggie from a drawer.

Nathan carefully slid the fine china onto the Formica countertop. She watched him glance around the kitchen and wondered what he thought of her little house. She'd painted the dated pine cabinets a crisp, glossy white when they moved in, and the Formica on the counters was a cheerful indigo-and-yellow plaid, but her place was like a fiberglass dinghy compared to his luxurious ocean liner of a home.

He leaned a hip against the counter and folded his arms across his chest. "The job you interviewed for today is at a good-sized company. Have you rethought your policy about not working for large corporations?"

Chloe dropped several scones into a baggie and kept her voice low. "I don't have the luxury of that policy anymore."

"Because of your grandmother?" His voice was soft too.

She nodded. "She's worth the compromise."

"I was hoping I had something to do with your change of heart," he said, moving to stand behind her. He lifted her hair from the back of her neck to press his lips on the sensitive skin as he trapped her against the counter with his body. Shivers of pleasure radiated down her spine.

She poked him in the ribs. "My grandmother is on the other side of that wall."

He took a step back. "And I haven't done anything she would disapprove of. In this kitchen," he added.

She turned and held out the filled baggie. "For your breakfast tomorrow."

He took the scones with a heavy-lidded look. "I'd rather have you for breakfast." That sent more than mere shivers racing through her. She was about to shush him when he continued, "But there's always the dressing room at Saks."

"You wouldn't dare." She choked on a laugh as she headed for the door.

He caught her wrist to stop her. There was no teasing in his voice or his face as he looked down at her. "When it comes to you, I'll dare many things."

The intensity of his gaze sent a tiny thrill of excitement and panic ricocheting around inside her rib cage. She stared up at him, feeling like a rabbit caught in the hypnotic spell of a snake.

"Keep that in mind," he said, releasing her wrist and waving her through the kitchen door in front of him.

Somehow she got through the polite good-byes. Nathan gave her a chaste kiss on the cheek at the front door before he headed for the car, his long strides making their modest walkway seem even shorter.

She stood watching as the Rolls glided into motion, noting with relief that the windows were as opaque as Nathan had promised.

As she came back into the living room, where her grandmother sat in her favorite chair, Grandmillie raised her hand in a warding-off gesture. "I wanted to see him for myself, so don't chew me out."

Chloe put her hands on her hips. "You might have warned me."

"What would you have done differently if I had?"

Chloe looked around at the immaculate living room, and her indignation sputtered out. "I would have helped you clean the downstairs and set the table. You must be exhausted."

"I got Lynda to help me with the cleaning in exchange for some scones."

"I'm confused." Chloe sat on the couch. "I thought you wanted me to marry him, but it sounded like you were trying to scare him away with all that talk about evil corporations."

Her grandmother spun the neck of her cane between her palms. "He's not what I expected."

"Better or worse?"

Grandmillie stared down at her rotating cane for a long moment before looking at Chloe. "He's not like your father's friends. They were all brilliant scientists, but they were—what's that word the teenagers use?—nerds. Easy for a smart woman to manage. Your Nathan"— Grandmillie shook her head—"he's not the manageable sort."

That surprised a snort out of Chloe. "That's an understatement."

"Sweetie, I was hoping he would be someone who would cherish you and take good care of you, but that man could hurt you." Grandmillie seemed to brace herself. "I could tell what you'd been doing in the car, and I can't find it in myself to blame you. He's a hottie too."

Chloe would have laughed at the second example of teenage slang coming so easily from her grandmother's lips, but she was too distressed by what Grandmillie was trying to tell her. "He's out of my league. I told you that at the beginning."

The cane hit the floor with a bang. "*No one* is out of your league, Chloe! But he's got a powerful personality that could break you in half."

"I've had some practice dealing with strong personalities," Chloe said. But Grandmillie's words had burrowed inside her mind to reinforce her own belief that she and Nathan were not equals.

Grandmillie harrumphed, but her tone was soft. "It's not your backbone I'm worried about, it's your heart."

How did she tell her grandmother this was just about sex? "My heart isn't involved."

Her grandmother leveled a stare at her. "You're not the sort to be intimate with a man without feeling something for him."

Chloe cringed at the knowledge that Grandmillie was right. Nathan had gotten to her, so she felt more than she wanted to. Serious physical attraction. Admiration. Pity.

That last one was the most dangerous. She felt sorry for the man because he did so much out of a sense of duty and so little out of a sense of fun. In fact, the only time he really let loose was when they made love; he could be almost playful. And that was the chink in her armor. "It won't last long enough for me to get emotionally involved."

"I wouldn't bet on that. He looked pretty smitten."

Chloe pushed up from the cushions and walked over to give her grandmother a kiss. "I'm going to clean up the dishes. Your scones were fantastic."

Grandmillie thumped her cane again but made no comment.

Chloe carried a load of dishes into the kitchen and placed them gently in the sink. Then she cut loose with a shimmy across the kitchen floor.

Grandmillie thought Nathan had looked *smitten*!

Nathan got in the elevator to his apartment. Instead of pushing the button to ascend, he leaned against the elevator wall, his arms crossed, his chin sunk on his chest. He'd been thinking about his meeting with Chloe's grandmother all the way home in the car.

Except for the moments when he'd been remembering what he and Chloe had done in the car before that. He shifted and settled his shoulders more firmly against the wall.

His plan to get Chloe a job at Trainor Electronics had taken a hit. Her dislike of corporations ran deeper than discomfort with the politics. It was personal. She might accept the offer, but only out of necessity. That didn't make him happy.

Even worse, Chloe's grandmother had invited him in and then tried to chase him away. She had weighed him and found him wanting.

It felt unnervingly similar to the way his father had judged him. And Chloe would respect her grandmother's opinion.

After seeing their cozy little house, he was even more resolved to help Chloe keep her grandmother there. It was the right thing to do. That meant an e-mail to Roberta about getting Chloe that position before she took another one.

He hit the "Up" button.

When the elevator doors opened, Ed was waiting for him, dressed in his usual uniform of white shirt and dark suit. "Was there a malfunction in the elevator?" his majordomo asked.

Nathan shoved off the wall and walked through the opening into the entrance hall. "No, I was thinking."

"Good to know your brain is still working, because I was starting to wonder." Ed jerked his head toward a doorway. "Ben is in the den with his doctor bag. He says you missed your appointment with him this morning."

"I had an emergency meeting." A wave of guilt and exhaustion broke over Nathan. He'd canceled the checkup with his friend at the last minute because he hadn't wanted to argue with Ben about whether he should be at work or not. "Don't worry. I'll let him poke and prod me to his heart's content."

Ed nodded. "You look tired."

"It's been a long day." He hadn't felt it until the elevator had stopped, and the evening stretched out empty in front of him. Despite knowing that Ben would lecture him, Nathan felt his spirits lift at the prospect of having something other than work to fill the next couple of hours.

Ed held out his hand, and Nathan shrugged out of his suit jacket in their familiar daily ritual. As he handed it to the older man, Nathan gave him an apologetic smile. "Thanks for worrying about me."

"Someone needs to," Ed muttered before he did his vanishing act.

Nathan squared his shoulders and walked down the hallway to the den. Ben lounged on the sofa, a rocks glass in one hand, the television remote control in the other. "I love watching television on your dime," the doctor said.

Nathan dropped into an upholstered armchair with a grunt.

"You were dodging me this morning," Ben said.

"I admit it."

Ben turned off the television. "How do you feel?"

"Fine."

The doctor gave a huff of exasperation and stood up. "I'm doing a full workup."

Nathan waved a hand in surrender. "I'm bone tired. But no headache or any other ache, no fever, no chills, no cough. I do solemnly swear."

"When you start quoting the Marine oath, I know you're feeling like hell," Ben said, but his tone had lost its edge. He flipped open the bag sitting on the coffee table and pulled out a stethoscope. "Just a quick checkup to earn my pay."

"Forget the pay," Nathan said. "Have dinner with me. As a friend."

Ben gave him a sharp look. "It's past dinnertime. Don't you have to read fifty reports and answer three thousand e-mails?"

Nathan rubbed a spot between his eyebrows. "I may have lied about the headache."

"I'll eat a second dinner because you have an excellent chef." Ben smacked the stethoscope against Nathan's chest. "Breathe in."

Nathan drew in several breaths as his friend moved the stethoscope around. He let Ben take his blood pressure and run a few other basic tests. "Satisfied?" he asked as the doctor folded the stethoscope back into the bag.

"You need rest," Ben said, picking up his scotch and taking a swallow. "Or you could have a relapse."

"We both know that's not going to happen."

"Which? The rest or the relapse?" Ben asked.

"Both." The only way he would stay in bed was if he could lure Chloe into it with him. And he would rest only after he'd made her come at least three times.

Ed walked in with a tray of hors d'oeuvres. "Would you like a drink?" he asked Nathan.

"Something with orange juice," Ben said. "He needs the vitamin C."

"A Manhattan." Nathan paused long enough to annoy Ben before adding, "With an orange juice chaser."

"You'll find several varieties of citrus fruit on the tray as well," Ed said.

"Good man," Ben said. "I'll hold him down while you force them down his throat."

"I should have known you two would conspire against me." But oddly he found the idea comforting rather than irritating. He picked up a miniature skewer of fruit and bit into a piece of pineapple.

Ben watched him with raised eyebrows. "An alien has taken over Nathan's body."

"Do you want me to eat this fruit or not?"

Ben sat down and turned to Ed. "What's for dinner? I've been invited to stay."

A look of surprise crossed Ed's face before he launched into the menu. Nathan frowned. "How long has it been since you last ate here?" he asked Ben after Ed left.

Ben looked up at the ceiling in thought. "A year, year and a half," he concluded.

"You should come more often."

"I come when I'm invited."

"You're my oldest friend. You don't need an invitation."

"What? I'm supposed to drop by in the hope that a miracle will happen and you'll be home and not working?" Ben swirled the scotch in his glass.

It was true that Nathan ate out most nights. "Ed and Janice know my schedule."

"If you think I'm calling your assistants to find out whether you're available for dinner, think again."

"Point taken." Ed returned with the drinks. Nathan grabbed the

Manhattan and took a gulp, savoring the burn in his throat. "I'm glad you were free tonight."

Ben gave him a crooked smile. "Actually, I need to make a phone call."

Nathan scowled as he grasped Ben's meaning. "Don't cancel something on my account."

Ben stood and pulled his cell phone out of his pocket before heading for the door. "Sometimes friendship comes first."

Nathan pushed up out of the chair and roamed over to the wall of windows, staring out at the city that never slept. When had he become such a lousy friend? He'd let himself pretend that the time he spent with Ben for medical and charitable reasons was enough.

Ben walked back into the room, and Nathan turned. "I'm sorry."

Ben came to an abrupt halt. "Definitely an alien."

Nathan raised his glass to his friend. "I'll do better in the future."

The two men returned to their seats and demolished the hors d'oeuvres before Ed announced dinner. Later, as they sat at the dinner table with coffee and brandy in front of them, Ben said, "I like this new Nathan. He's like the old Nathan, except he doesn't constantly badger me to play Space Invaders."

"Asteroids."

"A game where one stared at a computer screen and exercised only one's hands for hours on end," Ben said, leaning back in his chair. "Although your obsession led to Trainor Electronics, so it wasn't a total waste of time."

"My father is getting married Saturday."

"I'm invited."

Nathan felt his jaw go tense. "Why didn't you tell me?"

"You don't respond well when I bring up your father."

"Because you defend him."

"I try to explain him, so maybe you'll get your head out of your ass and talk to him." Ben's voice was sharp. "He may have pushed you in a direction you didn't want to go, but at least he didn't hit you."

When Ben's father got drunk, he'd become violent toward his wife and his son. Nathan's father had intervened on more than one occasion.

"That's not why I have a problem with him."

"Your mother suffered from clinical depression. It was a chemical imbalance in her brain. Your father didn't cause that. You didn't either."

Nathan had heard that from Ben before, but the guilt still ate at him. "She was under more pressure than she could handle."

Ben held his gaze for a long moment. "No one could have stopped her from taking her own life. Not your father. Not you."

Nathan knocked back the rest of his brandy as he tried to believe that. He placed the snifter carefully on the table before he met Ben's eyes again. "Are you going to the wedding?"

Ben nodded. "Are you?"

"Against my better judgment, yes."

Ben sat up in the chair, surprise written on his face. "Why?"

Nathan relaxed enough to let a faint smile curl his lips. "Someone talked me into it."

"Since it wasn't me, I sense the hand of Ed," Ben said, reaching for his coffee.

"You'd be wrong. Chloe persuaded me. In fact, she's my date for the wedding."

His friend choked on the hot beverage.

Nathan enjoyed Ben's reaction. "By the way, she doesn't work for me anymore." *For now.*

Ben grabbed a napkin to dab at the spewed coffee on his shirt.

"Hell, Nathan, you can't throw that poor woman into the viper pit that's your relationship with the general. For one thing, she'll run screaming as far away as she can get."

"You underestimate Chloe. She has an interesting theory that my father wants to share this new phase of his life with me."

Ben tossed the crumpled napkin on the table. "How could she have a theory? She's never met the man."

Nathan refilled his glass and took a sip of brandy, letting the heat of it join the alcohol already warming his stomach. He hadn't drunk this much since the night at the Bellwether Club. "She wasn't afraid of me. She won't be cowed by my father."

"Maybe she doesn't want to get in the middle of your power struggle."

"He's an officer. He'll behave at his own wedding."

"It's you I'm worried about," Ben said. "Why Chloe?"

Nathan was about to tell him it was none of his business until he remembered what a crap friend he'd been recently. "She's not Teresa."

"Is that supposed to be an answer?"

"I thought Teresa wasn't interested in the trappings. She lied about that." Nathan stared into the golden liquor in his glass. "Chloe really isn't interested. She considers them a barrier, not a bonus."

For once Ben had no smart comeback, and Nathan found himself wanting to talk about her. "I met her grandmother today. Grandmillie didn't approve of me."

Ben snorted. "What grandmother wouldn't want you as a grand-son-in-law?"

"Getting ahead of ourselves, aren't we?"

"You're the one meeting her family already."

"It seems only fair, since she'll be meeting mine."

Ben gave a bark of laughter. "I'd like to know the lady who feels you aren't good enough for her granddaughter. It would be refreshing. What did you do to put her off?"

"Exerted every ounce of my charm."

"Well, that explains it then." Ben turned his coffee cup on its saucer a few rotations before he looked up at Nathan. "Are you sure Chloe isn't just smarter than Teresa?"

Again, Nathan quashed the urge to tell Ben to go to hell. He scanned through all of his encounters with Chloe from the moment Roberta had introduced them to Chloe's rebuff of him in the kitchen that evening. She'd known exactly who he was from the get-go, and she'd actually tried to extricate herself from his sickroom on several occasions. He considered her openness about asking to be paid for her time, and then refusing compensation once they'd become involved.

But what really convinced him was her lovemaking. There was no artifice, no choreographed performance to impress him. Chloe was all fire and fun. A wave of longing roared through him and he shook his head. "She's smart, all right. But not in that way."

"If you say so." Ben went back to spinning his cup. "It will be interesting to watch you, Chloe, and the general square off."

Nathan debated for a few seconds. He'd planned to make love to Chloe on the jet, but he'd also resolved to be a better friend to Ben. "I'm taking the jet. Want to hitch a ride?"

"Is Ed coming?"

Nathan felt like a jerk. Of course, Ed would be going. He'd served under his father. But Nathan hadn't asked. He'd been so caught up in Chloe, he couldn't think of anything else. "I don't know."

"Well, if Ed's going, I'm in. If not, I don't want to be the third wheel."

"Give me a minute." Nathan shoved himself away from the dinner table to walk across the dining room and into the kitchen.

Ed and the chef were sitting at a round table in a corner of the kitchen, drinking coffee from thick white mugs, while a young man washed pots and pans in the gleaming stainless-steel sink. All three looked startled when Nathan appeared. Ed put his mug down. "Do you need more coffee?" he asked, starting to stand.

Nathan shook his head and waved him back into his chair. "No, I've been an ass."

The corners of Ed's lips twitched, but he didn't comment.

Nathan caught the movement. "You show great restraint," he said in acknowledgment. "In fact, I owe you an apology."

Now his butler looked worried.

"I never asked you if you're going to the general's wedding. I should have. And I should have offered you a ride on the jet," Nathan said.

"I accepted after Ms. Russell told me you were going," Ed said, "but I've booked myself a commercial ticket."

As the implications hit Nathan, he felt even worse. Because of his loyalty to Nathan, Ed had been willing to forgo the wedding of the former commanding officer he respected and admired, a wedding many of his oldest friends would be attending.

"You're a better man than I am," Nathan finally said. "I hope you'll accept my apology and join me on the jet." He made a mental note to reimburse Ed for the plane ticket.

Ed let his butler mask slip with a grin. "Hell, yes. It beats being crammed into some prop plane like a sardine."

Relief flooded through Nathan. He hadn't totally screwed up. "Thanks for not giving me a page 11."

Ed's grin faded. "You didn't deserve most of the ones you got."

Nathan didn't want anyone's pity, not even Ed's. "Yeah, I did, and I worked hard to get them."

The older man caught Nathan's tone and nodded. "I have to give you credit for your work ethic. You were a genius at getting under the general's skin."

"That particular genius was mutual." Nathan shoved his hands into his trousers pockets. "I should get back to Ben."

He pivoted on his heel and returned to the dining room to find Ben staring out the window as he sipped his coffee.

Nathan joined him. "Ed is coming, so you have no excuse for avoiding my company."

Ben turned away from the blaze of lights. "You're just recruiting reinforcements."

"Damn right I am."

Chapter 20

"A job at Trainor Electronics?" Chloe practically dropped her cell phone onto her turkey sandwich. She had just started her thirty-minute lunch break when Judith's call came through. Suspicion sank its claws into her. "What kind of job?"

"It's in marketing, an area you love." Judith read off the description. "You'd start off in a junior capacity, but there's a lot of upside. And listen to the salary." When Judith mentioned the number, Chloe was too stunned to speak, so Judith continued. "I don't want to put any undue pressure on you, but this would solve a lot of your financial problems and put a great signing bonus in my pocket. Not to mention it's a tech company, which is a field you like to work in."

"Who would I be reporting to?"

"The vice president of marketing . . . um . . . Phillippe Riviere. Roberta says he asked for you specifically, so you must know him."

"I met him the day Nath—Mr. Trainor got sick. For about three minutes."

"Well, you impressed the hell out of him in those three minutes."

Chloe pleated a corner of the paper from her sandwich as she debated how much to share with Judith.

"Why are you not jumping for joy?" her friend asked. "It seems like a no-brainer to me. Especially since we don't know yet if you got the position you interviewed for yesterday."

Chloe sighed. "I didn't want to tell you this because I didn't think it mattered anymore, but I'm dating Nathan Trainor."

Judith's silence was deafening. Finally, she spoke. "Sweetie, I don't know what to say. I think you'd be crazy to turn down this job. You'll have to make the decision about whether it's kosher to date your boss's boss."

"I'm afraid Nathan might have arranged the offer."

"I'm not going to speculate on what his reasons might be. I don't know the situation well enough."

"I think he feels sorry for me and Grandmillie."

"That's a better spin than I would have put on it." Chloe could hear Judith beating a tattoo on the desk with her fingernails. "I'm going to risk pissing you off, but you claim to value my cynicism. Once you accept the position, it's going to be difficult for Trainor to fire you without cause. There's no probation period; I checked because it changes my contract with them. You're a full-fledged employee right off the bat."

"Okay," Chloe said when Judith stopped.

"So if you break up, you'll still have a great job with a fantastic salary and benefits."

Chloe felt the tension clutching at her shoulders ease. "So you think it's all right for me to work there and date Nathan?"

Judith took a deep breath. "I think you won't be dating Nathan as long as you'll be working at his company."

"Oh." Considering Chloe kept telling herself her relationship with Nathan was short-term, she felt a surprising stab of pain at Judith's prediction. "I see."

"I'm being realistic, sweetie."

Chloe tried for flippancy to prove she was a realist too. "That's what I love about you." However, she wanted to hear what Nathan had to say about the job offer. "Let me just sleep on it. I'll call you tomorrow."

Chloe disconnected and slumped back into her chair before swiveling around to stare out the window of the conference room.

Was it absurdly conceited to think that Nathan had created a position just for her? He couldn't possibly care about her enough to foist his girlfriend on one of his vice presidents, could he? An annoying little voice in her brain piped up that Trainor Electronics was big enough so one extra employee wasn't going to affect the bottom line, which meant it might be a job custom-tailored for her.

No, it was more plausible that Nathan had heard about the opening and mentioned her name to Phil Riviere. That was a grand enough gesture when she thought about it with more humility. A recommendation from the CEO would be hard to ignore.

Either way, she faced a serious dilemma: Should she break her own personal code of ethics and work for a man she was dating? No, *dating* was too mild a word. Should she work for a man she was having wild, passionate sex with?

Chloe groaned when she realized that wasn't even the worst of it.

How would she feel when she and Nathan broke up, the inevitable outcome Judith had predicted? She might still see him in the corridor or on the elevator or in the lobby. How long would it take before she stopped looking at his hands and remembering how it felt to have his fingers deep inside her? Or staring at his mouth and thinking of his lips on her breasts or between her thighs? His gray eyes would no longer blaze with desire or gleam with mischief when he looked at her. She wouldn't get that delicious glow of satisfaction out of knowing that she could make him have fun.

She choked on a sob as a searing sense of loss hollowed out her chest. If this was how she felt just imagining it . . .

Slamming her palms down on the arms of the big chair, she shoved herself out of it to pace around the table as she faced the truth.

Grandmillie was right. She was in too deep with Nathan. It would be better to stop right now. She could accept the job at Trainor Electronics with a clear conscience and start the process of getting over him sooner rather than later.

She halted abruptly. "The wedding."

She couldn't leave him to face his father alone. The joy that exploded through her when she decided she would have another five days with Nathan convinced her that she'd made the right decision.

Not to go to the wedding, but to end the relationship before she fell any harder.

Nathan leaned back against the Rolls, the cold of the metal biting through his cotton shirt. He should have stayed in the car to read another report, but he wanted to see the way Chloe's face lit up when she spotted him. Yesterday, her obvious delight had hit him in the chest like CPR to a dying man: hard but life-giving. Something he couldn't name had shifted inside him.

The front doors of the office building swung open with a flash of sun on glass as another elevatorload of workers poured out into the damp, gloomy New York afternoon. He scanned the crowd for Chloe's face, his pulse rate settling back to normal when he didn't see it.

He went back to his reverie until a single figure came out the far door. The moment her toe hit the sidewalk, he knew it was Chloe. Every nerve in his body went on full alert, shouting, *That's the woman you want!*

He straightened away from the car and lifted his hand as he started toward her. "Chloe."

She turned and the anticipated delight flashed across her face. He lengthened his stride to reach her faster but slowed when her expression changed, dimmed by a shadow that looked almost like regret. Was she going to tell him she wouldn't let him buy her clothes? Or something worse?

"Chloe," he said again as he seized her shoulders and bent to kiss her, spectators be damned. Her lips were soft and warm and yielding. Her breasts under her jacket brushed tantalizingly against his chest. She gave a little mew of pleasure as he pulled her closer. He wanted to slide his hands down her back to dig his fingers into her behind and jam her hard against his erection. He contented himself with a quick pat on one perfectly curved buttock before he released her.

She tucked her hand in the crook of his arm. "It's a good thing I'm only a temp here. I'm pretty sure at least four people I work with are gawking at us."

"Once you're on the sidewalk, you're on your own time," he said, hauling her along with him toward the privacy of the big car. He bent his head to whisper in her ear the question that had been distracting him off and on all day. "Are you wearing panties?"

"Of course I am. It would shock the saleslady at Saks if I didn't."

"I told Oskar to take at least thirty minutes to get us to Saks." He pulled open the car door for her and helped her into the private warmth of the interior.

"Oh, great," she huffed as he slid onto the seat beside her. "Now Oskar knows exactly what we're doing back here."

"I pay Oskar a great deal not to speculate on what I'm doing." He sank his fingers into the tightly coiled satin of her hair and shook loose the neat bun, sifting his fingers through the glossy strands so they fell over her shoulders.

She shivered as the back of his hand brushed the side of her soft, ripe breast. "You can pay Oskar not to talk about it, but his thoughts are beyond your control."

"Oskar's may be, but I'll bet I can focus yours for the next thirty minutes." He wanted to push her down onto the black leather, tear off her panties, and plunge himself inside her, to feel her moving underneath him and around him. But she had a valid point about the saleslady. He reached for the top button on her blouse.

Chloe put her palm flat on his chest and pushed him away. "We need to talk business first."

Surprise made him yield to the pressure of her small hand. He leaned back as she shifted onto the facing seat and looked him in the eye. Her stern expression was undercut by the wild fall of her hair, and he couldn't stop a smile from curling the corners of his lips.

"Stop smirking."

Her annoyance made his smile go wider.

She looked out the window. "Judith called me about the position at Trainor Electronics."

That killed the smile. His e-mail to Roberta had gotten action faster than he'd expected. He waited.

She turned back to him, her back ramrod straight. "Did you pull strings for me?"

He shrugged. "I mentioned you were looking for a permanent position."

"When the CEO says something like that, it's pulling strings." She didn't look happy.

"Look, Phil Riviere knows how Rich Sinclair writes. He read the report you edited and was impressed. He wanted you in his department."

Her gaze on his face felt like a laser beam. She was weighing his words for their honesty. And they were true, as far as they went. She frowned. "Do you spend a lot of time in the marketing department?"

He tried to reroute the conversation by letting his voice drop to a rasp. "Are you afraid I'll distract you?"

"I'm very focused when I'm working," she said without reacting to his tone. "And that's not what worries me."

"What is it then?"

She shook her head and stared down at her hands. They were twisted into a knot on her lap. She straightened them out and flexed her fingers wide. "It's a very generous offer and a great position." She gave him an unreadable look. "I have a rule about not dating my boss."

"No one will know we're involved," he promised. Her job should bring her nowhere near the executive office, so they'd never have any reason to interact at work. Unless he needed to see her. He had a momentary fantasy of calling her up to his office and bending her over his desk. His erection throbbed again.

"You obviously know nothing about office gossip," she said before she looked away.

"Chloe, there are three levels of management between your job and mine. Why would anyone care?"

"I care," she said in a low voice.

"Phil wouldn't have hired you if he didn't believe you could do a great job. You'll be an asset to his department."

She huffed out a breath that sounded more unhappy than relieved. "All right." She scooted back to the seat beside him.

He tried to read her expression, but she was in profile to him. "So you'll take the job."

She turned her head, an imp of mischief dancing in her brown eyes. "I told Judith I'd let her know tomorrow."

"You are what's known as a tease," he said, sliding his hand around her neck to twine his fingers into her hair and tilt her head back. He nipped at the soft skin on the side of her neck before dragging his mouth down to lick the shadow of cleavage that just showed in the neckline of her blouse.

The intake of her breath made him harder, but he had a new plan. He slipped his hand up under her skirt, finding satisfaction in the fact that she let her thighs open. When he found the lace of her panties, it was warm and damp. He hooked it aside with his thumb and slid first one and then two fingers into the moist heat of her, stroking and flexing so she bucked up off the seat. He could feel her movements become more frantic, and he slowed his.

"Who's teasing now?" she gasped, her hands scrabbling at the leather seat as she rode his hand.

"I'm getting you ready." He leaned over and took her open mouth, using his tongue to echo the deliberate rhythm of his fingers. She whimpered and tried to push herself against his hand, but he shifted to ease the pressure.

She pulled her mouth away from him. "Ready for what?"

"The fitting room." He rubbed his thumb against her, loving the satiny slide of her private skin, trying to ignore the way her moan shot straight to his cock. "I want you desperate."

"I'm trying to be angry with you, but it's really difficult."

He pressed his thumb a little harder, gauging how far he could wind her up before she went over the edge.

"Especially when you do that."

He pulled his hand out from under her skirt, bringing his fingers up to inhale the fragrance of Chloe's arousal. Then he pulled a handkerchief out of his pocket and regretfully wiped the delicious moisture off his fingers.

She'd slumped back on the seat and was watching him through slitted eyes.

"If I tasted you, I wouldn't be able to walk into Saks," he said.

That made her smile, a triumphant curve of her full lips.

"Now *you're* smirking," he said.

"No, that's a grimace of sexual frustration," she said, smoothing her skirt down as she pressed her knees together.

The car came to a stop.

Nathan threaded his fingers through Chloe's and lifted her hand to kiss the smooth skin on its back. "I hope the fitting room has lots of mirrors."

Chapter 21

Chloe felt like a bundle of lit-up nerve endings. As Nathan helped her out of the car and escorted her to an unmarked bronze door on the side of the venerable retailer's Fifth Avenue store, she could feel every brush of her clothing, every whisper of air over her skin, every point of contact between Nathan's body and hers. It all fed the tightly wound knot of desire deep in her belly that was aching for release.

A tall, beautiful woman whose salt-and-pepper hair contrasted dramatically with her chocolate-colored skin stood just inside the door. "Ms. Russell, Mr. Trainor," she said, stepping forward with her hand outstretched. "I'm Faye LaBarre, your personal shopper. Let me show you what I've selected for you." Her deep voice moved in the cadences of the South, and her handshake was firm.

Nathan took Chloe's elbow as they followed Faye to a bronze-and-wood-paneled elevator. Just that casual touch sent fire burning through her veins. The elevator was small enough that Nathan's shoulder and hip brushed against her, and she had to quell the urge to lean into his body. Faye led them out into what looked like someone's living room. A plush beige couch and several chairs were arranged around an open space covered by a pastel Oriental rug. An elegant brass rack hung with dresses stood in the middle of it.

"May I offer you something to drink?" Faye asked, waving them toward the couch.

"Water would be great, please. And call me Chloe."

Faye's smile was as warm as her voice. "Sure thing, sugar. Mr. Trainor?"

"Nathan," he said with his own heart-grabbing smile. "Water for me as well."

Nathan settled onto the sofa, stretching out his long legs and sliding his cell phone out of his pocket. "I'll leave you ladies to your critical task."

Faye handed each of them a tall glass of water with a lime floating in it. Chloe took a gulp and turned toward the rack.

"Nathan forwarded me the sizes you gave him and explained about the wedding you're attending. I pulled together several ensembles I thought might work. Shall we begin?"

Chloe took another swallow of water and set the tumbler down on a glass-topped side table. She ran her damp palm down her skirt so she wouldn't get water spots on the beautiful clothes displayed in front of her. She saw with relief that they had tags dangling from them, so she'd be able to select by price.

She walked to the rack and casually glanced at one of the tags, biting back an exclamation of dismay. The only information on it was the size and the designer's name, and the name let her know it was exorbitantly expensive. She reminded herself that her appearance would reflect on Nathan, so she needed to swallow her pride, just this once.

Faye showed her each of the half-dozen outfits, naming the designer, describing the fabrics, and discussing the accessories. As Chloe hesitated in front of the array, Faye said, "If you don't like any of these, I have another rack for you to look at."

"My problem is deciding which one to try on," Chloe said, running her fingers over the beautiful embroidery on the skirt of one dress.

"Try them all on," Nathan said, startling her into spinning around. She'd thought he was engrossed in his cell phone, but instead he was lounging on the couch, his arms spread across the back, the glass of water dangling from his long fingers. "I'll help you choose."

"A gentleman after my own heart," Faye said, rolling the rack toward a wide door.

Chloe trundled along behind Faye into the huge dressing room, remembering Nathan's comment about mirrors as her image was reflected back at her from multiple angles. He had to be kidding about having sex here, since they had a very attentive personal shopper. Chloe was both relieved and frustrated.

"All right, let's try the Roberto Cavalli first since you were stroking it." Faye's tone invited Chloe to laugh along with her. "Would you like me to help you, or would you prefer that I give you your privacy?"

"I, um—" Chloe wasn't accustomed to having a dresser, but when she thought about the possibility of damaging one of the delicate and expensive pieces of clothing with her inexpert handling, she decided she could use some assistance. "Please stay. I don't want to ruin anything."

"With pleasure, sugar. You're going to look stunning in this." Faye was already unfastening the dress and slipping it off its hanger.

Chloe stripped down to her bra and panties so the other woman could drop the dress over her head. Faye zipped it up and then pulled a shoe box from the stack on the shelf at the top of the rack. "Now just slide your feet into these."

Chloe couldn't guess the cost of the dresses, but she knew her shoes, and the studded leather Sergio Rossi Mary Jane pumps were well north of a thousand dollars. She toed off her Louboutin knock-offs and reverently slid her feet into the sky-high heels. She started to lean over to fasten the straps, but Faye stopped her. "Let me get that for you."

Once the straps were buckled, Chloe couldn't take her eyes off her feet. "They're so beautiful," she breathed.

"Hmm." Faye sounded less than satisfied, and Chloe lifted her eyes to find the personal shopper gazing at her with an assessing eye. Chloe looked in the mirror. The dress fit her a little too well, in her opinion, the royal-blue lace fabric following every curve.

"Not for a wedding," Faye said. "It would work for an intimate dinner for two, though."

"I'm too buxom for it, aren't I?"

"No, sugar, it's too flat for you," Faye said.

Chloe hesitated. "Maybe I shouldn't show it to Nathan since it's not right for the occasion."

"Any man who's willing to wait while you shop should be rewarded with a look at you in that dress."

"Can I have your home phone number?" Chloe joked. "I could use you when I need a little ego boosting."

Faye chuckled as Chloe teetered past her on the high heels.

Nathan dropped his phone on the sofa beside him as she walked into the sitting area. She stopped in the middle of the carpet and held out her hands at her sides in a mute question. "It's a Roberto Cavalli."

He frowned as his gaze skimmed down her, leaving a trail of heat in its wake. "Come closer," he said.

Chloe walked to within three feet of him. The heels gave her so much extra height that she had to look down to meet his eyes. They were ablaze with wicked intent.

"Now turn slowly."

She rotated in front of him, knowing he was teasing her. "How many mirrors are in the dressing room?" he asked when her back was to him.

She threw him a glare over her shoulder. "Five—and Faye."

He gave her a light pat on the behind.

Chloe came all the way around to face him. "There's a security camera too."

"I'm a tech geek. Security cameras don't stand a chance against me." He leaned back. "You know why I like this dress?"

Chloe raised her eyebrows.

"It makes me want to rip it off you."

All the arousal she'd managed to tamp down burst back into full flame. "You don't rip a Roberto Cavalli."

"I suppose I could use scissors." He ran his fingertip down the side of her rib cage and along the line of her hip. "Cold steel against your soft, warm skin. That could be very erotic."

She sucked in a sharp breath. "I'd better try on the next dress." She tried to spin on her heel and nearly fell. He caught her by the hips, holding her until she found her balance. As she teetered back to the dressing room, she could feel the imprint of his hands on her skin, almost as though they'd burned through the lacy fabric.

"He liked it for all the wrong reasons," Chloe told Faye as the shopper unfastened the dress and helped her out of it.

"I've got the Carolina Herrera ready for you next. I have a good feeling about it."

The soft cotton fabric of the second dress slithered down over Chloe's skin, evoking the brush of Nathan's hands. She closed her eyes and took a deep breath to calm her racing pulse. The zipper sang as Faye ran it up her back. When Chloe opened her eyes, she knew this was the one.

The sheath skimmed her curves in a subtly sexy way, touching but not clinging. The pattern was an impressionist version of tweed in white, gray, and a rich, soft blue. What gave the dress a high-fashion twist was the way a different fabric, a sueded cotton in solid blue, formed wide straps in front but turned into a solid yoke in the back. It was fresh, sophisticated, and perfectly appropriate for an afternoon wedding in the South.

"Nailed it," Faye said. "And wait until you see the shoes."

She pulled a box marked "Dior" from the shelf and opened it to reveal pumps of gray taffeta embroidered with a dusting of blue spangles. As Faye lifted the shoes from the box, the beads threw a confetti of sparkles around the fitting room.

"I can't wear these," Chloe breathed. "They should be in a museum."

Faye knelt to help Chloe step into the shoes. Then she draped a featherlight shawl of cashmere around Chloe's shoulders in a swirl of blue. "For the church. I checked the weather, and it's all you'll need this time of year in North Carolina."

She handed Chloe a neat little handbag in textured metallic leather. "By Alexander McQueen. Just enough room for what you need to carry, with a little sheen to give the outfit edge."

Chloe stared at her multiple images in the mirror. She looked like . . . like a woman a billionaire would take to a wedding.

"All you need is jewelry," Faye said. "I thought Nathan might want to choose that with you."

"I can handle that myself," Chloe said. She was not accepting expensive jewelry from Nathan. It reminded her too much of the dismissal of Ms. Fogarty. With the salary Trainor Electronics would be paying her, she didn't need a diamond bracelet to sell anymore.

The Dior pumps were easier to balance on, so Chloe sashayed out to model for Nathan. He was drinking his water but put the glass down on the glass-topped coffee table with an audible clink when he saw her.

"This is the one," Chloe said, striking a pose with her hand on her hip.

"If you say so," he said, leaning forward. He gave her the same laser-focused assessment as she turned slowly without his prompting.

When she faced him again, he nodded. "It works for me at a distance. Now come closer so I can test the fabric."

Chloe stayed where she was. "To make sure it tears easily?"

His lips curved in a wicked smile. "No, to cop a feel."

"Oh, well, in that case . . ." Chloe started toward him, letting her hips swing.

He gave a low rasp of a laugh and came up off the sofa in a swift movement, startling her to a halt. He came around the coffee table in two long strides and, putting one hand behind her head and one on her bottom, pulled her hard against him for a kiss that nearly blew the top of her head off. He lifted his head and looked at her with heavy-lidded eyes. "Time to send Faye in search of some lingerie."

Chloe hadn't believed he meant it about the dressing room, but the seriousness of his intention was clear on his face. "We can't really do that," she hissed in a low voice. "The video will end up on the Internet or something."

"Trust me." He laced his fingers with hers and pulled her along behind him as he walked into the fitting room. Faye was unzipping the next dress for her to try on.

"You found the perfect dress," Nathan said, turning his charm on Faye, "but it needs lingerie to match. Would you mind choosing a few possibilities while we wait here?"

Chloe felt the embarrassment reddening her cheeks as Faye nodded with a knowing look in her eye. "I'll bring a selection." The personal shopper glided out of the dressing room, closing the door behind her with an audible click.

Nathan scanned the room from floor to ceiling. "Only one camera. They trust their customers." He dropped her hand and pulled a small black gizmo out of his pocket to fiddle with a couple of buttons. "Now let's leave the room empty for a moment." He opened the door for her.

Chloe stepped outside with Nathan following behind her. He closed the door and waited a minute before pushing more buttons on the gadget and pointing it toward the camera in the ceiling.

"I feel like I'm in a Julian Best movie," she said.

"Julian Best would sneer at something this basic," Nathan said, pocketing the gizmo. "But now the security video will show an empty room for as long as we need it."

Chloe felt the oxygen leave her lungs as Nathan held the door wide, his eyes blazing with desire. "We have to be careful with the dress," she squeaked as she walked through the door. Suddenly the multiple mirrors seemed shiny with sinful decadence.

"No ripping," Nathan promised, leading her to the center of the room and stepping behind her. He took the bag and shawl, and then unzipped her dress so expertly that she wondered how many times he'd done it before. She felt the drift of air on her bare skin, and then he was stripping the fabric from her shoulders and shoving it down over her hips.

As it puddled on the floor, Chloe stepped carefully out of the dress. Before she could pick it up, Nathan had hooked it up off the floor and tossed it over the stool set in one corner. "It won't be there long enough to wrinkle," he said.

Then he came up close behind her and splayed one hand over her belly to pull her against his erection while the other covered her breast. He was watching their reflection in the mirror, the heat in his eyes refracting from the glass and spreading through her body. "I'd like to take more time to enjoy this picture, but we have a deadline."

He skimmed his hand inside her panties. She knew he would feel how wet she already was. A low groan vibrated through him as he slipped his fingers into her. She shuddered with pleasure at the pressure. "Ah, Chloe, I want to do so many things to you right now."

"I just want you inside me," she panted.

And then his fingers were gone, leaving her feeling empty and yearning. He yanked her lace panties down to her knees, letting them fall from there. Chloe kicked out of them as she felt his fingers at the hook of her bra. The lace fell from her breasts, leaving her naked except for the spangled heels. The curves of her body seemed tender and vulnerable framed by the navy of Nathan's suit. When he wrapped his arm across her waist, the dark sleeve of his jacket looked and felt almost like a restraint. She shook with the intensity of her arousal.

He nipped at the side of her neck, driving her even wilder. She rubbed her bottom against the erection she could feel through the wool of his trousers. Another groan tore from his throat, and he released her abruptly to unzip his fly and pull a foil envelope from his pocket. She turned to take the condom from him and stroke it down over his cock, making him hiss and throw his head back.

He took her wrists and towed her to the hanging rack, spinning her back to it before he pulled her hands up over her head and wrapped her fingers around the bar. She held on tightly as he gripped her buttocks to lift her and open her thighs. She felt the head of his cock brush against her in a perfect combination of hard and soft. He brought her down as he flexed his hips upward, burying himself deep inside her. The delicious sensation of being filled all at once wrenched a cry of pleasure from her throat.

"Shh!" he warned, but he was smiling like a wolf, wild and predatory.

She wrapped her legs around his hips and locked her ankles behind him, using the bar to leverage herself hard against him. The friction sent a thrill spiraling through her, so she arched backward. He pulled away and thrust back into her, his fingers digging into the soft skin of her behind as he moved and angled her. Then his hair was brushing her shoulder as he bent to take one nipple into his mouth and graze it with his teeth. Pure sensation shot from her breast to the coil of tension deep in her belly. Her muscles rippled into a clench around Nathan's cock. He sucked at her breast and her muscles tightened again.

"That's it," he muttered against her skin before he lifted his head to capture her gaze. He shifted his grip and began to stroke in and out of her in a hard, driving rhythm. She watched the build of lust in his eyes as he pushed them both closer and closer to their release. She felt the moment of suspense as she balanced on the edge, and then her entire body seemed to burst into a supernova of orgasm, making her fling her head back and hang onto the rod for dear life as her internal muscles clamped around Nathan's sensual invasion.

She felt him seat himself even deeper to reach his own climax, nearly bruising her with the convulsive strength of his hands. For a long moment, they stayed bowed against each other, riding their climaxes together. And then he was cradling her in his arms as the aftershocks continued to shudder through her.

"You can let go," he murmured, taking all her weight. She unwrapped her suddenly cramped fingers from the bar and draped her arms limply over Nathan's shoulders. Gazing past his head into the repeating reflections of the angled mirrors, she got a delicious shock from the sight of his hands on her bare bottom. She shifted, her breasts brushing against the fabric of his jacket, which made her internal muscles shiver again.

He carried her to the upholstered chair in the corner of the fitting room and sat, moving her so she was curled on his lap.

"I never thought I'd ever do that." Chloe snuggled into his chest, loving the feel of his body heat through the cotton and wool of his clothes.

"Make love in a dressing room?" His voice was a low rumble against her cheek.

"Make love in Dior pumps."

He chuckled and ran his hand down the bare curve of her back to give her rump a quick squeeze. "If you want to greet Faye naked, it's fine by me, but I know how modest you are, so you should probably get dressed."

Chloe sighed. It was a shame to move when she felt so utterly sated and relaxed. "She knew what we were planning to do."

"I'm sure it's not the first time a man has been driven to strip the clothes off the beautiful woman he's buying them for."

Right. He was buying her these clothes for the wedding, and after that she would go back to being an employee. Her afterglow died like a burned-out lightbulb. Putting her palms flat on his chest, she pushed away from him and squirmed off his lap. "You should deactivate your camera jammer."

He caught her by the waist and dropped a kiss on the tip of each of her breasts, making her tremble as his lips sent delicious shivers spinning into her belly. He looked up at her. "You need to put your clothes on or I won't be able to stop touching you."

She couldn't resist tracing one of his strong, dark eyebrows with her fingertip, feeling the contrast of hair over skin over bone. The mesmerizing textures and stark angles of his upturned face caught at her heart. She had to swallow hard to banish the lump of regret lodged in her throat. "I don't want you to stop," she whispered.

Desire flared in his gray eyes and his grip on her tightened.

The clatter of a door opening shattered the cocoon of sexual enthrallment, and Chloe started. Nathan gave a growl of frustration and released his hold on her. "Ten seconds later and I would have been inside you when she walked in."

Chloe felt the heat of his words lick up the inside of her thighs as she snatched her panties and bra off the floor where Nathan had dropped them. "You'd better get out of here."

He crossed his legs and lifted an eyebrow. "Not that easy right now."

He looked so out of place, perched on the tiny curvy chair in the pastel dressing room. She gave a little snort of laughter as she hooked her bra and wrapped herself in the robe Saks provided for its customers. Nathan took out the small black box and aimed it at the camera before palming it and returning it to his pocket.

Faye bustled into the lounge area, making far more noise than necessary. Chloe was rehanging the dress as the personal shopper tapped on the dressing-room door.

"Come in," Nathan said, making Chloe scowl at him. As Faye walked in, laden with wisps of lace in various shades, he gave Chloe a bland look before saying, "Unfortunately, we have to cut our shopping spree short. We'll take all of those." He gestured toward Faye's armload. "And whatever of these Chloe liked." He waved toward the clothing rack. "And have them delivered."

Chloe started to protest. "Just the—"

Nathan silenced her with a look that said he had no time for arguments because he had something else on his mind. It was a look that set her on fire.

"Yes, sir," Faye said, unloading the lingerie onto a shelf. "I'll be outside if you need me."

"I like that woman," Nathan said when the outer door closed behind Faye. He stood and came up behind Chloe as she shrugged out of the robe.

"You can't buy all that," Chloe said, nodding to the lingerie. "It was just an excuse to make her leave."

Nathan kissed the side of her neck. "You're going to need a change of panties when I'm done."

She caught his gaze in the mirror, and he gave her a slow smile. As soon as she was dressed, he took her elbow and steered her swiftly through the store and into the waiting Rolls.

He was right. Her panties came apart at the seams thirty seconds after the car door closed.

Nathan lounged on the seat of the Rolls as it hummed along the highway back toward Manhattan. He remembered the soft, warm feel of Chloe curled in his lap in the dressing room, wearing nothing but sparkling high heels. Leaning back, he stared at the car's roof and let the memories of the afternoon spool through his mind. He felt a smile twitching at the corners of his lips.

The truth was he'd never intended to make love to her in the dressing room. Even with his video-camera trickery, it was a risky thing to do. But her half-shocked, half-daring responses to his teasing had kept him pushing until he couldn't stop himself.

If he got blackmailed for every penny he had, it would have been worth it.

He moved on to what they'd done together in the car in the rush-hour traffic when his phone vibrated in his jacket pocket. His pulse bounded as he anticipated seeing Chloe's name on the screen. Gavin Miller's name appeared instead, and he almost ignored the call in favor of returning to his daydream. However, the man would just pester him until they talked.

"Miller, I was cursing you earlier."

Gavin laughed, a dark sound. "Already losing the wager?"

"Your strategy is backfiring."

"Did I mention a strategy?"

"You suggested using all the resources at my disposal." Nathan remembered Chloe's look of consternation when she picked up the tag on the first dress. He'd been afraid she would refuse to even try it on.

"You shouldn't listen to anything I say about women. I'd been drowning my sorrows long before I called you that night."

"I thought your problem was writer's block."

"Cause and effect, my boyo, chicken and egg. Which came first? The betrayal or the block?"

"You've been drowning your sorrows again," Nathan said, hearing the slight slurring in Gavin's speech.

"It's after five o'clock, so that's socially acceptable." Gavin spoke with careful precision. "Who is this unusual female?"

Suddenly, Nathan didn't want to expose his relationship with Chloe to Gavin's harsh cynicism. "Why did you call me?"

"Ah, off-limits, I see. That's promising." Gavin sounded amused rather than annoyed. "I was just checking in on your progress, but I have my answer."

"Do you bother Archer too?"

"Archer is hard to bother. Or at least to gauge whether I've bothered him. That's why they call him the Iceman, I imagine. He seems focused entirely on football right now."

"What about you?"

"All I do is sit in my chair and stare at a blank computer screen. It's not conducive to romance. Nor am I in the mood for it."

Nathan thought of the foul mood he'd been in when the flu was raging through his body. Yet he'd still wanted Chloe. "The right woman will change your mood in a millisecond."

"Spoken like a man with experience. Wouldn't it be ironic if the computer geek beat out the jock and the novelist? I tip my hat to you, Trainor."

"That would be premature." He was miles from offering Chloe a ring.

"I'm not so sure. You sound like a different man. There's a note of hope in your voice."

"Do you put crap like that in your books?"

Gavin gave that same humorless bark. "Right now I'd be happy to put anything at all in a book." He paused. "When are we going to meet this extraordinary woman who doesn't want your riches?"

"When hell freezes over," Nathan said.

"Or right after you put a ring on her finger." Gavin's chuckle echoed in Nathan's ear as he ended the call.

Chapter 22

Grandmillie tapped her fork against her plate to interrupt Chloe's highly censored version of her shopping trip. "Sounds like you had a grand time at Saks. So what's bothering you?"

"What? Nothing." Chloe picked up her water glass and took a sip. She had been putting off the inevitable. "In fact, I have good news. I've been offered a really great job at Trainor Electronics. You won't believe the salary."

Silence met her announcement. Chloe glanced up to see a frown drawing down her grandmother's white eyebrows. She saw no condemnation in Grandmillie's face, only concern.

"I know," Chloe said in response to the unspoken comment. "But the job's in the marketing department, so I wouldn't be working directly for Nathan. He swears he just mentioned that I was looking for a full-time position, and Phil Riviere requested my resumé." She sat up straight. "I'm well qualified. I'll do a great job."

"Of course you will. They'll be lucky to have you," Grandmillie snapped. The worry came back into her eyes. "Your Nathan is putting you in a difficult situation."

"He says he's just trying to help me."

"He should have helped by finding you a job somewhere else."

Chloe knew that, but she also knew how she craved his physical presence. He seemed to feel the same way about her.

"What happens when someone at the company finds out about the two of you? Because they will." Grandmillie unknowingly imitated Judith by drumming her fingernails on the table. "No one will criticize *him*, but your abilities will be questioned."

Something shifted inside Chloe's chest, something that smothered that last tiny flicker of hope she'd been nursing without even realizing it. The hope that somehow it would be all right to take the job and keep Nathan too. For all her posturing to herself, she'd been secretly keeping that option open. Grandmillie's words stripped bare her self-deception as boiling-hot tears welled up at the thought of losing him.

Her grandmother leaned in to cover Chloe's hand where it lay fisted on the table. "I understand he's become important to you."

Chloe looked away as the tears spilled down her cheeks. "I make him laugh," she said, her voice quavering.

"You've become important to him too, or he wouldn't have gotten the job for you." Grandmillie's touch was gentle. "But he's not thinking of your best interests by keeping you at Trainor Electronics and risking your reputation. He's only thinking of his own wants."

Chloe blinked hard. Her voice came out raspy and low. "The relationship wasn't going to last anyway. I'll just end it sooner rather than later."

Grandmillie nodded her approval. "You've known him such a short time, it will be easier to do it now."

Chloe felt like her heart was being squeezed in a vise. There would be nothing easy about it. "I have an obligation to go to his father's wedding, but on Sunday I'll tell him we can't continue to see each other."

Grandmillie gave a sympathetic sigh. "It was like that with your grandfather. We couldn't be apart from each other, so we got married, because that was what you did in those days."

"And you ended up divorced."

"Do you think Nathan would marry you?"

Startled, Chloe looked at her grandmother. "It's only been a week."

"If it had been three months, do you think he'd propose rather than lose you?"

Chloe thought hard. She considered the high-powered, self-assured Teresa and her abrupt and permanent exit. Then there was the way Cavill had jumped to incorrect conclusions about her relationship with Nathan right off the bat. It looked like Nathan had a revolving door with women.

On top of that, she compared Nathan's huge home and multiple cars and aircraft to her tiny house and ten-year-old Toyota. She remembered the guest-room closet stocked with designer clothing and the casual way he'd told Faye they'd buy everything in the Saks dressing room.

"Would he sweep me away in a white Rolls to live in the penthouse of his castle?" She shook her head. "Only in a fairy tale."

Grandmillie gave her hand an affectionate squeeze before she let go. "You're a smart, sensible girl."

Chloe picked up her fork and speared a bite of chicken. She put it in her mouth, but it tasted like tears.

Just this once, she wanted to believe in fairy tales.

Nathan sat down at the desk in his home office and opened his e-mail program. Scanning down the endless list, he scowled at the mind-numbing subject lines of reports and memos and scheduling.

The contrast with the explosive pleasure of his earlier hours was too dismal. He flicked a finger across the screen to slam the program shut. The thought of Chloe sent him to a triple-password-protected folder marked "Prometheus."

A couple of hours later, he leaped out of his chair so fast it spun in circles as he paced away from his desk and back again. He had an idea about how to fix Prometheus, and he wanted to discuss it with someone. He glanced at his watch and growled in frustration. He couldn't drag Andrew Koenig, the project's manager, away from his wife and children at this hour. Then he remembered Ginnie Tsai, the assistant manager of the project. She reminded him of himself at that age, committed to the point of obsession. She would *want* to hear his idea, no matter what the time.

He went back to the computer, bracing his arm on the desk as he scrolled through the company's phone directory until he found her number and sent it to his autodialer. "Ginnie, it's Nathan Trainor. I might have a solution to our problem with the battery. I know it's late, but can you meet me at the R and D lab?"

There was a short pause before her voice came back with a tinge of pride. "I'm already there."

Nathan wasn't sure how to label the emotion that blew through him at her words, but it might have been joy. He'd found his tribe again.

It was after midnight when he left the lab and walked out of the doors of Trainor Electronics and into the foggy Manhattan air. Neon signs swirled colors through the night, and scattered knots of people still strolled the sidewalks. He'd told Oskar to go home so he could walk off the adrenaline sizzling through his veins.

He'd arrived at the lab to find Ginnie and half a dozen other team members awaiting him. When he explained his idea, they had practically vibrated with excitement. They'd torn the battery down to its microcomponents before starting to reassemble them in a white heat of creative exhilaration.

He'd been impressed with how they'd embraced his suggestion and expanded it, stretched it in new directions and layered their own improvements on it. There had been that rare electricity of pure thought sparking between all of them. He felt almost drunk on it.

He needed to share it with Chloe. His hand went into his pocket to wrap around his cell phone. Chloe would be sound asleep in her bed, hopefully dreaming her erotic dreams of him.

He released the phone as he imagined her in *his* bed. He could wake her up with a kiss and a long stroke down the sexy curves of her body. Her *naked* body, since this was his fantasy. She'd blink up at him with a sleepy, come-hither smile. He'd have to decide whether he wanted to tell her about the breakthrough before or after he made love to her. Maybe he'd tell her about it *while* he made love to her. He would whisper something very technical and watch her agile mind try to focus on it while he did his best to distract her by plunging himself inside her delicious heat.

As his cock hardened, Nathan winced at his self-inflicted frustration.

He kept walking, but the hunger for Chloe didn't lessen. He hit the autodial button for her number. It took four rings, but she picked up just as her voice mail began. "Nathan?" Her voice was husky with sleep. "Are you all right?"

"Beyond all right. I just left the lab. I think we've got Prometheus on the right track."

He heard the rustle of sheets as she shifted in some way. "I'm thrilled for you and your team." Her tone was warm and he could picture her smile. "I'd ask how you did it, but I'm pretty sure I wouldn't understand a word."

He chuckled, remembering his fantasy. "I won't bore you with the technical details, but I want to thank you."

"For what?"

"You sent me there. I'd forgotten where I started, what I was really good at. You reminded me that my job as CEO could take me out of the executive office." He let his voice drop low. "Working with the development team tonight was almost as good as sex with you."

She gave a half-pleased, half-embarrassed choke of laughter. "An intellectual orgy."

He injected even more innuendo in his voice. "One thing that would make this night perfect would be to get home and find you in my bed. Naked." The thought of his vast empty bed was depressing.

"By all means, send Kurt in the helicopter."

He heard the dryness in her voice, but he couldn't stop himself from showing his need. "What if I brought the Rolls and parked in front of your house?"

She laughed. She thought he was joking.

"If you agreed, I'd be there in thirty minutes," he said.

"No, I have to work tomorrow." But he'd heard the tiny pause while she'd seriously considered it. That would have to be enough.

Chapter 23

Chloe collated the various audit documents in a haze of fatigue. After Nathan's call, she'd tossed and turned the rest of the night, regretting her decision to say no to his crazy late-night proposal. She had so little time left with him. She should have thrown caution, good sense, and discretion to the winds and agreed to his insane idea of meeting in the Rolls. Instead she'd given up the bliss of seeing him and had gotten no sleep anyway.

She'd sealed the fate of their relationship this morning by calling Judith and accepting the job with Trainor Electronics. Judith had told her she was doing the right thing, but it didn't make Chloe feel less miserable. Especially since she would be starting there next week.

She sighed and rechecked the pile of documents before she shoved them into the jaws of the electric stapler. Her cell phone chimed with Grandmillie's distinctive ringtone. Chloe nearly ripped the pocket of her skirt in her haste to get it out. "Is everything all right?"

"It's fine." Grandmillie sounded testy. "I just called to tell you Oskar left a mountain of boxes and shopping bags in our front hall.

I figured you should know when you talk with your Nathan. You're seeing him after work, aren't you?"

"Oh," Chloe said, slumping back into the chair in relief. "Yes, he's picking me up in about twenty minutes. Is it really a mountain? I only wanted one dress and some accessories."

"You've got dress bags, shoe boxes, and a whole variety of assorted other boxes and bags."

"Oh, dear." Chloe curled even farther down into the chair. "What do I do with it all?"

"You give it back."

"I can try." Chloe had a feeling Nathan wouldn't accept the return of his purchases no matter which way their relationship went. "I have to wear one outfit to the wedding. If he doesn't take the rest back, I'll donate it to Goodwill." Chloe was talking to herself rather than Grandmillie.

"Let's not be hasty," Grandmillie said.

That made Chloe laugh in a slightly broken way. "You're a pip, Grandmillie. Remember I get the tax deduction for my donation."

"Hadn't thought of that." Grandmillie harrumphed and hung up.

Chloe couldn't help it. When she walked out the office doors and saw Nathan lounging against the Rolls, every cell in her body nearly exploded with joy. She could feel the stupidly happy smile spread across her face as he straightened and started toward her. When he swept her into his arms and dipped her low for a quick, dramatic kiss, she wanted to giggle like a teenager.

"That's not exactly being discreet," she said as he righted her.

He pulled her against his side and hustled her to the car. "I feel too good to worry about discretion."

"So you truly fixed Prometheus?"

He helped her into the toasty interior and slid onto the seat beside her, pulling the door closed. "I've at least gotten it out of a dead end. We'll see where the new road leads."

But she could see the exhilaration in his eyes. He saw success at the end of the road. Taking her face in his hands, he brushed his lips against hers with a strangely soft and reverent touch. "Thank you, darling."

Chloe's breath caught at his last word. "I, um, you're welcome."

He started to deepen the kiss, but she took hold of his lapels and gave him a little shake. He lifted his head. "Is 'darling' unacceptable?"

"No, no, not that. I love the word *darling*." Especially when it came from his lips. "I have to talk to you about all the stuff that got delivered to my house today. I only needed one outfit, but Grandmillie says it's a small mountain."

"We were in a hurry, remember? I told her I'd take everything."

He tried to kiss the side of her neck, but she shook him again. "All the lingerie. Not all the dresses and shoes and bags."

He shrugged. "She must have misunderstood."

"No, you misunderstood. I don't want to be showered with expensive gifts."

"Really?" He sat back as a look of cynicism flitted across his face. "You don't have a high opinion of women, do you?"

He was silent for a long moment before he said, "You're changing my mind."

Guilt ripped at her chest. He probably wouldn't feel that way in a few days when she chose the job over him. She needed to tell him the truth about her feelings for him now, before he wouldn't believe her. "It's you I want. Just Nathan. Not the CEO of Trainor Electronics. Not the billionaire who owns an apartment bigger than my block. All that only gets in the way."

He scanned her face as she spoke. She tried to will the depth of her emotions into her eyes and her words. He brushed back a little piece of hair that had come loose from her bun. "Everything in me says to believe you," he said.

Chloe reached out to lay her hand against his cheek. "No matter how often I told myself we were too unequal, I couldn't stop myself from wanting you."

Nathan's face tightened as he turned his head and kissed her palm. "There is nothing unequal about us."

"It didn't matter anyway. You made me forget about your cars and private doctors and designer clothes. It all evaporated." Chloe traced her fingertip over his lips. "You're extraordinary just being you."

For a moment, he looked younger and less commanding, his gray eyes clear and unshadowed, the lines around his mouth less marked. For a moment, he believed her. And then the CEO was back. "You have stronger principles than I'm accustomed to."

She sighed inwardly. "They haven't held up so well against you."

"That's good, because I'm about to do something very unprincipled." With that he stretched her out on the seat and used his mouth and hands to utterly destroy any resistance. Afterward, he lay with his head on her lap while she combed her fingers through his hair, memorizing the fine grain of his skin and the spikes of his lashes against his cheeks. She hated to bring up a touchy subject, but she needed some information about their upcoming trip. "Tell me about the wedding. I don't even remember where it is."

"Camp Lejeune, North Carolina," Nathan said, opening his eyes as he shifted restlessly. "Home of Expeditionary Forces in Readiness. We'll be flying down on my jet."

"On your jet. Of course," Chloe said, stroking his cheek to still his movement.

He gave her a sharp look. "One thing I've learned is that time has as much value as money. Possibly more. That's why I have a jet." His voice slowed and roughened. "And a private cabin is so much more comfortable than a commercial lavatory for certain activities."

Chloe shook her head at him. "No hanky-panky on the way down. It was bad enough having Grandmillie meet you after we'd been fooling around. I'm not making the same mistake with your father. I want to be able to hold my head high so I'm worthy of you."

"I have no interest in what my father thinks about you. All that matters is what I think."

Chloe didn't believe him. Any mention of his father set Nathan on edge. Whether he admitted it to himself or not, his father's opinion affected him. "You're going to the wedding, so you must have some interest in your father's feelings."

"I'm going because you talked me into it when I was still weak with the flu."

"Why don't you cancel, then? Say you have a business emergency." Chloe wasn't sure why she kept pushing him, but she felt this was important.

"Ed and Ben are counting on a ride with us on the jet." Nathan gave her a half smile as she sputtered at him about letting her believe he planned to make love to her. He shrugged, his shoulders moving against her thighs in a delicious friction. "I'll admit to being curious about my father's motives."

That was his vulnerability speaking. "I am too. You said it would be a full military ceremony."

"The general is a jarhead through and through, so there will be swords flashing." A shadow crossed his face and he tipped his head away, tension drawing his jawline taut. "I have something he might want for the wedding."

"Do you think that's why he invited you?"

He hesitated before he looked back at her. "No, he would have asked for it."

"What is it?"

"The family sword. Passed down through generations of military Trainors. He gave it to me in a last-ditch effort to persuade me to apply to the Naval Academy or West Point or anywhere that required a uniform and service to God and country." His eyes filled with regret, anger, and pain. "I took it to MIT and used it to slice bananas onto my cereal."

Chloe couldn't help it. A gurgle of laughter rose in her throat at the vision of a young Nathan using a long, gleaming saber to carve fruit. "That sounds like a difficult way to cut up bananas. I mean, you'd need really long arms . . ."

For a moment his eyebrows drew down and she thought she'd gone too far, but then the tightness in his jaw eased and he started to chuckle. "My roommate sometimes helped."

"So he held the banana over your bowl and you whacked at it with the sword." She chortled again. "You have to love teenage rebellion." Quelling her amusement, she held his gaze. "Take the sword with you to the wedding. Loan it to him for the ceremony. It will be symbolic."

"Of what?" The frown was back.

"Your relationship." She wanted to give him something before they parted ways. Maybe she could reopen the line of communication with his father. "Or rather, your wish to have one."

"I don't want a relationship with my father."

Chloe shook her head. "I don't believe that."

He levered himself off her lap and sat up. She got the message that he was not happy, but she wasn't going to quit. "He invited you for a reason. And you accepted for a reason. Don't blame it on the flu."

Chloe waited as he stared out the window. She'd counted to fourteen when he turned back to her. "I'll take the damned sword." The clenched muscles of his jaw eased into a wicked smile. "I can use it when we get back to remove your clothes more quickly."

She concealed her sense of triumph with an answering smile. "If you come near my Carolina Herrera dress with that sword, I'll break it in half."

He threw back his head and laughed. She sensed it was more to release his tension about the wedding than about her wit.

The car glided to a halt in front of Chloe's house. Nathan muttered a curse under his breath. "Come to dinner with me tomorrow," he said. "I want more than just an hour in the back of my car."

She wanted it too, more desperately than he knew. "I'd love to."

Surprise showed in the sudden lift of his brows. "That was easy. Why didn't I ask you before this?"

"You were terrified of rejection?"

He pivoted and pinned her against the seat, bringing his mouth beside her ear as his hand slid between her legs to touch the most sensitive spot on her body. "If Grandmillie wasn't timing how long it takes for the car door to open, I'd show you how I would overcome your rejection."

As his finger sent spirals of heat through her, Chloe murmured, "I already said yes."

"Damn," he said, withdrawing his hand. "So you did. Have dinner with me Friday as well. There's a Broadway premiere I want to take you to."

"I can't. I need to spend time with Grandmillie since I'll be gone all day Saturday."

He nodded but said nothing, watching her as though he were waiting for something more.

"What?" she asked, baffled.

"Invite me to spend the evening with Grandmillie too."

Shock made her blurt out, "Seriously?"

"I can bring dinner so you don't have to cook." His expression turned intense. "Grandmillie doesn't approve of me, so I need another chance to win her over."

"Grandmillie likes you just fine. She calls you my 'young man,' which is hilarious."

He looked offended. "Why?"

How did she explain that he was too brilliant, too rich, too sexy, and too powerful to be anyone's young man? And after this weekend, he would never again be *her* young man. "It makes you sound like a prom date, and you are so far beyond that."

That seemed to mollify him, because he smiled. "I have one thing in common with a prom date."

"You do?"

"I think about nothing except getting you out of your clothes."

Chloe gave him a light punch in the shoulder, grabbed her handbag, and hurtled out of the privacy of the Rolls.

Nathan exited the car behind her, lacing his fingers with hers as he accompanied her to the front door. "You didn't invite me for dinner, but I'll work on that tomorrow." He leaned down to kiss her. "I'll pick you up after work and you can change at my place. Would you wear the blue lace dress for me? As a favor."

So she would have two incredibly expensive dresses hanging unused in her closet after this weekend. Chloe knew when she was being manipulated, but she couldn't resist his request. "You are a devious and ruthless man, which is why I will wear the dress. Without any panties."

Nathan's look nearly set her on fire. "And you call *me* ruthless."

Nathan frowned at the array of unread reports and memos running down the computer screen in his home office. Leaving work at five o'clock every day to see Chloe cut into his working time, and he needed to catch up. He read through one memo twice without taking in a word. Irritated with himself, he pushed his rolling chair away from his desk and swiveled to face the windows where the lights of Manhattan blazed.

Today's encounter with Chloe had left him unsettled and restless. The sex had been great. It always was with her. When she'd said she wanted him for himself and no other reason, he'd believed her. Her emotion had been genuine, but there was a tinge of regret in it that made him uneasy. Instead of bringing them closer, her deeper feelings seemed to be putting a distance between them.

Then he'd spilled his guts about the family sword.

"Damn it." He vaulted out of the chair and paced across the room.

The thought that his father might want to wear the sword had hit him as he described the wedding ceremony to Chloe, and the rest had just spilled out. Even Ben didn't know he'd used the saber to slice bananas, the most disrespectful use he could think of for it.

He'd told her a shameful secret, but she wouldn't let him have a meal with her beloved grandmother. What did that say about their relationship?

He wasn't accustomed to feeling off balance with a woman. Chloe seemed so honest and straightforward, yet there were layers to her he hadn't begun to understand. It frustrated him. He wanted to know everything about her.

Tapping his finger against his thigh, he stared unseeingly out the window. Knowing too much could get messy. He usually preferred to stay safely on the surface with the women he dated. Things hadn't worked so well with Teresa because he'd allowed himself to hope for more.

He was falling into the same trap with Chloe. So why did it feel so good?

A buzzing sound came from his desk as his cell phone danced on the stainless-steel surface. The first word that sprang to his mind was *Chloe,* and he was across the floor in four long strides. But the name on the screen was "Luke Archer Cell."

Surprise made him answer the phone.

"Trainor, I need a favor." The quarterback's Texas drawl was stronger on the phone. "I got talked into buying a table at a charity dinner tomorrow night, and I need to fill it up. Miller's coming, so I'm asking you to come too. And bring a date."

Nathan sat down and tilted back his chair to prop his feet up on the desk. "Miller put you up to this."

"Miller? No, he's just willing to go along with it for a good cause. We're raising money for foster kids in the New York metro area."

"That's not what I meant. He wants to meet my date."

"Hell, based on what Miller says, *I* want to meet her." Archer said. "You work fast, man."

"As I told him yesterday, the meeting is premature. And I have no intention of exposing her to Miller's curiosity." Not to mention the fact that he wasn't about to give up an entire evening of having Chloe all to himself.

"Too bad," Archer said. "The silent auction has some damn nice jewelry, and all the proceeds go to the kids."

Nathan dropped his feet to the floor and sat up. He could buy Chloe something beautiful, and she wouldn't feel guilty about accepting it since it was given in the name of charity. Temptation sank its claws into him.

Archer must have read his silence because the quarterback said, "There's a listing of the items online. I'll text you the link."

"Did you donate a signed football?" Nathan asked, stalling.

"With four tickets on the fifty-yard line," Archer said. "Miller kicked in an entire set of autographed Julian Best books, along with a prop from the last movie."

Nathan huffed out a laugh. "Put me down for a TE-Genio 3-D printer." He could also get something Chloe would like at Tiffany's, donate it to the auction, and bid on it for her. But Archer didn't need to know that.

"Sounds high-tech. So you'll come."

"I'm sure I'll regret it, but I'll ask Chloe if she'd like to attend."

"Chloe. Nice name. I'll text you all the information."

Archer hung up and Nathan rested the cell phone on his thigh. Would Chloe be impressed or put off by the charity dinner? He shook his head. He never knew with her. Archer's arriving texts chimed. Nathan read the information before he hit Chloe's number on speed dial and lifted the phone to his ear.

"Nathan." Delight, caution, and surprise mixed in her voice.

"How would you feel about a change of plans for tomorrow?" he asked. "We've been invited to a charity dinner for foster kids. A friend of mine is sponsoring a table."

"Is it Ben?" She sounded pleased by the prospect.

"No, it's Luke Archer." He waited to see if she would recognize the name.

Silence hummed through the phone for a second. "Luke Archer the quarterback?"

"That's the one."

"Of course you're friends with Luke Archer."

"Maybe acquaintance is a better description," he clarified, still not sure what her reaction was.

"Well, I guess if it's for a good cause . . ." She gave a funny little laugh. "The Empire was my father's favorite football team. I watched Luke Archer win four Super Bowls."

"Then he'll enjoy your company more than mine. I've never seen him play." He'd buy the tickets Archer had donated to the auction as well as the planted jewelry.

"You're not a football fan?" Chloe sounded astonished. "I figured with your military background . . . the Army-Navy game and all that."

He made a wry face even though she couldn't see him. "When I was in front of a screen, I was playing video games."

"That makes sense." She gave a little sigh. "There's so much I don't know about you."

He didn't like her tone. It was almost sad. "We have plenty of time to find out all those things."

"Plenty of time," she echoed, but without conviction. "Oh my goodness! I just realized . . . What should I wear to the dinner?"

"You have all the outfits from Saks, so you can pick one of those." He allowed a touch of smugness in his voice. "It's cocktail attire."

"So I don't have to wear a long gown." Relief laced her words.

"I vote for the blue dress, as always."

"It might be a little, er, formfitting for a charity dinner."

He remembered how the stretchy lace outlined her hips and clung to the curves of her breasts. "Your form is what I love, so that works for me."

She caught her breath at the compliment. "All right, I'll wear it. But I'm not going commando at a public dinner."

"I knew I'd regret agreeing to Archer's invitation," he said, but he was smiling. He would enjoy seeing what kind of lingerie she chose for the sexy dress.

After he hung up, he had the thought that maybe he didn't want Archer and Miller seeing her curves. He balanced that against the prospect of peeling the dress off her on the way home from the dinner and decided to let his request stand.

Now he just had to fit a trip to Tiffany's into his schedule tomorrow.

Chapter 24

As she walked through the doors to cocktail hour at the ritzy midtown hotel, Chloe tightened her hold on Nathan's arm and pasted on her most confident smile. Honestly, she wouldn't have agreed to come if she hadn't known how thrilled her father would have been to meet Luke Archer.

A hostess dressed in a black suit walked up to them with a tablet in her hand. "Mr. Trainor and Ms. Russell, Mr. Archer asked me to escort you to him."

Nathan nodded and put his hand against the small of Chloe's back to indicate she should follow the young woman. "How did she know who we were?" Chloe asked in an undertone before she stepped in front of him.

Nathan looked uncomfortable as he shrugged. "They prep the hostesses with photos of major donors. It's part of the courtship dance. They make you feel important so you'll give them more money."

The hostess stopped and looked over her shoulder, so Chloe hurried forward. Nathan was a major donor. It shouldn't surprise her.

She made a surreptitious scan of their fellow guests as she walked through the chattering crowd. The women wore clothes that reeked of money, and the suits of their male counterparts clearly did not come ready-made off a rack. Thank goodness Nathan had sent the extra outfits to her house! She would have been woefully underdressed in her own clothes.

Of course, he looked superb in a midnight-blue suit with a light-blue shirt and yellow tie, his hair tamed into neat waves that brushed his collar. She caught several women casting envious glances her way, which made a smug little smile turn up the corners of her lips.

The hostess touched a guest's shoulder to clear their path. As the guest moved aside, Chloe saw Luke Archer, with his signature mane of blond hair, standing directly in front of her. His head was bent as he listened politely to the animated conversation of a petite blonde woman who had her hand tucked in his elbow. As Chloe and Nathan approached, he turned those famously piercing blue eyes on them. She realized the blonde woman wasn't quite as small as she'd thought. Luke Archer's height and broad shoulders just made her appear tiny.

"Good to see you, man," the quarterback said, gripping Nathan's hand briefly before turning to Chloe with a surprisingly easy smile and a charming Texas twang. "You must be Chloe. I'm Luke Archer."

His big hand engulfed hers and she wondered how many footballs he'd thrown with it. "I know. I'll never forget the eighty-two-yard pass you made to win the Super Bowl. My heart was in my throat as that ball flew through the air," she said. "I'm a great fan of yours." She nodded toward the rest of the room with a smile. "Along with everyone else here, I suspect."

He shook his head. "There are plenty of Patriots and Dolphins fans here." He turned to his companion. "Jane Dreyer, meet Chloe Russell and Nathan Trainor." The woman gave them a dazzling smile as she shook hands. She was about fifteen years older than Luke, had straight platinum-blonde hair, and wore a simple long-sleeved purple sheath adorned with a gorgeous collection of gold chains and bangles. "Jane is Gavin's literary agent," Luke added.

Chloe knew Gavin meant Gavin Miller, the author of the hugely successful Julian Best series. He was another of Nathan's acquaintances. She wondered what other famous people they would run into here.

"I'm trying to persuade Luke to write his memoir," Jane said. "You'd want to read that, wouldn't you?"

"Absolutely," Chloe said.

Luke shook his head. "Maybe when I retire from football."

"I've explained that he needs to write it now, while he's at the height of his career," Jane said, appealing to Chloe and Nathan again. "That will give him the broadest platform of readers."

"She makes a good point," Nathan said.

Chloe was surprised to see a flicker in the quarterback's air of steely confidence as he said, "I'm not much of a writer."

"Not a problem," Jane said. "I have some fantastic ghostwriters as clients."

"Where's Gavin?" Nathan asked, glancing around.

"He took my date to look at the auction items in the next room," Luke said, appearing relieved at the change of subject.

"We'll have to bid on some of those too." Nathan looked down at Chloe with a smile. "For the cause. I hear Luke donated an autographed football you might like."

"I'd love that, especially knowing it's supporting the foster kids," she said. It seemed safe to agree to that. An autographed football couldn't cost all that much, could it?

"Trainor, you actually came." Another tall man, this one dark where Luke Archer was blond, strolled up to the group accompanied by a young, very trim woman. "I didn't think you would." He turned a flashing smile on Chloe.

"Good to see you too, Miller," Nathan said with an amused edge to his tone. "Chloe, this is Gavin Miller."

Gavin projected a cynical, devil-may-care attitude in contrast to Luke's almost palpable discipline and self-control. The author's striking green eyes held a glint of mischief. Yet she noticed dark circles under them. "Chloe, the pearl beyond price, it's a pleasure to meet you." Instead of shaking her hand, he gave her a brief hug. "Allow me to present Elyssa Lauda, Luke's personal trainer. And a very lovely one at that."

That explained Elyssa's perfectly defined arm muscles, but Chloe was puzzled by Gavin's description of herself. As she shook hands with the trainer, she caught an exchange of glances between Nathan and Gavin, one warning, the other challenging. Something was going on between these men that Nathan hadn't clued her in on.

Miller maneuvered himself around to stand beside Chloe. "So tell me how you and Nathan met. Being a writer, I'm always interested in the backstory."

It figured he'd lead with an awkward question. "I worked for him, briefly. I'm temping between permanent jobs."

Interest flared in the writer's green eyes. "An office romance, then." He raised his dark eyebrows at her. "So you spent hours in his company and still agreed to go on a date with him. You're a brave woman."

Nathan slid his arm around her waist. "*Foolhardy* might be a better word," he said. "Not to mention the fact that for the first few days of our acquaintance, I had the flu."

Chloe was surprised he would admit that, but she played along. "And germs make him cranky."

"I'll bet." Luke joined the conversation, startling Chloe. She looked up to see the three men locked in a staring match.

"Chloe and I are going to take a look at the auction offerings," Nathan said. "We'll meet you at the dinner table."

He guided her away from the group toward another door, stopping a server with a tray of filled champagne flutes to take two of the slender glasses. Several people greeted him, but he just nodded and kept going, his arm like a steel band around Chloe's waist. As soon as they reached the next room, she slipped out of his grasp and turned to face him. "So what's going on with you, Luke, and Gavin?"

His expression became unreadable and he took a swallow of champagne. "Just some typical male posturing."

"About what?"

He looked away for a long moment. "You notice Gavin brought his agent and Luke brought his trainer."

"So?"

"I'm the only one who brought an actual date."

"How do you know those aren't real dates?"

"Because Luke and Gavin don't look at them the way I look at you. They don't find a way to touch them at every opportunity like I do you." Nathan smiled down at her with something in his eyes that made it hard to breathe. "They're jealous, plain and simple."

"About me?" Chloe was flabbergasted.

He slipped his arm around her again and brushed his lips against the side of her neck, sending shivers rippling over her skin. "I'm the only one who gets to do this. And this." He shifted his hand to press it against the thin lace covering the curve of her behind. The splay of his fingers reminded her of what they'd done before they'd dressed to come to the party. Heat bloomed between her legs.

"Stop distracting me," she grumbled. "Why didn't they bring real dates?"

"I assume they don't have any to bring." His lips curved into a gloating smile. "Forget about them, let's donate some money to the kids."

Chloe let him lead her to the first of a series of round tables dotting the room. Auction items were artfully displayed atop forest-green tablecloths. Well-dressed patrons were circling the tables, chatting and occasionally pausing to write on the bid sheets. Nathan threw a cursory glance at the first few offerings before his eyes lit up at the sight of Archer's autographed football. They'd been given a number when they checked into the party, and he scrawled it on the sheet along with his bid.

Chloe's eyes widened as she read the description of Luke's donation and realized it included four fifty-yard-line seats to an Empire game. Then she checked Nathan's bid and nearly choked. "I don't care how good those seats are, they're not worth that much."

"It's just a way to give money to the charity, darling," Nathan said. "I might as well get something that we'll enjoy in the process."

Chloe narrowed her eyes at him even as she savored being called darling, although he was probably doing that in an attempt to overcome her scruples. "You said you'd never seen Luke play, so you wouldn't enjoy the game."

"I'll enjoy watching you enjoy it." He towed her past three more tables before stopping in front of a display of jewelry laid in the distinctive blue-green boxes that marked them as Tiffany's. One box held a bangle bracelet in white gold covered with a random mosaic of small sapphires and diamonds that glittered in the spotlight over them. The other contained a pair of earrings—two long, dangling bars of white gold encrusted with the same pattern of sapphires and diamonds. They were stunning in their dazzling simplicity.

"What do you think of those?" he asked.

"They're beautiful. Both classic and modern," Chloe said cautiously.

"Like you."

She looked up to see him smiling at her. "That's a very nice thing to say. But do not bid on those. They must be worth a small fortune."

He glanced at the bid sheet. "Not even a tiny fortune." He picked up the pen and wrote his number, and a bid that was double the one before it.

Chloe gasped. "Nathan, stop! If you win those, I will not accept them."

He looked taken aback. "It's just a dona—"

"A donation. I get it, but you can't give those to me. It's bad enough that I took this dress and these shoes." She waved a hand down at her clothes.

He put down his champagne glass and wrapped his hands around her shoulders so he could lock his gaze on hers. "I want to give you things that will make you happy. What's wrong with that?"

She couldn't tell him that they wouldn't be together long enough to go to the football game or for her to wear the jewelry. "What's wrong is that I can't give you equally amazing things in return."

His eyes went dark with an emotion she couldn't decipher. "Is that really the problem? Because let me tell you what incredible things you've given me." His grip on her shoulders intensified. "You've given me Prometheus. I wouldn't have gone near it without you. I have a new perspective on my friendship with Ben, thanks to you. You're even forcing me to deal with my father." Heat flared in his eyes. "You've given me the pleasure of your beautiful body." He rubbed his fingers against the fabric of her dress, making her breasts ache with the desire to have him touch them the same way.

Then he floored her. "You've given me joy. I haven't had that in my life for a long time."

That did it. All the barriers and excuses she'd put up around her heart disintegrated into dust and blew away. She loved this overbearing, complicated, brilliant man to the depths of her soul.

Chloe wanted to stop time right then and there. To let herself bathe in this marvelous feeling, to soak in it and let it pour over her.

She had been fighting this love for so long. It felt good to relax into the emotion for just a few fleeting moments before she had to deny it.

"What is it, Chloe?"

He was far too attuned to her. She shook her head. "You can't buy me the jewelry." And she couldn't be in love with him. It was impossible.

She saw hurt in his eyes, sending a jab of guilt through her chest. She hated to cause him pain, yet all too soon she was going to do far worse than turning down some auction items.

"I said too much." He shook his head at himself. "No wonder you looked stunned. Forget about my outburst. Let's find Archer and Miller."

He tucked her hand into the crook of his elbow and laid his other hand over hers, but she could feel his withdrawal. He'd bared his emotions to her, and she'd rejected his honesty. Misery washed away most of the exultation she'd felt before.

As Chloe walked silently beside him, Nathan berated himself for dumping his issues on her. Her expression of shocked disbelief lingered in his mind's eye. He had hoped to make her understand how much he owed her, but all he'd succeeded in doing was to show her how screwed up he really was.

Bringing Chloe to this event was a mistake. Miller was watching her like a hungry hawk. Archer was sizing her up as though she were a first-round draft pick. And now he'd revealed things about himself she didn't want to know.

It wasn't a mistake. It was a disaster.

He needed to tell Miller and Archer to back off, and then he needed to gain back the ground he'd lost with her.

"I'm sorry," Chloe said into the silence. "I shouldn't be so ungrateful. It's lovely of you to want to buy me pretty things and football tickets. I want you to know I appreciate it."

Now she was apologizing. Chloe, who never backed down from him. He needed to get things back to normal. "I wasn't being nice. I was being an arrogant ass who tried to force something on you that you didn't want. Tell me I've forgotten how real people live or something along those lines."

She started, and turned to look up at him with a question in her eyes. He gave her his best master-of-the-universe look. Her gaze went soft and nearly undermined his determination to provoke her back into her usual tart self.

"Being generous doesn't make you an arrogant ass," she said, grazing her hand down his arm to lace her warm, slim fingers with his. He felt her touch right into his core. "You just need to keep it in proportion."

"I guess I've lost my sense of that," he said, wondering how true it was.

She smiled. "It must be hard not to when you're you."

Chapter 25

As she touched up her lipstick in the ladies' room mirror, Chloe tried to regain her balance after the emotional roller-coaster ride she'd just taken. She'd excused herself on the way to the table because she was finding it hard to breathe when she was anywhere near Nathan. His revelations and her reactions kept rolling over her like tidal waves.

On top of that, she had to face his two famous friends and the gorgeous women with them. Yes, she felt intimidated. If this were Nathan's office, she'd be fine, but the social setting made her feel out of her depth.

She tucked her lipstick back in the shiny clutch and squared her shoulders under the blue lace. At least she *looked* like she belonged here.

She walked out of the ladies' room only to be pulled up short by the sound of Nathan's voice coming from behind her. She spun around, but he wasn't in the subtly lit hallway. She started toward the sound, the heels of her crystal-studded Jimmy Choo d'Orsay pumps clicking on the marble floor as she tried to figure out where he was. The sign for the men's room indicated it was around the corner in the opposite direction, so that wasn't the source. She took a few more steps and spotted a partly open door. She hesitated, wondering if she should interrupt what might be a private conversation since he'd chosen to have it in a private room. Then she heard her name.

"Chloe's a smart woman," Nathan was saying. "She's already asked me what's going on. So lay off the interrogation, Miller."

"Will you tell her about the bet, or will that be our little secret?" That was Gavin Miller speaking, amusement coloring his tone.

Chloe froze. They'd made some sort of a bet about her?

"I say keep it to yourself." Luke Archer was in there too. "It might just make her mad."

The quarterback was part of it as well. And he thought she'd be mad.

"Why wouldn't she be flattered to know she won the bet for you?" Miller asked. "By the way, I can see why you chose her. She's got that certain something. Well done."

It sounded like Nathan had deliberately picked her for something. Was it about seducing her? Had he told them about that? Anger and humiliation welled up in her chest.

"You're both getting way ahead of yourselves." Nathan's voice sliced sharp. "I'll take Chloe home right now if you don't back off."

"Hey, talk to Miller, not me," Luke said.

Gavin's laugh felt like it was pounding against her temples. "You've got it bad, my boyo. I'll behave, if only so I can watch you guard your Chloe like a dog with a bone."

"You're an idiot," Nathan said, but he sounded more irritated than angry.

Chloe realized the discussion was ending and she needed to get out of there. Moving fast in the sky-high heels wasn't easy, but she managed to reach the safety of the ladies' room before the three men came out of their powwow.

She sank down on the same vanity stool she'd vacated a few minutes before. She could feel hot, furious tears welling up in her eyes. Would Nathan really have talked about sex with her to his two *acquaintances*?

She couldn't believe that of him. Yes, he was arrogant and over-bearing, but he wouldn't share their intimacy. He wasn't that kind of man. It had to be something else. She gulped in a few deep breaths to fight back the tears. Gavin had at least pretended not to be aware that she'd temped for Nathan, so he didn't know even the basic details about their relationship.

Then what on earth was the bet about?

She couldn't sit in the ladies' room much longer or Nathan would wonder what was wrong. She forced herself to stand up even though her knees felt wobbly. As she searched for her courage, Nathan's words echoed through her mind. She'd given him things he hadn't gotten from anyone else. The knowledge sent a surge of reinforcing strength up her backbone.

She smoothed the exquisite blue lace of her dress down over her hips. No stupid male bet was going to keep her from having her Cinderella moment. She would admire all the beautiful clothes, enjoy every bite of gourmet food, and tuck away memories of her conversations with all the famous people. Taking one last look in the mirror, Chloe walked out of the ladies' room and into the glittering crowd.

Although it was well after midnight, Nathan leaned on the railing of the terrace, gazing across the Hudson. The big river reflected the lights from both shores while a few sparkling stars managed to compete with the million-kilowatt glow. A sharp, chilly breeze flattened his shirt against his chest, making him shudder.

He stared into the night, knowing Chloe was there across the river, tucked into her bed. Would she dream of him, or would the distance he felt widening between them tonight send her dreams in another direction?

He gripped the cold metal of the railing as he frowned. Something had happened during the evening to make her pull away from him. All during dinner, he'd caught her slanting looks at him. And they weren't the kinds of glances that said she was thinking about sex in the Rolls. Although when they finally got away from the damned party, she had responded to his touch with an almost desperate abandon that had surprised him. She'd seemed to be channeling some pent-up emotion into making love. He just couldn't figure out what that emotion was.

Miller and Archer had stuck to their promises, carrying on perfectly normal conversations with Chloe. She'd held her own with them, even though on the way to the dinner she'd confessed to being nervous. An odd sense of pride swelled inside him. His Chloe didn't let anyone intimidate her.

Including him.

She still hadn't invited him to dinner with her grandmother. He respected her love and concern for Grandmillie, but it was putting a roadblock in their relationship. There had to be a way to get around it.

His smile faded as a realization hit him: Chloe didn't want to get around it. She showed no signs of frustration at having to snatch a few hours here and there with him. He was the one who kept badgering her for more time together.

Straightening away from the railing, Nathan paced back and forth across the tiled floor, reliving every minute of the last two weeks with Chloe. He examined each encounter, allocating words and actions into imaginary columns marked "she cares" or "she doesn't."

He stopped as something twisted in his chest. The final tally was inconclusive.

Pivoting on his heel, he walked back inside. There was one thing he could do to tip the scales in his favor.

Nathan walked down the hallway, trying to remember where the family sword was stored. Chloe wanted him to bring it to the wedding as a peace offering to his father. The irony of that was not lost on him.

He paced through the downstairs rooms, looking for the wooden case that held the antique artifact. Most of these rooms were used for business and charitable entertaining, so he didn't spend much time scanning the decor. The living room, dining room, and media room were a bust. He knew it wasn't in his office or den. That left the library, a room he'd expended some thought on setting up but then rarely occupied. As he entered, the aroma of leather and paper made him inhale in appreciation. He'd become so tied to his electronics that he'd forgotten the delights of physical books. He scanned the floor-to-ceiling bookshelves, enjoying the glint of gold leaf on bindings.

And there it was, sitting in its own niche on the shelves—a simple mahogany box, long and flat with two polished brass hasps secured with matching padlocks.

The sight of it churned up a storm of emotions. His earliest memories included that wooden container. It had been kept in the family china cabinet in every house they lived in. His father would open the cabinet's glass doors and lift out the box, placing it reverently on the dining room table. When Nathan was a little boy, he'd stood on a chair as his father unlocked the small padlocks and opened the hinged lid to reveal the sword and scabbard nestled in the custom-made compartments lined with blue-black velvet. He had learned the simplest version of the sword's story as soon as he was old enough to understand the words. As he grew older, his father added more and more detail until Nathan could repeat the sword's entire history.

On his twelfth birthday, Nathan had been given the solemn and weighty responsibility of caring for the sword. His father had handed him a flat, featherlight package wrapped in blue-and-gold-striped paper. Nathan opened it to find a pair of lint-free cotton gloves. He'd known immediately what they signified, since he'd watched his father wax and oil the sword while wearing a similar pair many times. His heart had leaped at this rare sign of his father's trust.

Of course, the trust had lasted only about two years. Once he and his father began their battle over Nathan's future, Nathan deliberately shirked his duty as sword polisher. He'd never done damage to the sword, though, even at the height of hostilities. He could be grateful for that.

Nathan walked over to the shelf and lifted the box down the way his father had, placing it on the huge leather-topped desk in the center of the room. The key lay on top of the box, since there were no children in his house who needed protection from the sharp blade. Or vice versa.

The brass of the key and the padlocks gleamed in the soft light of the overhead chandelier. Probably Ed's handiwork. Ed respected the sword as much as the general did. Removing the padlocks, Nathan flicked open the hasps and raised the lid.

He was struck by how utilitarian the sword was. In his memories, it glowed in its nest of velvet. But this was a weapon that had been used in battle on a regular basis. There were nicks on the blade to prove it. The basket hilt was dull steel with a tint of ancient rust, and its curlicues were not delicate ornaments but bold swirls and bars meant to protect its owner's hand from an attacker's slashing blade. The brass scabbard was a little fancier and more polished because it had been an officer's sword, but it also showed the scratches and dents of daily use.

His father had explained that you didn't strip clean a sword like this, because that would wash away its history. You oiled the grip and waxed the blade to preserve its integrity for the next generation. And Nathan had done just that for two years, first with his father coaching him through the steps, and then with his father simply sitting with him, sharing their heritage.

Nathan felt a clench of emotion at the back of his throat. He'd forgotten those times when the two of them would talk as he wiped the sword down with a soft cloth. His father had told him stories of his childhood, of his military training, and even of some of the missions he'd taken part in, although those were heavily edited. Nathan had shared information about school and sports and even his friends. He'd never discussed his fascination with technology, though. That topic brought a tightness to his father's jaw that Nathan had learned it was better to avoid. But those infrequent afternoons had been good ones.

That was what Chloe and her grandmother had all the time.

Nathan gazed down at the sword as he let the memories flow over him. Then he went rummaging through the desk drawers until he found what he was looking for: a box containing lint-free cotton gloves, baby oil, kerosene, a jar of carabellum wax, and several clean cloths. He'd known Ed would keep the supplies near the sword. Lifting the supplies out of the lowest drawer, he shook out the folded piece of felt that lay beneath them, spreading it over the desktop before he pulled on the gloves.

He slipped his fingers under the hilt and blade of the sword and laid it on the felt. Opening the jar of wax, he dipped a cloth in it and began to apply it to the blade with a touch so gentle the sword lay motionless on the felt.

Chapter 26

Chloe shoved the last bobby pin into her neatly twisted bun and scanned her reflection in the mirror. The foundation was doing a decent job of lightening the circles under her eyes. The last twenty-four hours had been tense and sleepless because she'd alternated between trying to persuade herself she wasn't in love with Nathan and wondering exactly what his bet was about.

How stupid was she? She'd known from the beginning that their relationship had an end date. Chloe just wished it wasn't so soon and that she didn't have to be the one to break it off. Although Nathan clearly wasn't in love with her, she kept remembering his statement that she'd brought joy into his life. As ticked off as she was about the existence of the bet, she still hated to cause him pain. Because she didn't want to hurt the man she loved.

With a huff of angry exasperation at herself and Nathan, she picked up her lipstick and carefully applied the rose color before tucking the tube into her Alexander McQueen handbag. She couldn't help running an admiring finger over the bag's metallic surface. Then she opened her closet door to check every detail in the full-length mirror.

It was extraordinary how much taller she looked because of the perfect fit of the dress. The sky-high heels lengthened her legs and gave her more height. She arranged the blue wrap around her shoulders, appreciating the way it brought out the blue touches in the dress and the shoes.

This was the armor she wore to face Nathan and his father.

She picked up the purse and went out into the living room to twirl in front of Grandmillie.

Her grandmother pursed her lips and nodded her approval. "I guess those designer clothes do have something special about them. Not that I approve of the ridiculous prices, but that dress looks like it was made for you."

"I feel like a million bucks," Chloe confessed. "Fortunately, the outfit didn't cost quite that much."

Grandmillie snorted out a laugh before a look of sadness crossed her face. "I wish you could buy prettier clothes for yourself all the time."

Chloe came over to kneel beside her grandmother. "No matter how great a job I have, I'd never be able to pay for this myself. I only agreed to buy this because I didn't want to embarrass Nathan in front of his father, especially since they have a strained relationship. I feel like I'm going to be examined under a microscope."

The sound of a powerful automobile engine signaled Nathan's arrival. Chloe gave Grandmillie a quick squeeze of the hand and an air kiss before she straightened. "Time to join the jet set."

"Cinderella going to the ball," Grandmillie said. "You deserve it."

Chloe scooped up the handbag and headed for the front door. The bell rang just as she turned the knob to open it.

The Nathan who stood on her front porch was every inch the CEO in a tailored navy suit, a white shirt, and a red power tie. The gleaming waves of his hair were subdued, and his black wing tips shone like mirrors. Even his face seemed carved into commanding angles.

"In full intimidation mode, I see," Chloe said, although her heart and her pulse leaped at the sight.

That loosened the tense set of his jaw. He gave her an appreciative scan and then brushed his lips against her cheek. "You are every inch my match."

"Me, intimidating?" Chloe shook her head, but she liked the idea.

"Beauty can be very formidable." He stepped into the foyer and glanced through the door to the living room. "May I say hello to your grandmother?"

"Of course." Chloe led the way through the door.

"You look worthy of my granddaughter," Grandmillie said.

He smiled and Chloe blessed her grandmother as the tension in his shoulders eased a bit more. "That's a high compliment," he said with a slight bow. Reaching into his pocket, he pulled out a business card and handed it to Grandmillie. "Dr. Cavill will be at the wedding, so I wanted to give you his partner's direct phone number, just in case you need it. Please don't hesitate to call for any reason at all."

Chloe held her breath, but Grandmillie didn't throw the card in his face. Instead she read the name on it. "Dorothy Scott. Nice solid name, and a woman. I like that."

Chloe cast a grateful glance at Nathan. She'd arranged for their neighbor Lynda to stop in a couple of times to check on her grandmother, but this was an extra level of care. Evidently Grandmillie was willing to accept it from someone other than Chloe.

He tucked Chloe's hand in his elbow. "We should be back by eight at the latest."

"I wish your father much happiness," Grandmillie said. "He's fortunate to get a second chance."

Chloe felt Nathan stiffen as he nodded.

He escorted Chloe out the front door and to the Maserati, open-ing the door and handing her in. As he steered the car down the narrow residential street, he reached across the gearshift to take her hand in his. Chloe used her other hand to trace along his knuckles. She loved the texture of his skin, the cradling strength of his grip, and the sense of connection she felt.

"I brought the sword," he said.

She twisted around to see a long, flat leather case lying on the backseat. He'd listened to her. "I think it's the right thing to do. The family sword should be a part of an important family celebration."

His grip tightened. "*Celebration* might be too happy a word."

"He must be so nervous," Chloe said.

"The general, nervous?" He slanted her a glance of disbelief.

"He's going to be a father again after thirty-odd years."

"Fatherhood didn't bother him. He just went on as he always did, steamrolling over everyone in his path."

"Remember what Grandmillie said about second chances? Maybe he's hoping to be a kinder father this time." She paused. "I won't say a *better* father, because he did something right in raising you."

He squeezed her hand before letting her go to steer the car through traffic. "I suppose he was a good example of what I didn't want to be."

"Sometimes that can be as useful as a role model." Chloe took a breath. "Maybe he just couldn't understand that you weren't like him. Your talents drew you in a direction he hadn't even thought of."

"He's never once come to Trainor Electronics," Nathan said. His jaw looked as though it was carved from granite.

"So he's as stiff-necked and stubborn as you are." But Chloe's heart broke for him. He'd built something spectacular, and his father wouldn't acknowledge it with his presence. "But you'll never con-vince me he's not proud of you."

Nathan made a sound of repudiation. She hoped that the loan of the sword would soften the general's attitude toward his son. The man must be an idiot if he couldn't see how magnificent the child he'd raised had become.

"What's the story behind the sword?" she asked.

"Family lore claims the sword was given to General Nathanael Greene by a British officer who served under Cornwallis in the Revolutionary War."

"Is that who you're named after?"

He shook his head. "My name comes from a Confederate general, Nathan Bedford Forrest, whose career my father particularly admires. He was a brilliant tactician, his men loved him, and his name struck fear in his enemies' hearts."

"He sounds like a good namesake. But tell me the rest of the sword's history."

"The officer gave Nathanael Greene his sword because he was impressed with the superb strategy General Greene displayed in retreating." Nathan gave a bitter laugh. "Greene presented the sword to one of his subordinates for bravery on the battlefield. That subordinate happened to be my ancestor, William Trainor."

"Did they actually use it, or is it one of those dressy swords for show?"

"It was used in battle. You can see the nicks and scratches and dents. It's called a three-quarter basket hilt sword, made by Samuel Harvey."

She was impressed. "So it must be valuable even apart from your family's connection."

"More than you know," he said with an odd note in his voice.

He swung the car onto an access road that led to a manned gate, showing his ID to the guard who waved them through. They drove around a hangar, and there was the now-familiar black-and-silver

Trainor Electronics jet standing on the tarmac. Nathan slotted the car into a marked space along the hangar's wall and twisted toward her in his seat. "Would you humor me with something today?"

She didn't trust his too-guileless smile. "That depends."

He reached into his pocket and brought out two Tiffany boxes. "I would like you to accept these as a loan just for today. Then you can return them to me."

"Forgive me for being suspicious," Chloe said, not moving to take the proffered packages, "but I still have a whole pile of Saks Fifth Avenue boxes in my closet that haven't been returned."

"I'll have everything picked up on Monday. You have my word." He continued to hold the blue boxes out to her. "I'd like to see if my choices suit you. Just for my own satisfaction."

"I'm on to your tricks," Chloe said. But it seemed ungracious and even unkind to refuse when he was so on edge. "But I'll pretend you fooled me this time."

She put one of the boxes in her lap and untied the white satin ribbon from the other one. Inside lay the sapphire-and-diamond bangle from the auction. Chloe touched the sparkling stones with her fingertip. "Your bid won."

He took the open box from her. "Now the other one."

She tugged the ribbon free and lifted the lid to reveal the matching earrings. "I have to admit, these are perfect for this dress."

Gratification lit his eyes. "My thought exactly. However, if you prefer to wear your pearls, please don't feel obligated to wear these."

The cultured pearl studs she wore were no match for Nathan's gift. She removed them and hooked the Tiffany earrings through her lobes.

"Let me help you with the bracelet," Nathan said. He deftly flicked it open before fitting it around her wrist and snapping it closed. He held her wrist to admire the bangle, his long fingers warm where they lay against her skin. With a swift movement, he lifted her arm to brush a kiss on the sensitive skin on the inside of her wrist, his breath tickling across her hand. "Thank you for indulging me."

As she watched the bracelet send a confetti of light dancing around the car's interior, Chloe knew it was herself she was indulging, and in more ways than wearing expensive jewelry.

Chapter 27

As the jet had gotten closer to landing, Nathan had become increasingly withdrawn, his gaze fixed on the blue sky outside the plane's window. When he no longer responded, his friends had stopped the friendly ribbing that was meant to relax him while it kept Chloe in a ripple of laughter all during the flight southward. Once they touched down, Nathan had collected the sword and escorted the group to the waiting limo, his shoulders held rigid.

Now Chloe sat in the limousine beside a silent Nathan while Ben and Ed chatted in the seat perpendicular to them. Despite all the constraints she felt, she wanted to soothe his strain away. However, the best she could do was lay her hand over his, stilling his fingers from drumming on the leather of the seat. She couldn't even say anything comforting to him since she didn't want to embarrass him in front of his friends.

So she intertwined her fingers with his and gave him her best smile of support when he glanced down at her for a moment. She was rewarded with a softening of the lines around his mouth. He lifted her hand and kissed the back of it.

Chloe caught the quick look of concern Ed cast Nathan's way. So she wasn't the only one who'd noticed the tightness in his jaw.

The limo swung past brick gates and wound through the military base. Chloe caught glimpses of people dressed in everything from full dress uniforms to various shades of camouflage. It struck her that Nathan had worn Marine Corps colors too, and she wondered if he was aware of it.

The limousine glided to a halt outside a large brick church with white trim. A clot of young men and women in dress uniforms walked through the church's door, their posture impeccable. When Nathan swung the car door open, the soft, warm air felt like summer. Autumn had not yet arrived in North Carolina.

"The general picked his wedding date right. This is one of the three days the weather isn't miserable here," Ed said, as he exited out the other side.

Once again, Nathan offered Chloe his hand. This time, though, she had the sense that she was the one giving support, as his grip was firm to the point of near discomfort.

Ben came around the car. "We'll go find our own seats," he said. "You see if you can track down the general before the service begins."

Nathan nodded as he hefted the sword case and led Chloe toward a side door of the chapel. "You've been here before," she said.

"Every Sunday for all the years we were stationed here."

She tried to think cool thoughts as she almost jogged to keep up with his long strides, but when he pulled open the door, she sighed in relief as a cloud of cool air billowed out. He towed her through another door into a small carpeted room. A tall silver-haired man in the dark-blue jacket and black belt of a Marine officer's dress uniform stood with his back to them, his hat tucked under his arm. He was speaking with a short, wiry gray-haired man, also in uniform, who was facing them.

Nathan's grip on her hand became crushing, but he wore a mask of polite indifference on his face. "Uncle Fred, it's good to see you," he said.

"Nathan, you son of a gun," the shorter man said, a grin creasing his tanned skin. "Glad you could make it."

The silver-haired man pivoted slowly, as though he wasn't sure what he would find behind him. Chloe's breath hitched as she saw his face. There was no question he was Nathan's father. The resemblance was extraordinary, right down to the way the general's hair waved away from his forehead.

"Dad, Uncle Fred," Nathan said, "I'd like you to meet Chloe Russell."

She had to tug her hand loose from his to hold it out. "General Trainor, it's a pleasure," she said.

The older man was wearing white gloves, and he quickly stripped his right one off before taking her hand in a dry, firm hold. "A delightful surprise to meet you," he said, his deep voice carrying a noticeable southern drawl. He gave her a quick penetrating look before shifting his gaze back to his son.

Chloe felt invisible as the two men locked eyes. They were matched in height and breadth of shoulder. The father was only slightly thicker through the waist than his son.

The general held out his hand to Nathan. "Thank you for coming."

For a moment, she was afraid Nathan would spurn his father's handshake, but he briefly gripped the outstretched hand before holding up the leather case. "I thought you'd want this for the ceremony," he said.

The general's attention had clearly been on his son and not on the luggage he carried, because surprise flickered in his eyes. "You thought right," he said, taking the case.

Nathan nodded. "Congratulations."

Then he took Chloe's hand and started toward the door. She wanted to scream in frustration. The two men hadn't exchanged more than a dozen words, and those had been stiff and formal. When Nathan suddenly halted, she happily came to a stop, hoping he would offer something more to his father. He didn't turn but simply looked over his shoulder to say, "I'll need the sword back after the wedding."

She had partially swiveled so she could see the general's face. A strange look crossed it—a mixture of shock and gladness.

Then Nathan was moving again, and she was being towed along with him. She threw an apologetic smile to Uncle Fred, who nodded back with a rueful look.

"You and your father look so much alike," she whispered as they approached the double doors that led into the nave of the chapel.

"And there the resemblance ends," he muttered, relinquishing her hand when a young Marine offered her his arm to escort her down the aisle.

"Bride or groom?" the young man asked, so he could seat them on the proper side of the church.

"Family on the groom's side," Chloe said.

"We'll sit with Ben and Ed," Nathan contradicted from just behind her. "They're up near the front."

Chloe glanced around as she paced up the aisle beside her escort. When Nathan had mentioned a chapel, she'd expected something small and intimate. This was a huge open space of white walls lit by arched stained-glass windows under a ceiling supported by heavy, dark trusses. Row upon row of straight wooden pews marched down the nave in a neat military progression. She wasn't sure how big a battalion was, but she imagined you could fit one in the church.

As they got closer to the altar, the pews were filled from the aisle to their midpoints. She spotted Ben and Ed three rows from the front and steered her escort toward them. Nathan gestured her aside so he could slide in first, giving her the aisle view.

Ed and Nathan exchanged murmurs, neither of them looking happy, and she suspected Ed was trying to persuade Nathan to sit in the front pew. On the bride's side there were several family members, but the groom's family pew held only one older couple and a single man.

Nathan must have followed her gaze because he said, "Those are my other two uncles and my aunt-in-law."

Chloe hesitated, but the pew looked so empty. She'd persuaded Nathan to bring the sword. She should at least attempt to push him another step toward reconciliation with his father. "I think we should sit up there. Otherwise the bride's side wins."

He looked down at her with an odd glint in his eye. "You're being Machiavellian again." He turned and said something to Ed before taking her hand. "You've played on my competitive nature."

She gave him a dazzling smile as they stood and walked to their new seats. This time Nathan sat between her and his relatives, creating a barrier to conversation. He nodded to his uncles and aunt but didn't offer to introduce her.

"You're being rude," she whispered.

"I'm keeping you out of trouble."

"Trouble for me or for you?"

"Both." He laced his fingers with hers and stared straight ahead. She felt his nerves in the sporadic press of his fingers and saw it in the tiny tic of a muscle in his jaw.

"At least we have a chance against the bride's side now. There are only eight of them. And they're all short," she whispered.

His grip on her hand eased, and the corner of his mouth twitched.

The brash, festive notes of a trumpet rang through the church, making her start. A door near the altar opened to allow General Trainor and Uncle Fred to walk through it with the measured pace of soldiers on parade. They took their positions and stood ramrod straight and unsmiling.

The trumpet was joined by the organ in the "Trumpet Voluntary." Chloe twisted in her seat to see a young man and woman, in uniforms from two different services, pace up the aisle in that same controlled stride.

"My cousins Emily and Christopher," Nathan murmured. "Navy and Air Force."

Behind them came one woman, dressed in a simple sheath of peach satin, holding a bouquet of cream roses.

"Angel's sister, Sarita." Nathan's voice went tight.

As Sarita reached the front of the church, the music changed to the "Wedding March," and the congregation stood. A small woman wearing a short, floating cream chiffon dress started down the aisle. Her bouquet held peach roses, and the same flowers were woven into the dark-brown braid circling her head like a coronet. As she came closer, a waft of air-conditioning flattened the chiffon against the bride's stomach, and Chloe could see the telltale swell of pregnancy.

She turned forward as the bride passed and caught an expression of such heartbreaking joy and uncertainty on the groom's face that tears pricked at her eyes.

"Your father loves her," she whispered.

He glanced down at her. "He loved my mother. He loved me. It made no difference in how he treated us."

Chloe sucked in a breath as the truth hit her. Nathan disliked Angel because his father treated her differently—better—than he had his first wife. He didn't want his father to be kinder and more considerate of his second wife. It would make his mother seem less worthy somehow. She could understand and even sympathize with his feelings, but they would separate him from the father whose approval he still sought.

She tucked her hand into the crook of Nathan's elbow, hoping she could pull some of the tension from him.

The minister motioned them to sit, and the ceremony proceeded. When Nathan's father kissed his new wife, he did so with a tenderness and passion that brought forth a soft, collective sigh from the female wedding guests.

"We ask the congregation to precede the bride and groom from the church for the traditional arch of sabers," the minister announced before he gave the blessing and the organ and trumpet once again swelled into triumphant sound.

Chloe was excited about seeing the famous crossed swords. As the family followed the three wedding attendants down the aisle, she noticed the curious gazes aimed at Nathan and her. People at the base were interested in the famous prodigal son.

They came out the doors to find four Marines indicating where guests should stand on either side of the walk leading from the church. The southern sun shed enough heat to make it uncomfortably warm, but the bulk of the guests were military and stood straight and tall in their dark jackets with their white hats on. As soon as the last guest exited, Chloe heard a barked command from inside. Into the light marched a Marine with two lines of four of his fellow soldiers following him in perfect unison. They proceeded between the two walls of guests until their leader snapped another command. The two lines halted, pivoted, and drew their swords as one, holding the sabers point down until two more Marines reopened the church doors.

The bride and groom emerged and stopped as the honor guard's commander brought his troops to attention, their swords held upright against their shoulders.

"Present swords," he ordered.

The sword tips crossed, forming the arch. General Trainor and Angel trod solemnly through the arch. As they passed, each pair of

Marines lowered their swords back to their sides until the couple reached the final two. Those brought their sabers down in front of the wedding couple, forcing them to a halt. The honor guard's commander lowered his voice to say, "You must kiss the bride to pass."

"By whose orders?" the general snapped back.

"Cupid's, sir," the commander said, breaking into a grin.

"Never heard of him," the general said. "Must be some rock from Washington." Everyone except the honor guard laughed. They were still standing stiffly at attention. "Well, at least it's an order that won't get me in trouble." He bent and kissed Angel softly on the lips.

The obstructing swords were lifted, and the guests applauded as the general and his bride slid into a waiting limousine. The sword bearers returned their weapons to their scabbards with a snick of metal, and the crowd dispersed to their cars.

Chloe had been so caught up in the beauty and precision of the ceremony that she hadn't noticed the perspiration trickling down her spine. As Nathan drew her toward their limo where it waited just across the road, she grimaced at the dampness. "That's an impressive way to make an exit," she said.

"The Marines are good at pomp and circumstance," Nathan said in a tone that indicated he wasn't impressed at all.

Ed and Ben caught up with them.

"Why couldn't they do that indoors?" Ben complained, blotting his forehead with his coat sleeve.

"Marines don't feel heat or cold," Nathan said with that same edge.

"The hell they don't," Ed said. "They're just tougher than a little weather."

"I thought it was magnificent," Chloe said.

"They know how to put on a show," Ben agreed, standing aside as Nathan handed Chloe into the backseat.

She slid gratefully onto the cool, smooth leather. The driver had placed glasses of iced water with lemon slices in the cup holders.

Chloe snatched one up, drinking down half of it in one long, deliciously chilled gulp.

Ben dropped onto his seat and grabbed another glass. "What I wouldn't give to just pour this over my head," he said.

"The officers' club is air-conditioned," Nathan said as he folded himself in beside Chloe. He surprised her by taking her hand. She scooted closer to him since he seemed to want her physical presence.

After a short drive, the limousine drew up in front of another white-trimmed brick building. This one had two long, covered porticoes leading to the doors. Once again, they followed a crowd of uniformed guests into the club, where air-conditioning welcomed them. They passed walls covered with the Marine insignia and arrived in a large room with deep blue patterned carpeting, brass chandeliers, and white linen–covered tables set around a parquet dance floor. Classical music played softly as the bride and groom stood near the door greeting their guests.

Chloe decided not to comment on how the bride radiated happiness, but it was true. Maybe it was because she was pregnant, but Angel's face glowed, her smile lighting up every time she received a guest's good wishes. When she looked up at her new husband, the smile both grew and softened.

Nathan's grip on her hand became tighter the closer they got to the newlyweds. She reached across and laid her other hand over the back of his, making her borrowed bracelet glitter. "I won't leave you, I promise," she murmured.

"I'm sorry," he said, easing the pressure.

Then it was their turn. Chloe braced herself, wondering what sort of greeting Angel would give them. From what Ed had told her, Nathan had not been cordial toward the woman he considered his mother's usurper.

But the bride's smile did not falter or dim. "Nathan, you were so good to come," she said, putting her hands on his shoulders so he would bend to let her kiss his cheek. "I know it wasn't easy for you."

Chloe felt him stiffen. "It seemed like too important an occasion to miss," he said. "Angel, meet Chloe Russell." He moved Chloe forward so she stood in front of him almost like a shield.

"Best wishes to you for a happy future," Chloe said, holding out her hand.

Angel drew her in for a hug. "Thank you, my dear. I feel as though I'm carrying our future with me," she said, resting one palm on the soft swell of her stomach. "Strange miracles sometimes happen."

A shudder passed through Nathan. Chloe quickly moved sideways to get him away from Angel. That brought them face-to-face with General Trainor.

"Congratulations, sir," Nathan said, squaring his shoulders and offering his hand to his father.

Ironically, Nathan's posture was more rigid than the general's. The older man pulled his son in for one of those quick, hard hugs men give each other. Chloe let her hand slide loose from Nathan's arm so he couldn't use her for that shielding maneuver again.

When the general stepped back, Chloe could see a glitter of moisture in his eyes. Hope bloomed in her chest. The father was prepared to embrace his son. Now she just had to get Nathan to meet his father halfway . . . or even a quarter of the way. She got the sense that General Trainor would be willing to go the extra distance.

The general touched the hilt of the antique sword that hung in its scabbard on his belt. "Having this with me for the ceremony was something I hadn't hoped for and probably didn't deserve. Thank you for your generosity."

"You're thanking the wrong person," Nathan said, putting his arm around Chloe's waist to nudge her in front of him. "She's responsible for the sword's presence."

When disappointment shadowed the general's eyes, Chloe wanted to stomp her stiletto heel hard on the arch of Nathan's foot. "He's exaggerating," she said. "I'm sure you know that Nathan doesn't do anything he doesn't want to." She deliberately did not look at Nathan to see how he reacted to her statement. Instead she stood on tiptoe to give the general a peck on the cheek. "Many congratulations, sir. You and Angel make a lovely couple."

"Well, she's lovely, and I make us a couple," Nathan's father said, a spark of humor on his face. He took both of Chloe's hands and gave them a squeeze. "It's good to have you here, young lady. I'm glad my son brought you." He gave Nathan a shrewd look. "Or you brought my son. Either way works for me."

Chloe slanted a look up at Nathan. His brows were drawn together in what she thought might be regret. "I wish you and Angel happiness together," he said. "I think you've earned a chance at it."

His father's posture stiffened and Chloe waited to see what that meant. "That's a good wish," the general said, "and a surprising one. I accept it with humility and gratitude." He shifted his gaze back to Chloe. "Stick with him, Chloe. We Trainor men improve with age."

She gave the general a smile as they moved away to let the next guest offer congratulations. Nathan led her toward the bar across the room, muttering, "Let's get something to dull our senses."

"Is it that hard to be civil to your father?" she asked with genuine puzzlement.

He stopped in the middle of the dance floor and frowned down at her. "Civil, no. Sincere, yes. Celebrating his marriage to his pregnant girlfriend is not something I'm able to feel joy about."

"You sounded sincere when you said he deserved a chance at happiness. And it surprised him."

He gave a tight smile. "Surprising the general is an accomplishment in itself." He looked down at the floor. "My mother's mental health issues were not his fault. He didn't handle them well, but he didn't create them." He took a deep breath. "No one deserves to go through the hell of having his wife commit suicide."

He lifted his eyes to hers, and they were bleak with pain. She wanted to wrap herself around him and make him forget. Instead she cupped her palm against his cheek, feeling the satin of his freshly shaved skin. "You don't need a drink. You've forgiven him."

He made a gesture of disagreement. "There's a difference between understanding and forgiveness."

"One leads to the other."

"You're an eternal optimist." He took her hand away from his face and used it to move her toward the bar again. "A glass of champagne and a scotch on the rocks."

"Here you are, Mr. Trainor." The bartender handed the slim glass flute to Nathan with a smile before he picked up a scotch bottle. He was a short, sturdy man, his sandy hair shot through with streaks of silver.

"Thanks," Nathan said, passing the flute to Chloe as recognition dawned in his eyes. "Dino Sparks," he said. "I can't believe you're still here. How are you? And when the hell did you start calling me Mr. Trainor?"

The two men shook hands. "You're a big shot in New York now," Dino said, going back to pouring the scotch.

"I wouldn't be if you hadn't taught me everything I know about electrical wiring."

Dino's face lit up, but he shook his head. "I showed you a few tricks, that's all. You got smarter than me fast."

"Chloe, I'd like you to meet my mentor, Dino. I did a lot of my best tinkering in his workshop. I think I still owe him a replacement tone probe amplifier." The lines around Nathan's mouth had lightened as he introduced them.

She shook hands with the bartender. "I love meeting Nathan's old friends. Did he ever blow anything up?"

Dino burst out laughing. "Ever? He caught something on fire at least once a week."

Nathan grinned. It was like watching him when he slept; he became a younger, more carefree version of himself. "I did it on purpose, you know."

"He liked to set off the fire alarm," Dino said, nodding. He looked around and lowered his voice. "Just to annoy his father."

Chloe wished Dino hadn't mentioned the general, but Nathan's grin didn't waver. "And it worked," he said with relish.

Just as she was about to prod Dino for more stories, Uncle Fred's voice boomed through the loudspeakers. "General and Mrs. Trainor invite everyone to join them on the floor to share their first dance as a married couple."

The lilting strains of a waltz swelled through the room as the general led Angel to the center of the room. After a second of standing in perfect stillness, Nathan's father spun his new wife into a graceful turn in time to the music. Guests lined the edge of the dance floor, watching the couple move together with fluid ease. After one circuit of the floor, the general barked, "Does no one know how to follow a simple order? Get out here and dance."

Laughter rose from the crowd, and a few couples did some tentative box steps. None could hold a candle to the general and his bride.

Suddenly, Nathan took the champagne flute from Chloe's hand and set it on the bar beside his scotch. "Let's give them some competition."

"Wait . . . what?"

"We're obeying the general's orders." He wrapped his arm around her waist and propelled her toward the dance floor while she tried to walk slowly, hoping the music would change. She was wearing high slender heels and a straight skirt, not optimal waltzing attire. Not to mention the fact that she hadn't had a waltz partner in, oh, ten years at least.

The music was still going when Nathan led her onto the parquet and turned her around to face him. She took a deep breath and put her left hand on his shoulder, feeling the solidity of him through the light wool of his suit. When he put his hand on the small of her back, she felt a zing of exhilaration along with her nerves. Then he took her right hand in his, his arm strong and firm so she could rely on it for guidance. They stood still, looking into each other's eyes for a moment as the music came to the end of a phrase. She shifted her grip on his shoulder, and he gave a tiny nod.

Then he was spinning her around the floor with the same expertise as his father. For the first few steps she was stiff with worry that she would stumble and embarrass both of them.

"You're thinking too much," Nathan murmured as he stopped twirling to allow her to catch her breath and balance for a split second. "I'll support you."

"I—" Chloe shut up as he swung her into another dizzying circle. He flattened his palm on her back and pressed her closer so their bodies were touching. Now she could feel the shift in his weight, the subtle lean to one side or another, the change of angle in his elbow, and she could let him take her wherever he wanted.

She forgot they were competing with the general. She forgot that Ed, Ben, and a platoon of Marines were watching. She even forgot the bet. It was all Nathan, his gray eyes locked on her face, the strength of his arms enveloping her, the heady feeling of melding together both bodies and minds to move as one. She wanted the music to go on forever.

But it stopped and applause rippled around them.

Nathan finished the turn and brought them to a halt, his eyes lit with something like the same elation she felt. "You make a good partner in all kinds of situations," he said.

Her delight dimmed at his ambiguous words. All the realities of the situation crashed back into her.

"I see those dance classes your mother forced you to take weren't wasted." General Trainor walked up to them, his arm around Angel's waist. He smiled at Chloe. "The mothers of all the teenage girls got up the money to start a dancing class, but they needed partners. So the teenage boys got to attend free, which made their mothers apply serious pressure."

Nathan didn't smile. "Once we found out we were not only allowed, but expected, to put our arms around the girls, it wasn't so hard to persuade us."

Chloe smiled for him. "I can imagine the hormones raging in that room."

"My cousins Brenda and Sally went to that class," Angel said. "They spent half their time moving the boys' hands back up to their waists."

Chloe slanted a glance up at Nathan. He still refused to smile. When she looked back at Angel, the other woman gave her an almost imperceptible shrug, as if to say they had both tried their best.

Fortunately, another couple came to speak with the newlyweds, so Chloe tugged Nathan off the dance floor.

"You know, I actually enjoyed dancing with you," she said. "Until you ruined it by making it about your father."

Although he didn't flinch, she could tell that she'd startled him. "It wasn't about my father when we were dancing." He stroked his thumb over the skin on the inside of her wrist. "I wanted to waltz you right out of the room and into a closet where I could lock the door and have you up against the wall." His voice was low and intense.

"That was only because you thought you were winning the dance contest." But his touch and his words sent a streak of electric arousal up her arm and back down low in her belly.

"No, it was because your body and mine were perfectly attuned. I could practically feel your thoughts through my hands. I wanted to be inside you with that happening."

Chloe swallowed hard as his words vibrated through her, spinning into a tightly coiled ball of sheer desire between her legs. "Where's that closet you mentioned?" she managed to choke out.

His thumb went still as his grip on her hand tightened. "I can find one in sixty seconds flat."

For a moment she was tempted. Their time was running out and she wanted to store up memories. She glanced around and caught sight of Ed and Ben, talking earnestly to a group of uniformed men and women. She shook her head. "Maybe later. Right now, we have to be good guests."

"I see I'll have to ply you with champagne."

Raising her eyes to his face, she nearly went up in flames in the heat of his gaze. "Totally unnecessary. Just dance with me again."

He smiled with a wicked edge. "Don't they say dancing is a vertical expression of a horizontal desire?"

"Except we're planning to stay vertical with our desire."

"We're very adaptable that way."

Chloe's phone shrilled in the special tone reserved for calls from Grandmillie. One small, selfish part of her wanted to cry out in disappointment at the interruption of this hot and sexy banter with Nathan. But her heart twisted with fear as she fumbled at the catch of her handbag. Grandmillie knew where she was. Only an extreme emergency would cause her to call Chloe.

"It's your grandmother," Nathan guessed as he scanned her face. The hungry glint in his eyes faded as concern took its place.

She nodded as she swiped her finger across the phone's screen and lifted it to her ear. "Grandmillie? Are you okay?"

"It's Lynda. I'm at the hospital with Millie. She didn't want me to call you, but I thought you'd want to know."

Chloe reached out blindly to take Nathan's hand as the word *hospital* walloped her with dizzying force. He closed his fingers around hers in a comforting grip.

"Thank you for overruling her." The buzz of conversation was making it hard to hear her neighbor's voice. "Wait, let me find a quieter place to talk."

Without a word, Nathan put his arm around her waist and led her toward a side door. It opened into an empty hallway. He released her and pulled the door closed, shutting out the noise.

"I'm here," Chloe said. "What happened?"

"She blacked out and fell again. She called me when she came to because she didn't want to bother you at the wedding. Since it's Saturday, I took her to the hospital. She's awake and speaking clearly, so there doesn't seem to be any permanent damage. The doctor says she'll be okay."

"This is the second time in two weeks," Chloe said, rubbing at her chest as though she could unravel the knot her heart was clenched in.

"That's why I thought I should call. I made her give me her cell phone so it would do that special ring. I practically had to wrestle it out of her grip."

"Lynda, you are so wonderful." Chloe could barely speak through the tears of appreciation.

"Hey, Millie's been great to my kids. If it hadn't been for her, I wouldn't have found out about Joey's problems with the third-grade bullies."

"I don't know if she told you, but I'm in North Carolina right now. I'll get back as soon as I can." Guilt crashed over Chloe. Nathan would insist on taking her back to New Jersey. He might not see his father again for another two years.

"I hear you took a private jet there." Lynda gave an admiring whistle. "Millie says to tell you not to rush back. Stay and enjoy the wedding or she'll sign up for Crestmont the minute she gets out of the hospital."

Chloe could hear her grandmother's voice in her mind, and it made her smile through her concern. "Sounds like she's back to her usual self."

"Just a minute," Lynda said. Chloe heard some rustling and clicking. Then Lynda spoke again, her voice low. "I didn't want her to hear me, but I think she's scared. Not about being in the hospital but about falling again."

"I'm worried about that too," Chloe said as regret pinched at her. She'd been too busy with Nathan to pay close enough attention to Grandmillie's health issues. "We need to find out why it keeps happening."

"Another doctor just came in, so I've got to go. Don't worry, Pete's home with the kids, so I can stay until you get back."

"Thank you so much," Chloe said, trying to project the overwhelming gratitude she felt through the phone, but Lynda has disconnected.

Chloe lowered the phone.

"I've already texted the pilot to prep for takeoff, and the limo is waiting at the door," Nathan said, looking up from the phone he held in his palm. "We need to let Ben and Ed know the jet will be back for them. You can tell me what happened when we're on our way."

She shook her head. "I want you to stay here. It's your father's wedding day. You shouldn't miss it."

Nathan slid his phone into his breast pocket. "I'm not letting you go alone. End of discussion." He started toward the door.

She didn't have the time or the strength to argue with him, so she allowed him to escort her back into the dining room. The music had changed to something more contemporary, and the dance floor was filled with uniformed couples flinging their bodies around with gleeful abandon.

Ed and Ben, however, were still in conversation with the same group with whom she'd noticed them before. Nathan took her hand and strode through the crowded room. Guests gave him appraising glances and moved out of his way, just as they did for his father.

When Ed saw Nathan, he stepped out of the group. "What's the problem?" the older man asked.

"Chloe's grandmother is in the hospital. I'm taking her home to New Jersey. The jet will come back for you and Ben."

Ed looked at Chloe and evidently didn't like what he saw. "I'll come with you. I can help with logistics while you stay with Ms. Russell."

Chloe opened her mouth to protest, but Nathan squeezed her hand and nodded. "We'd appreciate that."

Ben joined them. "What's going on?"

Nathan explained again. "Let's say good-bye to the general and head out," Ben said instantly.

"Please, don't leave on my account," Chloe said as guilt piled on guilt. "Your friends are here. I feel terrible about taking you away."

"I'm a doctor," Ben pointed out. "I'll be a hell of a lot more useful than some computer nerd."

Ben's insult had the odd effect of comforting Chloe. He was treating her as part of this tight circle of Nathan's friends.

Nathan's smile flashed briefly. "You'd be as useless as I am without your fancy medical equipment, which my technology powers."

"We can insult each other or we can get Ms. Russell to her grandmother," Ed said. "The general and Mrs. Trainor are at zero nine hundred."

Ben gave Chloe a rueful shrug as he let her pass with Nathan. "Thank you," she said, meaning it. If he spoke with the doctors, they would take Grandmillie's case seriously.

Nathan led her up to his father and Angel. "Our apologies, but Chloe has a family medical emergency," Nathan said. "We have to head back up north immediately."

"Oh, no, I'm so sorry," Angel said, enfolding Chloe in a hug. "We send our prayers with you."

"I'm the one who's sorry to take everyone away early," Chloe said. "But my grandmother is in the hospital."

General Trainor held out his hand to Nathan. "It was good to have you here."

Chloe could hear the depth of sincerity in the general's voice.

"It was good to be here, sir," Nathan said, gripping his father's hand a little longer than a mere handshake. Chloe willed him to say something further.

"The sword!" the general said, his free hand going to where the hilt should have been. "I put it in the office for safekeeping."

"Keep it," Nathan said. "It belongs here with you."

Chapter 28

Chloe spent the short ride to the airfield explaining what had happened to Grandmillie and apologizing for taking everyone away from the wedding. All three men waved away her apologies. As usual, the limo drove directly up to the jet's steps. When they passed the door to the cockpit, Nathan leaned in to say, "Kurt, we're in a hurry."

"Yes, sir," the pilot said, his tone eager. "I've been looking forward to opening up this baby's engines."

The copilot came out to lock the door closed, and then the jet was roaring down the runway. As soon as they were airborne, Ben leaned forward. "Tell me everything you know about your grandmother's health."

"Honestly, I don't know a lot, because Grandmillie doesn't like me to worry," Chloe said. "However, I know she fell for no apparent reason two and a half weeks ago. Her doctor thought she might have had a mild stroke, but there was no permanent damage that he could find."

Ben asked her several more questions, most of which she couldn't answer.

"Do you have her doctor's phone number?" Ben asked. "With your permission, I could speak with him directly."

Chloe wanted to hug him. "Yes, of course, you have my permission." She pulled out her cell phone and gave Ben the number. He unbuckled his seat belt and moved to the back of the cabin to make the phone call.

She watched his retreating back with concern. Why didn't he want to talk to the doctor where she could hear him?

"He doesn't want to scare you with medical jargon," Nathan said, taking her hand.

Chloe shifted her gaze back to him. He was looking at her with a combination of understanding and what might have been envy. He skimmed his thumb over her knuckles. "I guess this is the flipside of caring about someone so much. You worry."

She felt the burn of tears at the back of her eyes as she nodded. "Love makes you vulnerable. But I'd rather worry all the time than not feel it."

Nathan looked down at their hands. "I'm beginning to understand that."

"That was a nice thing you did, telling your father the sword belongs with him."

There was an odd, almost uncertain note in Nathan's voice as he said, "I'm hoping I won't need it."

"Your father was really glad you came to his wedding," she said.

"He said he was."

"Don't you believe him?"

His hold on her tightened, and he raised his eyes to hers. They were shadowed. "I might. I just have to wonder why."

"Because you're his son and he has every reason to be proud of you."

He shook his head. "You don't know my father."

Chloe leaned over the arm of her seat to get closer to him. "I know what I saw in his eyes when he looked at you, and it was pride, pure and simple. He may not understand your passion, but he knows what you've accomplished with it."

She saw the muscles of his throat work as he swallowed, but he shook his head. "He was just savoring his victory in getting me down there."

She wanted to shake him. "You generally have a pretty high opinion of yourself, so I don't get this whole unworthy-son attitude."

Ed gave a muffled cough that she was pretty sure masked a laugh.

"What did your father want you to do with your life?" Nathan asked, ignoring his butler.

Chloe thought about it. "I don't know. He mostly told me about *his* life, but we didn't have a family tradition like yours." She began to understand just how deeply Nathan felt he had let his father down, and she grew angry with the general. "You know, it's your father's fault."

Nathan sat back, his eyebrows raised.

She went on. "He should have had more children if he was so determined to have one in the military. It's just genetics."

Nathan looked at the ceiling.

Chloe grabbed his forearm and shook it. "What I'm trying to say is that your father was wrong in trying to force you into a mold you could never fit. He should have been buying you the latest computer hardware available instead of teaching you how to polish a banged-up old sword. He was looking backward and you were looking forward. I'll let you figure out which is more constructive."

Nathan brought his gaze down and leveled it at her, making her feel as though she was being drilled through with a laser.

Ben chose that moment to walk back to their seating area. "Your grandmother's doctor filled me in on the tests he's run—" He stopped as he ran into the tension vibrating in the air. "What's going on here?"

"Chloe is explaining that my father should have had more children if he had his heart set on continuing the military tradition," Nathan said in an even tone.

"I never thought of that, but it makes sense," Ben said, settling into his seat.

"Enough," Nathan said. "Drop it."

Chloe was happy to change the subject. She was trying to promote a reconciliation between father and son, not make Nathan furious. She nodded to Ben. "Did the tests show anything?"

"They suggest a few possibilities, but I'm not going to make a diagnosis when I've never met the patient, much less examined her," Ben said.

"Thank God you're a better doctor than shrink," Nathan muttered.

Ed intervened, turning the conversation to neutral topics. Chloe listened with only half her attention as she worried about Grandmillie.

The one thing that kept her anchored was the feel of Nathan's warm, strong hand around hers. Even when his anger flared, he hadn't let her go.

Once the jet touched down, the trip to the hospital was a blur of Nathan guiding her through doors, past nurses' stations, and down corridors. People and barriers just gave way before the force of his combined charm and authority. Ben helped with the medical staff and Ed handled logistics, but Nathan was the leader of the group.

They arrived outside Grandmillie's room, and Chloe stopped to take a deep breath, bracing herself for what she might see in the hospital bed.

Nathan took both her hands in his and turned her to look at him. "The nurses all say she's fine."

"But they don't *know* her." She was afraid to find Grandmillie diminished in some way.

"Do you want me to go in with you?"

There was such kindness in his eyes and such strength in his grip that she wanted to lean on him. But she shook her head. "I need to talk to her alone about what happened."

He gave her hands a light squeeze and released them. Chloe pushed the door open more forcefully than necessary and walked in.

Grandmillie lay on her back with her eyes closed, while Lynda sat reading a magazine in a chair alongside her. A couple of monitors blinked by the bed, and an IV line ran to her grandmother's arm. Her usually well-groomed white hair was loose and tangled on the pillow. She looked tiny and frail between the shiny metal railings of the bed.

Anguish slugged Chloe in the chest.

"Chloe!" Lynda said, dropping the magazine. "That was fast."

Grandmillie's eyes snapped open, and she turned to frown at Chloe, all the spit and vinegar back in her face and voice. "I told you not to leave the wedding early."

"Nathan has a very fast jet," Chloe said, trotting to the bed so she could kiss her grandmother's cheek. Tears filled her throat, and she had a hard time saying, "I'm glad to see you're still your usual bossy self."

"I'm due a little more respect than that, young lady," Grandmillie said, but she wrapped her arms around Chloe's neck and drew her in for a hug, a rare show of affection from her independent grandmother.

Chloe returned the hug with feeling, holding her grandmother's thin body as carefully as a baby bird. When they separated, Chloe caught a watery gleam of tears in Grandmillie's eyes, bringing back the air of fragility. Chloe had to blink hard to hide her own reaction. She sat down in an empty chair and took her grandmother's hand before she looked over at Lynda. "Thank you a thousand times over for taking such good care of her."

"Don't mention it." Lynda came around the bed and bent to give Chloe a peck on the cheek. "I'm going to leave you two alone while I get a sandwich in the cafeteria."

Chloe wondered if Nathan was still outside but decided it was too hard to explain him to Lynda. So she just nodded and turned her attention back to her grandmother. "Now tell me what happened."

Her grandmother sighed. "It was the same as the last time. I was in the kitchen making a turkey sandwich. I started to feel short of breath and a bit anxious. My heart felt as though it was flopping around in my chest. I got light-headed and then everything went dark. When I woke up, I was lying on the kitchen floor. I checked the clock and only a couple of minutes had passed." Her hand trembled a little in Chloe's. "As soon as I could, I called Lynda."

"Why didn't you just press the button on your necklace?"

"Phooey! I didn't want all the fuss of an ambulance."

Chloe blew out a breath of exasperation. "If you were having a heart attack, the EMTs could actually help on the way to the hospital."

"I wasn't in any pain, and I wasn't unconscious for very long. I knew I wasn't having a heart attack."

Chloe laid her other hand on top of Grandmillie's. "You have to take better care of yourself for my sake. What would I do without you?"

All weakness fled from her grandmother's face as she smiled at Chloe. "Child, you'd be just fine. You're a strong, bright young woman with a big heart. You'll find a way to fill it when I'm gone, but I don't plan to kick the bucket just yet."

"If you aren't more careful, your plans may not matter." Chloe locked her gaze on her grandmother. "Promise me you'll push the button next time this happens. Otherwise I'm going to quit my job and stay home with you all day long."

Grandmillie's eyebrows rose. "You do that and I'll move to Crestmont."

As she tried to stare down her grandmother, Chloe felt a giggle rise in her throat. "If you move to Crestmont, I'll . . . I'll . . . I don't know what I'll do, but you won't like it." She let the giggle loose.

The corners of Grandmillie's lips twitched upward. "Two Russell women trying to out-threaten one another isn't pretty, is it?"

"Especially since I lost."

"Keep that in mind," Grandmillie said. "I may be old, but I've still got my wits about me."

"Still, will you promise me?" Chloe pleaded.

"Oh, fine. I promise." Her grandmother freed her hand and patted Chloe's cheek. "Since you were gracious enough to admit defeat."

"Now let's talk about what the doctor says," Chloe said, since she'd gotten her concession.

"So far they've all just talked a lot of gibberish filled with acronyms because they don't know what's wrong with me."

"Luckily, I've brought a translator. Ben Cavill is here."

"He's the fellow who insisted on giving me his emergency phone number." But Grandmillie looked pleased.

"Nathan and his butler, Ed, are here too."

"Good heavens, it's a regular tea party. Help me tidy up my hair."

As Chloe wove Grandmillie's hair into a neat braid that fell over her shoulder, the fear that had sunk its claws into her eased its grip. If her grandmother was worried about her hairstyle, she must be feeling close to normal. She straightened Grandmillie's hospital gown and smoothed the sheets out before going back to the door.

Stepping out into the hallway, she spotted Ben consulting with a young blonde woman wearing a lab coat. Just beyond him, Nathan and Ed were engrossed in conversation. Ben saw her and waved her over. "Dr. Scarpetti, meet Chloe Russell, Millie's grand-daughter."

Nathan walked up to stand beside Chloe. He was close enough that the hem of his jacket brushed against her arm as he moved. She resisted the urge to take a step sideways so she could feel the warmth and comfort of his body against hers.

She and Scarpetti shook hands. The doctor's grip was firm but brief, as though she needed to get on to the next task. "I've agreed to let Dr. Cavill examine Mrs. Russell even though he's not affili-ated with this hospital," Scarpetti said. "He's seen all of our test results and the records we received from your grandmother's PCP so he can bring you up-to-date. Now if you'll excuse me, we're short-staffed." She strode away.

"But—" Chloe started to follow the doctor.

Ben held up his hand to stop her. "She's doing us a big favor in allowing me to see Millie, so let her get to her rounds. With your permission, I'd like to go in to see your grandmother now."

"Yes, of course. Thank you so much. I told her you were here."

"And she didn't curse my name?" Ben said. "She wasn't very happy with me when I insisted she take my phone number during Nathan's flu."

"Actually, she's looking forward to hearing her diagnosis in plain English."

"I can't promise that," Ben said, giving her a wry smile before he headed down the hallway toward her grandmother's hospital room.

"Ed's going to pick up some food for everyone. Any requests?" Nathan asked.

"Any kind of sandwich is fine," Chloe said as she realized she was, in fact, ravenous.

The butler walked off in the opposite direction, and Chloe stood alone with Nathan. The adrenaline that had been fueling her through the crisis seemed to drain from her body all at once, and she shivered, regretting that she'd left her wrap in the limo.

Nathan stripped his jacket off and swung it around her shoulders like a cape. The smooth satin of the lining slid over her bare arms, enveloping her in the heat of his body and the exotic scent of his soap. Pulling the lapels together across her chest, she closed her eyes and inhaled.

"There's a lounge this way," he said, steering her toward a set of double doors, his arm around her waist.

At last she allowed herself to lean into him. It was heaven to be cocooned in his scent, supported by the strength of his arm, and warmed by the feel of his body against her side. She simply followed wherever he led her without thought or question. It was a relief to let go for a few moments.

"Sit," he said, maneuvering them both onto a green vinyl sofa without letting go of her. Chloe sank onto the hard cushion and snuggled in closer to Nathan's side.

"How was she?" he asked softly, his breath stirring the hair on top of her head.

Chloe's breath caught on a swallowed sob. "Much better than I hoped. In fact, she seems fine. It was just at the beginning, when she was lying still with her eyes closed, that she looked so small and frail." She sniffled, and Nathan fished in his pocket to offer her a small packet of tissues. It startled her to see the mundane little item in the long, elegant fingers of such a powerful man, but she took it gratefully. "I still want to see her as the loving but formidable grandmother of my youth, but she's not anymore. As I've grown up, she's grown old. I don't want to face that truth."

His arm tightened around her. "She's still pretty tough, you know, at least on me."

"Her mind and her spirit are," Chloe said, smiling a little. "But her body is betraying her. She and I both need to deal with that fact."

"Let's find out what's causing her falls before we worry about the long term." He rubbed his hand up and down her arm over the fabric of his jacket. "When Ben has a better idea of the situation, he'll refer Mrs. Russell to a top specialist. We'll have her moved to the appropriate hospital."

Chloe sat up straight as the implications of what he was saying sank in. It was so tempting to let him use his money and influence to get Grandmillie the best medical care available. She could almost justify it because it was for her grandmother, not herself. But she couldn't allow it when she needed to break the bonds of their relationship, not add to them. Reluctantly, she shook her head. "That's generous of both of you, but I can't accept any more of your help."

She felt him stiffen. "It's for your grandmother's benefit."

She slid sideways on the cushion, forcing him to drop his arm from around her waist. "She's *my* grandmother, not yours or Ben's."

He frowned and hesitated for a second, as though choosing his words carefully. "Your grandmother's well-being is important to me because you are important to me."

Chloe didn't want to hear this. She stood up.

"What is it?" he asked. His eyes narrowed as he scanned her face, not liking whatever he saw there.

She took a few strides away before turning to look him in the eye. "I had hoped—" She took a deep breath. "I had hoped to do this in a different place, in a different mood."

"Do what?" He rose from the sofa and took a step toward her. She halted him with a sharp gesture, but he still towered over her.

She could see suspicion building in the tightness of his jaw and the tense set of his shoulders. He could read her too well. She dropped her hand. "We can't continue to see each other now that I'm going to work at Trainor Electronics. It's not a good idea."

There was a long silence as he simply looked at her. She watched his face, waiting for hurt or anger, but he held whatever he was feeling in check.

"You're fired." He crossed his arms over his chest. "Problem solved."

Tears burned in her eyes as she shook her head. "Don't you see? Our relationship was going to end anyway. You're so brilliant and rich, and I'm, well, I'm just a temp."

"You don't think much of me if you believe that matters."

"Out in the real world it matters. I haven't been living in that since I met you. I've been hanging out in penthouses, driving in Rolls-Royces, and flying around in jets and helicopters. It's not who I am."

"None of that changes who *I* am, so it shouldn't impact who *you* are."

Now she could hear the pain in his voice, and it tore at her. She wrapped her arms around her waist. "You've earned it."

"I got lucky. People wanted what I created."

"My father invented lots of things people wanted. He didn't have a penthouse or a jet." Chloe said something she never thought she would. "He didn't have the drive or the discipline you do. He wouldn't work hard enough to build what you've built. You give thousands of people the ability to pay their mortgages and send their children to college. It's daunting."

He closed the distance between them and took hold of her shoulders, his eyes scorching. "You've seen me hallucinating. You've seen me naked. I'm a man like anyone else."

Chloe lifted her chin in an attempt to appear strong and certain, even as her heart was being slashed by every word. "No, you're different. You live in the stratosphere, and that's where you belong. Without me."

He held her as they stared at each other. His grip was hard but not punishing. She tried to memorize what this last touch felt like.

He dropped his hands and walked away to stare out the window, combing one hand through his hair. When he turned back to her, anger made his jaw hard and his eyes opaque. "I can't tar you with the same brush as Teresa. You couldn't have engineered my bout with the flu. But you are a damned skillful opportunist."

Chloe had expected this, even deserved it, but she still felt as though he'd drawn back his fist and socked her in the stomach. "When someone you love depends on you, you can't always make the decisions you want to," she said evenly. "You offered me the job without any prompting from me."

"I offered you the job so I could screw you in my office whenever I wanted to."

Even though she knew he was lashing out because she'd hurt him, his crudeness made her angry. "And you wanted to win your bet, didn't you?"

"What the hell are you talking about?" he said, but she caught the flash of guilt in his eyes.

"I heard you talking to Gavin and Luke about using me to win. That's why you took me to the charity dinner. Was screwing me in your office part of the wager?"

He gave her a long, level look. "You are so far wrong about that."

"Then why didn't you tell me about it?"

"It wasn't relevant."

"It involved me, so I think it was relevant."

"You don't know what you're talking about." He looked away, his lips pressed into a thin line.

"How can I, when you won't tell me?" His refusal to explain made her angry. With jerky movements she unhooked the earrings from her earlobes and removed the bracelet from her wrist, holding them out to him.

He yanked his gaze back to her before he reached out and scooped the jewelry off her palm. The anger that had fueled him seemed to evaporate as he closed his fingers on the sparkling baubles. His voice was hollow as he said, "I hoped you would keep them."

"You know I can't."

When he lifted his eyes to hers, she nearly cried out at the desolation in them. Maybe she was wrong. Maybe he'd felt more for her than she believed. But it didn't matter now. She had made her decision.

Without thinking she reached out to him, but his expression made her pull back her hand as though she'd gotten too near a bonfire. Except this bonfire burned with the cold of a glacier.

"I'll need my jacket," he said, nodding toward her.

"Of course." She'd forgotten she was still wearing it. Shrugging the warm garment off, she held it out. He took it in a way that avoided even brushing her fingertips. When a shiver ran through her, she wasn't sure if it was from the air-conditioning or from the icy contempt radiating from Nathan.

"Tell Ben and Ed I'll be in the Rolls," he said as he settled the jacket over his broad shoulders.

She opened her mouth to say good-bye, but he'd already pivoted toward the door. All she could do was watch him stride away from her.

She wanted to throw herself facedown on the plastic of the sofa and wail, but she had to keep herself together for Grandmillie.

Looking down, she realized she still had Nathan's tissues clutched in her hand. She opened her fingers and smoothed the crumpled packet back into its neat, rectangular shape. This would be the memento she treasured as the last thing he ever gave her.

Chapter 29

Nathan strode along the sidewalk with his shoulders hunched and his hands shoved in his pockets. He'd left Ben and Ed at his apartment. He didn't feel good about that. But he didn't feel good about anything right now, which was why he was headed for the R and D lab on a Saturday night.

He hoped no one else was pathetic enough to be there, because he was damned lousy company.

As he walked, he felt another wave of disbelief and anger roll through him, and cursed under his breath. He hadn't known Chloe long enough for it to hit him so hard.

This was Gavin Miller's fault, with all his tripe about finding a woman who didn't care about the money and the power. Nathan yanked his cell phone out of his jeans pocket and scrolled to the writer's number.

"You are a prize ass," he growled when Miller answered.

"So I've been told, but what's my specific crime tonight?"

Nathan was pissed off to hear amusement in the other man's tone. "Your moronic wager."

"More trouble with the opposite sex. I shouldn't be surprised. Meet me at the Bellwether Club. I'm buying."

He didn't want to be at his home. He didn't want to be at Trainor Electronics. He might as well go to the club and get drunk.

He pivoted in the direction of the club. "Be there in twenty."

"You look like hell," Gavin said as he slouched into the leather chair across from Nathan. He wore jeans, like Nathan, but with a black turtleneck and tweed jacket.

"You look like someone pretending to be a writer." Nathan had already tossed back one scotch and was sipping his second.

The waiter slid an empty crystal tumbler onto the table in front of Gavin. "Will you be sharing the scotch, sir," he asked, nodding to the bottle on the table, "or would you prefer bourbon?"

"I'll be comradely and drink with my friend, despite his foul mood," the writer said, picking up the scotch and pouring it before the waiter could. "Now tell me your tale of woe, Trainor."

"I came to drink, not talk."

Gavin took a swallow of his drink. "You could have done that alone."

"You said it was on you." Nathan wasn't ready to admit what was bothering him.

Gavin spun the bottle around so he could read the label. "You should have ordered more expensive scotch." He waved the waiter over. "Take this away and bring a bottle of the Macallan, 1989. Unless Bill Gates has drunk it all already."

"Are we celebrating the end of your writer's block?" Nathan asked, having a rough idea of the price of the bottle Gavin had just ordered.

The writer threw him a sardonic glance. "If you're going to drown your sorrows, you should do it with something worth the hangover."

Nathan remembered how depressed he'd felt about work until he got back into the R and D lab. Being unable to write must feel something like that to Gavin. "Sorry."

The other man shrugged. "I can live on my backlist royalties for the rest of my life, but other people are counting on this book."

"You're miserable without your creative outlet."

"Aren't we the sensitive psychoanalyst?" Gavin grimaced. "In order to need an outlet, I'd have to have some creativity left in me."

"You think it's not there, but it's building up. If you don't use it, you'll have a core meltdown." Nathan tossed back the last of his scotch as the waiter approached with a tray holding two tulip-shaped glasses, wide at the bottom and tapering to the top, and a simple clear bottle of dark-amber liquid with the year 1989 prominent on its label.

As the waiter reverently poured the single malt, Gavin said, "I appreciate the image of nuclear disaster, but I'm just a commercial hack. At worst, it would be a cherry bomb going off."

The waiter placed the bottle on the table and stepped back. "I hope you'll enjoy the Macallan, sirs." Clearly he felt they weren't paying such a rare beverage the attention it deserved.

Nathan picked up the glass and inhaled the heavy, complex scent. "Nice." He took a sip and let it sit on his tongue, savoring the flavors of spice, nuts, and wood.

"You get a little bit of fruit at the finish," Gavin said after swallowing his first taste.

Nathan drank the rest of the scotch in one gulp, just to be a bastard. He poured another and stared down into the dark-brown liquid glowing with red highlights. He could feel Gavin's gaze on him.

"Quit stalling," the other man said. "What's got you abusing one of the world's finest single malts?"

"My own stupidity."

"That goes without saying."

Nathan waited for more, but Gavin just took another sip of scotch. The whiskey burned through Nathan's veins, loosening all the controls he'd put on his emotions. "Damn it, she chose the job over me."

The writer sat up. "Chloe dumped you? Start at the beginning. This should be a good story."

Nathan told him about the flu epidemic and Chloe's abrupt promotion to executive assistant. "Ben basically forced her into coming to my apartment," Nathan said. "She tried to say no every step of the way. She's the strangest combination of ruthless determination and soft heart. The determination is all for her grandmother, so she kept negotiating more and more money every time I asked her to stay, but I think she only agreed to do it because she felt sorry for me in my sickly condition."

"Sorry for you? Sure, I believe that," Gavin said.

"You've met her. She wasn't at all intimidated by me." It had been the apartment and the cars and the jet that had bothered Chloe. Nathan, she'd treated as an equal. Until now.

"Well, she would have to be a criminal mastermind to have engineered a flu epidemic and then maneuvered her way into becoming your temporary assistant, so I'll give you that. It sounds like she took full advantage of the situation, though."

Nathan had accused her of opportunism too, but he shook his head. "She wouldn't take anything of significance from me until I offered her the job."

"We're back to the job."

Nathan drank a slug of single malt, letting it scorch down his throat. "I made sure she got a job at Trainor Electronics."

"You *are* an idiot."

The truth of that had smacked Nathan in the head a few hours earlier. "I hated having to snatch an hour here and there with her. I thought we could spend more time together if she worked in the same building."

Gavin gave a long, low whistle. "You have swallowed the hook, line, and sinker, my friend."

"She needed the job," Nathan said. "She supports her grandmother, who's having health issues." He'd spoken with Ben earlier. His friend was nearly certain that Millie Russell's problem was a simple and treatable heart arrhythmia. Relief had surged through Nathan at the news. He did have it bad.

"So you got on your white horse and rode to her rescue."

"Trainor Electronics employs thousands of people. What difference does it make if HR offers a position to someone who has both the skills and the need for it?"

"The difference is you're sleeping with this someone. People would have found out, and Chloe, if she has the integrity you claim she does, would have felt like crap."

"Maybe Chloe was right." Nathan stared at the outrageously expensive bottle of scotch. "Maybe I've become insulated from the real world."

"The plot thickens."

"Today she wouldn't let me get a specialist for her grandmother, who fainted and fell. When I pushed, she told me she was ending the relationship because it was wrong for her to be involved with her boss."

"She works for you?"

"No." Nathan glared at Gavin. "I may be besotted, but I'm not brain-dead. She works about three levels below me in the organization chart, in an entirely different department."

"*Besotted.* Nice word," Gavin said. "Is that what you are?"

Nathan ignored him. He didn't know the answer to that. "She told me our relationship wouldn't have lasted anyway because it was too unequal."

Gavin held his glass up to the light, tilting it this way and that. "She has a point."

Nathan slammed his glass down on the table so hard some of the precious whiskey sloshed out. "I was a military brat. I grew up on bases in run-down housing with an alcoholic mother and a father who tried to force me into the Marines. All this"—he swept his hand around the opulent room—"doesn't change who I am."

"Sure, sure." Gavin looked unconvinced.

"And then she threw the bet in my face."

"You told her about the bet?"

"No, she heard us talking at the charity dinner, so thanks to you for adding to the problem." Nathan glared at Gavin.

"She must have been flattered when you explained it to her."

"I didn't. I was too pissed off."

"I can see you handled it well, so let's cut to the chase." Gavin leaned forward. "Do you love her?"

"No one can fall in love in two weeks." But he wasn't sure about that. Facing the prospect of life without Chloe made him feel bleak at best, despairing at worst. "I'm just pissed off." He knew he was repeating himself.

"I'm the last person who should give advice to the love-lorn . . . or the pissed off," Gavin said, "but I want you to think about this. If Chloe walked through that door right now and said she'd made a terrible mistake, how would you feel? You don't have to tell me. Just think about it."

Nathan turned his head toward the heavy mahogany door that led into the bar and imagined Chloe pushing it open and looking around the room until she spotted him. Her face would light up the way it did when she walked out of that accounting firm and saw him leaning against the Rolls. She would head toward him, swaying on those high heels she loved so much.

His heart squeezed hard in his chest, and he closed his eyes with a grimace.

"Yup, you've fallen hard," Gavin said.

A blast of light jerked Nathan awake. He opened his eyes and slammed them shut again as the sunlight jabbed into his eyeballs like a set of possessed screwdrivers.

"You have a visitor." Ed's voice sent the same screwdrivers plunging into his eardrums.

"Isn't it Sunday?"

"Yes." Something clinked on the bedside table, and Nathan slitted an eye to see a steaming mug. His stomach heaved as the usually welcome aroma of coffee hit his nostrils.

"I don't have visitors on Sundays." He rolled away from Ed and the light until a stupidly hopeful thought whispered that it might be Chloe. He lifted his head enough to look over his shoulder and then laid it back down with a groan. "Who is it?" he managed to growl.

"You should find that out for yourself."

The chipper little voice got louder. Nathan knew he shouldn't ask, but he couldn't stop himself. "Is it Chloe?"

"No." Ed's tone was flat and disapproving. Nathan couldn't tell if the disapproval was aimed at him or Chloe. Or both.

"Then tell whoever it is to go to hell." The misery that Chloe's name had temporarily banished flooded back through him.

"That wouldn't be a good idea."

"I'm sorry to barge in on you like this, son, but I don't have a lot of time." This had to be a nightmare, because the new voice sounded like his father.

Nathan pushed himself up onto his elbow even though the shift in elevation tightened the vise currently clamped around his head. He squinted at the two shapes silhouetted against the windows, trying to distinguish faces. "Sir?"

One shape stepped forward. "I have to catch a flight out of JFK at fifteen hundred hours. Angel and I are headed for Vienna."

It *was* his father. Long years of training made Nathan straighten and then wince at the new crash of pain. "Sir, if you'll give me a minute," he said. He wasn't going to stagger around the room clutching his head in front of the general.

"I'll wait in your study," his father said. "Ed, this young man could use a batch of your patented hangover killer."

Nathan searched for condemnation in the general's voice but found none.

"I'll get right on it, sir," Ed said as he accompanied the general out of the room.

Nathan crawled out from under the covers and hoisted himself off the bed, stumbling into the bathroom to fill the sink with cold water and dunk his head in it. It didn't stop the pain, but it cleared away some of the cobwebs.

He braced his arms on the counter and let water drip from his hair into the sink as memories of the day before came spinning back into his brain. Chloe looking scared but determined as she told him they'd have to break off their relationship. Chloe looking angry as she challenged him about the damned bet. Ed and Ben hammering at him in the Rolls about what he'd done to upset Chloe. Gavin telling him he had it bad and then ordering another bottle of scotch. Over it all a dark, colorless blanket of pain and loss.

He submerged his head in the sink again and held it under until he had to come up for air. Grabbing a towel, he headed for his dressing room. He dressed in gray slacks and a black tee, combed his damp hair into some order, and made his way down to the study, every step seeming to jar his teeth in his jaw.

He found his father standing in front of one of the bookcases, scanning the spines of the books. The general was wearing civilian clothes—a white polo shirt and crisply pressed khaki trousers, which made him seem unfamiliar. As Nathan crossed the room, the general turned. "I see you still have Jordan's *Campaigns of General Nathan Bedford Forrest.*"

"You gave it to me," Nathan said, holding out his hand to his father. "My apologies for my greeting. I wasn't expecting company this morning."

The general gripped his son's hand, making Nathan feel as though the bones of his fingers were grinding together.

"I needed to return something to its rightful owner," his father said. He went to the big desk and picked up the sword case, carrying it to where Nathan was holding himself upright by leaning on the back of a leather wing chair. His father held out the case with both hands.

"I told you to keep it," Nathan said. "I broke the family tradition."

The general took a deep breath. "I know I made you feel that way, and it was wrong. You've brought honor and glory to the family name in a way that's different from my way. But that doesn't make it less than my way. In fact, you've already accomplished much more than I have in my lifetime."

"That's not true, sir." Nathan's clouded brain was having a hard time processing his father's words.

"I don't regret how I raised you, because it's made you the man you are, and I'm damned proud of that," the general continued.

"I do regret the distance between us. I'd like to change it." He offered the sword case again. "Even if you can't see your way to closing that gap, I want you to have the family sword in your keeping."

Nathan released the chair and took the sword case, holding it in both hands as the general had while he stared down at it. It felt like a ceremony of some sort, this passing of the sword. He lifted his gaze to his father's, realizing suddenly that it was like looking at his own eyes in a mirror. "I'm honored, sir."

The general gripped Nathan's shoulder. "You've earned it, and that's the greatest honor of all."

Nathan took the case back to the desk and set it down as he focused on what his father had said about closing the distance between them. He turned back to the general. "Why now?"

"May I?" his father asked, pointing to one of the chairs.

Nathan nodded and took a seat opposite his father. He didn't know if he wanted to hear this or not.

The general clasped his hands on his knees. "As much as I love Angel, I refused to marry her because of you."

Nathan rocked back in the chair. "What did I have to do with you and Angel?"

His father looked up at him from under his eyebrows. "I was afraid it would cause a permanent rift between us, one that could never be repaired. I had always hoped . . ." He shook his head. "Then Angel told me she was pregnant. Once I got over the shock, I realized what a selfish fool I was. I proposed on the spot."

The general clenched and unclenched his hands a couple of times before he continued. "She turned me down flat. Said she wasn't going to have a shotgun wedding with a reluctant groom. I had a hell of a time convincing her I wasn't marrying her just because she was having our child."

Nathan felt an unwilling spike of sympathy for his father.

"When she agreed to marry me, there was only one thing missing from my happiness." The general stopped to clear his throat. "That was you, son. I realized I had to get over my infernal pride and make the first move. And the second one," he said, nodding to the sword. "If I need to make a third, fourth, and fifth move, I will, because you deserve that from me."

"Your first move was the wedding invitation."

His father nodded.

"You make it sound like a game of chess. Or a Nathan Forrest campaign." Nathan wasn't sure he liked that.

The general sighed. "That's just the way I know how to describe it. I'm a soldier, so I talk like one." He skewered Nathan with his so-familiar eyes. "It doesn't make me mean it less when I say I love you. I don't deserve it, but I'm asking for a second chance with you."

Nathan thrust himself out of his chair, wincing as his head pounded. He stood on braced legs with his hands shoved in his pockets. This was territory he hadn't expected to cross. He met his father's gaze, trying to read what was behind it. He caught the movement of his father's fists, clenching and unclenching again. The general's posture was rigid in a way that went beyond his military training. He was waiting for Nathan to reject him, but he was prepared to accept that and try again and again.

Nathan thought of all the angry things he'd wanted to say to his father, all the accusations of making his childhood hell and every one of his achievements seem worthless. Even worse, blaming his father for driving his mother to suicide. He realized his father would sit there and let him spew ugliness at him, maybe even agree with what he said.

"I give you credit for courage, Dad," Nathan said.

All the tension went out of his father. "Thank you," he said with more gratitude that Nathan's statement warranted.

"For saying you have courage? You've already proven that in combat."

"For calling me Dad."

Nathan hadn't realized he'd said it. It must have been because he'd gotten lost in the past, so it had spilled out unconsciously.

His father stood and held out his hand. Nathan put his in it and they pulled each other in for a short, powerful embrace. He could feel his father's strength the way he had as a child.

As they separated, his father said, "You're a generous man, son. You could have dragged me over the coals about what I did to you and your mother."

"I figure your pride was already taking a severe hit. I wasn't going to pile on."

"My pride?" His father made a sound of disgust. "Let me tell you something about that. You should take pride in your work and pride in keeping your barracks neat and pride in service to your country and your fellow man. But when it comes to people, pride is nothing but a high, wide wall you build between yourself and the ones you love."

Nathan knew about that wall, because he had built one just as sturdy. It wouldn't be easy to get around it to meet his father halfway.

The general cleared his throat. "Angel and I were hoping to stop back here on our return trip. Maybe we could have dinner with you, Ed, and Ben, and that nice young lady you brought to the wedding. Chloe, wasn't it?"

An image of the dinner table with all those people sitting around it rose up in Nathan's mind. It sparkled with laughter, warmth, and love because Chloe was part of it.

At that moment, Nathan understood three things. First, he wanted Chloe at that dinner more than he'd ever wanted anything in his life. Second, he had to tear down the wall he'd put up to protect his pride. Third, he was willing to make as many moves as it took to get her back.

"Dad, you're a genius. It *is* possible to fall in love in two weeks."

"You're confused, son. You're the brilliant one in this family."

Nathan shook his head gingerly. "Right now, I'm less confused than I've ever been in my life."

Chapter 30

Chloe wanted to put her head down on her new desk at Trainor Electronics and wail. Ever since Nathan had walked out of the hospital lounge, she'd been fighting her way through a storm of emotions that had left her both keyed up and wrung out.

Relief had come first when Ben had told her that Grandmillie's heart issue was an arrhythmia that was easily treatable. After he'd given her the news, she'd collapsed into a chair in the hospital lounge and sobbed.

But once that worry was removed, guilt, loss, and pain had swept in to drop a weight on her chest that made it hard to draw in a full breath.

She'd flinched at Ben's bafflement when she told him not to call the cardiac specialist he wanted to refer Grandmillie to. Ed had looked puzzled and then concerned when he returned with gourmet sandwiches and Nathan wasn't there to share them. Grandmillie kept giving her searching looks as Chloe dealt with doctors, nurses, and various other personnel at the hospital. By Saturday evening, she'd fallen asleep in the lounge chair in Grandmillie's room, awakening only when a nurse tucked a blanket around her.

On Sunday Grandmillie had been released from the hospital, so Chloe had busied herself with making her comfortable in her bedroom until her grandmother had commanded her to stop fussing. Then she'd pried the truth out of Chloe and stroked her hair while Chloe sobbed into the blankets on Grandmillie's bed. The only thing she hadn't shared with her grandmother was the mysterious bet.

"You fell in love with him, didn't you, child?" Grandmillie had said gently.

Chloe had started to protest, to say she just felt guilty about hurting him, but her grandmother's question forced her to admit the truth. Her heart had paid no attention to the warnings she'd given herself about his money and his power and his genius. She'd found the man behind all those intimidating trappings, and she wanted to love him for the rest of her life.

Chloe slumped down in her chair as despair swamped her all over again. She couldn't afford all this wallowing. She had to focus on work. Her new boss had e-mailed her a boatload of reports and memos to read so she'd be up to speed on the project she'd been assigned to. Opening the first file, she made herself concentrate. Her brain was clicking away, absorbing the ins and outs of the product's development, until she reached the end of the report, where a series of people had made comments. There was Nathan's name attached to an astute suggestion about renaming the product to avoid comparison with a competitor. The phrasing and tone were so distinctive that she could hear his voice saying the words. The same voice that had whispered hot, sexy suggestions in her ear as he moved inside her.

She put her hand over her mouth to stifle the sob that threatened to wrench itself from her throat. She needed to get out of there to pull herself together. Grabbing her handbag, she headed for the ladies' room in the hallway. As she passed the elevator, the doors slid open and Nathan stepped out the elevator, wearing one of his perfectly cut suits, his hair waving just down to the collar, his head turned as he spoke with the woman beside him.

Every molecule in Chloe's body leaped with sheer happiness at the sight of him. Her heart hadn't gotten the memo that she was no longer allowed to love Nathan. Then her brain sent a wave of misery rolling over her, nearly knocking her to her knees.

Chloe didn't care what anyone thought. She stumbled to the bathroom, slamming open the door and dodging into the first open stall. Latching it closed, she leaned against the stainless-steel wall and let the tears flow silently down her cheeks.

She couldn't do this. Seeing Nathan was like showing a starving woman a perfect chocolate éclair and then telling her she couldn't touch it.

She scrabbled in her bag for her cell phone. Before she speed-dialed Judith's number, she stuck her head out of the stall to make sure no one else was in the room.

"Hey, Chloe, what's up?" Her friend's familiar voice steadied her.

"I'm really sorry, but I can't continue at Trainor Electronics." She took a deep breath and fumbled for a reason. "I feel like I'm here under false pretenses."

"You mean because you're involved with the big boss?"

"*Was* involved with him. We broke up on Saturday. I just saw him for the first time since then."

She heard Judith blow out a breath before she said, "Well, you predicted it would end. I told you the job has no probation period, so he can't fire you as revenge. My advice is for you to tough it out until you get over him. Time heals all wounds, and the great salary and benefits will help the process along. And I'm not saying this because of my fee."

Chloe rested her forehead against the cool metal wall. "Judith, I did something stupid. I fell in love with him."

"Oh, damn. I was afraid of that."

"I hurt him, Judith. I did the same thing all the other women did. Used him for what he could give me."

"That's garbage and you know it."

"It feels like that to me. And he believes it." Chloe felt her decision come into focus. "I'm sorry, but I have to resign."

Judith's sigh sounded in Chloe's ear. "Okay, sweetie. Can you at least tell Roberta in HR that it's a family issue? It's almost true."

"Of course. I'll make it clear you were shocked and disappointed by my decision. I don't want to damage your relationship with Trainor Electronics."

"I know you don't. You're too nice for this whole mess. And I'll keep working to get you placed, so don't worry about that."

Chloe thanked Judith and hung up. She felt a curious sense of lightness. Guilt about the way she'd gotten the job had been weighing on her.

She marched out of the stall to touch up her makeup before taking the elevator to the HR floor. Once Roberta got over her astonishment, she was surprisingly sympathetic, saying she understood the issues of having elderly relatives. Chloe wished she didn't have to leave a company where the employees were treated so well. It proved that corporations weren't all heartless.

Chloe walked out of the HR office and headed back to the elevator. She reached for the "Down" button and then drew her hand back.

She wanted to see Nathan one more time. To tell him she'd been wrong to take the job. She didn't expect him to want her back, but she hoped he would think better of her. If he ever thought of her again. The contempt in his eyes on Saturday indicated he might dismiss her from his mind as not worth the trouble.

She stretched her hand out again, hesitated a moment, and pushed the "Up" button.

Chloe stood in front of the desk where it had all started. It seemed incredible that in just two weeks she'd experienced so many highs and lows.

As she waited to find out if Nathan would see her, she remembered the first time they'd made love, and Nathan's words as he'd walked away from her in the hospital. Maybe this was a bad idea.

"Mr. Trainor is available now," Janice said. She was a pleasant-looking fortyish woman, with short brown hair and a slight midwestern twang. She gave Chloe a smile. "I hear you did a great job when I was sick."

"Thanks." Chloe couldn't manage any more conversation because flutters of nerves were tightening her throat. She shifted her grip on her handbag and strode past Janice to pull open the big door into Nathan's office, bracing herself for whatever he might sling at her.

His desk was unoccupied, so she turned toward the windows. He was standing with his back to them. She could see the breadth of his shoulders, the length of his legs, and the way he had his hands thrust into his trousers pockets, but his face was in shadow. Not helpful.

She closed the door, walked halfway across the carpeted floor, and stopped, holding her bag in front of her body with both hands.

"How's your first day of work going?" Nathan asked.

His mundane question threw her off balance. "I, um—it's not."

He moved forward a step and waved to a chair. "Tell me about it."

She ignored the invitation to sit. "I came to tell you that I've resigned."

"Is Phil that hard to work for?"

"No, of course not." What was going on here? "I resigned because what I did was wrong. I shouldn't have accepted the job, knowing that we were . . . involved. My only excuse is that I feel responsible for Grandmillie."

"I understand that."

Chloe flung her arms out. "Why are you being so polite? You hated me on Saturday. And I deserved it."

His shoulders lifted and fell on an expelled breath. "Not hated, but you struck a serious blow."

"I don't blame you for anything you said. I acted like the worst kind of opportunist."

He took another step forward. "Look, neither one of us behaved well. I engineered the job here for my own convenience. If my motives had been as altruistic as I claimed, I would have found you a position at another company. So let's say we both could have done better and leave it at that."

"Oh. All right." She'd expected—maybe even wanted—more emotion from him. This calm, rational conversation was depressing. Their relationship hadn't been deep enough for her presence to bother him a mere forty-eight hours after it ended. Well, that proved what everyone had told her all along, and it made her want to curl up in a ball and weep. "Fine. I just wanted you to know." She half turned.

"Chloe." She pivoted back, a stupid little flame of hope coming to life in her heart. "My father came to see me yesterday. He brought back the sword."

The flame flickered out. "I thought you told him to keep it."

"I did." Nathan took another step in her direction. "You were right about the wedding invitation. He wanted a second chance."

"Are you giving it to him?" Chloe held her breath for his answer.

He didn't answer her directly. "He told me pride is a wall that separates you from the people you love. He said that he was willing to make the first move and the second move and as many more moves as it took until I agreed to give him that chance." He kept walking toward her as he spoke.

Her heart turned a somersault in her chest. "How many moves did it take?"

He stopped several feet away from her. "Two." She could see his face now, but it was unreadable.

"I'm glad." She'd wanted that for Nathan and his father. She decided to ask one daring question. "So you believe in second chances?"

"For some people."

Chloe could barely breathe. "Which ones?"

His gray eyes were focused on her face. "The ones I love."

She swallowed her pride because she couldn't help herself. "Am I one of those people?"

Nathan closed the distance between them, coming so close that she could see shadows under his eyes and a dusting of stubble that showed he hadn't shaved. He looked down at her and uttered one word. "Yes."

And then she was locked in his arms, her mouth against his as she wrapped her fists around his lapels to pull them closer together. He kissed her with a desperation that echoed her own, his embrace so intense it made her struggle to breathe.

He lifted his head a fraction of an inch away from hers. "Tell me I'm one of those people for you, Chloe."

"I love you, Nathan. I didn't mean to. I didn't want to. Everyone told me not to, but I couldn't stop it."

He smiled in a way that made her knees go weak. "I'm irresistible."

"To me." She pulled his head down to give him her kind of kiss, one that held an apology and a promise.

When she ended the kiss, he shifted his hands to her shoulders, holding her away from him. "You've brought so many good things back into my life, darling. I have so little to offer in return."

That last statement struck Chloe as funny. "I don't mean to be materialistic, but you've offered me a lot of things. Jewelry from Tiffany's, clothes from Saks Fifth Avenue, airplane rides, dinners at gourmet restaurants."

"And you've thrown most of them back in my face," he pointed out.

"You still don't get it. All I want you to offer is yourself."

He released her and held his arms out from his sides. "That's what I'm doing. All I am is yours."

"That's a heck of a lot," Chloe said, her heart squeezing with overwhelming joy as she threw herself against him so he closed his open arms around her. She stood on tiptoe to kiss him again.

"I need to explain the bet," he said, his voice serious.

A tremor of apprehension shook her. "Do I want to hear this?"

"I'm not sure, but you deserve to know." He led her to the couch and sat her down beside him in an echo of their scene in the hospital lounge. Not the image she wanted right now.

He swiveled to look at her. "Remember Teresa?"

Chloe nodded. "She had great shoes."

Nathan smiled briefly. "The night before you came to work for me, I found out she lied to me about our first meeting. I'd thought she might be different from the other women who just wanted something from me, but—" He shrugged. "I met Gavin and Luke that night. We got drunk together and made the wager you heard us talking about."

Nathan took both her hands in his warm, strong grip before he continued. "We each had one year to find a woman who chose us for ourselves and not our money or power or fame. If we failed, we had to forfeit something very important to us. But if we won, we won a lot more than just the bet."

"So you think you've won?" Happiness raced through Chloe.

"Darling, I'm sure of it. But I don't care about the wager. Knowing you love me is all I need to be a rich man."

Epilogue

A few months later

Even though the interior of the Rolls was toasty, Chloe snuggled up to Nathan, stroking her hand down the satin of his tuxedo lapel. "I still can't believe I get to walk into these fancy parties holding hands with the best-looking man there," she said.

Nathan threaded his arm around her waist under the velvet cape she wore. The warmth of his palm on her hip seeped through the thin blue silk of her evening gown. "I used to hate those parties. Now I spend them thinking about how I'm going to make love to you once we leave. It's a significant improvement." His hand slid lower.

Chloe trapped his wandering fingers under hers. "You said we have one stop to make before we go home, so no wrinkling the dress." She tilted her head up to give him a hot look. "Yet."

He gave her thigh a quick squeeze before moving his hand to a less dangerous spot. "Do you think Grandmillie will have fired her new companion by the time we arrive?"

Chloe chuckled. "No, she likes Taleesha. She says she's a woman of good sense. I'm so relieved."

"Hank at Jersey Caregivers must be even more relieved."

"Grandmillie is particular about who she spends her time with." Chloe sighed. "I knew she would be."

"She's allowed." Nathan shifted on the seat so Chloe found herself plastered against him. "Phil gave me an earful today about how selfish I was to force you to leave Trainor Electronics. He had lunch with your boss and heard all about the great work you're doing for Allitel."

"At least I'm not working for a competitor," Chloe said as gratification made her grin. Judith had found her the job three weeks after she'd resigned from Trainor Electronics. Chloe had made Nathan swear not to intervene in any way, so she knew she'd gotten the position on her own merits. "It's almost as good a company to work for as Trainor."

"And the location is convenient." Nathan bent to kiss the side of her neck.

Delicious shivers danced down over Chloe's breasts at his touch . . . and at the thought of her occasional lunchtime visits to Nathan's office. They would barely manage to wolf down one of the sandwiches Janice ordered for them before Nathan would have her stretched out on top of his desk or bent over one of the armchairs.

"Dad says you need to come down to visit Allitel's regional office in Raleigh. He wants to take you out to dinner at a great restaurant he knows there." Nathan picked up her free hand and toyed with her fingers. "I might join you there."

Nathan and his father were finding their way to a new relationship, but he still liked to have Chloe around when he was with the general. The Marine had taken a liking to her, and it softened some of the edges of his forceful personality, making it easier for Nathan to connect with him. Angel's presence also helped, and Nathan was coming to terms with the prospect of having a very young half sibling. In fact, Angel had asked him to be the child's godfather, much to Nathan's initial consternation but ultimate pleasure.

"I'm sure I can come up with an excuse for a road trip," Chloe said, "as long as you're coming too." Especially now that Grandmillie had Taleesha.

Nathan's hold on her tightened. "You didn't really think I'd let you go without me."

"Well, you went to Japan for four days alone."

"Only because you wouldn't quit your job and come with me."

Chloe laughed. He had suggested she do that, which had made her heart flutter with delight because he wanted her company that much.

The Rolls glided to a stop, and Chloe peered out the window. They were parked in front of a brownstone adorned with fantastic gargoyles and ornate curlicues, all thrown into high relief by dramatic up-lighting. A small black shield was attached to the wall beside the door with the gold initials *B. C.* intertwined.

"What is this place?" she asked.

"The Bellwether Club."

"This is where you made that bet." Chloe sat back.

"Yes, and I brought you here to prove that I won."

"Luke and Gavin already know me," Chloe said, not moving from her seat. Although she now considered the two men friends, she hadn't quite forgiven them for the part they'd played in the four most miserable days of her life.

"They need to see the ring," Nathan said.

Chloe wiggled the fingers of her left hand to make the sapphire and its surrounding diamonds flash in the light. She still felt like a bit of a show-off wearing it. "It doesn't seem real yet."

He lifted his hand to take her chin and turn her face toward his. "Darling, there's nothing more real than what we have between us." The playful gleam was absent from his eyes as he said it.

He kissed her and pushed the car door open, taking her hand to help her out of the car. "Now let's go rub it in."

A staff member met them by a marble-topped table decorated with a giant bouquet of flowers, taking Chloe's cape and Nathan's overcoat. "Ms. Hogan is waiting for you in her office."

"Ms. Hogan?" Chloe threw a questioning glance at Nathan as he led her down a wide hallway carpeted with jewel-colored Oriental rugs.

"Frankie Hogan is the keeper of the betting paperwork. She's also the owner of the club." He ushered her into a cozy room furnished with plush green wing chairs and a warmly glowing fireplace.

The inner door was open, and a slender woman stood framed in it, her white pageboy catching gold glints from the fire. She wore a pantsuit so dark Chloe couldn't tell exactly what color it was. "I'm Frankie Hogan. Welcome to the Bellwether Club," the woman said, the rasp of her voice reminding Chloe of smoky Irish bars. "You must be Chloe Russell."

"I am." Chloe shook Frankie's tiny hand. "A pleasure to meet you."

"I told them all they had to bring in the women who had the misfortune to fall in love with them," Frankie said, but a twinkle in her eye took the sting out of her words. She scanned Chloe's face for a long moment. "Come in."

Chloe followed her through the door into a large office that looked nothing like the rest of the club. It was brightly lit and held clean-lined modern furniture designed for function as well as form. Steel-framed French doors gave onto a garden featuring a sensuous abstract sculpture, now dusted with snow.

Frankie stopped in front of what appeared to be a cupboard door before she turned to Chloe. "Let's see the ring."

Chloe held up her hand, the bright light glittering off the facets of the gems.

"Nice," Frankie said, throwing an approving glance at Nathan. "Substantial but not ostentatious."

Nathan laughed. "I had to balance my desire to let everyone know she belonged to me against Chloe's accusations that I don't live in the real world."

"Ha!" Frankie barked as she typed in a combination that opened the door. Behind it was a massive utilitarian safe with a dial and a slot. Frankie put her body between the dial and her two guests as she twirled it. Then she pulled a strangely shaped key from her pocket and fed it into the slot.

"No biometrics?" Nathan asked. Chloe loved that his inventor's mind was always working.

"I'm not having someone cut off my thumb to open a damned safe," Frankie said, swinging the foot-thick door open.

"Wise," Nathan said.

The older woman pulled out a leather portfolio, shuffled through the papers in it, and removed a thick cream-colored envelope. "I understand you've decided I should mark the still-sealed envelope with 'wager satisfied' and my initials. You wish me to retain it until the end of the one-year time frame of the bet."

"That's correct," Nathan confirmed.

Frankie carried the envelope to her desk, where she picked up a black fountain pen, scrawled the two words and her initials on the vellum, and blotted it.

"Why not just shred it since you've won?" Chloe asked, a little miffed that the bet would linger on.

"We want to destroy them—or reveal them—all at the same time." He took Chloe's hands in his and faced her. "We were gambling with the most important of our possessions: our hearts. A wager like that deserves the respect of ritual."

"And gamblers are superstitious," Frankie said, putting the envelope back in the portfolio and closing the safe. "Nathan here doesn't want to jinx his chances of marrying you."

"Seriously?" Chloe said, giving him a skeptical look.

"Better safe than sorry," he said, lifting her hands to kiss first one and then the other, his lips firm on her skin. "It's not easy to find a woman brave enough to love me for myself."

Chloe could feel his touch along all the nerve endings in her body.

"We have rooms upstairs," Frankie said, her tone dry. "But first your friends are waiting for you in the bar where this sentimental bet began." The club owner held out her hand to Chloe again. "I expect a wedding invitation."

"You're at the top of the guest list," Nathan said.

As they left Frankie's office, Chloe said, "Let's make a deal."

Nathan groaned. "You always come out on top in these negotiations."

"I thought you liked me in that position," Chloe said, enjoying the quick intake of Nathan's breath. "Anyway, this one's easy. You tell me what you wrote on that piece of paper in Frankie's safe, and I'll have a drink with Luke and Gavin."

All the teasing went out of Nathan's expression. "Let's go somewhere more private."

He led her down the hall to a small hexagonal room furnished with a round, leather-topped table surrounded by four dark wooden chairs upholstered in matching leather. A circular gold-and-wine-patterned Oriental rug covered the floor. Closing the door, he pulled out a chair to seat Chloe before turning another one toward her and sitting down himself.

"We agreed to wager something that was not only valuable in and of itself, but which would cause us pain to lose." He crossed his arms on his chest. "I considered the pair of paintings in my bedroom. They would bring a lot of money at auction, but I could replace them with different ones. Another possibility was the first battery I invented. That had significance to me, but it wasn't intrinsically valuable, except maybe to a computer geek."

He uncrossed his arms and leaned forward in his chair. "So I wagered the family sword."

Chloe gasped. "You must have been really drunk."

"It was desperation that drove me. I knew there was something wrong with my life and I needed to make a change." His gaze burned with intensity. "You didn't just save the family sword. You saved *me*."

"Love saved you," Chloe said. "I was just lucky enough to be the one you gambled on."

He stood and drew her up against him before he lowered his head and kissed her. She understood he wanted to do more than just *say* he loved her. He wanted her to feel it deep down in her bones.

"I love you too," she breathed against his lips.

For a long moment, they stood pressed together, absorbing the emotion swirling around and through them. Then he slid his hand down to the curve of her behind.

"There's something I've been meaning to ask you all night," he said.

She looked up to find a devil in his eye. "What's that?"

"Are you wearing anything under that dress?"

"Just my skin," she said, injecting a little seduction into her voice.

"That's what I thought." And then both of his hands were cupping her bottom, rubbing the silk against her. "I want to tear this dress off you and have you right here on the Oriental rug."

"You did that last night, only on a different Oriental rug," she said, her breath catching as his fingers traced lightly down between her buttocks.

"Damn Miller and Archer for stopping me," he muttered before opening the door and gesturing toward the stairs. "Let's get this over with so I can have you naked in the car."

Anticipation rippled through Chloe. She slipped her hand under Nathan's tux jacket and gave his muscular butt a quick squeeze. He grinned, but corralled her hand to steady her up the elegant staircase.

At the top of the stairs, he led her into a room that was so stereotypically "men's club" she nearly laughed out loud. "I can't believe Frankie decorated this place," she said.

"She did it as a swipe at the other clubs that wouldn't let her in. She decided to out-club them, as she puts it." Nathan swept his gaze around the room. "There they are."

The two men stood as they approached the table set by a tall, arched window. Luke sported a blue blazer, white button-down shirt, and khaki slacks that gave his well-muscled, athletic frame an elegantly tailored look. The black turtleneck and slacks Gavin wore under his tweed jacket made him appear lean and slightly piratical.

Gavin stepped forward first, giving her a peck on both cheeks. "A pleasure, Chloe. I see you made the entirely wrong decision to tie yourself to Trainor here. How much did he have to pay you to wear that ring?"

"You're contradicting yourself," Chloe said, amazed as always that the writer could make his insults sound so charming. It was something about the self-mocking light in his dark eyes.

"Or maybe it's merely an oxymoron," Gavin said with a wink.

Luke offered his hand and said in his Texas drawl, "Best wishes on your engagement." He shook Nathan's hand as well. "Congratulations on winning your fiancée. You're a real competitor."

Chloe always liked Luke's straightforward courtesy, but she caught the hint of steel when he called Nathan a competitor.

Gavin waved his hand at an ice bucket. "We've ordered a 1928 Dom Pérignon to celebrate this happy occasion."

"My favorite," Chloe said. She had a feeling she didn't want to know what the bottle of champagne cost.

The glasses were filled and distributed as they stood. Gavin lifted his flute in the center of their circle. "Here's to Nathan drawing a queen into his royal flush. We wish you health, happiness, and a long life together."

Luke brought his glass up. "Here's to putting seven points on the board on the opening drive. I predict a championship season."

Since she was next to Luke, Chloe put her glass into the cluster. Despite the rocky start, she'd gotten fond of Nathan's two friends. "Here's to burning all three envelopes by the end of the bet."

Nathan touched his flute to Chloe's, looking into her eyes and saying, "The true prize in this wager was not *my* heart. It was yours. Winning your love makes me the luckiest man in the world."

Chloe couldn't speak past the emotions squeezing her throat.

Nathan tossed back his champagne in one gulp and removed her half-empty flute from Chloe's grasp. Taking her hand and interlacing his long, powerful fingers with hers, he nodded to Luke and Gavin. "I wish you both good luck. And now I'm going to take my fiancée home and show her just how much I mean what I said."

DON'T MISS
THE QUARTERBACK ANTES UP,
THE NEXT BOOK IN
NANCY HERKNESS'S
WAGER OF HEARTS SERIES.

Luke Archer is the superstar quarterback for the New York Empire and a media darling because of his good looks, talent, charm, and longevity. He's facing the prospect of retirement from the game he has lived, breathed, and loved for his entire life. If he can't be on the field, he doesn't want to be anywhere near football, so what will he do with the rest of his life?

He's contemplating this dilemma with deep depression when he meets Nathan Trainor and Gavin Miller in the bar at the Bellwether Club. There, they make their potentially life-changing wager of hearts: find a woman who loves them for themselves—not their money, power, or fame.

Little does Luke know that his game changer works right in the luxury condominium building where he lives. Miranda Tate is the hardworking and highly ethical assistant concierge, and when Luke nearly gets her fired, he finds he has a lot to make up for before he can win the love of his life.

Coming in summer 2016

DISCUSSION QUESTIONS

1   Nathan does whatever he can to be different from his father, yet Chloe notices that he shares many of the same mannerisms and attitudes. Is it possible to completely throw off the influence of our parents? Or is their impact on our younger selves always going to affect our future behavior?

2   Is there anyone in your life whom you would be willing to make significant personal sacrifices for, the way Chloe does for Grandmillie? Who would it be and why?

3   Much of the book's conflict comes from the vast gap in economic status between Chloe and Nathan. Would the story have played out differently if both were wealthy or both middle-class? How would it have been affected if Chloe were the billionaire and Nathan the temp?

4   Nathan and his father's relationship is strained because his father believes in tradition, while Nathan focuses on progress. In which direction does your own thinking lean? Why do you feel that way?

5   Ed, Ben, and Grandmillie are secondary characters, yet they have great influence on the protagonists. Who are the secondary characters in your life who have shaped you? And whom do you think you have helped shape?

6   Chloe and her Grandmillie are fiercely independent, which sometimes stands in the way of asking for the help they need. Nathan and his father also cling to their pride, which keeps them from reconciling. Can any trait be considered harmful if taken to an extreme? What trait defines you, and has it ever caused problems?

7   The Marines are an important—although not always positive—part of Nathan's childhood. What do you see as the pros and cons of a military upbringing?

8   Frankie Hogan founds the Bellwether Club because she is denied access to other prestigious social venues due to her gender and lack of social background. Are high-powered women considered a threat to high-powered men? Do you believe there is gender equality in the workplace and/or in society today?

9   When Nathan finally returns to the research-and-development department, he realizes that his persistent unhappiness has been caused at least partially by the lack of a creative outlet. Gavin Miller admits that he doesn't *have* to write for his living anymore, but he's miserable when he can't. Does everyone have something they need to do to stay sane and happy, some outlet that relieves stress? What is yours?

ACKNOWLEDGMENTS

A thousand thank-yous to all the people who generously poured their time, talent, thought, and expertise into making *The CEO Buys In* the best book it could be. My deepest gratitude goes to:

JoVon Sotak, my incredible editor, who shepherded my book through all its many phases and iterations, and who came up with the inspired idea of giving my hero a military father, adding a whole new depth to his character. She rocks!

Jessica Poore, Marlene Kelly, and the Montlake Author Relations team, an amazing, high-energy group of professionals who support my books in a myriad of ways.

Jane Dystel and Miriam Goderich, my fabulous agents. I sometimes have to pinch myself to make sure I'm not just dreaming that they represent me.

Andrea Hurst, my fantastic developmental editor, whose brilliant, insightful suggestions not only strengthened this book but the whole Wager of Hearts series.

Sara Brady and Tara Doernberg, my superb copy editors, who wield their considerable expertise on matters of grammar and style to make my book sparkle like a diamond.

Jill Kramer, my terrific proofreader, who uses her fine-tooth comb to catch my mistakes and inconsistencies and gives my book that gleaming professional polish.

Elizabeth Turner, my excellent cover designer, who was endlessly patient and painstaking in her work to capture my vision for this book, as well as the series, and turn it into its current gorgeous reality.

Miriam Allenson, Lisa Verge Higgins, and Jennifer Wilck, my astoundingly talented and downright fun critique group, who applaud my work's strengths and pinpoint its weaknesses. They are my lifeboat.

Rebecca Theodorou, who developed the thought-provoking discussion questions for this book's readers to ponder and debate. That degree in English lit comes in handy sometimes.

Jeff, Rebecca, and Loukas, whom I love with all my heart. You all keep me anchored in the real world.

ABOUT THE AUTHOR

Photo © 2003 Phil Cantor

Nancy Herkness is the author of the award-winning Whisper Horse series, as well as the Wager of Hearts series and several other contemporary romance novels. Three Whisper Horse novels were nominated for Romance Writers of America RITA™ awards.

Nancy is a member of Romance Writers of America, New Jersey Romance Writers, and Novelists, Inc. She has received many honors for her work, including the Golden Leaf Award, the Maggie Award in Contemporary Romance, and the National Excellence in Romance Fiction Award. She graduated from Princeton University with a degree in English literature and creative writing.

A native of West Virginia, Nancy now lives in New Jersey in a Victorian house twelve miles west of the Lincoln Tunnel with her husband, two mismatched dogs, and an elderly cat.

For more information about Nancy and her books, visit www. NancyHerkness.com. Nancy also loves to connect with fans online:

Facebook: https://www.facebook.com/nancyherkness
Blog: http://fromthegarret.wordpress.com/
Twitter: @NancyHerkness
Pinterest (with a board for each of her books): http://www
.pinterest.com/nancyherkness/